Ana Huang is the #1 *New York Times*, #1 *USA Today*, and #1 *Sunday Times* bestselling author of over a dozen contemporary romances, which have collectively sold twenty-three million copies worldwide. Her subgenres range from sports to billionaire and suspense, but all of her books feature her signature blend of steam and swoon.

Her work has been translated into thirty-four languages, and she has been featured on *Good Morning America*, *The Kelly Clarkson Show*, *The Drew Barrymore Show*, *The Washington Post*, and more.

A BookTok phenomenon, her breakout Twisted series has over two billion views on the platform. It is currently in development for television at Netflix.

Ana is also a crossword-puzzle enthusiast and an avid traveler. She's visited nearly forty countries, several of which have served as inspiration for her books.

BOOKS BY ANA HUANG

GODS OF THE GAME

A series of interconnected standalones

The Striker

The Defender

The Keeper

KINGS OF SIN

A series of interconnected standalones

King of Wrath

King of Pride

King of Greed

King of Sloth

King of Envy

King of Gluttony

TWISTED

A series of interconnected standalones

Twisted Love

Twisted Games

Twisted Hate

Twisted Lies

IF LOVE

If We Ever Meet Again (Duet Book 1)

If the Sun Never Sets (Duet Book 2)

If Love Had a Price (Standalone)

If We Were Perfect (Standalone)

THE DEFENDER

THE MULTI-MILLION COPY BESTSELLING AUTHOR

ANA HUANG

PIATKUS

PIATKUS

First published in the US in 2025 by Bloom Books,
An imprint of Sourcebooks
Published in Great Britain in 2025 by Piatkus

5 7 9 10 8 6 4

Copyright © 2025 by Ana Huang

Internal images © nikiteev/Depositphotos, studioworkstock/
Depositphotos, imdproduction/Depositphotos

The moral right of the author has been asserted.

A CIP catalogue record for this book is available from the British Library.

ISBN 978-0-349-44227-3

Printed and bound in Great Britain by Clays Ltd, Elcograf S.p.A.

Papers used by Piatkus are from well-managed forests
and other responsible sources.

Piatkus
An imprint of
Little, Brown Book Group
Carmelite House
50 Victoria Embankment
London EC4Y 0DZ

The authorised representative
in the EEA is
Hachette Ireland
8 Castlecourt Centre,
Dublin 15, D15 XTP3, Ireland
(email: info@hbgi.ie)

An Hachette UK Company

www.hachette.co.uk
www.littlebrown.co.uk

To finding your comfort person.

PLAYLIST

Natural
Imagine Dragons

Crush
Jennifer Paige

Baby Boy
Beyoncé ft. Sean Paul

Dangerous
Limi

Eyes Don't Lie
Isabel LaRosa

Feels
Kiiara

Breathless
The Corrs

Finally Found You
Enrique Iglesias ft. Sammy Adams

Ruin My Life
Zara Larsson

Talk That Talk
Rihanna

Digital Get Down
*NSYNC

Here Without You
3 Doors Down

Photographs
Rihanna

Meet Me Halfway
Black Eyed Peas

Hanging By A Moment
Lifehouse

Clarity
Zedd ft. Foxes

CONTENT NOTES

This story contains explicit sexual content, profanity, violence, and topics that may be sensitive to some readers.

For a detailed list, please visit anahuang.com/content-warnings

AUTHOR'S NOTE

This story takes place in London, so it uses the British term "football" instead of soccer. Unless otherwise stated, football as it's used here always refers to soccer, not American football.

Please also note that certain details about the Premier League and Champions League schedules have been modified for story purposes.

With the exception of fictional teams in this universe, all clubs will be referred to by their city name only and not their official club name (ex: Madrid instead of Real Madrid and Manchester instead of Manchester United or Manchester City).

CHAPTER 1

VINCENT

IN MY DEFENSE, THE PUB DIDN'T HAVE AN EXPLICIT *NO Miniature Pigs* rule. The owner was a stickler about no cameras and no fighting, but when it came to adorable porcine companions? Not a single warning until he spotted Truffle in my arms and lost his shit over "unhygienic animals."

Ironic, considering his pub was called the Angry Boar. You'd think he'd be more understanding when it came to swine.

"It's not your fault," I told the teacup pig nestled in my arms. "Mac doesn't like any living thing, human or animal. Besides, I bet you're cleaner than half the people in there."

Truffle snorted in agreement.

"So much for our big night out," Adil grumbled. "We won our first match against Holchester this season"—an expected chorus of jeers erupted at the mention of our longtime rival—"and instead of celebrating, we're out in the cold. Literally."

My team was gathered on the pavement outside the pub, trying to decide what to do next. So far, the only thing we'd agreed on was that pigs were cute, and pub rules sucked.

"Whose fault is that? I told DuBois not to bring Truffle." Stevens gestured at me. "That's *my* pet, but our dear ol' captain decided to make him the team mascot instead."

"Captain's privilege," I said with a grin. "I can make anyone the team mascot, so watch your mouth or you'll find yourself in a costume instead of a kit during next week's match."

The earlier jeers morphed into laughter and good-natured ribbing. The tips of Stevens's ears turned red, but he took my words in stride, as I knew he would.

I was only messing around. My role as a captain of Blackcastle, one of the Premier League's top football clubs, included a lot of things—giving team talks, operating as the middleman between management and players, making sure these Neanderthals behaved both in and out of the changing room—but it didn't include team mascot assignments. Not officially, anyway.

Unofficially? I had the power to elevate anyone's pet to the lauded role of team mascot. Tonight, that honor belonged to Truffle, the cutest pig you'd ever see.

"Okay, enough about the pig," Adil said. "Where are we taking this party? Your house? Another pub? Neon?"

"How about Legends?" Asher named a famous American sports bar whose London branch was as popular as its New York one. "I know the owner. I can easily get us a last-minute private room."

"Yes to Legends, no to the private room," Stevens said. "No offense, lads, but I'm not trying to be part of a sausage fest all night. I'd rather meet some girls."

"You can meet them, but you wouldn't know what to do with them," Adil cracked.

"Oh, that's rich coming from you. When's the last time *you* were on a date?"

"As a matter of fact…"

A ping from my phone distracted me from their inane argument.

📅   **THE DAY** *(Do Not Contact)*

Oh, fuck. It was midnight, which meant it was October third. THE DAY.

With all the stress leading up to the Holchester match and then the high of winning, I'd almost forgotten.

My stomach bottomed out, and any interest I'd had in continuing tonight's celebration vanished.

I'd set the annual reminder for myself five years ago. It was an act of masochism, considering I couldn't do anything about it—not without hurting the people I loved, hence the *Do Not Contact* note.

But I needed the evidence that it was there. That I *could* do something about it if I wanted to. The question was…did I want to?

Truffle let out a small squeal. *Double fuck.* I was squeezing the poor thing so tightly with one arm that he was squirming.

"Sorry, buddy." I loosened my hold, but the knot in my throat remained.

It would be so easy. I had the information stored on my phone. All I'd have to do—

"DuBois, you down?" Asher's voice interrupted my mental spiral.

I jerked my head up. "What?"

"Legends. You down?"

"Um." I tried to think through the buzzing in my ears. It was funny how a single reminder could flip my mood upside down. "Nah. You guys go. I'm calling it a night."

Asher's brows pulled together. "You okay? You look a little pale."

"I'm fine, just tired. Adrenaline crash, I think."

He didn't look convinced. "Tell me if you're about to have a heart attack or something. Scarlett would never forgive me if I let you die in the middle of the street."

I cracked a small smile. Besides being our team's star striker, he was also my sister Scarlett's boyfriend.

Asher and I were once massive rivals, but we developed a begrudging friendship after he transferred to Blackcastle from Holchester and started dating my sister. I was convinced she used him to spy on me sometimes because, well, she was my sister, and sisters were universally nosy.

"I promise I'm not going to drop dead." I reluctantly handed Truffle back to Stevens. I'd adopt him for the weekend, but I'd already "kidnapped" him from Stevens's parents earlier when Stevens took them around to meet the team. "I'll see you guys on Monday, okay? Enjoy Legends."

The other players groaned and complained good-naturedly about me abandoning them, but they didn't stop me from hailing the next taxi home.

I sank into the back seat and gave the driver my address. Thankfully, he either didn't recognize me or didn't make a fuss of it because he simply started driving, no questions asked.

THE DAY (Do Not Contact).

I rubbed a hand over my face. I couldn't shake the reminder from my brain, and I hated how much power it held over me after all these years. More than that, I hated *myself* for giving it that power in the first place.

My phone vibrated. I shot upright, my heart rate skyrocketing to dangerous levels. It was completely improbable, but maybe—

No. It was just Scarlett.

I wiped a hand over my face again and took a calming breath before I answered.

"You picked up." Her surprise was evident over the laughter and what sounded like a truck backing up in the background. "I thought you'd still be out with the team."

"Nah." I forced an even tone. "They went to Legends, but I wasn't feeling it so I'm going home."

"Since when do you turn down an excuse to party?"

"Since I'm not twenty-one anymore."

"Please. Don't act like you've grown up *that* much when you spent two weeks in Ibiza over the summer."

"Hey, you don't know what I did in Ibiza. Don't assume."

"Everyone knows what you did, Vincent. It was in the tabloids."

"Yeah, because tabloids are famous for being the arbiters of truth."

Scarlett scoffed, but her voice softened with her next question. "How are you holding up?"

My shoulders bunched. Of course. *That* was why she called. She was the only other person in the world who knew about my fixation on October third.

"Fine," I lied. "I barely thought about it. Too distracted by today's match."

To her credit, she let my blatant lie slide. I don't think she expected me to tell the truth; she just wanted to make sure I knew she was there if and when I spiraled.

"Good," she said. "I'm here if you need me."

"I know. Love ya, sis."

"Love you too, idiot."

I smirked at her familiar sign-off, but my smile faded soon after I hung up. I wished I were more like Scarlett when it came to these things. She didn't give a fuck about her version of October third, but me? I couldn't stop obsessing over it once or twice a year.

I finally arrived home. I paid the driver and hopped out, my footsteps crunching on gravel.

A lot of players preferred to live in outer London for more space and privacy, but I'd chosen a swanky five-bedroom house right in the heart of the city. Too much quiet was an invitation for unwanted thoughts.

I reached the entry gate, ready to punch in my security code, when a small movement caught my eye. The hairs on the back of my neck prickled.

The gate was already open.

It swayed in the night wind, the motion so subtle I would've missed it if I hadn't been standing so close. A low creak rippled through the silence.

I thought I'd locked it when I left that morning, but maybe my memory was playing tricks on me. My security system would've alerted me if anyone had tried to break in. Right?

I entered the front garden and firmly locked the gate behind me. I held my breath as I walked to the front door, grabbed the doorknob, and twisted.

It didn't budge.

I exhaled a sigh of relief. I must've forgotten to secure the gate earlier after all.

Once I was inside, I flipped on the lights and debated whether to watch TV or play a video game before bed. I was too amped up to fall asleep, and I needed a distraction.

I tossed my keys in the shallow dish by the door and was about to make my way to the game room when something caught my eye for the second time that night.

A small box sat next to the key holder. It was wrapped in brown paper and tied with a red ribbon. No note as far as I could tell—nothing to indicate who'd put it there because I sure as hell didn't put it there myself.

A metallic taste filled my mouth. The hairs on my neck prickled again, this time in frantic warning, but morbid curiosity got the best of me.

I opened the box.

I stared at its contents, unable to believe my eyes.

"What the *fuck*?"

CHAPTER 2

BROOKLYN

"NO, NO, NO. DON'T DO THIS TO ME. COME ON." I JABBED at my phone like that would somehow charge its battery, but no dice. I caught one last glimpse of my pastel fruit-print wallpaper before everything turned black. "*Dammit.*"

That was what I got for doomscrolling social media during the cab ride to my dad's house *and* for not charging my phone before I left home.

I was almost at my dad's place, and I normally wouldn't freak out this much if I weren't waiting for a call from my mom. She said she had something important to tell me, and getting her on the phone was usually harder than trying to break into MI5 headquarters. If I missed today's call, I probably wouldn't hear from her again for another two months.

"We're here." My unsmiling driver dropped me off in front of a familiar Georgian-style house. Not a very friendly guy, but he didn't talk and he got me here in one piece, so five stars.

I thanked him and exited the car, my worry over missing my mom's call replaced by a stomach full of nerves. They were little fluttery things that zipped inside me like a hive of bees ready to explode, and the closer I got to the door, the stronger they buzzed.

Was it weird to feel this anxious about dinner with a parent? Maybe, but the truth was, after a year and a half of living in the same city, my dad still felt like a stranger. I knew he loved me in his own way, but we'd yet to have a single conversation that didn't revolve around football or small talk.

I guess that was inevitable when we both worked for Blackcastle— me as a sports nutrition intern, him as the head coach and manager (yes, my dad was *the* Frank Armstrong).

I get why he defaulted to the topic of work when we were together, but I hoped we could finally have some real father-daughter bonding time tonight.

I rang the doorbell. My dad answered it in record time.

"Wow. You're dressed up." I took in his suit and tie. He hated suits and ties. I was flattered that he was making such an effort, but now I felt underdressed in my sweater and jeans. "You look really nice, but the restaurant's dress code isn't that strict."

His brow furrowed. A flash of confusion crossed his face before the groove between his eyes deepened. "Shit."

My stomach plummeted. "You forgot."

I should've reminded him yesterday, but I'd called out "sick" and missed the Holchester match (though I did watch it online after). He didn't like texting or talking on the phone, so I relied on our shared work hours to talk to him.

"No. It's on my calendar. I didn't forget about dinner, but I forgot to call and tell you we have to postpone." He looked like he'd rather walk into a den of lions than have this conversation. "Vuk is in town, and he wants to meet tonight to discuss some team business. I tried to get out of it. I couldn't."

Vuk Markovic was Blackcastle's owner. He lived in New York and was pretty hands-off with club operations, but when he was in town, everyone jumped to accommodate him.

"Oh!" I forced a bright smile. "I totally understand. We can take a rain check. No big deal."

"I'm sorry." A hint of apology softened my father's gruff voice. "I meant to tell you sooner, but I got caught up in pre-meeting prep. It was all last minute."

"It's okay." My voice pitched higher on the last syllable, and I blinked back an alarming burn behind my eyes. What was *wrong* with me? I couldn't be tearing up over a postponed dinner when I'd gone through much worse shit without so much as a flinch. "I get it. Really. We'll have plenty of opportunities for dinner later. Work is more important." I cleared my throat and waved my phone in the air. "Do you mind if I come in and charge this for a bit though? It's dead, and I'm waiting for a call from—from someone."

I almost said *Mom*, but bringing her up was a sure way to nuke the conversation.

"Go ahead. I have to run, but make yourself at home." He handed me a wad of cash. "Feel free to order in."

"Thanks."

We awkwardly hugged goodbye. Then he was gone, and I was alone in the silence.

I swallowed the lump in my throat. *No crying.* I didn't care that no one was around to see it. If I cried over something as stupid as dinner, I'd never forgive myself.

I took a deep breath, straightened my shoulders, and marched upstairs, where I found a charger in my dad's office. By the time I plugged my phone in, I'd shoved my wayward emotions into a box where they belonged.

The cash he gave me burned a hole in my pocket, but I wasn't hungry anymore.

I checked my cell. It'd charged enough to turn on again, but there were no missed calls. San Diego was eight hours behind London so it was still early there, but I couldn't sit around all night waiting for my mom.

I dialed her first instead. As expected, it went straight to voicemail. "Hey, Mom, it's me. Just wanted to check in since you said you wanted to talk today. Um, you're probably busy with Harry and Charlie, but give me a call back when you get this." Harry and Charlie were my stepfather and half-brother, respectively. "Oh, say hi to them for me. 'Kay, bye." I hung up and dropped my head back with a groan. "I'm *such* a loser."

I was young, hot, and single in London, and my Sunday plans revolved around my parents *who weren't even here*.

"Fuck this." I sat up straight, my self-pity sharpening into a sudden burst of motivation.

I had friends. I had a life. Why was I wallowing like a grounded teenager?

I checked my phone again. Twenty-five percent charged. *Good enough*.

I unplugged it and left.

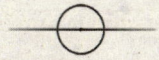

Thirty-five minutes later, I arrived at one of the poshest mansions in London. The white, four-story behemoth occupied a prime lot in the city's most expensive neighborhood, and no matter how many times I visited, I never quite got over how grandiose it was.

Only the best for world-famous footballer Asher Donovan and his girlfriend, Scarlett DuBois, who also happened to be one of my best friends.

Scarlett and I met right after I moved to London, when she saved me from a potential mugger outside a nightclub. She'd pushed the guy away, I'd clobbered him with my bag, and we'd been thick as thieves ever since.

"Brooklyn!" Her face lit up when she opened the door and saw me. "This is a surprise."

"I'm so sorry for dropping by unannounced. I hope this isn't a bad time. Dad bailed on dinner, and you mentioned yesterday you were craving the fruit tarts from that bakery you like, so..." I held up the bakery's signature pink-striped bag. "I didn't come empty-handed."

"It's not a bad time. You didn't have to bring a gift—though I'm not going to turn it down—and I'm sorry about dinner." Scarlett's voice softened. "I know you were looking forward to it."

"It is what it is." I was already intruding on her Sunday; no need for me to trauma dump as well.

I'd flirted with the idea of hitting the pubs solo after I left my dad's house, but I wasn't in the mood to deal with men. I'd much rather be with friends.

Thankfully, Scarlett didn't seem put out by my sudden appearance. She chatted away as she led me through the house, which was as opulent on the inside as it was on the outside.

Scarlett was the type of girl who preferred fish and chips to foie gras and leggings to couture, but she lived with Asher, the king of flash. This was actually his second home in the area. His other mansion was on the outskirts of London, but it was too far from work for Scarlett so he'd bought something closer to the city center.

My eyebrows shot up when we passed by an indoor construction site instead. Planks of wood littered the floor, and there was a bunch of heavy-looking equipment that looked like they could do some serious damage if you got on their bad side.

"Are you still renovating? I thought you were done."

"So did I," Scarlett said wryly. "But the studio didn't turn out quite the way we imagined, so we have to make some tweaks. Asher wants to add an indoor arcade as well, so we'll be renovating for at least another two months."

Scarlett was a former prima ballerina turned teacher at the prestigious Royal Academy of Ballet, also known as RAB, but Asher was the one who'd insisted on installing a private ballet studio in their new house. That man was so head over heels for her, it would be alarming if it wasn't so endearing.

"Indoor arcade? Faaaancy," I teased. "You should ask him to build a spa—one that's fully staffed and open to friends and family. He'll do it. You know he would."

"I'm not asking my boyfriend to operate a spa out of our house. It wouldn't be very practical, would it?"

"That's the problem with you Brits. Too much focus on what's practical and too little focus on what's *fun*. What's the point of dating a famous footballer if you can't indulge in a little extravagance?"

Scarlett bumped my hip with hers. "Then *you* date a footballer and ask him for the spa."

We entered the living room, where we promptly flopped onto our favorite couch and split one of the fruit tarts. I ate healthy most of the time, but I wasn't opposed to the occasional treat.

"Tempting, but I'm afraid you snagged the only good one in the bunch." I'd been around athletes my whole life. I'd even dated a few of them. Unless you liked commitment issues, cheating, and gaslighting, it was best to steer clear.

"What's the only good one in the bunch?" Asher appeared in the doorway. His hair was damp, his skin was sweaty, and he was so incredibly, devastatingly handsome that it hurt a little to look at him.

I meant that in a purely objective way. Even if he wasn't dating one of my best friends, I wouldn't go for him. He wasn't my type—like I said, I didn't do athletes—but I could appreciate a fine specimen when I saw one.

He walked over to us.

"You are." Scarlett tilted her head back so he could kiss her on the lips. "We're talking about dating footballers."

"Yeah?" Asher glanced at me with amusement. "Didn't know you were browsing around that market, Brooklyn."

"I'm not, which is why I said Scarlett got the only good one. No offense, but I'd rather die than date any of your teammates."

Asher laughed. "As someone who has to share a changing room with them, I don't blame you." He came around and sat on Scarlett's other side. They exchanged a smile, one so intimate and knowing it could only exist between two people who'd already envisioned forever with each other.

Another lump formed in my throat.

I was happy for Scarlett. She was one of the kindest people I knew, and she'd gone through a lot, including a freak car accident that ended her dream career early. She deserved true love.

But seeing her and Asher together underscored how unmoored I'd been feeling. It wasn't even about the lack of romance in my life; it was about being someone's priority. Having an anchor. Knowing there was a person out there who would be my first call if shit went down and vice versa.

I loved my friends. They had my back and I had theirs, but they had other priorities too. As for my family...well, that was a whole other story I'd prefer to leave on the shelf.

I was a balloon drifting aimlessly through the crowd while everyone around me found their tethers.

It sucked.

The sound of the doorbell interrupted my slow descent into wallowing again.

"That's our takeaway." Asher moved to stand. "I'll get it."

"No, you guys stay here. I can get it." I jumped up, eager for the chance to do something besides feel sorry for myself. "I need to stretch my legs anyway." I left before they could argue.

Maybe I should head out after I got their food. I didn't want to be *that* friend who dropped by unannounced, ate their food, then left.

Besides, what was sadder—spending Sunday night alone in your dad's house or playing third wheel to your friend and her boyfriend?

Scratch that. I didn't want to know.

After two wrong turns—I swear, this house was a maze—I made it to the foyer. I opened the door, expecting to see a random delivery person.

Instead, I was greeted by a distressingly familiar face: light brown skin, dark brown eyes, and full lips that slowly curved into a smile that would make most women swoon.

Key word: *most*.

My own smile vanished. "Oh. It's you."

CHAPTER 3

VINCENT

"DON'T SOUND SO HAPPY TO SEE ME, BUTTERCUP. I'LL GET the wrong idea." I suppressed a laugh at Brooklyn's eye roll.

I hadn't expected her to answer my sister's door, but I wasn't complaining. Riling her up had been one of my greatest joys in life since we met after a charity football match last summer. She'd already been friends with Scarlett, but none of us had known she was interning at Blackcastle yet.

Her addition to the team had been a welcome surprise; her relation to Coach had not, since the only thing worse than trying not to overstep with Coach's daughter was trying not to overstep with Coach's *hot* daughter.

Long, wavy blonde hair that shimmered like gold in the sunlight. Big blue eyes. Full lips and an adorable smattering of freckles across her nose. It was like God had sent her specifically to test me—I mean, us. The team in general.

"Apparently, you're as bad at reading expressions as you are at reading Holchester's plays." She arched one brow. "What was that mess with Lyle yesterday?"

"Good job for cherry picking the *one* time I let him score. Don't forget, we won yesterday's match."

"Thanks to Asher."

"Does your boss know how bad your match analyses are? Because all Blackcastle staff should have a baseline knowledge of football, which you clearly don't."

"Is it bad analysis if I point out how you misjudged Lyle's pass and fucked up the interception?"

"Wow. I didn't realize you watched me so closely during our matches." I placed a hand over my chest. "I'm flattered. Truly."

"Please. I work for the club. It's my job to follow every player closely."

"Yeah? Then what was Stevens doing fifteen minutes into the first half?"

"His job, unlike you."

I didn't think anything could make me laugh today, but the sound that came out of my mouth was as genuine as it was unexpected.

Brooklyn may look angelic, but she had the tongue of a viper. It was oddly attractive.

I shouldn't enjoy verbally sparring with her so much. She was the manager's daughter, which meant he would rip my balls off if I looked at her the wrong way. On top of that, she was one of my sister's best friends, which meant Scarlett would *also* rip my balls off if I looked at her the wrong way. It was a lot of potential danger for one girl.

The problem was, I'd never liked playing safe.

Brooklyn's mouth curved. Her eyes dropped to the takeaway bags in my hands. "Did you rob the delivery guy on your way in?"

"It's not robbery if he handed the food over willingly." By pure coincidence, I'd arrived at the same time as Asher and Scarlett's takeaway, so I'd offered to bring it in myself. The delivery guy agreed and promptly asked for a selfie afterward. I obliged; everyone was happy.

"Are you going to let me in, or are you waiting for the food to get cold first?" I drawled.

She wrinkled her nose but stepped aside. "Does Scarlett know you're coming?"

"Nah. I just happened to be in the neighborhood."

That was a lie. No one "just happened to be" in this neighborhood, but I'd spent the day seesawing between fear, anger, and confusion. If I didn't tell someone what happened soon, I was going to explode.

After I opened the box last night—technically this morning—I'd immediately packed a bag and checked into a hotel. I didn't know what the "gift" giver's intentions were, but I wasn't going home until I'd changed the locks and upgraded the security system. It was better to be safe than sorry.

Brooklyn and I entered the living room. Asher was the first to see me.

"Shit, DuBois, you miss me already? I just saw you yesterday." He shook his head. "You're getting clingy."

"Fuck off. I'm here to see my sister. You're like a wart on an otherwise cute little toad. Unwanted, but part of the package."

"Play nice, boys," Scarlett warned, but a hint of amusement gleamed in her eyes.

I set the takeaway on the coffee table and explained what happened with the delivery.

Asher and Scarlett had ordered enough food to feed a small village, though most of it was healthy stuff like grilled chicken and vegetables. We had to be careful with our diet during the season, so the only "fun" foods were courtesy of Scarlett.

"Actually, I think I'm going to head out," Brooklyn said when I tried to hand her a plate.

"What? You just got here!" Scarlett protested.

"I know, but I already ate so I'm not…" Brooklyn trailed off. She glanced at her phone, her brow furrowing.

I put the plate down and leaned back. My bullshit radar clanged like a firehouse bell in my head. Brooklyn lived too far away for a quick drop-in, and she wasn't the type to leave a social gathering simply because she couldn't participate in an activity. This was the girl who arbitrarily gave up alcohol for a month over the summer and *still* outlasted everyone at the club.

Something was wrong. What did she see on her phone? Was it related to work or personal?

More importantly, why did I care?

"Sorry, I have to take this, but I'll text you later, okay?" She hugged Scarlett goodbye. Her eyes met mine briefly over my sister's shoulder. A small frisson of…something sparked in my blood.

I uncapped my water and took a swig, swallowing the sudden urge to ask her to stay.

Then she was gone, leaving nothing but a trace of perfume in my lungs.

Asher and Scarlett did most of the talking while we ate. Neither questioned why I'd showed up unannounced, but without Brooklyn here to lighten my mood, the weight of the past twenty-odd hours settled heavy on my shoulders again.

I finally spoke up toward the end of our meal. "I have to tell you guys something, but you can't freak out."

Scarlett set her fork down and eyed me with a mixture of intrigue and wariness. "Okay…"

I gave them a quick rundown of what happened after I parted with the team last night. "I opened the box and found this."

I retrieved the item from my pocket and set it on the table.

Asher and Scarlett stared at it, their baffled expressions mirroring what I'd felt when I first saw it.

It was a doll. A large, painstakingly detailed crochet doll of me, to be exact, complete with a buzz cut, black button eyes, and a full Blackcastle football kit. Instead of my name on the shirt, it featured the letters BFF.

"BFF? As in Best Friends Forever?" Asher sounded confused. "What the fuck?"

"It could mean that. It could mean Big Fucking Failure. Who knows? There was no note or anything. Just the doll."

In the grand scheme of things, it could've been worse. The intruder could've left a severed body part or a stalker-y surveillance photo of me, but the innocuous nature of the doll somehow made it more insidious. I didn't know what they wanted. Why would they go to the trouble of breaking into my house, thereby risking arrest, just to leave a basic "gift"?

"God, this is creepy. Please tell me you went to the police." Scarlett picked up the doll. Leaned in. Flinched. "They even got your scar right."

I had a faint white scar on my knee from a childhood injury. Most people didn't know about it. It was too small to see from afar, and magazines usually airbrushed it out of my photoshoots.

I hadn't noticed until Scarlett pointed it out, but whoever crocheted the doll had nailed the exact shape and size of the scar.

A chill swept down my back, but I took the doll from her and forced a blithe tone. "If a fan is dedicated enough to make this, they're dedicated enough to know I have the scar. It's not a secret."

"Normal fans don't break into your house," Asher said. "You have a stalker, or at least someone obsessive enough to do something like this. Scarlett's right. You need to go to the police."

"An intruder is not the same as a stalker, and absolutely not. I don't want the press catching wind of this and making it a big thing. We have Champions League matches coming up. I can't afford to be distracted."

I doubted the police would even care. Yeah, breaking and entering was a crime, but nothing got stolen and I hadn't received any threats. What were they supposed to do?

"It *is* a big thing," Scarlett argued. "You weren't home this time, but what happens if they come back while you're there? You could get hurt."

"Someone's coming by tomorrow to upgrade the security system. Whoever did this"—I held up the doll—"isn't getting in again."

"Did you see anything on the cameras?" Asher asked.

"Uh." I rubbed the back of my neck. "Cameras were on the fritz last week, and I haven't gotten the chance to fix them yet."

"Jesus." He groaned.

Asher was way more security-minded than I was, but he also had more, uh, *enthusiastic* fans than me. The man was usually hounded by paparazzi everywhere he went.

Don't get me wrong. I had my issues with the paps too, as well as piles of fan mail every week. But my fanbase felt more restrained compared to his, and I'd never had a reason to worry about them stepping out of line—until now.

"Do you think it's the same person who left you the note on your car?" Scarlett asked.

A few weeks ago, I'd left training to find a note tucked under the windscreen wiper of my car. It congratulated me on renewing my sports drink sponsorship. Pretty standard stuff except for one thing— the words were cut out from magazines, making it look like a ransom letter from some nineties movie.

I'd chalked it up to a prank, but Scarlett's question had me viewing it from a whole other angle.

"I have no idea." I'd tossed the note immediately after getting it.

"You shouldn't go home until we figure out who this person is and what they want," Asher said. "Doesn't matter if you upgrade your security. They could be dangerous. Remember what happened to Tyler Conley?"

I grimaced. Tyler Conley was a famous pop singer who got hospitalized months ago after an obsessed fan followed him home and stabbed him three times before a neighbor heard his screams and called the police. Thankfully, he'd pulled through and his attacker was currently in prison, awaiting trial, but he'd since become the poster boy for the dangers of fame.

I had no desire to be another Tyler Conley.

"Go to the police," Scarlett repeated. "Even if you think it's not a big deal, it should be on record."

I hated to admit it, but she was right. "I'll go later tonight."

"Forget the hotel. Move in with us until they catch the creep," she said. "Our security is unbeatable, thanks to Asher's paranoia"—Asher shrugged in agreement—"and our address isn't publicly available. Yours is."

"I can't do that. A hotel is *fine*."

"Yes, you can, and no, it isn't. A hotel is too open to the public. You're my brother. As annoying as you are, I'm not letting you die on my watch."

"You're being dramatic."

Yet warmth trickled through my veins at her words. I hated making my sister worry, but it was nice to know I wasn't in this alone.

Although we weren't biological siblings, Scarlett and I had always been close. Our parents adopted us when we were babies, and we looked nothing alike, which was why people were often surprised to find out we were related. She was pale and petite, with black hair and gray eyes; I was tall and muscled, with brown eyes and light brown skin that spoke to my biracial background.

We lived together as young kids, but we were separated after our parents divorced. She grew up in England with our mum; I moved to Paris with our dad, where I went to an international school. But we'd always spent the summers and holidays together with one parent or the other, and we'd gotten even closer after I moved to London a few years ago to play for Blackcastle.

"As long as you don't mind the construction, we have plenty of room here," Asher said.

Arguing was useless. Scarlett and Asher were both stubborn as fuck.

"Fine," I said. "I'll move in. Just don't do any weird couple shit while I'm here, okay?"

CHAPTER 4

VINCENT

I LASTED SEVEN DAYS IN THEIR HOUSE.

After I agreed to move in, Asher went back to my house with me to pack a full duffel. I also checked out of my hotel, (reluctantly) filed a police report, and went ahead with the security upgrades on Monday.

As expected, the police were less than impressed by my problem. They thought it was normal weird shit celebrities had to deal with, but they were also big Blackcastle fans and assigned an obligatory detective to my case. I had little faith they would find the intruder, but at least it was on record.

However, the most pressing problem was the fact that I was now living with my sister and her boyfriend. It was a big house, but when we were forced to live under one roof with construction and copious amounts of PDA, even Buckingham Palace wouldn't be big enough.

I could deal with the noise and piles of sawdust everywhere. I could even look past Asher and Scarlett's kisses and cuddle time on the couch, but I drew the line at anything that made me want to upchuck.

That line was crossed on day seven. Asher and I usually went home from practice together, but I had to run some errands first.

When I returned to the house, the contractors were gone, but the faint strains of classical music filled the air. It appeared to be coming from the ballet studio.

"Hello?" I called out. "Lettie? You home?"

I walked toward the studio, my senses on high alert. My heartbeat thundered through my entire body as every worst-case scenario ran through my mind. Last week's incident had heightened my paranoia, and while I didn't think a burglar would stop for a Beethoven intermission before they robbed the place, I couldn't fathom why Asher or Scarlett would be playing music in a half-finished studio either.

I stopped at the door. It was closed, but the music was *definitely* coming from inside.

You know that saying, curiosity killed the cat? Well, I understood firsthand how that cat felt because instead of minding my own damn business the way I should've, I opened the door.

"Jesus!"

"*Fuck*!"

"Vincent!"

"Have you heard of knocking first?!"

"Why would I knock when this is supposed to be a *construction site*?" Bile splashed up my throat as Scarlett and Asher jerked away from each other, their faces bright red.

Neither of them was naked, thank God, but they didn't have to be for me to figure out what they'd been doing. Mussed hair, rumpled clothing, guilty expressions—the implications were clear.

Scarlett was sitting on the barre with her legs wrapped around Asher's waist, and I needed to find the nearest bottle of bleach to drown myself in.

"No. Nope. Abso-fucking-lutely not." I turned right around and marched to my room. I didn't give them a chance to say anything else.

I was an open-minded person. I'd come to terms with my sister dating my teammate and I understood, theoretically, that they engaged in normal couple activities.

But there was no way I could continue to live here after almost walking in on them having sex. I lucked out this time, but the longer I stayed, the greater the chances of me clawing my eyes out.

I needed to find a new place to crash. ASAP.

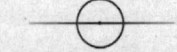

THREE DAYS LATER

"I'm so freaking excited we're flatmates now!" Adil flopped onto the couch next to me with the zeal of a hyperactive golden retriever. "The captain and the midfielder, living under one roof. It's going to be a blast. We can read Wilma Pebbles late into the night. Watch *Love Island* together. Go for a morning jog at sunrise." His face lit up. "We could even have our own reality show! We'll call it *Blackcastle Behind the Scenes: The Lives of Footballers On and Off the Pitch*." He waved his hand through the air, as if he were presenting an imaginary marquee.

"*Love Island* isn't on air right now, and that's a little long for a show title," I said dryly, keeping my eyes trained on the TV screen before us.

"Greatness requires more words." He settled deeper into the couch. "Whatcha watching?"

"New Nate Reynolds." I was a big fan of Reynolds's action thrillers. "I think they're getting to an important part of the plot, so if—"

"Awesome. Is this the one where he tries to stop the cyberterrorists from taking down the US electrical grid?"

I held back a sigh. So much for a quiet evening.

I'd moved into Adil's house two nights ago, and I was already reaching my limit.

Don't get me wrong. He was a great guy, and I really appreciated him letting me crash here. He was also the only guy on the team who didn't live with a partner or have disgusting hygiene habits, which was why I'd turned to him after I bolted out of Scarlett and Asher's place.

Ideally, I'd suck it up and move back home, but every time I thought about it, my muscles tensed like I was bracing for a punch I couldn't see coming. The intruder had done a number on me, and although I hated being ruled by fear, I needed to keep my shit together for the team's sake. I couldn't risk distraction before or during a match, so home was still a no-go.

Unfortunately, while Adil was welcoming, he was also a little *too* friendly. Not in a creepy way, but in a "we must hang out twenty-four-seven and I'll talk your ear off every minute" type of way. So far, the only alone time I'd had when I wasn't sleeping was in the shower.

"That was the previous installment," I said in response to his question. "Listen, I'm happy to chat later, but I prefer to watch—"

"You know which movie of his is criminally underrated?" Adil bulldozed over my attempt to end the conversation. It wasn't malicious, just oblivious. "*The Grey Dogs*. It's an indie film, not a big action blockbuster, but I thought it was very heartfelt. Honestly, he has the range to play different characters—"

"Adil." I placed a firm hand on his shoulder. "I appreciate your enthusiasm regarding Reynolds's acting career, but let's pause those thoughts until the movie is over, okay?"

He bobbed his head. "Okay."

I was blessed with two minutes of peace and quiet (unless you counted the explosions onscreen) before Adil spoke again.

"Dude, how much do you think they spend on special effects for these movies? And do you think Reynolds does his own stunts? I heard he does, which is *crazy* because what do you mean he really jumped from all those cliffs? I wanted to be an actor for a minute when I was little, but there's no way…"

I groaned as Adil rambled on about every stunt from Nate Reynolds's filmography. Thank God the captions were on because I couldn't hear a word the actors were saying.

I was an extrovert, but I wasn't extroverted enough to live with Adil.

I needed to find a new place to stay. Again.

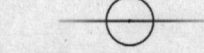

ANOTHER THREE DAYS LATER

The only other teammate I would've considered rooming with was Noah Wilson, our goalkeeper. He was clean and quiet, but he also had a preteen daughter. Living with them would've been weird, and I doubted he would've agreed anyway.

So Noah's place was out, which left me with no other option but a hotel again. The police didn't have any leads on the intruder, but the more days that passed, the more tempted I was to move home.

"No way," Scarlett said firmly when I brought it up over weekend brunch. "That's how stalkers and weirdos get you. They wait until you think the danger has passed, and then *bam*! They Tyler Conley you. Next thing you know, you're bleeding out on the kitchen floor with knife wounds all over your body."

Asher and I winced in unison. We were seated in the back of the restaurant with Brooklyn and Scarlett's other best friend, Carina Vu, who'd been caught up on my intruder situation. Thankfully, no one bothered us beyond a few double takes.

"Someone's been listening to too much true crime." I took a sip of coffee. Even though half my family was British, I'd never gotten on the tea train. I was more of an espresso person.

"It's called *true* crime for a reason," Carina said. "Don't underestimate how fucked up the average person can be."

"I'm surprised someone's stalking you to begin with." Brooklyn gazed at me with innocent doe eyes. "There are so many more interesting celebrities in this restaurant alone."

Asher coughed out a laugh while I cocked one eyebrow and set my cup down. I leaned in slightly, just enough to make her shift in her seat. "You talk so much shit, yet you're obsessed with my life. Projecting much?"

"Please. I couldn't care less about your life." Her voice was airy, but her gaze dipped to my mouth for a fraction too long before it darted away.

Too late. I caught it. Every damn time, I caught it.

My pulse kicked up a notch. "You care enough to follow my every move during a match."

"I told you that was for work." A flush crept up her neck. "Is this what it's like to have a narcissistic personality? It must be exhausting to make *everything* about yourself at all times."

I smirked, knowing exactly how she'd react to the challenge in my voice. Her gaze dropped again to my mouth—right where I wanted it—before she caught herself and glared at me. "Keep deflecting, buttercup," I drawled. "One day, you'll admit the truth, and I'll be right here to accept your apology."

"Sure," she said, sweet as pie. "Or maybe the intruder will do us all a favor and take you out before then."

Surprise flared, and for the second time since the break-in, Brooklyn pulled an unexpected laugh out of me.

Some people might've found her statement morbid, but I appreciated her light-hearted roast. I wasn't good at coping with serious issues in a serious way. It was a character flaw that I should probably work on in therapy, but the world was shitty enough without me adding my woes to it.

The mental spiral I suffered every October third was the most wallowing I allowed myself.

"Better hope not, or I'll haunt you forever," I said. "If you think I'm bad now, wait until I'm a ghost. I'll be insufferable."

A grin touched her mouth before she quickly flattened it into a straight line. But the sparkle of laughter remained in her eyes, and that was enough to make me smile back.

When I returned my attention to the rest of the table, our friends had stopped talking and were staring at us with varying degrees of amusement, exasperation, and curiosity, respectively.

"If you're done bickering, let's get back to the issue at hand," Scarlett said dryly. She was used to my verbal sparring with Brooklyn. "I still don't like the idea of you going back home, even with added security. Are there other friends or teammates you can stay with? I still think a hotel is too public."

She had a point. I'd already been recognized twice in the lobby, despite my attempts to go incognito. "Unfortunately not. No one else has a living situation that would work for a flatmate."

"I would let you sleep on my couch, but it might be too uncomfortable," Carina mused. "It's a cheap couch."

I patted her shoulder. "It's the thought that counts."

I'd known Carina for years. She was like another sister to me, and there was zero chance either of us would develop an attraction for the other. Staying with her wouldn't be weird, but she lived in a one-bedroom flat and I couldn't sleep on a couch during football season. Our physical performance team would kill me.

"If you don't know anyone who has a spare room, maybe I do," Scarlett said thoughtfully. "It has to be someone who's vetted, lives alone, and won't freak out over the fact that you're, well, *you*. Someone like…" She trailed off.

A beat of silence passed before every head swung toward Brooklyn.

Her fork froze halfway to her mouth. She lowered it slowly, her eyes darting around the table. "No. Absolutely not."

"You said you were planning to rent out your second room anyway," Carina pointed out.

"I never said that."

"You should've." Asher dumped fuel on the fire like the bastard he was. "A spare room in London is too valuable to leave empty. Vincent is annoying, but at least you know he's not a psycho."

"Thanks," I said.

"Anytime."

"This is ridiculous. He's not moving in. He wouldn't want to live with me anyway." Brooklyn turned an expectant gaze my way. "Right?"

It took me an extra second to respond. "Right."

On paper, it was a terrible idea. If Coach would kill me for looking at her the wrong way, he would torture *then* kill me if I shacked up with his only daughter—his ridiculously beautiful, sharp-tongued daughter, who knew exactly how to get under my skin and who somehow managed to make me want her more with every insult she threw my way.

On the other hand, Brooklyn's setup was pretty perfect per Scarlett's specifications. She lived alone in a big flat that was close to our training grounds, she wasn't a serial killer, and she smelled nicer than anyone else I knew. That last point was weirdly prominent in my mind.

"No, wait, I really think we're onto something." Carina wouldn't let it go. "Vincent needs a place to stay; Brooklyn will get extra cash. I don't see what the issue is. It's a win-win."

Pink blossomed across Brooklyn's face. "The issue is we *can't* live together. We'll drive each other nuts."

"How do you know? You've never lived together before," Carina said. "It's better than finding some rando from Gumtree."

"I just know." Brooklyn released an exasperated sigh. "Vincent, back me up here."

I opened my mouth to do exactly that, but the words that came out weren't the ones I'd intended. "Carina has a point."

"*What*?" She gaped at me. "You just said you didn't want to live with me!"

"I don't." I sniffed trouble from a mile away, but the more she pushed back, the more I wanted to prove her wrong.

What could I say? It was the contrarian in me.

The wheels in my head spun. The Coach threat was significant, but as far as I knew, he and Brooklyn didn't spend much time together. The chances of him randomly dropping by her flat were slim.

It would take some finessing, but we could keep our flatmate situation a secret from him. It wasn't like I was going to stay there forever.

I explained all this (minus the Coach part). Brooklyn didn't look convinced.

"Look, it's your home. You can let me in or not," I said. "But it's interesting how *adamant* you are about it. It's almost like you're scared."

Brooklyn straightened immediately. *Bingo.* I knew that would get to her.

Goading her always felt like winning some secret game we played, and I'd just scored a major point.

Scarlett groaned and covered her face with her hands. She probably regretted putting forth Brooklyn's place as an option, but it was too late. The train had already left the station.

"Scared of what?" Brooklyn demanded.

"Of not being able to control yourself around me."

She sputtered out a sound that was half laugh, half scoff. "Do you hear yourself? That's the sound of your delusion and ego colliding. Trust me, I'd be able to control myself just fine."

"Prove it." I leaned forward until I was close enough to count the faint freckles dotting her nose and cheeks. Her eyes were a deep sapphire in the late morning light, and I could smell her perfume again—something fresh and citrusy, like a lemon grove on a warm summer day. "Let me move in with you."

Her eyes sparked. Her nostrils flared.

And I knew I had her before she even opened her mouth.

"Fine," she said. "But I'm charging you double for rent."

"Deal." I settled back against my seat, my chest aglow with satisfaction and a tingle of something else.

Scarlett dropped her head to the table. Asher rubbed her back, a shit-eating grin on his face. Next to him, Carina sipped her drink, her expression neutral save for the smirk lurking in the corners of her mouth.

As for me? I was already making plans for my stay at Brooklyn's place.

This was going to be fun.

CHAPTER 5

BROOKLYN

I'D BEEN MANIPULATED, AND I HAD NO ONE TO BLAME but myself.

One second, I was eating my eggs at brunch. The next, Vincent was at my door with a duffel slung over his shoulder and a cocky smile on his face. "Hey, roomie."

"Don't call me that. You are a temporary tenant. That's all."

"Okay, buttercup."

I didn't know why he'd picked that nickname for me, and I wasn't going to give him the satisfaction of asking, but it irritated my soul.

His grin widened at my grumble of annoyance. Cockiness aside, it was a nice smile. A lethal one, even—white teeth, a shadow of a dimple, and devilishness mixed with just enough warmth to make you feel like you were the only person in the world.

I refused to fall for it. Vincent DuBois might be able to charm everyone else he met, but I'd known he was trouble from the moment we met. There was something about him that made my entire body tense when he was nearby. He was like the moon to my tide; his mere presence altered my gravitational field.

"You've been here before with Scarlett, so I'll skip the tour." I shut the door behind him after he walked in. His shirtsleeve brushed my arm on his way past, and a small tingle slipped down my spine.

See? My self-preservation instincts were already screaming. He was bad news, but it was too late for me to back out. If I went back on my word, he'd win, which would be unacceptable.

Brooklyn Armstrong did not lose, especially not to arrogant, annoyingly attractive players like Vincent DuBois.

"That's fine," he said easily. "Just tell me where you want me."

I side-eyed him as I led him to his room. The corners of his mouth twitched, but I refused to respond to his double entendre.

Besides, he wasn't going to be so amused when he saw what I'd prepared for him.

I bit back a grin as I opened the bedroom door. "I took the liberty of redecorating for you. I hope you don't mind."

"You didn't have to—" Vincent stopped dead in the doorway. His duffel hit the floor with a thud as he took in his new home for the foreseeable future.

Up until last night, I'd used the spare bedroom as extra storage space for my clothes and workout equipment. All those things had been cleared out. In their place were stuffed animals—dozens and dozens of them. Pink pigs, purple horses, giant pandas and little dolphins. Plushies of every shape, size, and category crowded the small space like a kid's estate sale gone wild, and a one-eyed doll that may or may not have been haunted sat on the shelf opposite the bed.

I'd gotten the toys courtesy of my neighbor. As luck would have it, she was a collector whose therapist recently convinced her to "release her attachments to the past." When I saw her post offering the plushies at a discount in the building's group chat, I immediately jumped at the opportunity.

I tied the look together with sparkly fuchsia sheets and lace-trimmed pillows.

"Do you like it?" I asked, the picture of innocence. "I read somewhere that stuffed animals can make a place feel homier, and I really want you to be comfortable here."

Vincent may have manipulated me into letting him move in, but that didn't mean I couldn't have a little fun at his expense.

He picked up the nearest stuffed animal and examined it. A minute later, he set it back down with exquisite care and looked me straight in the eyes.

I held my breath, my chest ballooning with anticipation.

"I *love* it," he said. He radiated so much sincerity, my teeth ached. "I can't believe you went to all this trouble for me. I'm honored."

My gaze narrowed. Not a hint of sarcasm in his voice; not a trace of irritation on his face. *Bastard.*

"I'm nothing if not a good host." It was time to switch tactics. "Since you'll be staying here for a while, we should go over the house rules."

Vincent leaned against the doorframe and crossed his arms, the picture of insouciance.

"Let's hear 'em," he drawled. Despite growing up in Paris, he didn't have a strong French accent. It was probably because he'd attended international school and spent every other summer in the UK. But there were certain moments, like these, when a flicker of it slipped in so smoothly it was like it'd been there all along.

My spine tingled again, this time more insistently.

I ignored it and ticked off the rules on my fingers. "No smoking indoors."

"I don't smoke."

"No hogging the bathroom, TV, or other communal amenities.

The hot water runs out quickly, so don't, you know, spend too much time in the shower." I emphasized the last part.

I wasn't an idiot; I knew what guys were doing when they took more than ten minutes in the shower.

Vincent's eyes gleamed with laughter. "Noted."

I ran through a handful of other rules before I reached the grand finale. "And…" I paused for dramatic effect. "No bringing girls over. Ever. I don't want random people coming in and out of my flat."

That *had* to be a dealbreaker for him. He was good-looking, single, and famous. Women threw themselves at him every day, and according to the tabloids, he didn't exactly resist their advances. There was no way he could resist bringing someone over.

Vincent's brow creased.

Triumph sparked until he spoke again.

"Brooklyn," he said, "I have absolutely zero interest in bringing other girls over."

There it was again—the subtle change in his tone, followed by a tiny swoop in my stomach. His reply sounded innocuous at first, but his faint emphasis on the word *other* sent my mind cartwheeling in a dozen directions, each more dangerous than the last.

Was the emphasis pure semantics, in that I was already a girl living here so anyone else he brought over would be an "other" by default?

Or did he mean he had zero interest in bringing other girls over because…

No. I wasn't going there. It didn't matter anyway. Vincent and I would never be more than quasi-friends and temporary flatmates. He was probably just trying to fuck with me, per usual.

"Stop it," I said.

"Stop what?"

"Stop trying to charm me."

His eyes flooded with surprise, and I immediately wanted to snatch my words back. *Shit.* I'd fucked up.

A slow smile spread over his face, turning his shadow of a dimple into a lethal weapon. "I wasn't trying, but I'm happy to hear you're charmed."

"Oh, shut up. You know what I meant."

"Not really."

I blew out a sigh. This wasn't how I'd imagined his move-in going. At all.

But I'd be lying if I said a *tiny* part of me wasn't glad he was here to take my mind off my mom's latest bombshell. She'd called when I was at Scarlett's house, and I wished I'd never picked up.

My stomach cramped. I shifted my gaze away from Vincent and resisted the urge to bite my nails. I'd kicked the habit years ago, but the possibility of relapse reared its ugly head every time I was stressed.

"Let's move on," I said. "Towels are in the linen closet across the hall if you need them. I'm heading out early tomorrow to run errands, so don't wait up for me."

Vincent's eyebrows rose. "What errands do you need to run *that* early on a weekday?"

My nails made it halfway to my mouth before I caught myself. "This and that."

I didn't mention that I hadn't received a job offer from Blackcastle yet, so I was exploring other options for when my internship ended in late December. If the club wanted to keep me on, they would've said something by now.

To be honest, I wasn't sure if I even wanted to work for Blackcastle full-time. I definitely wanted to stay in the sports nutrition field, but as much as I liked the team, I didn't love being the only female on staff. I was also sure some of my coworkers thought I'd gotten the internship because of my dad. My glowing performance reviews didn't matter as much as the revelation that I was Frank Armstrong's daughter.

"Is this related to why you missed the match against Holchester?" Vincent followed me out of the room and into the kitchen.

"No." *Yes.* I'd interviewed for an open nutritionist role at a local gym. It was a big step down from the Premier League, but a job was a job. That was the only day they could see me, so I'd called in sick and snuck out for the disastrous interview.

Long story short: my potential manager was a pig who couldn't stop ogling my chest or making sexual innuendos, and I ended our meeting early by calling him a shrimp-dicked weasel.

Anyway, I didn't get the job.

Scarlett and Carina were the only ones who knew the details. I wasn't telling anyone at Blackcastle I was looking at other employers until they officially ended my internship without a job offer, which seemed like the proper thing to do.

"What about the text from two weeks ago?" Vincent leaned against the counter while I assembled the ingredients for a salad.

"What text?"

"The one you got at Scarlett and Asher's house. You looked like someone told you your dog died."

I froze. Vincent was the last person I'd expected to pick up on my mood shift. I was always the perky, upbeat one, and I'd cultivated that image so strongly, most people never noticed when I became subdued.

It was my superpower. Smile for the world, crash out in silence. The perfect shield against unwanted pity.

I should've guessed Vincent would crack that shield the way he did everything else. That was *his* superpower.

"Sorry. I didn't mean to pry," he said when I didn't respond. He wasn't smiling anymore. "But you looked upset that day, and I—" He cleared his throat. "I want to make sure you're okay. Since we're now flatmates and all. Can't have you spiraling when we're in the same flat."

A ball of emotion lodged in my chest. I breathed past it and summoned a bright smile. "Oh, that. It was a stupid message from, um, an old coworker. Nothing major." I busied myself with the salad so he couldn't see my face.

There had been no ex coworker. In reality, my mom had received my voicemail and texted me her big news.

I'm off to brunch so can't talk, but I'm pregnant again! I'm finally getting a daughter! Will discuss later. xo

Finally getting a daughter. Implying she didn't have one already.

It wasn't my mom's intention to make me feel invisible; it never was. But that made it worse. Careless cruelty always cut deeper than intentional malice.

"Speaking of upset, we can't tell my dad you're living here." I washed a handful of cherry tomatoes and dropped them in my salad. "I know we already said we won't, but I have to mention it again. He'll freak out."

"Trust me. I have no plans to say anything to him. I like living too much," Vincent said dryly.

"Does he know about your intruder situation?"

"Not yet." Vincent glanced away. "I'm not sure it's worth bringing up."

"It worried you enough to move out until the police get a lead on this guy. Or girl," I amended.

"That's more for Scarlett's sake than mine." His smile returned, but it didn't quite reach his eyes. "I appreciate your concern though. Between the custom bedroom decor and this"—he gestured between us—"I'm starting to think you like me."

I scoffed. "There's no *this*. I'm only asking so I know what not to say in front of my dad."

Despite my dismissal, a twinge of concern nagged at me. The intruder was probably a one-off thing, but what if it wasn't? Fans did wild stuff all the time, but it only took one person going off the rails for tragedy to strike.

An image of Vincent bleeding out on the floor like Tyler Conley flashed through my mind. The twinge tightened into a knot.

I'd held off on interrogating Vincent about the situation. He had enough people fussing about it without me piling on, but my blithe comments didn't mean I was indifferent to the danger.

We weren't best friends, but for better or worse, he'd become an indispensable part of my life in London. If anything happened to him, my world wouldn't be the same.

"Don't say anything." Vincent's mouth set in a stern line. "I'll handle it."

"Sure." I hesitated, debating, before my voice softened. "It's okay to feel scared. I know it's not 'socially acceptable' for a guy to show weakness or whatever, but if someone breaks into your house, anxiety is normal."

His gaze flew to mine.

No tingle this time—only a beat of breathlessness that stretched out like a sigh. Warm, heavy, knowing.

Ninety-nine percent of our conversations revolved around playful jabs and insults. That was the dynamic we were most comfortable with. But every now and then, we'd drop our guards, and those moments would feel deeper than they did with anyone else *because* they were so rare.

It was how I knew they were real.

Vincent's throat moved with a swallow. He held my gaze for an extra millisecond before shifting his attention to the counter.

"Good to know." A trace of huskiness deepened his voice, but when he spoke again, it was gone. "Thanks for letting me stay here, even if it's to prove a point." He tossed out a grin. "No hotel concierge can match the personalized service I've received so far. Five stars. No notes."

Our earlier moment splintered into twin shards of relief and... disappointment? No, that couldn't be right.

"I do love proving a point." I resumed making my dinner and drizzled a bit of balsamic vinaigrette over the salad. "Also, just so we're clear, I'm not a concierge, mother, *or* maid. You're responsible for your own chores and cooking, and if you slack off"—I pointed a fork at him—"I'm kicking you out onto the street. Got it?"

He gave me a laconic salute. "Yes, ma'am," he drawled. His eyes glittered with amusement. "Don't worry. You won't even notice I'm here."

CHAPTER 6

VINCENT

"HELP. I'M DYING." STEVENS SANK ONTO THE CHANGING room bench with a groan. "I swear Coach is a masochist because who comes up with drills like that? They're inhumane."

"Stop whining," Samson said. The Nigerian winger gently shoved Stevens's shoulder. "You're a professional. Act like it."

"A professional sufferer." Stevens looked up at me with puppy dog eyes. "Captain, *do* something."

I laughed and pulled my shirt over my head. "Sorry, man, Samson's right. You gotta toughen up or we'll never beat Milan this weekend."

"Fuckin' Milan. Don't worry. We'll beat 'em." Stevens raised his voice. "Right, boys?"

"Fuck yeah!"

"We're going to kick their ass!"

"Blackcastle til the end!"

Raucous agreement filled the changing room. It was interspersed with laughter and the usual shit talking, though it was more subdued today than usual. Training had been brutal, and the pressure was on to deliver during this weekend's match.

Since we topped the Premier League last season, we'd automatically qualified for this year's Champions League, or UCL, Europe's most prestigious club football competition. Our next hurdle was clearing the knockout stages to make it to the semi-finals in the spring. I felt good about our odds, but we had some tough matches ahead.

"How's the new flatmate situation going?" Asher asked. He'd already showered and changed. How the fuck was that possible when we only finished training ten minutes ago? "Did Brooklyn spike your protein shake with laxatives yet?"

"No, and don't give her any ideas. You know she'd do it."

"Don't tempt me. I have plenty of ideas, but I'll keep them to myself for Scarlett's sake. Just don't piss me off, yeah?"

"Fuck off, Donovan." But I was smiling.

I'd been living with Brooklyn for almost a week, and it was going surprisingly well. We had the same schedule, the same cleaning habits, and the same diet. She took an absurdly long time in the bathroom every morning, but I hogged the television every other night, so it was a fair tradeoff.

That being said, I was never letting my protein shakes out of my sight again.

I was about to head for the showers when the changing room fell silent.

"DuBois!" Coach's voice boomed through the sudden quiet. Every head swiveled toward me. "My office. Now."

A low chorus of *oohs* sprang up from the rest of the team. I swear, it was like captaining a bunch of schoolboys.

"Shit. What did you do?" Asher asked.

"No fucking clue."

I walked toward Coach's office, my steps heavy with trepidation.

He hadn't called me to his office out of the blue since Asher first transferred to Blackcastle. Our rivalry at the time had cost us the league final, and Coach had been furious.

But Asher and I were friends now, so that was no longer an issue. Training had gone smoothly today, and the club's overall performance this season was stellar.

I racked my brain for other reasons why Coach would want a sidebar but came up blank.

"Close the door and sit down," he said when I entered his office. He sat behind his desk, his expression inscrutable.

I did as he asked, my unease growing by the second. "What's this about, Coach?"

He steepled his fingers beneath his chin and regarded me for a long moment. "You've been keeping a secret from me."

My stomach plummeted to my feet. *Shit*. Had he found out I was living with Brooklyn? If so, did he think we were sleeping together?

A dozen images of my immediate future flashed through my mind, each bloodier than the last.

Me getting strangled by Coach.

Me being pummeled to death by one of his paperweights.

Me meeting the lethal end of his letter opener.

I gulped and shifted my attention to his desk. That was a mistake. The first thing I saw was a photo of Brooklyn smiling up at me from beside his computer. She was wearing a yellow sundress and her hair was shorter, but her smile and the sparkle in her eyes were the same.

"Vincent!" Coach's voice yanked my eyes back to him. His brows settled into a frown so deep, I was afraid his face would get stuck that way. "Is there anything you want to tell me?"

"Not particularly, no," I hedged.

"So someone didn't break into your house after the Holchester match?"

Fuck, I was going to die—*wait, what?*

I was so sure he was going to bring up Brooklyn that it took my brain a beat to process his words.

The intruder. *That* was the secret he'd discovered—not the fact I was living with his daughter.

My lungs expanded with air again. "It's not a big deal," I said, trying to hide the relief in my voice. "I filed a police report and they're looking into it. They're not too worried. Neither am I." That wasn't totally true, but I wasn't going to whine about it to Coach.

Coach's eyebrows rose at my response. "Then why aren't you living at home?"

How did he—*Adil.* He was the only person who would've spilled to Coach. That little rat. I was going to murder him.

"I'm waiting until the contractors finish upgrading my security system," I lied. "They're backlogged, so it's taking longer than expected."

"Where are you living now?"

"A hotel."

"Which one?"

"The Hyde Regency."

Coach's eyes narrowed. A minute ticked by, followed by another. Beads of sweat dotted my hairline, and right when I thought he'd call me out on my bullshit, he gave a curt nod.

"Next time something like this happens, I want to hear it straight from you," he said. "We don't keep secrets on my team. My players are my responsibility, and I'm invested in your well-being on and off the pitch. So any time you run into trouble, you come to me. Do you understand?"

"Yes, sir."

"Good. Now get out of my office. And DuBois?"

I paused with my hand on the doorknob.

"Don't be too hard on your teammates," he said. "They're just looking out for you."

Translation: don't kill them, or you'll have to answer to me.

As annoyed as I was with Adil, Coach was right. Adil didn't have a malicious bone in his body. If he told anyone about my situation, it was out of genuine concern.

I sighed. I couldn't even be angry in peace.

"I know," I said. "I appreciate you looking out for me, Coach."

Another nod, then I was gone.

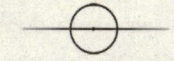

BROOKLYN

Damn him.

I thought I could put Vincent off with his ridiculously pink room and a list of strict chores, including a full cleaning and laundry day every week, but the man was like Teflon. Every attempt I made to get under his skin bounced off him and backfired on me instead.

I stood in the doorway between the kitchen and the living room. The hum of the vacuum filled the flat as Vincent moved through the flat, oblivious to my presence. He wore nothing except for a pair of sweatpants, which hung just low enough to toe the line between casual and criminal. His arm and back muscles flexed every time he pushed the vacuum forward, and I hated that I noticed.

Chores weren't supposed be sexy. They were supposed to be mundane, but watching a shirtless, slightly sweaty Vincent DuBois be domestic on a Friday night was anything but mundane.

My eyes lingered on the sculpted planes of his shoulders, and a weird sensation tightened in my stomach.

He'd lived here for only five days, and I was already desperate for him to move out. He took up too much space. Too much oxygen. If we kept this up for much longer, I was going to suffocate from the lack of air.

"If you keep staring at me like that, I'm going to have to charge admission." Vincent's drawl floated above the noise before he cut the vacuum off. He turned to where I stood, his mouth tugging up into a knowing smirk as I quickly dragged my eyes up to his face.

Heat blazed from my neck up to my cheeks. *Not so oblivious after all.* "You're living in my flat," I reminded him. "I should be the one charging *you* admission."

"You do. I pay rent—rent that's double the market value, by the way."

"Well, I should charge you more for...for indecent exposure."

His eyebrows rose. Amusement glided through his eyes. "How so?"

"It's unnecessary to vacuum with your shirt off. I didn't sign up to see that." I gestured at his bare torso. The lighting caught on the ridges of his abs, and I couldn't help counting them. *One, two, three...six, seven, eight.* Of *course* he had an eight-pack. He was such an overachiever. "If I wanted to see a half-naked man, I'd go to *Magic Mike Live.*"

His amusement sharpened into a devilish gleam. He walked over, stopping close enough for his body heat to sink beneath my skin. My muscles involuntarily clenched when he propped an arm on the doorframe beside my head.

"Does my half-nakedness bother you, buttercup?" His voice was like silk, pitched so low I strained to hear it over the sudden roar of my pulse.

My unwelcome reaction to his proximity brought in a rush of annoyance. How was it possible he smelled like soap and fresh laundry when I could see the faint sheen of sweat on his chest?

"Yes." I met his eyes and willed myself not to breathe in too deeply. "It's inappropriate."

"If you think this is inappropriate, wait till you hear I sleep naked."

A lightning-quick image of his naked form tangled up in his sheets flashed through my head. It was gone in a blink, but it was enough to warm my blood.

I clenched my teeth. I hated hormones sometimes.

"What you do when you sleep is none of my business. That's in the privacy of your room. But when you're in a common area, please refrain from unnecessary clothing removals," I said, well aware I sounded like a prude. "How would you feel if I walked around with my shirt off?"

I knew I'd set myself up before the words finished leaving my mouth.

A flare of heat darkened his eyes, and the warmth in my blood turned downright scorching. "I don't know," he drawled. "Why don't you try it and I'll tell you?"

A flame flickered low in my stomach, but I raised my chin, my tone cool and clipped. "No, thank you."

I couldn't think of a wittier reply. I was too furious with myself for letting him get to me.

It's almost like you're scared.

Scared of what?

Of not being able to control yourself around me.

Vincent had baited me into letting him move in because I wanted to prove that he didn't affect me, but was he right? Was taking off his shirt and having a sexy voice all it took for me to lose our invisible challenge? I didn't even *like* the guy in that way. He was objectively gorgeous, but arrogant. Funny, but annoying. Charming, but utterly infuriating.

No. The dust in the air must be clogging up my common sense. I could absolutely control myself around Vincent, and there was no way in hell I'd let him think otherwise.

"While we're on the subject of impropriety, you might want to wear a thicker shirt," Vincent said, his voice suddenly strained. "Or... something else."

I blinked. "Excuse me?"

His gaze flicked to my chest. I looked down, horror consuming me when I discovered what he was talking about.

I never wore a bra at home, and I'd resisted changing that habit after Vincent moved in. Underwire was too uncomfortable to bother with even when there was man in my house.

It hadn't been a problem—until now. Despite the warmth in the flat, my nipples had hardened to the point that they were clearly visible through my thin cotton T-shirt.

I instantly crossed my arms, my skin flushing hot and cold. The flame in my stomach flickered again, but I ignored it and looked up at Vincent.

His gaze lingered on mine, all traces of amusement gone. His jaw was tight, and the weight of his stare sent a shiver ghosting down my spine.

For a second, neither of us moved. Silence stretched between us, thick and charged, until I forced a reply from my throat.

"It wouldn't be inappropriate if you didn't look." My heart beat a little too fast for my chest. I wasn't making sense, but any words were better than that taut, electric tension from earlier. "You shouldn't be staring at...*them* anyway." I couldn't bring myself to use the anatomical term. It sounded too sexual for an already precarious situation.

"It's hard not to," he said wryly. "They're right there."

Fresh embarrassment washed across my face. "Who's the one who can't control themself now?"

"I never said I could control myself around you."

My pulse tripped.

"I can," he added with a hint of roughness. "But I never said it."

"Semantics." It came out breathless and a little angry as I tried to wrangle my runaway hormones back into submission.

Maybe I was ovulating, and Vincent's soap was infused with some sort of weird pheromone. That was the only possible explanation. We'd known each other for over a year, and I'd never reacted to him this way before.

Then again, we'd never been this close before—his breath grazing my skin, his scent filling my lungs, the warmth between us a palpable, living thing.

The corner of Vincent's mouth tipped up, but the amusement in his eyes was still buried beneath a flicker of heat. "I'm not a saint. If you walk around looking like that, I'll notice." His jaw flexed again. "So I'm merely suggesting you find a way to remedy the problem, or I'll think you're purposely trying to tempt me."

Trying to tempt him? He wished. I'd only try to tempt him if I wanted him, which I *didn't*.

This had gone on long enough. I needed to regain control of the situation.

"That sounds like a personal problem. If it bothers you so much, you can always move back home," I said. No more semi-flirting or sexual innuendos. We had to return to our regularly scheduled programming of insults and verbal spars, ASAP. "Forget your new security system. I bet your personality is enough to ward off any women who might think of setting foot in there." There. That was better.

I expected Vincent to counter with his usual cocky grin and a flippant remark. Instead, he froze, the color draining from his face. His breath quickened before he dropped his arm from the wall and stepped back, chest heaving. Tension ran up the cords of his neck and across his jaw, and any sparks from earlier evaporated.

It all happened in the space of seconds.

Confusion bloomed. My insult had been a standard one, as far as our relationship went. Why was he reacting like I'd punched him?

"Vincent?" I asked tentatively. "Are you—"

"I'm going to take a shower." He cut me off.

He turned abruptly and walked away, leaving me alone to wonder what the hell just happened.

CHAPTER 7

VINCENT

I LEANED FORWARD, PRESSING MY FOREHEAD AGAINST the shower tile as hot water pounded my back. My heartbeat was finally returning to normal, but the knots in my back and shoulders remained.

I didn't know what happened. She mentioned me moving home, and my body just revolted. Cold sweat. Faint nausea. Full-body chills.

I knew she'd been joking, but that hadn't stopped the physical onslaught. It'd been so sudden and unexpected, I couldn't think of what else to do except leave. Immediately.

I closed my eyes and took a long, deliberate breath.

I didn't get panic attacks, not even on the pitch. I'd been anxious the night someone broke into my house, but I thought I'd gotten over it. Someone leaving a stupid doll wasn't a big deal, right? I hadn't been physically harmed.

But I'd forgotten what a mindfuck it'd been until now. I'd moved out before I could grapple with the consequences of that night, and Brooklyn's words had dragged a shit ton of baggage to the surface.

It wasn't about harm done. It was about the violation—the knowledge that someone had been in my personal space, touching my things and doing God knew what else before I came home. Who was to say they hadn't rifled through my drawers or planted secret cameras everywhere?

That kind of unease burrowed under your skin and stayed there, no matter how many locks I changed or new security measures I installed.

You can always move back home.

My throat tightened, my mind spinning images of what that would look like—the constant checking over my shoulder, startling at every creak and rattle. The vague sense of dread every time I walked through the door. The inability to feel safe in my own fucking house.

Yes, I could hire a physical security team, but I hated the thought of strangers hovering over me, watching my every move. Besides, bodyguards wouldn't change anything. My hang-ups were psychological. I could hire a hundred bodyguards, and the thought of sleeping at home would still fuck with my head.

I couldn't do it. Not yet.

The violation was too fresh. I'd get over it with time or maybe therapy, but those things took, well, time, and I didn't have any to spare right now. Not when it was the middle of the season and we were contenders in the UCL. I needed to be laser focused on the game, which meant I couldn't return home until the police caught the perp (unlikely) or the thought of sleeping in my own bedroom didn't make me break out in a cold sweat.

Until then, I had to stay put at Brooklyn's place—no matter how much she tempted me.

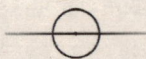

I didn't talk to Brooklyn again all weekend. I went to training on Saturday and spent Sunday at Adil's house, playing video games. I needed a little space from her after our weird, tension-charged moment on Friday.

I'd teased her about staring at me as a joke. I felt her eyes on me the entire time I'd been vacuuming, and I couldn't resist the opportunity to get under her skin. But fuck, being that close to her and seeing how flustered she was…it wrecked my self-control. The fact she hadn't been wearing a bra was the cherry on top.

Even now, days later, the memory of her nipples straining against her T-shirt brought a rush of heat to my groin.

I willed the image away as I entered the flat on Monday evening and tossed my keys in the bowl near the door. The last thing I wanted was to return home with an ill-advised erection.

The faint sound of computer keys clacking came from the kitchen. I followed it and found Brooklyn sitting at the tiled island. A pair of black-rimmed glasses perched on her nose while an untouched green smoothie sat on the table next to her. Her brow furrowed with concentration as she typed away.

She was so engrossed in her work that she didn't hear me enter. Every once in a while, she'd stop typing to scribble something in her notebook. Her face would light up, and she'd return to her laptop with renewed zeal.

The corners of my mouth kicked up. She looked inexplicably adorable and somewhat intimidating when she was so focused, like a kitten who wouldn't hesitate to claw your eyes out if you interrupted mealtime.

"You should take a break," I said. "That smoothie looks too good to go to waste."

"Jesus!" Brooklyn startled. She slammed her laptop shut, her face turning pink. "How long have you been standing there?"

"Long enough to watch your dinner get cold." I walked over and pulled up the stool next to hers.

"I'm not that hungry."

"Too busy writing one-star reviews on TripAdvisor?"

"Too busy compiling a list of ways to kill someone without getting caught." She gave me a sweet smile. "For curiosity's sake, of course."

"Of course," I drawled. "I wouldn't expect anything less."

Our eyes connected, and a beat of charged silence hummed between us before I tapped a gentle finger against the temple of her glasses. "I didn't know you wore glasses."

"I don't. I mean, I do, but I don't need them." She tucked a strand of hair behind her ear in an uncharacteristically self-conscious gesture. "I only wear them when I need to be productive. It's a weird trigger. When I put them on, my brain instantly switches to work mode."

It was a good thing she didn't wear them all the time because those glasses were sexy as hell, but I kept that thought to myself.

"What are you working on?"

"Updated meal plans for the team. My performance evaluation is coming up, so I want to make sure that they're, um, good."

Normally, I would've zeroed in on her suspicious verbal stumble if I weren't so distracted by another part of her reply.

"Final evaluation, huh?" I said casually. "What are you doing after the internship?"

"I haven't decided yet."

Something tugged at my gut. Hard.

I knew she was an intern and that all internships eventually ended, but I'd foolishly assumed she'd take a full-time job at Blackcastle afterward. She was a great nutritionist, and her dad was the manager, for Christ's sake.

"I see." I cleared my throat, not wanting to dwell on why the prospect of her leaving upset me so much. "Speaking of Blackcastle, I forgot to tell you. I talked to your dad last week." I summarized my conversation with Coach. "I told him I'm staying at a hotel, but I'm not sure he buys it. We'll have to be extra careful."

"The police still don't have any leads?"

"I don't think they're even looking." I kept my expression studiously neutral. I'd recovered from my anxiety attack on Friday, but any mention of the intruder situation still sent a wave of unease through me.

Brooklyn groaned. "They have to. I don't want you living here forever."

"Because you find me too irresistible and you're afraid you'll throw yourself at me sooner or later," I said with a wise nod. "I understand."

"Not that again." She crossed her arms. Thankfully, she was wearing a bra today. "Can you think of any other conversation topic? This one's getting old."

"Old but true."

My knee accidentally grazed hers. An electric spark jolted up my leg, and from the way her breath caught, she felt it too.

We joked about each other's self-control, but there was a glimmer of truth to our words that neither of us wanted to acknowledge—an ember of attraction buried beneath the wisecracks and feigned nonchalance. Maybe it was purely physical, or maybe it was something more. Either way, it was safer to treat it as a joke. There was no risk or vulnerability in a joke.

"You're insufferable," Brooklyn said, moving her leg away. Yet she lingered, her body angled toward mine as if the distance between us hadn't quite registered yet.

"I've been called worse."

She huffed out a laugh.

A new silence fell, lighter than the last but simmering with something unspoken.

Heat pulsed across my skin, and it took me a second to realize it wasn't metaphorical but literal—sweat beaded on my forehead and dampened my shirt, making it stick to my skin. I'd been so distracted by Brooklyn that I hadn't noticed the thick, suffocating warmth until there was a lull in our conversation.

"Is the AC broken?" I asked, breaking the quiet. "I'm roasting in here."

Most London flats didn't have air conditioning. Brooklyn's was one of the rare exceptions, but I didn't hear its steady hum in the background. The weather was unusually warm for October, and we still needed to run the AC in order to sleep comfortably.

"It gave out this morning. I already let the landlord know, but he can't fix it until—*what are you doing?*" Brooklyn squeaked when I pulled my shirt over my head and tossed it on the floor.

It helped. Barely.

"What does it look like? I'm cooling off." Now that I'd noticed the heat, I couldn't *stop* noticing it. It seemed to intensify with every passing second. If I splashed water on myself, it would probably sizzle. "I'd take my bottoms off too, but I figured you wouldn't appreciate me walking around without trousers."

"I don't appreciate you walking around without a shirt again," Brooklyn sputtered. "Put it back on! We just talked about this the other night."

"Relax, buttercup." I hopped off my stool and strode to the fridge. I opened the door, a welcome blast of cold air hitting me in the face. "You work for a men's football club. It's nothing you haven't seen before."

"That's at work, not in my own home. It's different."

I grabbed a water from the bottom shelf. "How so?"

"It just is. This is the fourth time you've taken your shirt off in front of me, and you've only been here for a week."

She'd counted. Interesting.

I closed the fridge, turned, and cocked an eyebrow. "Remaining fully clothed in communal spaces wasn't one of your flat rules."

"It is now."

"You can't retroactively add a new item to the flat rules."

"Yes, I can. It's my flat, which means they're my rules." Brooklyn's gaze remained fixed on my face even as I closed the distance between us again.

"Admit it. You *are* scared," I said.

"I have no idea what you're talking about."

"I'm talking about the fact that you're staring at my face like I have the map to the Holy Grail engraved on there—*or* like you're determined not to look anywhere else because that would be too tempting."

"Is this hell? Am I in hell? I *must* be if you're here and I'm forced to endure the same back and forth every three days." Despite her scoff, a telltale hint of pink tinged her cheeks.

"Answer the question, buttercup."

"You didn't ask a question. You said I'm scared, which I'm not." Brooklyn lifted her hair from her shoulders. I absolutely did not notice how the movement exposed the delicate curve of her neck or the way her pulse fluttered beneath her skin. "If anything, *you're* scared of *me*."

I let out a disbelieving laugh. "Why would I be scared of you?"

"For the same reason of not being able to control yourself. Tell me you're not staring at my neck and thinking about kissing it right now."

"I hate to break it to you, but necks aren't a turn-on for me," I lied. "I'm not a vampire. But if you want to talk about staring, let's talk about the way you *ogled* my abs the other night."

"I wasn't ogling. I was...counting." The pink on her cheeks darkened. "Eight-packs are so over. I prefer dad bods. They're way cuddlier."

"Liar."

"Egomaniac."

We stared each other down, our words bristling with heat and an unspoken challenge. The air crackled like static before a storm.

Brooklyn wasn't wrong about me being attracted to her, but I wasn't wrong about her being attracted to me either. I would bet on it. In fact...

An idea sparked in my head, one so bold and audacious that I couldn't help but let out a slow grin.

"There's a way to end this debate once and for all," I said. "Let's bet on it."

"Excuse me?"

"A bet. Let's see who'll cave and kiss the other first. We'll be living together for a while. We might as well make things interesting."

Brooklyn snorted. "That just sounds like an excuse for you to kiss me."

"No, because I wouldn't kiss you. *You'd* kiss *me*." I spread my hands in a matter-of-fact gesture. "That's the point of the bet."

It was genius. I was a little worried at how easily she got under my skin, but competition was hardwired into my DNA. Even if I *wanted* to kiss her, I wouldn't because I wanted to win more.

That was the beautiful irony of the bet—it gave us "permission" to kiss the other, but it effectively ensured we wouldn't, thereby keeping us safe from emotional vulnerability and any other consequences that might arise if we ever gave in to our attraction.

"That's the dumbest thing I've ever heard," Brooklyn said, but it wasn't a no. She was as competitive as I was. "Hypothetically, let's say I agree. What would the winner get?"

"Bragging rights and…" I searched for another prize. "A thousand pounds."

"A *thousand pounds*?" Her jaw dropped. "Not all of us make a star athlete's salary."

"Fine. Bragging rights and a hundred pounds, plus the knowledge that you were right and the other person can't resist you."

Childish? Sure. Fun? Absolutely.

Rolling with a stupid wager was infinitely better than whatever might've happened the other night if my unwanted but perfectly timed anxiety attack hadn't interrupted us.

"What are the parameters of the bet?" Brooklyn asked.

Got her. Hook, line, and sinker. "Nothing illegal or coercive," I said. "Everything else is fair game. The kiss also has to be voluntary and purposeful. CPR doesn't count. Neither does getting trapped under mistletoe or tripping and falling on the other person."

"Kisses are mutual. How are we supposed to determine who initiated it?"

"Come on. One person has to lean in; the other has to meet them. It's like porn. You know it when you see it."

"That isn't clear enough."

"Yes, it is. There's no reason to get hung up on such a small detail unless you're thinking of caving already." I shrugged. "Come on, buttercup. Yes or no. Are you in or out?"

Her nostrils flared. I could see the debate raging inside her because it was the same one I'd have if I were in her position.

On one hand, she couldn't resist a challenge, especially when it came from me. She wanted to prove to me—and maybe herself—that she *wasn't* attracted to me and that, even if she was, her self-control was stronger than mine. The hundred pounds didn't hurt either.

On the other hand, a kiss might land us in trouble with Blackcastle, which had a strict no-fraternization rule. Our platonic flatmate situation didn't violate it, but any romantic or sexual contact—like a kiss—*would*. The violation could get us fired, suspended, or at least heavily disciplined in whatever manner HR saw fit.

However, that was only *if* the kiss happened and *if* they found out. It would be one kiss shared by two people who both had something to lose. If we didn't tell anyone, how would Blackcastle know?

"What's the proposed time frame?" Brooklyn asked, dodging my question.

"For as long as we're living under the same roof."

She drew her bottom lip between her teeth. I could practically hear the gears turning in her head.

"Fine, but only because I can't wait to prove you wrong." She held out her hand, her eyes steely with determination.

I grinned and shook it. It was small and soft, but her grip was like iron.

Although there was a 95 percent chance our bet would end in a draw, that didn't mean I wouldn't try my best to outplay her. "May the best flatmate win."

CHAPTER 8

VINCENT

I WAS FLEXIBLE WHEN IT CAME TO A LOT OF THINGS, BUT there was one time-honored ritual I refused to miss: my Tuesday night dates with Channel 4.

Forget pubs and parties. The only place I wanted to be at that time was on the sofa, parked in front of a flat-screen TV with a cold drink in hand and a bowl of popcorn in my lap.

I relaxed into my seat, my shoulders loosening at the familiar intro music. My phone was on silent, and—

"What are you watching?"

I glanced over and nearly choked on a kernel of popcorn.

Brooklyn had been holed up in her bedroom all evening. I hadn't expected to see her again until the next morning, but there she was, waltzing into the living room and wearing the most indecent piece of clothing possible: an oversized football shirt. Nothing else. No shoes, no makeup, just a Blackcastle shirt that skimmed the bottoms of her thighs and showed off miles of bare, tanned skin. Her hair spilled over her shoulders in glossy golden waves, and she looked so fucking good

I had to physically restrain my jaw from dropping.

The kernel went down the wrong pipe. I erupted into a fit of coughs and grabbed my drink, my eyes watering. I gulped it down while Brooklyn sank down next to me on the sofa with a deceptively innocent smile.

"Are you okay?" She patted me on the back. "Do you need CPR?"

That sneaky little minx. We were one day into our bet, and she'd already fired the first shot.

Here's a secret: for most guys, especially athletes, an oversized shirt was the hottest thing a woman could wear. Forget lingerie and heels. Seeing a member of the opposite sex in our favorite club's gear was pure kryptonite.

Brooklyn hung out with footballers enough to know that. She was playing to my weakness, but I'd be damned if I lost to a piece of athletic wear.

"I'm fine." I got my coughing under control. "To answer your question, I'm watching *The Great British Bake Off*."

I purposely didn't look at her.

I can do this. I saw people in shirts every day. She was no different.

But just in case, I stared straight ahead and pictured Adil's hairy legs poking out from beneath her top instead.

"Again? Do you watch anything else?" Brooklyn eyed the screen with dubious interest. "You're obsessed with this show."

"Because it's the greatest show ever made." I couldn't believe that was even a question. "Don't tell me you've never experienced the brilliance that's *Bake Off*."

"I've watched a few clips. It's fine."

I whipped my head around to gape at her. "It's *fine*? You think the show is just *fine*? What's wrong with you?"

Forget visions of Adil. Her blasphemy effectively killed the power of her shirt.

"Nothing is wrong with me. Believe it or not, people *can* have different tastes in television."

"Sure, if you're talking about literally anything else. But *Bake Off* is an institution. It's universally beloved."

"Clearly not."

I reached over and placed the back of my hand on her forehead. It was distressingly cool. "No fever, which means you're not sick and delirious. You just have bad taste." I dropped my hand. "I'm so sorry. That condition is incurable."

Brooklyn snorted. "You're overreacting. I didn't say I hated it. I said it's fine, which is the equivalent of giving it a C. That's a passing grade."

"It deserves more than a C." My indignation rose by the minute. "You can't get the full experience from a few clips. Watch this episode with me. If you still don't love it by the end, I'll let it go."

"Are you sure? I don't want to intrude on your personal time."

"No, you—" I stopped short. *Wait a minute.*

Brooklyn stared back at me, the picture of innocence, but the gleam in her eyes gave her away.

Oh, she was good. She'd baited me into committing to an hour of her company when I was at my weakest (i.e. relaxed, at home, and watching *Bake Off* while she wore that damn outfit like a weapon). I couldn't withdraw my invitation without admitting my weakness, so I gritted my teeth and reassured her that she wouldn't be intruding *at all*.

Our joint viewing started off strong. Brooklyn fell silent, and I was sucked into the drama of Pastry Week. It was my favorite week.

Then, about ten minutes in, Brooklyn "casually" stretched her legs. The shirt rode up on her thigh, revealing another sliver of skin.

The contestants onscreen blurred. My jaw clenched, and I stared harder at the TV, willing my peripheral vision to die for the next fifty minutes or so.

Old socks. Smelly boots. Bloody sores.

I focused on mental images of the least sexy things I could think of.

My pride was at stake here. I could *not* give in this soon, no matter how nice she smelled or how soft her skin looked. One kiss wasn't worth the lifetime of gloating she'd lord over me if I lost.

Brooklyn yawned and stretched her arms over her head. Her sleeve grazed my arm, and a flicker of electricity darted over my skin.

I tensed.

Screw this. It was time to fight back.

I followed her lead and pretended to yawn. I leaned back, lazily stretching my arms and draping one over the back of the couch. The move was a classic for a reason—it worked.

My fingertips brushed the curve of her shoulder. I was close enough to feel the heat of her body, but that meant the reverse was also true.

I shifted in my seat. My thigh touched hers, and I had to suppress a smile when she stiffened.

That's right. Two can play at this game.

From that point on, it was a choreography of deliberate-disguised-as-unintentional attacks.

Brooklyn leaned into my embrace; I brought my arm fully around her shoulders.

She reached across me for popcorn, bringing her face perilously close to mine. From this distance, I could count each freckle scattered across her nose and cheeks and feel the soft warmth of her breath against my skin.

I turned my head, daring her to close the gap between us.

She didn't, and I didn't, but the possibility was there, humming in the background.

Neither of us spoke. Our communication was broadcast through our actions, and for the first time since I got hooked on *Bake Off*, I was only half paying attention to the weekly challenge.

The judges' commentary drowned out the heavy thumps of my heart. This entire bet was a catch-22—I was torturing myself as much as I was her with every "accidental" touch and glance. But that was what made it fun, and seduction attempts aside, this felt nice—us sitting on the couch, watching my comfort show together. I wasn't tempted to prove myself by filling the silence with funny stories or interesting tidbits. I could just...be.

By the time the showstoppers were judged and the episode wrapped, Brooklyn and I were snuggled closer than a real couple, but I refused to admit defeat and pull away first. Apparently, she felt the same way, so we were stuck in a tangle of limbs on the couch.

"So? What do you think?" I made a conscious effort not to inhale too deeply. Her head was tucked beneath my chin, and I was convinced she'd added some secret aphrodisiacs to her shampoo. No hair product should smell *that* good. "Did you change your mind about the show being just fine?"

Conversation was good. Conversation distracted me from how close her hand was to a certain private part—not enough to cross a line, but enough that I knew she was doing it on purpose. Well, I wasn't falling for it. Not today.

"It's better than I expected," she admitted. "But I'm still not convinced it's as great as you say it is."

My mouth parted. "Unbelievable." How could she say that after Pastry Week? It was famously one of the best weeks! "I was right when I said your bad taste is incurable."

"This coming from a guy who drinks protein shakes that taste like old gym socks."

"How—have you been stealing my shakes?"

"I took a *tiny* sip of one because I was curious." Brooklyn pinched her thumb and forefinger together to indicate how small her infraction was. "I'm a nutritionist. I couldn't help it. But don't worry, I learned my lesson because it was the most disgusting drink I've ever had."

"Your job isn't an excuse for committing an offense."

She huffed out a laugh. "You're such a fucking drama queen. No wonder you love reality TV."

"That's probably true," I acknowledged. I loved the messiness of reality TV. Sure, most of it was scripted, but some of it wasn't. It made me feel better, knowing I wasn't the only one who had to deal with weird people and fucked-up situations.

"Have you ever tried baking some of the stuff from the show?" Brooklyn asked.

"Once. I almost burned down my kitchen."

She lifted her head to stare at me. "You're joking."

"I swear. Firefighters came and everything. It was humiliating. My craving for blueberry pancakes made me the butt of my neighborhood's jokes for weeks." I grimaced. "Anyway, I never tried to bake again."

She burst into a fresh bout of laughter. "Oh, I would've paid *good* money to see that. Please tell me there are pictures."

"I'm glad my suffering amuses you." But my mouth curved with reluctance. It was impossible to hear her laugh without wanting to smile too.

We were still wrapped around each other, but our stubborn defiance had softened into something that felt almost normal.

We had to leave the living room eventually, but the moment felt too good for me to let go yet.

"What were you really working on yesterday?" I asked.

Brooklyn raised a quizzical brow.

"In the kitchen, before I came in," I clarified. "No one gets *that* excited about creating meal plans."

"Oh. That." Her smile faded. A second later, she disentangled herself from me and scooted over on the sofa. Cool air rushed in to fill her absence. It was a technical win for me in our silent battle, but I mourned her warmth too much to celebrate.

I dropped my arms, resisting the urge to draw her back into my embrace.

"If I tell you, you can't laugh," she said.

I nodded, my curiosity piqued. Besides, laughter was the last thing on my mind when she looked so unsure. The sight tugged at my chest harder than it should.

"Every year, ISNA—the International Sports Nutrition Association—gives out awards to high achievers in the field. The recipients are usually people who've been doing this for decades. But this year, they created the Innovator Award to recognize nutritionists who are early in their careers but are driving innovation in the field. The winner gets a twenty-thousand-dollar cash prize and mentorship from a veteran practitioner. I found out about it last week, and I was working on the application when you came home." Faint pink bloomed across her cheeks. "It's a long shot, but the prize would be a game changer for me. It's the first time I've ever qualified for an ISNA award, so I got really excited."

"That's incredible." My brow furrowed. "Why did you think I'd laugh?"

"I don't know." She smoothed a hand over her thigh, her expression self-conscious. "When I say it out loud, it seems so out of reach. It's like telling someone I want to win an Olympic medal."

"That's not the same thing. You beat out thousands of applicants for the Blackcastle internship, and you're doing a damn good job. Winning an award for something you're great at isn't a long shot; it's deserved."

Some people dismissed Brooklyn as a nepotism hire, but a little birdie in HR told me they had no idea who her father was until she reached the final round. They only found out because they had to run the obligatory background screening.

Surprise flared in her eyes. We rarely gave each other compliments, but I meant what I said. She deserved that prize as much as anyone else.

"I see why they made you captain." Her smile returned in increments. "You're good at pep talks."

"Only if I believe what I'm saying," I said. "So how does it work? What do you have to do to win?"

"It's like applying for college. I need three letters of recommendation, a personal statement, and a CV listing relevant achievements and experiences, plus optional items like press coverage or journal publications. If I'm a finalist, I'll have multiple rounds of interviews." She bit her bottom lip. "The deadline is in two months, so I really need to focus. The personal statement will be the hardest part."

"At least the rest is fairly easy. Everyone at Blackcastle will give you a great rec. Hell, I'll write you one, if you want. Seriously."

Another flare of surprise, this time accompanied by a softness that made my heart twist. "I appreciate that, but they want diversified recommendations so I can only have one from Blackcastle." Her expression turned rueful. "Anyway, it would be weird to get all my recs from a place I'll no longer be working at."

I straightened. Her words hit me like a punch in the gut. "Wait. You're leaving?"

Her internship ended after the new year, but I'd assumed she would stay on as a junior performance nutritionist. Her leaving hadn't even occurred to me.

"It's not up to me," she said. "They haven't made an offer."

"That makes no sense. You're the best intern we have."

"Maybe, but I'm not the only intern. They can only hire so many people."

"Bullshit. The only other intern is Henry, and he's mediocre, at best." In fact, fuck Henry. He was a nice enough guy, but if he was the reason Brooklyn had to leave, I hated him (respectfully).

"It's subjective, I guess." She shrugged. "Enough about me. What about you? How do you feel about the club's odds of winning the Champions League?"

She wasn't subtle about her deflection, and I could respect that. But I could also be angry about the way Blackcastle was treating her.

"Pretty good." I swallowed the desire to call the HR director and ream them out. That would be stepping way over the line. Knowing Brooklyn, she would hate that. "We're kicking ass so far, but we haven't played our toughest competition yet."

We were in the league phase of the UCL. Teams played each other only once during this phase, and while we'd notched several wins so far, matches against Madrid, Barca, and other top clubs loomed in the coming weeks. We couldn't afford to slack off.

"There's a lot of pressure to make it to the finals from both the club and my agent. He thinks I have a solid shot at getting the Zenith ambassadorship if that happens," I added. I wasn't sure why I'd added that last part. To prolong the conversation? To impress Brooklyn?

If there was any brand deal capable of the latter, it was Zenith, a major global name that sold shoes, clothing, sports equipment, and every other athletic item you could think of. Unlike its competitors, who added new faces every year, Zenith was notorious for sticking to one or two ambassadors over the course of a decade. Ben Evers, its current ambassador for men's sports, had been with them for twelve years. He recently announced his retirement from swimming, and rumors were flying about Zenith's alleged search for his replacement.

Someone from their exec team contacted Lloyd, my agent, to set up a meeting. They didn't say what it was about, and I didn't want to get my hopes up, but it had to be about a potential sponsorship. I couldn't think of another reason they'd want to meet.

"Zenith. Wow." Brooklyn's eyebrows rose with reluctant admiration, and I'd be damned if that didn't spark a glow in my chest. "I feel like you're already the face of everything. Cologne, deodorant, clothing...I can't walk through a single Tube station without seeing your face plastered all over the walls."

"Then my plan for world domination is working."

I was only half-joking. I had more sponsorships than anyone at Blackcastle, including Asher. Lloyd was worried that would lead to "brand dilution," but I wasn't going to be at the top of the game forever. I might as well take advantage of it while I could.

The money I got from sponsors was my safety net. If I got injured tomorrow and had to quit football, I'd still be set for retirement. I earned more from my brand deals than I did my Blackcastle salary, and I'd invested that extra cash wisely.

But—and I'd never tell anyone this—the other reason I loved working with brands was because of the validation. Every deal was proof that they believed in me and that I deserved to be here.

I wasn't good enough for everyone, but I was good enough for someone.

"I hope you stay at Blackcastle," I told Brooklyn. "It wouldn't be the same without you."

She obviously didn't want to talk about it, but I couldn't let her go without sharing how I felt. I'd been in her shoes before. I'd waited for offers that never came, and I'd been passed over for opportunities that I worked my ass off for.

I couldn't change Brooklyn's employment circumstances, but I could make sure she knew she was appreciated. Her presence made a difference, regardless of what HR did or didn't do.

Her face softened. "Thanks." A smile played on her lips. "I think you'll get the Zenith deal whether you make it to the finals or not. You're you."

"Is that a compliment?"

"Usually, no, but in this case, yes. Don't read too much into it," she warned. "I'm delirious from lack of sleep."

"It's not even ten yet, Grandma."

"I woke up early, slacker."

My smirk mirrored hers as we fell back into our comfortable banter. Our brief moment of vulnerability had passed, but the echoes of it lingered, smoothing the edges of our insults.

"I'm going to bed." Brooklyn let out a genuine yawn and stood. "I have a long day tomorrow." She hesitated, then said, "Thanks for inviting me to watch the show with you. It was...fun."

"Anytime. Night, buttercup."

"Goodnight."

I waited until she disappeared into the hall before I cleaned up the living room and went to bed.

It wasn't until I turned off the lights that I realized I hadn't thought about our bet at all after we started talking. My guard had been completely down. If she'd made her move then, I would've fallen for it.

I covered my eyes with my forearm. *Fuck*.

CHAPTER 9

BROOKLYN

I WASN'T A BIG ASTROLOGY PERSON, BUT THE PLANETS had to be misaligned. There'd been too many strange occurrences for any other explanation.

First, there was the bet with Vincent, which set off alarm bells the minute he suggested it. I loved a good challenge, but competing with him to see who could seduce the other first was a bad idea on every level. One, it would force us to interact *more*, as if living together weren't enough. Two, winning the bet would mean violating Blackcastle's anti-fraternization policy, though I supposed no one would know if we didn't tell them. And finally, three, as much as I hated to admit it, I did find him infuriatingly attractive.

I thought living with him would kill his appeal because most guys were messy, dirty, and gross. He was the opposite. He cleaned, he cooked (sort of), and he folded laundry flawlessly. I kept running into him on his way out of the bathroom, and he used the world's best-smelling aftershave. It was infuriating.

None of that was enough to make me kiss him. Not even close.

But it was enough to make me uneasy.

The unease was exacerbated by our strangely enjoyable *Bake Off* night. I'd gone into the living room hoping to win our bet early. He was a guy, and guys couldn't resist a girl in a football shirt. That was a universal fact. But instead of getting him to kiss me, I'd started... having fun. Talking to him, snuggling against him (albeit reluctantly), and having a real conversation without our usual insults and snark. It was the standout night of my week, so that was unsettling.

Now, my dad and I were at our long-postponed dinner, and he didn't look right.

Correction: he looked *nice*, which wasn't right. The planets were definitely out of sync.

Frank Armstrong famously lived in athletic wear. He once made national news for showing up to a black-tie fundraiser in slippers, but here he was, dressed up in a suit and tie.

"Who invented this thing?" he grumbled. He tugged on his tie, his expression pained. "How can anyone eat comfortably when they're slowly choking to death?"

I stifled a laugh. "You don't have to wear a tie, Dad. A jacket is fine."

"I thought that was part of the dress code."

"It's not."

"Every other guy in here is wearing a tie."

"You *can* wear one if you want, but it's optional." I pulled up the restaurant's website on my phone and showed him the text. "See?"

"Oh, thank God." The tie was gone in an instant. "I don't get the whole dress code thing. I know this is supposed to be fancy, but I've been to a few restaurants like this. None of their chicken is better than Nando's."

"At least it's quieter. We can actually hear ourselves talk," I said lightly.

With its linen tablecloths, crystal chandeliers, and embossed leather-bound menus, the restaurant was definitely fancier than what either of us was accustomed to.

Despite his considerable salary as one of the Premier League's top managers, my dad was extremely lowkey. Maybe I should've picked a more casual spot for dinner, but I'd wanted to do something special.

When I packed up everything and left California after finishing grad school and getting accepted into Blackcastle's internship program, I had no idea how the move would go. I just knew I couldn't stay in San Diego and watch my mom fuss over her new family anymore.

I also figured it was time to get to know my father better. We hadn't lived in the same city since I was two, when my parents divorced and my mom moved out of the UK, vowing to never return. I'd spent a handful of summers with my dad as a teen, but he mostly worked, and I mostly ran around London, flirting with boys and eating my weight in scones. We'd never truly bonded, though that hadn't stopped him from being overly protective whenever he stepped away from the pitch long enough to realize I was of dating age.

Our dynamic hadn't changed much this time around, but I was determined to make an effort. My mom was a lost cause, but if I could salvage my relationship with one parent, it would be worth it.

My dad cleared his throat. "Sorry, Brooke," he said, apparently remembering the restaurant was my idea. He was the only person in the world who called me Brooke. "I didn't mean to complain. I'm sure the food will be great."

"It's okay. The reviews are good, so hopefully they weren't lying."

I took a sip of water. He laid his napkin across his lap.

I racked my brain for a fun conversation topic, but I couldn't think of anything except football and *The Great British Bake Off*, which my dad most certainly didn't watch.

Why hadn't I made a list of things we could talk about beforehand? *So stupid.*

Our silence stretched into painful territory until a server came to take our orders. After he left, quiet descended again, heavier than ever.

"So—"

"How—"

We spoke at the same time.

"You go first," I said right as he insisted, "You go first."

Another beat of silence.

"How did your meeting with Vuk go?" I finally asked. I didn't know much about the club's mysterious owner, but he kind of terrified me. He looked like he could snap you in half with his bare hands if you so much as breathed the wrong way.

"Good," my dad said. "He's happy with the team's performance."

"That's good."

"Yep, very good."

This was almost worse than silence. If we kept this up, and I had a nickel for every time we uttered the word "good" during dinner, I could fund the ISNA award myself.

Our painful small talk continued past our appetizers and into our mains. The weather, the traffic, our plans for the weekend—every topic felt forced and stilted. It was a complete one-eighty from my easy conversations with Vincent.

I wish he were here. The thought came to me with sudden force.

I'd never craved Vincent's company before. We worked together and had a lot of mutual friends, so he was always just...there. But no matter how much he provoked me or how often we argued, we never had a problem talking to each other. I could say anything or nothing to him and feel comfortable about it.

If he were here, he'd find a way to engage the table in a debate about volcanoes or something, and I wouldn't want to crawl out of my skin from the awkwardness.

I cut into my salmon with more force than necessary. Forget misaligned planets. I must've entered another dimension entirely if I was missing Vincent DuBois, of all people.

"Have you talked to your mother lately?"

My knife slipped and hit the porcelain plate with a clang. A nearby couple stopped eating to side-eye me, but I was too busy gaping at my dad to notice.

Rule number one in the dysfunctional relationship I had with my parents: don't talk about the other person in front of them. Ever.

The last time I violated this rule, I'd subjected myself to an hour-long tirade about "narcissism disguised as enlightenment" (age sixteen, my father's words), so him willingly bringing her up over dinner portended nothing short of the apocalypse.

I checked our surroundings for fire and brimstone before responding. "We've messaged a few times." *Once in the past month.* "Why?"

My dad took a bite of his steak, chewed, and swallowed before he said, somewhat cautiously, "I heard she's pregnant again."

I gave up on the salmon and set my knife aside. "She is."

I wasn't sure where my dad was going with this. He didn't know my mom's new family was one of the reasons I'd moved to London. He thought I'd moved because I wanted to work for the Premier League, which was true. It just wasn't the whole truth.

"How are you, uh, holding up?" he asked.

Maybe he was more observant than I gave him credit for.

"I'm happy for her," I lied. "I already have one half-sibling. What's one more?"

Don't get me wrong, I really did like my half-brother. Charlie was two years old and the cutest, happiest baby in the world. If I could hang out with him sans my mom, I would do so in a heartbeat.

But that was the thing. It was impossible to separate them. Obviously, they shouldn't be separated considering how young he was, but my mom hadn't any qualms about leaving me with a neighbor or random babysitter when I was that age. She'd never looked happier to be a parent than she did now, and I couldn't help feeling like I'd been her trial run. A thirty-day-free membership she'd accidentally signed up for and forgotten about for the past twenty-seven years.

None of this was Charlie's fault, but I couldn't help the way I felt either.

"How are you taking it?" I asked my dad.

He flicked his eyebrows up like that was the world's stupidest question, but he didn't want me to feel bad about it. "Your mother and I have been divorced for over two decades. She could give birth to a two-headed llama, and I wouldn't care."

Some of my tension eased, and I snorted out a laugh. "How did you know she's pregnant?"

"We still have some mutual friends. I didn't ask. They brought it up first."

"Ah." I had no illusions about my parents "coming to their senses" and getting back together. I wouldn't support that anyway; they were the worst fit for each other. They only married because they'd had a brief fling when my mom lived in the UK. She got pregnant with me, they tied the knot because that was what they were supposed to do, and after what my mom repeatedly told me were the "worst, most stressful years" of her life, they split in a legal battle that made World War II look civil.

But while my mom had moved on, dating a string of men who

wove in and out of my childhood and teenage years until she settled down, my dad never remarried. He was too obsessed with work.

"Have you thought about dating again?" I asked.

He was only in his late forties. There were plenty of women his age who would be thrilled to go out with him, and I sincerely thought he needed something other than work to keep him occupied.

"Absolutely not," he said firmly. "Managing the team is already a handful. I don't need the stress of a relationship on top of it."

"A good relationship is worth the occasional stress."

"In your twenties, yes. When you're my age? Not worth it." My dad cleared his throat. "What about you? Have you, uh, met any nice blokes here?"

"'Nice blokes'? That's *such* a dad thing to say," I teased.

"I should hope so, since I am your dad."

"Valid, and no, I haven't met anyone serious. I've been on a few dates, but they haven't gone anywhere."

I thought London would be a goldmine of British-accented hotties in perfectly tailored suits. While they *did* exist in certain pockets of the city, I'd neglected to factor in personality, work schedules, and general emotional availability when daydreaming about my great romance abroad.

My dad's brows pinched. "You have? With who? Why didn't I know about them?"

"Because they weren't important." I feigned exasperation, but secretly, a warm glow spread through my stomach. I didn't want him micromanaging my life, but this was the closest we'd ever gotten to a normal father-daughter conversation. "I promise, if I go on more than...five dates with a guy, I'll let you know."

"Five?" he sputtered. "That's too many. A second date is worth a heads-up."

"No way. First dates are for putting out feelers. Second dates are for confirming that the first date wasn't a fluke."

"What about the third, fourth, and fifth?"

"Third is the first true test for a potential relationship. Fourth is when it's getting kind of serious. Fifth is when it gets serious enough for me to alert friends and family."

"That makes no sense."

"It's just the way people do it these days, Dad."

His frown deepened. "Fine," he grumbled. "But it better not be one of those whirlwind things where you're married by the third date."

I wrinkled my nose. "Don't worry. I have *no* plans to marry anyone by any date at this time."

Theoretically, I liked the idea of marriage. Practically, I was nowhere near ready for that type of commitment.

"Good. You're young. You should be building your career and having fun. But not *too* much fun," he added quickly. "I trust your judgment. Just don't get involved with any footballers." He pointed his fork at me. "They're bad news. Great work ethic, terrible monogamists. Trust me. I hear their changing room chatter. I used to be *part* of the changing room chatter."

"Dad, please. I wouldn't date a footballer if they offered me a million pounds and a Lamborghini."

He nodded, apparently satisfied.

We returned to our meals, but my mention of a Lamborghini made me think of Vincent again. He drove a Lambo—midnight blue, fully customized, retailed for three hundred grand *without* the customizations.

He wasn't obsessed with sports vehicles the way Asher was, but he'd gone all out for the one he did own.

I wasn't going to lie. It was a sexy car.

I snuck a peek at my phone. No new messages—not that I'd been expecting any. I certainly hadn't been expecting one from Vincent.

What was he up to anyway? He'd been in the shower when I left, but it was Friday night. Famous footballers didn't stay home and watch TV on Friday nights. He was either out with his friends or... on a date.

Our bet didn't exclude us from dating other people. It would be weird to keep it going if either of us entered an exclusive relationship, but non-exclusive flings? Not prohibited under the rules.

A piece of fish stuck in my throat. I coughed and quickly gulped down the rest of my water, but I drank it too fast and started coughing even more.

My dad's brow creased. "Are you okay?"

"Uh-huh," I gasped. My eyes watered, but the coughing eventually subsided, and our server stopped hovering nearby like he was afraid I'd choke to death on his watch.

It was fine. I was fine.

I didn't care where Vincent was. He could do whatever he wanted, and so could I.

CHAPTER 10

VINCENT

"I CAN'T BELIEVE YOU'RE LIVING WITH COACH'S daughter." Adil shook his head. "He'll murder you if he finds out."

"Which is why he won't find out. *Right*?" I pinned the midfielder with a glare.

He gulped. "Uh, right."

It was Friday night, and Asher, Adil, Noah, and I were seated at a corner booth in the Angry Boar. The rest of the team was scattered throughout the pub.

I'd debated telling my friends about the bet, but it didn't feel right. As silly as it was, the wager was between Brooklyn and me only. I didn't want to bring other people into it, and I didn't need them telling me what a bad idea it was either.

I already knew it was a bad idea. I'd originally thought it was genius, but I quickly realized anything that brought me closer to Brooklyn was playing with fire. That shirt stunt she'd pulled the other night was diabolical.

But it was still easier to manage my *mild* attraction to her within the confines of a bet than to let it sprawl free, twisting and turning down roads that might end in humiliation, heartache, or worse.

Not that I thought it would get that far. It was just a precaution.

"You have to ask yourself—why are you risking the Boss's wrath by living with her?" Asher mused. While I usually called Coach, well, Coach, Asher always referred to him as the Boss. "Maybe it's because you have a crush on her."

My glare pivoted from Adil's face to his.

He smirked, and I wondered for the millionth time why my sister couldn't date someone who was less of a fuckhead.

"Scarlett's the one who suggested we move in together. You were there."

"Yeah, I was there when you basically dared her to let you move in. Why would you have done that unless you have a crush on her?"

"He has a point," Adil said.

"Stay out of it. You weren't even there." I turned to Noah. "Wilson, back me up."

"No, thanks," he said. "I think they're right."

I gaped at him. "You too?" This must've been how Caesar felt when Brutus stabbed him.

He shrugged, a small smile playing on his mouth when Asher high-fived him.

"I should've left you to mope at home alone," I grumbled.

Noah looked like he would've been perfectly happy with that, but no one twisted his arm and forced him to come out with us. I mean, I may have insinuated this was a quasi-mandatory team bonding night, but I hadn't held a gun to his head.

That being said, if his daughter wasn't sleeping over at a friend's place, he wouldn't be here, and I wouldn't blame him. It was tough raising a ten-year-old on your own, which was why I didn't take it personally whenever he declined our invitations.

I did, however, blame him for ganging up on me with Asher and Adil. He was the last person I'd expected to betray me.

"It's okay to have a crush on Brooklyn. I do. A teeny-tiny one," Adil said. "I feel bad that she has to live with you though."

"What's that supposed to mean?" I asked, insulted.

"It means she's a smoke show and you're not." He gave an apologetic shrug. "Sorry."

"Watch it," I growled over Asher's laughter. Even Noah was smiling at my expense. See? Traitors, all of them. "You're still on thin ice for ratting me out to Coach."

"I apologized for that already!" Adil complained. "Besides, I'm just telling the truth. I've seen both your legs. Hers are way better, which is crazy, because you're the pro athlete and she isn't."

Asher's laugh escalated into a cackle. Noah turned his head, his shoulders shaking.

I kept my indignation for another minute before I broke. My mouth curved, and I tossed a crumpled-up napkin at Adil in defeat. "You're such an asshole."

"A truthful one. I mean, you must be saint to live with her and not want to, you know." He waggled his eyebrows, and just like that, I wanted to kill him again.

"Want to what?"

If he noticed the dangerous edge in my voice, he didn't show it. "See if she looks as good out of her clothes as she does in them." He propped his chin in his hands, a dreamy look entering his eyes. "Those legs. That smile. That ass—*ow*!" He howled and clutched his shin beneath the table, his starry-eyed expression contorting into a pained grimace. "What the hell was that for?"

"Sorry," I said. "Didn't know your leg was there."

"So you kicked your foot into the air for no reason?"

I shrugged. "I needed to stretch my legs."

I took a sip of my drink, ignoring Adil's dramatic moans and Asher and Noah's knowing smirks.

Whatever they were thinking, they were wrong. I hadn't kicked Adil on purpose because the way he talked about Brooklyn made me want to tear his head off his shoulders. I certainly didn't care that he or anyone else might've noticed how long her legs were, or how beautiful her smile was, or how her ass was sculpted enough to deserve its own exhibit in a museum.

Like I said, his shin simply got in my way. It wasn't like I'd kicked him hard enough to injure him.

While Noah and Asher consoled Adil, who pitifully asked for more ginger beer in order to feel better, my mind wandered toward a certain flatmate again.

I'd caught a glimpse of her before I hopped in the shower earlier. We didn't get a chance to talk, but she'd been all dressed up for... who?

She wasn't with her friends, at least not the ones I knew. Scarlett was visiting our mother for a "girls' weekend," and Carina had a new side gig that required her to work tonight.

Was Brooklyn out with other friends? Or was she on a date?

An unpleasant sensation slithered through my veins. I shifted in my seat, resisting the urge to text her.

There was no way she was on a date. I lived with her; if she met someone, I would've heard about it. Right?

"Incoming." Asher's voice derailed my train of thought. "I think this one's for you, DuBois."

I glanced up to see a leggy brunette sauntering toward us, dressed to kill in a minidress and heels. The outfit was a bit impractical for a pub, if you asked me, but she looked good enough to turn every other head in the place, so I guess it did its job.

Her attention was laser focused on me. She resembled a young Megan Fox, and normally, I'd be into it, but I couldn't summon more than a passing whiff of interest when she stopped at our table. One puff, and it was gone.

"Hi," she said breathlessly. "I'm so sorry to bother you, but my family and I are all *huge* Blackcastle fans. I know the pub has a no-picture and no-autograph rule, but I just had to come by and tell you that."

"Thank you." I smiled, aiming for polite but not flirtatious.

It didn't work.

She lingered by the table, chatting up a storm about our last match and our prospects for the UCL. I was impressed. She knew her stuff, but when she pivoted and invited me to a club for an "after-party," I had to decline.

"Sorry, I have to turn in early tonight," I said. "But it was great talking to you. I hope you have fun at the club."

Her face fell. She walked away, clearly disappointed.

When I looked at my friends again, they were staring at me with a mix of amusement and disbelief.

"Damn. That was brutal," Asher said.

"What? I was nice about it," I said defensively.

"Yeah, but Vincent DuBois, turning down a hot brunette?" Adil whistled. He'd finally recovered from my kick and was back to his usual self. "Are you *sure* you don't have a crush on someone else?"

I sighed. "Stop acting like a twelve-year-old. We're not in school anymore. Besides, I don't have a special preference for brunettes."

"Right." He nodded wisely. "You like blondes."

I didn't dignify that with a response.

"I'm going to grab another drink." Noah stood. "Anyone want anything?"

"I'll go with you." Adil jumped up. "Afterward, let's do a drive-by and see what the other guys are up to."

"That's not what a drive-by is." Noah gave me a pained expression as he walked away, Adil talking his ear off the entire time.

Asher also excused himself a minute later to use the loo. I was alone for the first time since I arrived, and instead of joining one of the other Blackcastle tables, I picked up my phone.

I hesitated before I typed a quick message and hit send.

> What are you up to?

A minute passed. No response.

I rubbed a hand over my mouth. Maybe I should've gone with Noah and Adil to the bar after all.

Just when I thought it was a lost cause, a new text popped up onscreen.

BROOKLYN

> I'm at dinner with my dad. Wbu?

With her dad. *Not a date.* The vise in my chest loosened.

> Hanging out at the Angry Boar with the team

> They're playing our song

The Angry Boar was one of the few pubs in town with a jukebox. Mac's wife was a big music fan, and he'd installed it for her. Proof that even old grumps had a romantic bone or two.

BROOKLYN

> ???

BROOKLYN

How much have you been drinking? We don't have a song

I beg to differ

I Hate Loving You. Riley K.

Three dots popped up, disappeared, then popped up again.

BROOKLYN

One, I don't believe for a second that they're playing teen pop in a London pub

BROOKLYN

Two, we've never listened to Riley K together

BROOKLYN

Three, you know that song is about love AND hate, right?

1) Believe it

2) No, but it made me think of you

3) Obviously

BROOKLYN

We don't love each other

We don't hate each other either

The three dots reappeared. I stared at the screen, my breath stalling in my lungs. Time slowed to an unbearable pace, but when the dots finally died, they didn't give way to a new message.

My text was the last one in the thread.

"Who died?"

I jerked my head up as Asher slid back into his seat. "What?"

"You're glaring at your phone like it personally offended you." He nodded at my cell. "What happened?"

"Nothing." I quickly moved the device to my other side, away from him. "I was just going through some emails."

Asher opened his mouth, but thankfully, Adil and Noah returned in time to distract him from further interrogation.

While Adil regaled us with the story of how he'd dared Samson to dance on camera to the Riley K song (which had indeed been playing, thank you very much), I checked my phone again. *Just in case.*

A red bubble graced my Messages app.

My stomach flipped. I tapped on the notification and skimmed the new text. It was only three words, but it was enough to make me smile.

BROOKLYN

No. We don't.

CHAPTER 11

BROOKLYN

LONDON'S UNUSUALLY WARM WEATHER LASTED through Halloween weekend. After that, a flip switched, and November dawned crisp and cold enough to make my teeth chatter when I stepped outside.

Luckily, today's schedule kicked off with an indoor presentation to the whole team on nutrition. Jones, the club's head of nutrition and my boss, ran the meeting with his assistant Rory. The other intern, Henry, and I were on hand to assist.

Even though I was the one who'd put the presentation together, I still listened intently while Jones discussed the importance of carbohydrates as fuel, different carb options, and ideal portion sizes. The players should already know this stuff, but it was smart to refresh their memories every once in a while.

"Is it just me, or are the lights in here way too bright?" Henry muttered. "I have the worst hangover."

I gave him a tight smile but didn't respond.

"What did you do this weekend? I went to Neon and—"

"Shhh." I kept my voice as low as possible. "Not now."

I tolerated Henry on a good day, but moments like these made me want to bang my head against a wall.

People freaked out when they discovered I was Frank Armstrong's daughter, but no one batted an eye at the fact that Henry was Jones's godson. Armstrong was a relatively common last name, so I was able to hide my parentage until I basically got the job. My dad was completely hands-off when it came to my internship. Henry couldn't say the same. Plus, he had the work ethic of a stoned frat boy, but I was the one who constantly had to prove myself while he skated by on the bare minimum.

Welcome to Blackcastle, home of the Nepotism Double Standard Olympics.

"We have a few more slides. Then I promise I'll let Coach torture you on the pitch," Jones said to scattered laughter. "Brooklyn, why don't you take over this last part?"

I straightened, my stomach fluttering as all eyes turned toward me. Jones hadn't given me any heads-up that I would be speaking today.

Thankfully, I knew the presentation like the back of my hand. My initial surprise quickly dissolved as I launched into an overview of how to make healthy versions of different foods and how to substitute empty calories with whole foods.

That was my favorite part of this job. I didn't believe in restrictive diets, and while pro athletes were much more disciplined than the average person, they would be better served if they *enjoyed* what they ate. Sustainability was an important part of performance optimization.

"We created some guides and games to help you remember this info later," I said. "I can—"

"Thank you, Brooklyn." Jones cut me off. "We're out of time, but this is only the first week of our monthly cycle. Next week, we'll focus on practical applications of the concepts we learned today…"

I snapped my mouth shut. My teeth ground together before I forced myself to relax.

I thought games were a fun way to engage the team, but Jones thought they were "infantilizing." I mean, yes, Sports Nutrition Bingo wasn't a peer-reviewed journal article, but we were dealing with footballers. If anyone liked a good game, it was them.

Jones kept talking. So much for running out of time.

I held back a sigh. I ignored Henry when he tried to engage me in conversation again about his night out at Neon and scanned the room instead.

The players all sat in front of their respective lockers. Most were paying attention, but a few were definitely zoning out. Stevens kept sneaking peeks at his phone, and every minute or so, Adil would whisper something to an exasperated-looking Noah.

My gaze skimmed over Asher and landed on Vincent. Like the others, he was dressed in a black-and-purple training kit. His long-sleeved shirt hugged his muscles, and the purple contrasted perfectly with his dark coloring. He lounged against his locker, his expression intent as Jones finally ceded the floor to Greely, the assistant coach. My dad wasn't here. He rarely attended presentations, so Greely often stepped in for him until the actual training started.

Vincent must've felt my eyes on him because he turned his head, ever so slightly, toward me.

Our gazes met, and my pulse slowed to a breathless crawl.

We hadn't talked much since our texts on Friday night. I'd spent all weekend in my room, working on the ISNA application, but every so often, images of our messages would float through my head.

We don't love each other.

We don't hate each other either.

Two sentences that encapsulated our long-standing dynamic. For over a year, we'd held fast on the middle ground between love and hate. Neutral, convenient, *safe.*

But our new living situation had upended that entire dynamic. I couldn't escape him anymore. He was always there, taking up space and filling up my thoughts, and the more time we spent together, the further I inched away from the middle ground.

Unfortunately, I wasn't headed in the direction I wanted, but I couldn't find a way to reverse course.

Vincent's gaze flickered at the edges, his expression inscrutable. We were across the room from each other, yet I could practically smell the subtle spice of his aftershave and feel the warmth of his skin against mine.

My heartbeat thundered in my ears. He leaned forward, and—

Loud chatter broke out. The tension fractured, and blood rushed to my face as I realized the team had been dismissed.

Players swarmed toward the exit. Vincent remained in his seat, his gaze holding mine for an extra beat before he stood and followed them out to the pitch.

It wasn't until he was out of sight that I released a shaky breath.

Our moment had lasted less than a minute, but like our texts, it lingered on my mind far longer than it should've.

While the team trained outside, Henry and I returned to our joint office. Thankfully, he'd stopped regaling me with tales of his tequila-fueled birthday party—for a nutritionist, he drank quite a lot—and I was able to focus on my work. Hours passed, and I was about to head out when Jones called me to his office.

"Good luck," Henry said without taking his eyes off his screen. He was reading a fitness article that conveniently featured a half-naked photo of a Victoria's Secret model.

Good luck? What was that supposed to mean?

My stomach pinched with nerves as I entered Jones's office and took the seat opposite his.

It's fine. He's not going to fire you. I only had a month or so left in my internship, and I'd been a model employee. Well, except for that time Henry asked me to "please fetch some tea" for him, and I dumped a heap of salt in there instead of sugar. He never asked me to get him a drink again.

"You did a good job on the presentation today," Jones said. "Minus the part about the games at the end."

"Thank you," I said politely, fighting the urge to sigh.

Jones had worked at Blackcastle for fifteen years. I respected him, but I secretly thought he was a bit too rigid. It was either his way or the highway. There was no room for argument.

"I wanted to talk to you because I received your recommendation request for the ISNA Innovator Award," he said. "That's an extremely prestigious prize."

"It is." I wasn't sure what else to say, and I worried my reply came off a bit condescending because it was so obvious. "I would really appreciate a recommendation if that's possible. You're so well-respected in our field, and a letter from you would go a long way in helping me with my application."

I discreetly wiped my palm against my thigh. If Jones refused to recommend me, I was toast. He was my direct manager; there was no way I'd advance to the final round without his support.

I had to make it to the final round. Maybe I'd win, maybe not, but becoming a finalist was about more than the money. It was about proving to myself that I had what it took to succeed and that I hadn't wasted the past ten years of my life on something I was only okay at.

"I'm happy to write you a recommendation," he said. I breathed a silent sigh of relief. *Thank God.* "You're a great intern. Some of your suggestions are unorthodox, but you work hard and you know your stuff. I've told you this before in your performance reviews, so I won't repeat myself. However…"

I tensed again, my relief fading as quickly as it'd popped up.

"I'm curious why you didn't email me about it until last week. Henry asked me for a letter months ago."

My stomach sank. Of course Henry was applying too, even though he didn't need the money.

"I didn't know about the Innovator Award until then," I admitted. "It's my fault for not being on top of it. I emailed you as soon as I found out, but I truly apologize if the timing is too tight."

I'd stopped paying attention to fellowships and awards once I got my master's degree since I wasn't eligible for most of them anyway. The oversight was on me.

"I see," Jones said slowly. "It's important to stay up to date on industry news. Just a tip for the future. But like I said, of course I'll write you a recommendation. You're an Armstrong. It's a given." He chuckled, but I didn't join him.

My skin prickled. I heard his implication loud and clear: my relation to the head coach outweighed my actual job performance. Perhaps his Armstrong quip was a joke. If it was, it wasn't funny.

Between me and your godson, *there are a lot of Blackcastle legacies in the mix.* I bit back my sarcastic reply and remained silent instead. It wouldn't be smart to antagonize my supervisor right after he agreed to write me a letter of recommendation, no matter how hypocritical he was being.

"There's another reason I wanted to talk to you," he said. "As you know, your internship ends after the holidays. There are extremely limited openings on our permanent team, but we would love to bring you onboard as a junior nutritionist. HR will email you the official offer letter later today, but I wanted to tell you myself."

My breath stalled. I blinked, my brain scrambling to reconcile his words with my earlier conviction that I'd be jobless come the new year.

Junior nutritionist. It was one step up from intern, but it was a *job*. A full-time, salaried one with benefits at a top Premier League club. I wouldn't be forced to ask my dad for money or work under some gym bro named Chad.

This was what I wanted…so why were there knots in my stomach?

"That's great!" I masked my conflicted feelings with semi-feigned excitement. "I'm honored. Thank you so much."

We went over a few logistical details before Jones dismissed me. I returned to my office, the knots multiplying by the second. I couldn't pinpoint where they were coming from, and it pissed me off.

What was wrong with me? Why couldn't I be happy for once? The job offer was a *good* thing. It proved that I deserved to be here—unless my dad broke his no-intervention rule and influenced their hiring decisions. Unlikely, but possible. Or maybe Jones and HR factored in our relationship themselves and decided it would be bad form to essentially fire their boss's daughter.

You're an Armstrong. It's a given.

My head pounded. I was dying to know whether Henry also got an offer, but he was already gone for the day.

For once, I would've appreciated his endless rambles. At least they would've saved me from my own thoughts.

I turned my computer off, grabbed my bag, and texted my group chat with Scarlett and Carina on my way out of the building. I'd planned to work on my ISNA essay tonight, but I didn't want to be alone. Besides, regardless of how I felt about the Blackcastle offer, I should celebrate. Right?

I texted my friends to let them know about the offer.

They'd talk me up. I could always count on my friends for perspective, and—

"Want a ride?"

My steps faltered at the familiar voice. I turned, my stomach tightening for an entirely different reason as Vincent sauntered toward me. He'd changed out of his training kit and into a long-sleeved T-shirt and jeans. A gym bag hung over his shoulder, and he looked infuriatingly gorgeous for someone who'd spent the afternoon running drills in freezing weather.

I shook my head. "I'm good. I drove to work." Sometimes we carpooled, but those instances were rare since we didn't want to tip my dad off to our living situation.

"Your car will still be here tomorrow. I can get you home much faster." Vincent fell into step with me. He smelled like clean soap and subtle cologne, an unexpectedly devastating combo that had me holding my breath in case it made me do something stupid, like take him up on his offer. "A Lambo beats a VW any day."

"Speed limits still exist, you know."

"Not for me. *Kidding*," he said when I side-eyed him. "Though I bet I can talk my way out of any speeding ticket."

"If you're trying to convince me to ride with you, you're failing miserably." I pushed open the double doors. A sudden gust of wind stole into my lungs, and I quickly picked up my pace. This was my least favorite part about living in the UK. When fall and winter hit, I was tempted to fly straight back to sunny San Diego. "Besides, I'm not going home first. I'm celebrating with the girls." Scarlett and Carina hadn't replied yet, but it was an easy excuse.

"Celebrating what?"

"Blackcastle offered me the junior nutritionist role. I just found out today."

Vincent's eyes brightened. "That's amazing. Congratulations."

"Thank you."

My mind flashed back to our night on the couch, when I'd admitted that I might have to leave the club soon.

I hope you stay at Blackcastle. It wouldn't be the same without you.

I'd never admit it, but his words hit me in the feels at exactly the right time. I'd needed the reassurance more than I thought, and I hadn't expected to get it from Vincent, of all people.

A golf ball lodged itself in my throat. He might have moved out by January, and if I turned down the offer, I wouldn't see him every day anymore.

It wouldn't be the same without you either. I hadn't said those words out loud at the time, but I'd felt them deep in my gut. And that feeling was back in full force.

Vincent's brows dipped. "You don't sound too excited. I thought you wanted an offer."

"I do. I mean…" I trailed off. The desire to spill all my woes to him crowded my throat, but I held back at the last minute. The Blackcastle parking lot was *not* the right place to ambush someone with an impromptu therapy session. "I need to think about it first. I don't want to rush into a decision."

"I can help." His dimple flashed. "Pros versus cons. Pro: stay, and you'll see me every day, even after I move out. Con: leave, and you won't."

I laughed, my chest lightening for the first time since I left Jones's office. "That's not how a pro/con list works, but thanks. It did help. I guess I'm turning down the offer after all."

"You say that now, but—" Vincent cut off abruptly.

We'd reached our cars, which were conveniently parked next to each other. I followed his stare to the hood of his Lamborghini, where a plain brown envelope was tucked beneath his windshield wipers.

It could be nothing, but considering what had happened the last time someone left him an unexpected gift, I understood why it'd freak him out.

Another chill swept through the lot. I shivered, missing the warmth of my cramped but heated office.

The muscles in Vincent's neck stretched taut. His earlier playfulness disappeared as he walked over and retrieved the envelope. He opened it, his expression inscrutable.

The silence ballooned until I couldn't take it anymore. "What does it say?"

His jaw flexed. After a tense beat, he handed me the note without a word.

I took it. A moment later, my blood iced because the "note" wasn't a note at all—it was a photo of the doll his intruder had left him last month. It was propped against a plain white background with no distinguishing marks. Next to it, little round red marbles spelled out one sentence.

Did you like your gift?

CHAPTER 12

VINCENT

I HAD TO GIVE PROPS TO WHOEVER WAS BEHIND THE DOLL and photo. They'd mastered the art of creeping me the fuck out with seemingly innocuous items.

Either they owned a replica of the doll they'd "gifted" me, or they took this picture before they broke into my house, sat on it, and waited until my guard was down before giving it to me.

"This is so fucked." Brooklyn looked a little green. "Who *does* this? It's like something out of a B-grade horror movie."

"I know." I scanned the car park, on high alert for any suspicious people or sudden movements.

Nothing. It was eerily empty.

Cold snaked down my spine.

It'd been a month since the intruder broke in—just enough time to lull me into a false sense of security. I'd convinced myself the break-in was a one-time thing, but the photo plunged me straight into paranoia again.

The taste of copper filled my mouth. My skin felt too tight for my body, and I wished I could change out of it the way I did my training kit. Be someone else for a day and leave Vincent DuBois behind.

I'd worked hard for my success. Most of the time, I loved it, but then shit like this made me rethink everything.

"Are you okay?" Brooklyn winced. "Sorry, that was a stupid question."

"No, it's fine. I'm okay." I rubbed a hand over my face and tried to think.

Whoever left the photo was long gone. I could check in with building security, but they were pretty useless for anything other than basic patrols.

Although the lot was closed to the public, it wasn't impenetrable. Just last year, someone snuck in and keyed Asher's prized vintage Jaguar. We all knew it was one or multiple Holchester players, but the cameras didn't catch them, and we couldn't prove it.

"What are you going to do?" Brooklyn asked. She was still holding the photo, but she looked like she wanted to throw it in a trash bin and set it on fire.

"Bring it to the police and hope they'll finally get off their ass long enough to do something." They'd been almost as useless as Blackcastle security. I was convinced the detective on my case had forgotten about it altogether.

"I'll go with you."

"You don't have to do that." I took the picture back from her. "Go celebrate with your friends. I can handle this on my own."

"I'll take a rain check. I won't be able to enjoy it anyway." A half-hearted smile touched her lips, though her eyes remained worried. "We're in this together, roomie."

My stomach sank. "Shit. Do you think they know where we live?"

Now that the intruder had found me at home and work, my new

(if temporary) lodging seemed like a logical next step for them.

"I don't think so. I was joking with the roomie comment," Brooklyn said quickly. "I don't really think they're going to show up at the flat and…I don't know, stage a naked photo shoot with the plushies or something."

I snorted out a laugh, but my mind churned with worry.

Should I hire a bodyguard? Some players had personal security teams, but I'd never received enough threats to justify the invasion of privacy. The thought of someone following me around twenty-four-seven made my skin crawl.

Plus, if I hired security out of the blue, the media would go wild with speculation. What if the attention emboldened the intruder to pull bigger stunts? I couldn't risk it. Not yet.

"We should take my car to the police station. It's less conspicuous. After that…" Brooklyn flicked a wary glance around the lot. "We should go somewhere besides home for a bit, just in case."

A knot eased in my gut. The situation was still "fucked," as she put it, but her determination to figure it out with me made it a little less daunting. No matter how bad things got, there was comfort in knowing I wasn't alone.

"Do you have a particular place in mind?" I asked.

Her brow furrowed for a minute before it smoothed. She smiled, her eyes regaining their usual sparkle. "As a matter of fact, I know just the spot."

Our visit to the police station was brief. I handed the photo over to Detective Smith, who promised he'd look into it and contact me if they got any leads.

It was the same spiel as the first time, and it didn't inspire great confidence. I'd thought about hiring a private investigator, but after asking around, I was told there wasn't much even the best P.I. could do for me. I was better off sticking with the police.

Luckily, I was so distracted by my current surroundings, I didn't have time to dwell on how much I wanted to grab Smith and shake him until an ounce of care fell out of his overgrown mustache.

"I can't believe you brought me here." I looked around with a disbelieving laugh. "I haven't been to one of these since I was twelve."

"I thought you might like it." Brooklyn grinned. "Everyone is so caught up in what they're doing, they won't pay attention to you unless you threaten to beat their high score. And even if they do notice you, they probably won't recognize you."

I clutched my chest in mock hurt. "Ouch. Way to kick a man when he's down."

"I like to take advantage of any situation when I can." She patted my shoulder. "But you have to admit, the chances of finding a football fan here are slim."

I had to agree. We were at SQ3, an arcade on the outskirts of London. Neon lights illuminated the dark space while the sounds of beeps and explosions from various games filled the air. A majority of the customers looked like teenagers, and Brooklyn was right—they were so engrossed in their games, Godzilla could stomp through the entrance and they wouldn't notice.

A place that offered anonymity *and* mindless entertainment? It was perfect.

"Pick your poison," she said after we retrieved a suitable amount of arcade coins. "*Kick It Pro*? *Pac-Man*? Simulation racing?"

Hmm.

I scanned the options and landed on an empty table in the corner.

"How good are you at air hockey?"

She followed my gaze and shrugged. "I'm decent."

Spoiler alert: she lied. She wasn't decent; she was *really fucking good*.

"*Merde*!" I cursed when she scored on me for the third time in a row. "Decent, my ass. What, did you play in the air hockey Olympics or something?"

"Oops. Did I forget to mention I spent a lot of time in arcades when I was little?" Brooklyn said, innocent as a lamb. "My mom's favorite salon was next door to one. I was too young to join her, so she'd give me some cash and drop me off while she got her weekly mani-pedi."

My brow creased at the mental image of a young Brooklyn playing games by herself while her mum luxuriated in a salon. "How old were you?"

"Seven or eight."

"And she left you alone in an arcade for hours?" I stared at her, stunned. "Is that even legal?"

"She became friends with the arcade owner and had them keep an eye on me. I was fine. I didn't get kidnapped or anything."

"She could've brought you with her. Salons aren't child-free spaces."

"Yeah, well, she liked her alone time." Brooklyn's tone was casual, but she carefully avoided my eyes as she lined up her mallet for her next shot. "We went to salons together when I was older. It's not a big deal."

Fuck that. It was messed up for her mother to leave her *underage child* with strangers because she "liked her alone time." I didn't care if she was supposedly friends with the arcade owner. All sorts of people came in and out of these places, and the owner had probably been too busy to keep a close eye on Brooklyn.

I didn't have children, but even I knew that was borderline parental neglect.

I swallowed my argument. It wasn't my place to question Brooklyn's relationship with her mother, but I'd never met the woman and I already kind of hated her.

No wonder Brooklyn rarely talked about her. We'd lived together for two weeks, and I'd yet to see her call or mention her mum a single time.

"How did she react when you told her you were moving to London?" I asked.

Brooklyn took her shot. The puck stopped an inch short of making the goal. "She was fine with it."

"Do you talk to her often?" I had a feeling I knew the answer, but I wanted to hear it from her. This was the first time she'd opened up about her family, and I was desperate for more. I shouldn't be; this skirted too close to an emotional connection when that was the last thing I wanted or needed. But I couldn't stop myself if I tried.

"We talk when the occasion calls for it." Brooklyn blocked my return shot. "She has a two-year-old and is pregnant with her second child, so she has her hands full. Plus there's the time difference..."

"Third."

"What?"

"She has you and the two-year-old. She's pregnant with her third child."

Brooklyn faltered. Pink crept over her cheeks, and she glanced away for a split second before meeting my eyes again. "Right. I meant my second half-sibling. I worded it weird."

Did I say I kind of hated her mother? I was wrong. I hated her, full stop. Brooklyn wouldn't slip up like that if someone hadn't reinforced the sentiment that she wasn't a "real" member of the family.

Maybe I was leaping to conclusions without knowing the full story, but I suspected I was at least half-right.

"What about you?" she asked. "What's your relationship with your mom like?"

I went along with the deflection. She'd helped me by not mentioning the intruder after we left the police station, and it was my turn to return the favor.

Still, I had to consciously unclench my teeth and breathe through my rising irritation at her mum before I answered. "It's pretty good. We haven't lived together since I was six, but Scarlett and I would alternate summers and holidays with our parents, so I still saw her often."

Most people looked back at their childhood with rose-tinted glasses, and I was no exception. When I thought back on those days, I didn't remember my parents' fights and passive aggression; I remembered walks along the Brighton Pier, lazy afternoons by the seaside, and hands sticky with candy floss. Our mum would often buy Scarlett and me ice cream cones if we answered her trivia questions correctly.

She wasn't perfect, but she did the best she could with what she had. I never forgot that.

"We don't talk every day, but I know she's there if I need her, and vice versa. Honestly, it's better if we don't talk every day," I added. "She's always on me about settling down and giving her grandchildren. There are only so many questions she can ask about my love life before it gets awkward."

"If you need backup, I'm happy to talk to her and explain why you procreating is a bad idea for the world in general."

"You're right. Society couldn't handle all that charm. Don't want to break any more hearts than I already do."

Brooklyn's lips flattened into a straight line. She managed to keep her serious expression for maybe ten seconds before she cracked and broke out into a laugh. "You're delusional." She said it with more indulgence than usual.

I grinned even as an inkling of guilt wormed through my chest.

I'd told her the truth about my mum—my real mum, the only one I'd call by that title—but my relationship with my *birth* mother was more complicated. For one, it existed solely in my imagination, and I hated that it was a part of my life at all.

My birth mum had never reached out. Never contacted me, never showed an interest in my life even when I signed with the Premier League and was later named captain of Blackcastle.

My parents had been transparent about my adoption since I was old enough to know what that meant. Apparently, my birth dad hadn't been part of the process at all. He may not have even known I existed, but I'd grown up fantasizing about meeting my birth mother, if only to see what she was like. However, her silence all these years was cold, clear confirmation that she wanted nothing to do with me no matter how rich or successful I got.

I didn't know why she gave me up, but it was the uncertainty that killed me—the possibility that, from the moment I was born, someone had already judged me "not good enough."

I didn't tell Brooklyn any of that. It was hard enough to admit it to myself without exposing my neuroses to innocent bystanders.

We finished our air hockey match without bringing up our families again. She won the first round, but I beat her by one point in the second. After that, we moved on to the pinball machines until hunger overtook us and we stopped for a quick food break at the attached bar. It didn't have any tables, just high tops, so we ate while standing.

"I can't believe we've been here for three hours." Brooklyn checked her watch. "I could've sworn we just got here."

"You know what they say—time flies when you're having fun."

We were surrounded by loud teenagers and bad pop music, but I didn't care. This was exactly what I'd needed after the photo shitshow.

"Thank you for this." I gestured around us. "I know it's not how you imagined spending the evening, but I appreciate you hanging out with me. I'm sorry I fucked up your job offer celebration though."

"You didn't fuck it up," Brooklyn said. "I had fun too."

Her usual playful exasperation was gone, and she sounded sincere, almost shy, as she looked at me.

The pop song in the background transitioned to another one that sounded exactly the same. Or maybe it sounded different. It was hard to tell beyond the sudden pounding of my pulse.

Diners streamed past us, either headed to the bar or back to the arcade, but I barely noticed. They all blurred into one giant, faceless mass behind her.

No matter where we were or how many people were around, Brooklyn could make the rest of the world fall away with one glance. I couldn't explain how or why. She just…did.

Her gaze darted to my mouth and back up again. I swallowed, my throat dry. I'd never noticed before, but there was a tiny freckle right above her upper lip.

The urge to lean forward and kiss it gripped me.

I dipped my chin. Brooklyn's lips parted, but she didn't pull away when I moved closer to her. In fact, she leaned in a fraction of an inch, her expression softening like she *wanted* me to kiss her, and—

And she'll win the bet.

The reminder of our wager blasted between us like a fire hose of ice water. I jerked back, the warmth in my chest turning to sludge.

The desire to kiss her was still there, but I couldn't give in to it. I wanted her to want me, and I needed her to make the first move. That was the only way I could be sure.

Brooklyn straightened, her cheeks flushing a faint pink.

"Do you know how to play pool?" I asked, somewhat abruptly. "Be honest." I was cynical, but when it came to her, I was also weak. I wasn't ready to return to our status quo, and we had a few more hours before the arcade closed.

She shook her head.

"Good." I swept the crumbs from our finished meals onto one tray and carried it to the nearest rubbish bin. Anything to get away from the cloud of disappointment in the air. "Let's go. The evening's not over yet."

CHAPTER 13

BROOKLYN

I DIDN'T KNOW THE ARCADE HAD A POOL ROOM UNTIL Vincent pointed it out. It wasn't a classic arcade game, but it worked out in our favor because we were the only people here.

"Loosen your grip and hold the cue like this." Vincent leaned over me to adjust my form. "Let your wrist hang naturally. It shouldn't be curved inward or outward toward your body; it should create a straight line with your forearm."

"Are you sure? This feels unnatural."

"Positive." I couldn't see him, but the amusement in his voice came through loud and clear. "You're good at air hockey; I'm good at pool. Trust me."

"Fine," I grumbled. "But you better not be sabotaging me."

He laughed, the sound low in my ear.

The awkwardness from the end of our meal was gone, but that meant I was back to being just a little too aware of his presence—the heat of his body, the scent of his cologne, the brush of his shirt against my back.

I set my jaw and tried to focus on mastering my grip. It was difficult. Between my job offer, the photo, our surprisingly candid conversation over air hockey, and our near-kiss during dinner, the day had been an emotional rollercoaster.

At least, I thought it was a near-kiss. The vibes had been there, and he'd moved so close...

But then he'd pulled back like he'd been burned and hadn't said a word about it since, so maybe I was wrong. Maybe I'd been sucked in by the illusion of intimacy that came from spending hours alone together.

So stupid.

The worst part wasn't mistakenly thinking he wanted to kiss me. The worst part was that I would've let him—bet or no bet.

Vincent had always been gorgeous, but the recent glimpses of his vulnerability tugged on my heartstrings in just the right way. The world loved the player, but I liked the flawed human underneath even more.

So, SO stupid.

"Good." The warmth of his breath slid over my skin. "Just like that."

Fuck. My entire body tightened as a shiver ran down my nape all the way to my toes. I didn't have a praise kink, but his voice, paired with those words, did things to me that reason couldn't explain.

I didn't even know what he was—

"Your form's perfect now." He released my hand and straightened.

Oh. Right. That was what we'd been working on while my brain rolled into the gutter.

By the time Vincent came around the other side of the table to face me, I'd wrestled my rogue hormones under control.

I stood, my face smoothing into what was hopefully a neutral expression.

"How about we make this more fun?" He selected his own cue stick from the wall. If our earlier proximity affected him the way it had me, he didn't show it. "Every time one of us sinks a ball, the other person has to reveal a secret."

"That hardly seems fair. I'm the novice. I'll be the one spilling all my secrets while you sit back and log them in your little blackmail book."

His eyes glittered with laughter. "I don't have a blackmail book, but thank you for the idea. Besides, haven't you heard of beginner's luck?" When I remained skeptical, he shrugged and said, a little too casually, "Or do you have that little faith in yourself?"

Damn him. He always knew how to get me.

I wasn't proud of it, but I took the bait and, as expected, I had to watch him sink the first ball of the night.

"Cough it up, buttercup," Vincent said over my groan. "What's secret number one?"

I searched for something small but significant enough to satisfy him. "I didn't have my first kiss until my senior year of high school. I was the last person in my friend group to kiss a boy, and everyone nicknamed me Pope Innocent because, well, you know."

He stared at me. A beat passed, and then—laughter. Deep, rich laughter that started as a chuckle and gradually escalated into guffaws.

"It's not funny," I protested even as a giggle rose in my own throat. "Seventeen-year-old me was traumatized! It wasn't a good kiss either. It was like making out with a slobbery toad."

He placed his hands on the table and dipped his chin, his shoulders shaking. "Pope Innocent," he choked out. "Oh, that's good."

I tried to remain stern, but the giggle slipped out before I could stop it. It was followed by another, and another, until I was doubled over, my stomach aching from laughter.

"I'm sorry your first kiss was such a terrible experience," Vincent said when we finally gathered ourselves. "I hope you've had better ones since then."

"Don't worry." The high from my amusement lingered, and my voice ran a touch breathless. "I have."

Our eyes met. My skin tingled, but the sensation washed away when he gestured toward my pool cue. "Your turn."

I shook off the buzz and leaned over, adopting the form he'd taught me. *Focus.*

But I didn't make my first shot, or my second, or my third. Vincent missed one but sank the other two.

Frustration chafed beneath my skin. I didn't expect to win, but I *had* to make at least one shot. Otherwise, my pride would never recover.

I scanned the table for the best opportunity and chose a ball near the middle. It wasn't as close to a pocket as some of the others, but the angle looked promising.

I hit it above its center and knew immediately I hadn't used enough force, but at least it was moving in the right direction.

Come on. I strangled my cue stick with a white-knuckled grip. The ball rolled slowly toward a corner pocket. Did it have enough momentum to make it, or was it going to lose steam partway there? *Go in. Go in. Go—*

It fell into the pocket with a soft thud.

"Oh my God." I clapped a hand over my mouth. I stared at the table, half expecting the ball to pop back out with a "Gotcha!" It didn't. "Holy shit, I did it! I did it! I sank a ball!"

I jumped up and down with a small squeal. I didn't care if I looked like an idiot. I was too damn happy about scoring a point.

Ha! Take *that*, pool gods.

When I finally calmed down enough to claim my prize, I glanced across the table and saw Vincent watching me with a half smile. It disappeared when my gaze caught his.

"Your turn to spill a secret." A thrill of anticipation bolted through me. "What's it going to be?"

He didn't hesitate. "I own one pair of underwear."

"*What*?"

"One *style* of underwear," he amended. "Most people won't see it anyway, and sticking to one style frees up mental space to focus on other things. I buy them a dozen at a time."

"Wow," I huffed. "I tell you juicy secrets, and you tell me about your underwear-buying habits. This is starting to feel like an unfair trade."

"Your last 'secret' was about kicking someone in the balls in middle school."

"One, he was bullying my friend, and two, that was funny."

"Not to that poor kid's balls."

"Then it's a good thing they're not part of this game."

A small dimple creased his cheek. "Fair enough." He chalked his pool cue and shrugged. "But if you want better secrets, you'll have to earn them."

Like most people, I needed motivation. Winning was a strong one, but *nothing* kicked my ass into gear like spite. If someone even hinted that I couldn't do something, I'd run myself into the ground before I proved them right. That was true in school, at work, and now, with pool.

Fortunately, I was a fast learner. Vincent was still beating me by five points, but I held my own, and soon, we were trading secrets at a steady rhythm.

He told me he cheated on a math exam because his dad wouldn't take him to a football match unless he got an A; I told him I asked my mom for a school fundraiser donation and used the money to buy a fake ID instead.

He told me he got attacked by a raccoon once during a trip to the States and had to get rabies shots; I told him I went to the wrong class my first day of college but was too embarrassed to leave, so I sat through an entire lecture on quantum physics.

"When I was fifteen, I babysat a neighbor's kid and saw him take his first step," Vincent said when it was his turn to share again. "After his parents came home, I said he was *so* close to walking so they should keep an eye out for it. He stood and walked up to them a few minutes later, and they freaked out. I never told them the truth."

I stopped examining the table and looked at him. A pang hit my chest at the mental image he painted. "That was really nice of you."

"It's not a big deal." He sounded a little embarrassed. "I just didn't want to take the milestone away from them."

The pang deepened. "It's a big deal to them, even if they don't know about it. Anyway." I cleared my throat and nodded at his cue stick. "It's your turn."

As expected, he scored again. He'd had the perfect shot lined up.

I mulled over what secret to share. I'd used up most of the insignificant ones. I was staying far away from the topic of my family, so I settled on a tangential admission instead. "I initially majored in sports nutrition because my dad was—*is*—this legend in the sports world, and I guess it was a way to feel closer to him since we didn't spend much time together when I was young."

The words flowed out with surprising ease. We'd shared half a dozen secrets by now. They started off silly, but there was something about this moment that unraveled a deeper thread in me.

The room was a judgment-free zone, and despite our history of insults, I didn't worry for a second that Vincent would weaponize what I told him in here.

"And now?" He watched me carefully. "How do you feel about it?"

"Now, I read nutrition blogs for fun and willingly spend my days working with footballers, so you tell me," I said.

His chuckle made me smile in return.

Vincent and I resumed our shots. He notched a victory two turns later, but I couldn't even be mad about it.

Somewhere along the way, it'd started being less about the game and more about the conversation.

"Congratulations. You now know more about me than anyone else in my life, including Scarlett." Dry amusement gilded his voice.

"Wow." I placed a hand over my chest. "I'm honored."

"You should be. I don't tell just anyone about my underwear-buying habits."

"So what you're saying is, I'm special."

"That's exactly what I'm saying." Vincent sat on the edge of the table, his posture relaxed, but there was an undercurrent to his words. A slight intensity that lit up my nerves one by one like tiny campfires in the night.

My quippy response died halfway up my throat.

Without the game to distract me, I was agonizingly aware of his presence again. Of the electric thrum in the air and the hooded, almost sensual way his eyes held mine.

Don't fall for it. It's calculated.

Vincent had always been charming, even when he was being annoying, but the bet cast suspicion over all our interactions. Was the glimmer of attraction genuine, or was he simply trying to prove a point? He wanted me to admit *I* wanted him, but I couldn't let him have the satisfaction, especially since it would never amount to anything.

I turned my head, breaking the spell. The little fires blinked out, and cool air rushed into my lungs once more.

A silent beat passed before Vincent slid off the table. "I'm going to get us some water." Was it me, or did his voice sound slightly strained? "I'll be right back."

"Sounds good."

He disappeared into the main arcade, and I finally allowed myself to fully exhale.

I checked my phone for new messages. I had texts from Scarlett and Carina congratulating me on the job offer, which I responded to with a quick thank-you. Then, before I could stop myself, I clicked into Instagram and looked up Vincent's private, personal profile. We were mutuals, but we never interacted in the app. Maybe there was something there that would help me win the bet.

Unfortunately, he wasn't super active. His last upload was a photo from Paris taken months ago. There was nothing that gave me any new insight into who he was, what he liked, or how I could seduce him into kissing me first.

"Do you need a pool partner?"

I hastily closed out of the app and looked up. *Not Vincent.* I should've known from the voice alone, but I was so startled by the unexpected question that it took my brain a minute to catch up.

The newcomer looked like he was around my age. Auburn hair, hazel eyes, crooked smile. Cute.

"I'm already playing with someone," I said apologetically. "He's getting a drink, but he's…" His accent suddenly clicked. I straightened, a thrill of recognition shooting through me. "Wait. Are you from the States?"

"Yep. La Jolla, born and raised."

"No way! I'm from La Mesa." La Jolla and La Mesa were both part of San Diego County.

"No shit? We're practically neighbors." His face lit up. "I'm Mason."

"Brooklyn." I grinned, my initial reserve falling away.

There were plenty of Americans in London, but I hadn't met anyone from my hometown until now. There was something about running into a fellow San Diegan abroad that created an instant bond.

Mason and I struck up an easy conversation. He was a year older than me, worked in corporate marketing, and had moved to London a month ago. He lived nearby and was exploring the neighborhood when he'd stumbled upon the arcade.

"I got my ass kicked by a teenager at *NBA Jam*, so I figured I'd try my hand at pool," he said sheepishly. "But if you already have a partner, I don't want to intrude."

"You're not intruding. If we find a fourth person, maybe we can play doubles."

I wasn't sure how Vincent would feel about that, but—actually, where *was* Vincent anyway? It didn't take that long to get water.

Mason smiled down at me. He really was handsome. I should've been flirting up a storm, but I couldn't stop my thoughts from wandering toward a certain footballer.

"I'd love that," he said. "I—"

"Love what?"

Deep. Smooth. Velvet edged with the tiniest hint of irritation.

My heartbeat quickened for a split second.

I turned and nearly walked straight into Vincent's chest. He was standing so close I could see the faint twitch in his jaw as he eyed Mason with barely veiled suspicion.

"We were saying how we could play doubles." I took one of the two water bottles from his hands. "This is Mason, by the way. Mason, this is Vincent."

"Do you two know each other?" Vincent's tone was light, but the near-imperceptible edge sharpened.

"We just met," I said. "But it turns out we both grew up in the San Diego area. Isn't that crazy?"

"So crazy."

I narrowed my eyes at his flat response. Vincent's default when meeting new people was guarded friendliness. Where was this hostility coming from?

"Hey, man." Mason held out his hand. After a long pause, Vincent shook it. "Do I know you from somewhere? You look familiar."

"Vincent's a footballer. He plays for Blackcastle," I said when Vincent took too long to respond. Seriously, what was wrong with him? He was never antagonistic unless the other person was an asshole, and Mason had been nothing but cordial so far. "You've probably seen him on TV. Or in the ads plastered all over the Tube."

"Ah. That must be it." Mason shrugged. "Sorry, I'm not a big soccer fan."

Vincent's jaw flexed again. I couldn't tell whether it was because Mason didn't know who he was or because he'd called football "soccer."

"Don't worry about it." His smile lacked any semblance of warmth. "Well, it was nice to meet you, Mason, but we have to get back to our match."

I was appalled by his curt dismissal, but Mason took it in stride. "Yeah, of course. And listen…" He rubbed the back of his neck, his sheepish expression returning. "I hope I'm not overstepping here, but are you two, uh, dating?"

"No." My answer came swiftly, followed by a laugh. "We're friends. Coworkers, really. And flatmates. *Temporary* flatmates." The words spilled out in a jumble. "We're a lot of things, but we're definitely not dating."

Mason's smile widened. "Got it. In that case, do you want to exchange numbers? I don't know anyone in London besides my coworkers, and they're all thirty years older than me. It'd be nice to hang out with someone my age."

I glanced at Vincent, who had moved toward the pool table. The muscles in his neck pulled taut as he racked the balls, his expression indifferent.

"Sure. It's always good to have another friend in the city." I returned my attention to Mason, annoyed at myself for even caring what Vincent thought. "Give me your phone."

I entered my number and texted myself so I had his contact info too. We said goodbye, and he was gone.

Vincent didn't wait a minute before he pounced. "Leave it to you to make a new friend in five minutes," he drawled. The edge was still there, softer, but noticeably present.

"You were gone for more than five minutes, and you were so rude to him." I crossed my arms. "What the hell was that anyway?"

"How was I rude? I shook his hand and said it was nice to meet him."

"It's not what you said. It's the way you said it."

"Are you policing my tone?"

"Are you being deliberately obtuse?"

Vincent straightened and faced me. His irritation was starkly obvious now, its severity highlighted by his frown and the tense set of his mouth. "Fine. I don't like him. Happy? There's something about him that feels off."

"You met him for two minutes. He was literally so nice."

"Ted Bundy was nice, and look how that turned out."

"You're ridiculous." I'd reached the end of my patience, but I didn't feel like arguing, so I switched topics instead. "What took you so long anyway? You could've just grabbed some water from the vending machines."

"I did, but someone recognized me. It turned into a whole thing." Vincent glanced at the doorway leading to the main arcade. It was only then that I noticed the group of teenagers watching us and whispering. "We should leave before they call more of their friends over."

I didn't argue.

Thankfully, no one ambushed him on our way out, and we rode the entire way home in silence.

We'd been getting along so well, but I should've known that wouldn't last. Bet or no bet, Vincent and I were destined to be at odds.

CHAPTER 14

BROOKLYN

AT FIRST GLANCE, IT SEEMED LIKE VINCENT AND I HAD reverted to our old ways after the arcade—lighthearted insults and the occasional eye roll peppered with shameless attempts to win the bet. He walked around shirtless so often, he might as well have been allergic to tops; I did yoga smack dab in the middle of the living room, dressed in my best ass-flattering leggings and a sports bra. I buttered him up by joining him on Tuesdays for *Bake Off* while he "coincidentally" needed to cook at the exact same time as me every night.

We both knew what the other was doing, so we were on guard. But that didn't change the fact that something had shifted imperceptibly since our afternoon together. I couldn't pinpoint what it was, but it was there, a slight ripple disturbing the glassy surface of our relationship.

It wasn't the renewed threat from his intruder, though that had definitely put us on edge. The police didn't think the photo on his car was "actionable," whatever that meant, so Vincent had doubled security at my flat. More cameras, more locks, and a motion sensor system that scared the crap out of me when I came home one Saturday afternoon to find a laser pointed at my forehead.

He kept his Lamborghini, but he also bought a discreet black Range Rover for everyday errands because the Lambo was too recognizable and he didn't want people following him home.

It might have been overkill considering we hadn't had issues with fans showing up at my flat so far, but it was better to be safe than sorry.

We were on the same page when it came to his intruder, so no, that wasn't the issue.

My thoughts swirled as I tried to relax with a hot shower.

Was it his reaction to Mason? If I didn't know better, I'd have thought Vincent was jealous, but I'd casually mentioned how Mason and I were texting, and he'd continued eating his dinner like I hadn't spoken.

What else could it be? The silly secrets we'd shared? The mere exposure effect from seeing him all day, every day? The glimpses of the man beneath the player, and the annoying realization that I couldn't dismiss him as another overhyped jock with an overinflated ego and the depth of a kiddie pool?

A part of me already knew there was more to him than what he showed the world. We'd had too many conversations for me to truly believe he was all brawn and no brains. But seeing him let his guard down at the arcade, if only for a little bit, drove that home deeper than I would've liked.

It doesn't matter. A bet was a bet, no matter how much I'd softened toward him. I couldn't forget that with the emotional stakes of it all— the potential humiliation of losing to Vincent DuBois, coupled with the knowledge that he would be right and that I *couldn't* resist him after all.

Soft moments had to remain just that. Moments.

I turned off the shower with a squeak of metal and dried off. I wrapped a towel around myself, stepped into the hall, and—*fuck*.

Vincent rounded the corner at the exact same moment that I exited the bathroom. We froze in unison.

This wasn't the first time we'd run into each other fresh out of the shower. However, this *was* the first time he'd seen me practically naked. I'd forgotten to do laundry earlier, so the only towel I had on hand was a minuscule one that barely covered my private parts.

Vincent's gaze slid down the length of my body before it came back up to my face. His jaw ticked, but he didn't say a word.

Heat suffused my cheeks. I was tempted to dash into my room and lock the door, but if I turned, he'd probably see my butt hanging out from under the towel.

I wanted to win the bet, but not at the expense of my dignity.

"You're dressed up," I said in an attempt at small talk. *Cool. Casual. Totally not freaking out over the fact that my nipples are one shrug away from popping free.* "On your way back from a date?"

Instead of his usual trainers and T-shirt, Vincent wore a perfectly tailored blazer and dark jeans. The jacket emphasized the broad width of his shoulders, and I detected the subtle, spicy scent of his cologne.

He looked good. Really good.

His inscrutable expression fell away, replaced with a hint of his dimple. I winced, mentally kicking myself for making it sound like I cared whether he was out on a date or not.

"Just got back from a meeting with my agent, actually," he said. "Zenith wants to have dinner next week, so we were coming up with a game plan."

Surprise replaced my self-consciousness. "So the rumor's true? They're looking for a new ambassador?"

"Seems like it. My agent says they're putting out feelers now. The CEO and the rest of the exec team will be at the dinner, and Lloyd thinks that means I'm already on their shortlist. He did some digging around. He's pretty confident it's down to me, Alarik Filipović, and Rene Martin."

Alarik Filipović was a twelve-time Grand Slam champion while Rene Martin was the reigning king of F1. They were tough competition, but Vincent was a legend in his own right. Besides, he was a hundred times more charismatic than either of those men, though I'd never tell him that. His ego was inflated enough.

I opened my mouth to make some sort of quip about him always coming in third since *Sports UK* recently named him the third-best player in the Premier League, but the words died in my throat.

One, that was kind of mean, and two, he didn't look cocky. He looked anxious. A frown creased his brow, and tension disrupted the usually confident set of his shoulders.

"Are you nervous about the exec dinner?" I asked instead.

"A little." He ran a hand over the back of his neck. "I really fucking want this sponsorship, Brooklyn."

My chest clenched. I was so used to arrogant, self-assured Vincent that this moment of raw honesty hit me harder than expected.

"Listen. I have no idea who they'll choose in the end, but out of all the athletes in the world, you're in the *top three* shortlist. That's already incredible," I said. "Clearly, they see something in you, or they wouldn't have invited you to dinner. As long as you don't dump a glass of wine over their heads or, I don't know, choke to death at the table, you'll be fine. There's nothing to be nervous about."

Vincent's face softened. His dimple made a brief reappearance. "You giving me a pep talk, buttercup?"

"If that's what you want to call it." I arched an eyebrow. "I've never seen you this nervous over a potential sponsor. What's so special about Zenith? Besides the money."

Thanks to his current brand deals, he was already raking in millions on top of his hefty Blackcastle salary. He wasn't exactly hard up for cash.

"The validation, I guess," Vincent said after a long pause. "It's not the best motivator, but I like how stable and long-term their deals are. They don't chase trends the way most other brands do. If Zenith chooses someone to be their ambassador, it means they have faith in them and the longevity of their career. And...I suppose it would just be nice to work with a team who believes I'm worth that much investment of their time and loyalty."

Investment, faith, loyalty. His words struck me hard.

Was that why I'd been dragging my feet on the Blackcastle offer? I'd wanted it for the validation, and I got it. But was Jones really invested in mentoring me and helping me grow, or was I destined to spend my time at the club working twice as hard for half the recognition?

I swallowed past the sudden knot in my throat.

"I get it," I said. "But—I'll say this once and only once—you're Vincent fucking DuBois. You're the captain of Blackcastle. You've won a World Cup. You don't *need* validation from outside brands."

It was a pep talk for myself as much as it was for Vincent, and my words came out fiercer than I'd intended.

There was a beat of surprise before the corner of his mouth kicked up. "Turns out you're pretty good at pep talks." Another pause. Then, "You should come with me."

"To..."

"The dinner. I can bring a plus-one, and Lloyd doesn't count. I was planning to fly solo, but I'd feel a lot better if you were by my side."

I ignored the way my pulse sped up. "What am I, your emotional support nutritionist?"

"No," he said with a straight face. "You're my emotional support flatmate."

Laughter bubbled in my throat. Damn him and his ability to make me smile even when I didn't want to.

"So?" he prompted. "You in?"

I hesitated. Going as his plus-one sounded an awful lot like a date, even if it was to a business function.

"It's not a date." It was as if Vincent had read my mind. "I'm not even paying. Zenith's picking up the bill."

"Cheapskate."

"Freeloader," he corrected. "If you're going to insult me, get the term right."

My lips twitched. "What if my dad finds out? He'll want to know why we went to a brand dinner together."

"Brooklyn." Vincent leveled me with a disbelieving stare. "Do you think your dad gives a shit about Zenith or marketing?"

He had a point.

My dad was laser focused on the game itself. He considered everything else a distraction, including the pre- and post-match press conferences, which he'd labeled as a "ridiculous waste of time."

Fortunately, his tunnel vision meant it was easy to hide my flatmate situation from him. Unfortunately, it meant I didn't have a good excuse for saying no.

"Fine. I'll go," I said. "But if the food is shit, or anyone at the table uses the word 'synergy,' you owe me a meal and twenty pounds."

Vincent chuckled. "Deal."

His response lingered in the air. My skin pebbled with goose bumps, and I realized with horror that I'd been in my towel this entire time.

My tiny, barely adequate towel, which I'd somehow forgotten about.

The same revelation appeared to hit Vincent at the same time. His smile vanished, and we hastily stepped back from each other.

"Well." I pasted on a smile. *Pretend you're wearing real clothes.* "Goodnight."

Vincent kept his eyes firmly on my face. "Goodnight."

I waited for him to turn his back before I sprinted to my room, closed the door, and locked it for good measure. I glanced at my reflection.

Yep, definitely a good thing I didn't leave while he was watching. My butt was hanging out like nobody's business.

I changed into pajamas and flopped onto my bed. I couldn't stop replaying our hallway interaction in my head.

In hindsight, I should've used the towel situation to my advantage. If I couldn't have gotten him to kiss me, I could've at least tortured him a bit. But the moment hadn't felt right, and I didn't want to win with something as obvious and heavy-handed as nudity. I had limits.

My phone pinged with a new text. I picked up my phone, grateful for the distraction.

MASON

What are you up to?

We'd been texting since the arcade, but he hadn't asked me out and I hadn't encouraged him to. Casual, no-strings-attached flirting was way more fun.

Working on my ISNA application. Nothing exciting. What about you?

MASON

At happy hour with some coworkers

MASON

> One of them just started singing Celine Dion a cappella, in case you're wondering how this is going

> See, this is why you ALWAYS say no to coworker hangouts outside the office. They always end with Celine Dion, resentment, and/or vomit. Not great either way

MASON

> Haha I'll keep that in mind

MASON

> On the upside, one of them told me about this great Italian restaurant in Notting Hill

MASON

> Want to go with me next Friday? My treat

My stomach twisted. I'd jinxed myself because that was, for *sure*, a date invitation. *So much for no-strings-attached flirting.*

I drew my bottom lip between my teeth. Mason was single, attractive, and easy to talk to. Best of all, he had no ties to or interest in football. He was honestly the best dating option I'd had all year... so why was I hesitating?

My thumbs hovered over my phone screen. I had to type three words. That was it.

I'd love to. See? Simple.

So why couldn't I do it?

You giving me a pep talk, buttercup?

You should come with me.

So what you're saying is, I'm special.

That's exactly what I'm saying.

I groaned and turned on my side. I glared at the wall separating my room from Vincent's, wishing I could scrub my brain clean of his voice.

> I might have a work thing that night. Can I confirm and get back to you?

MASON

> No problem. Just lmk when you're free, and we'll make it work

MASON

> Only if you want, of course :)

His easy understanding only made me feel worse.

Why couldn't I get out of my own way? And why couldn't Mason give me butterflies the way a certain other, off-limits person could?

I let out another groan. I rolled onto my stomach and buried my face in my comforter, the memory of Vincent's face floating through my head.

I really hated myself sometimes.

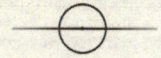

VINCENT

I could hear Brooklyn breathing.

It was physically impossible, given how thick the wall was between our rooms, but I swore I detected her soft inhales as I lay in bed, staring at the ceiling.

Every time I closed my eyes, the image of her in that towel seared itself into the back of my lids—long legs, tousled hair, and more bare skin than was decent. I couldn't erase it any more than I could erase the dozens of other memories that'd imprinted on my mind. There was a full Brooklyn Armstrong gallery up there, but I'd rather not visit tonight. It was too dangerous, so I kept my eyes wide open. Unfortunately, it only helped a little bit.

I could still feel her presence through the wall, warm and soft and just the right amount of prickly. She'd surprised me with her pep talk, and I'd surprised myself when I invited her to the Zenith dinner.

I shouldn't have done that. I had a hard enough time resisting her at home without bringing her to business meetings. But fuck, she just…comforted me. When I talked to her, I felt like everything would work out. She didn't try to kiss my ass, and if she said I was good, I was good.

There weren't many people in my life I could trust like that. I was going to be surrounded by sharks at that dinner. I needed someone who was on my side, even if their tongue was sharper than any blade.

I turned my head. A beam of moonlight sliced through the darkness and illuminated the wall separating us. The shadows of dozens of stuffed animals loomed in the background.

My lips curved. Brooklyn was a menace for pulling that stunt—I sneezed every time I entered my room because there were so many damn plushies—but I had to admire her creativity.

Honestly, I was surprised she hadn't tried to seduce me in the hall. She was competitive as hell, and after an initial flurry of attempts to win our bet—like I couldn't see right through her yoga pants scheme— her efforts had died down.

Was she distracted by something, or someone, else?

Maybe she's busy with Mason. The unwelcome thought shoehorned its way into my head, and my smile faded.

I'd had to force myself not to react when Brooklyn told me they'd been texting. I really didn't like that guy, but I didn't blame him for chasing her. If she weren't the coach's daughter and she didn't work at Blackcastle, I would've done the same thing.

As it stood, our bet was the closest thing we'd ever have to a relationship.

I resisted the urge to knock on the wall and see if she was still awake. That would be corny as hell. Plus, if she *was* awake, I'd rather not torture myself picturing all the things she could be doing—like texting a certain American who was tactless enough to hit on her in front of another man.

Yeah, Brooklyn and I weren't a couple, but he hadn't known that before flirting with her, had he?

Something green and oily poured through my blood. I clenched my jaw and yanked my gaze away from the wall. I resumed staring at the ceiling, where I tried to count pet pigs instead of thinking about my flatmate.

One Truffle.

Blond hair.

Two Truffles.

Mischievous smile.

Three Truffles.

White towel and tanned skin.

Low voice.

Words that nearly killed me with their fierce sincerity.

You're Vincent fucking DuBois...You don't need *validation from outside brands.*

A fist squeezed my chest. I rubbed a hand over my face and stared ruefully at the clock. It wasn't even eleven.

This was going to be a long night.

CHAPTER 15

BROOKLYN

"I HATE TO SAY IT, SWEETIE, BUT I DON'T THINK calligraphy is your calling." I set the latest handwritten thank-you card aside. "I'm so sorry."

Carina stared forlornly at the remaining stack of blank stationery in front of her. "I know. I had high hopes, but my writing is atrocious."

Scarlett, Carina, and I were huddled around the coffee table in my flat. Carina wanted to open a greeting card shop on Etsy and was currently practicing her calligraphy. Spoiler: it wasn't going well.

I loved the girl, but trying to decipher her handwriting was like trying to decode a Cold War cipher text.

"I thought you liked working at the art gallery," Scarlett said. "What happened?"

"It folded. Turns out the owner was embezzling money and ran off to the Caribbean with his mistress. I went in last night and everything was cleared out except for a stained rug and a pile of Post-its."

Scarlett winced. "Oof."

"Yeah. I didn't even get paid for my last two weeks of work."

"Look on the bright side." I aimed for cheerful optimism. "The story's so absurd, you could totally turn the experience into a screenplay. Pitch it to Hollywood, and *bam*! Instant fame and fortune."

"I don't think it's as easy as you make it sound," Carina said dryly.

"No, but it's *possible*." I squinted at the thank-you card. Were those Ns or Rs? "More possible than creating a greeting card empire, I'm afraid."

Being a good friend meant knowing when to support your girl's delusions and when to dish out some tough love.

Carina blew a strand of hair out of her eye in silent agreement. "I swear, I must've pissed off the career gods or something because I have the worst luck when it comes to second jobs."

I couldn't disagree.

Her lifelong dream was to visit the penguins in Antarctica. She'd been saving for years, but trips to Antarctica were ridiculously expensive, and her executive assistant's salary didn't go far in London to begin with. That was why she was determined to find the perfect side gig.

So far, she'd worked as a tutor, a barista, a professional survey participant, a gallery receptionist, and most recently, an aspiring but failed Etsy seller. All of them had ended in disaster.

"You could try the barista gig again," I said. "My local café is hiring, and your coffee's gotten, um, better."

Scarlett's eyes widened. "What are you doing?" she whispered when Carina was distracted with organizing the stationery. "She can't make coffee. She'll go to prison for murder!"

"I'm trying to help," I whispered back. "*You* come up with ideas then."

Scarlett was being dramatic, but Carina's coffee probably *could* wake the dead (not in a good way). The memory of her attempt at a vanilla latte was still burned into my tongue.

"No. The only coffee-related activity I'm cut out for is drinking it." Carina sighed while Scarlett and I released small, simultaneous exhales of relief. "I'll find something, but thanks for looking out. Sorry I'm such a buzzkill tonight."

"You're not being a buzzkill. I'd much rather be here with you guys than at some shitty bar with overpriced drinks," I said.

"Exactly." Scarlett stretched her arms over her head. "Besides, if we went out, we wouldn't be able to watch Carina butcher her calligraphy in—ah!" She squeaked with surprise when Carina crumpled a sheet of paper and tossed it at her. It hit her right on the nose.

"That's not funny," Carina said through a glimmer of laughter. "My cursive isn't the best, but it's legible."

Scarlett lobbed the paper ball back at her. This time, it got stuck in Carina's hair. "Your Ns look like Rs."

"Those letters naturally look alike!"

"Then how do you explain your Ts and Js?" I jabbed a finger at the thank-you card.

Carina's eyes narrowed. "Et tu, Brute?"

"I'm just telling the truth. Don't kill the messenger."

The three of us stared at each other. There was a moment of contemplation before we dove for the table at the same time, and our night exploded into a full-blown paper ball fight.

"My Ts. Do *not*. Look like Js!" Carina punctuated her words with surprisingly accurate lobs.

Forget Etsy. She should pitch for Major League Baseball.

"Yes, they do!"

"That's slander!"

"It's only slander if it's not true!"

"Brooklyn, look behind you!"

I squealed and ran behind the couch, my stomach cramping with laughter. My hair was weighed down with what felt like a dozen pieces of paper, and I ducked right as a particularly large projectile went sailing over my head. Our screams and laughter filled the flat.

Thank God Vincent wasn't here to see us acting like a bunch of children on a Monday night.

Honestly, even if he were, I wouldn't care. I needed this. I'd been slammed with work, and I was stuck on the ISNA application, which was due in a month. A silly night in with my friends was just what the doctor ordered.

Our "fight" lasted until we ran out of paper. Our laughter gradually subsided, and we collapsed onto the couch in a happy, tired heap.

"Where's Vincent?" Scarlett asked after we caught our breath. "Don't tell me you killed him already."

I snorted. "No. He went out to help Adil with holiday shopping or something." It was only mid-November, but Adil was notoriously enthusiastic when it came to buying gifts. "Living with him hasn't been so bad. At least he's clean and does his chores."

That was the upside. The downside was the number of times we inadvertently saw each other half-naked around the house.

Vincent's sculpted abs flashed through my mind. Heat prickled my neck, and I firmly shoved the image aside.

"See? I *knew* it would work out!" Carina grinned.

"Mmhmm." I avoided their eyes and plucked a stray paper ball out from between the couch cushions.

I hadn't told them about my bet with Vincent yet. I felt bad about lying to them, but I was nervous about how Scarlett would take it. Sure, she was the one who'd suggested he move in, but I didn't think she expected us to be anything other than platonic.

She also didn't seem like the type who'd freak out if we kissed, but I couldn't risk it. I valued her friendship too much.

I probably should've thought of that before agreeing to the bet. That was what my impulsiveness got me. Constantly trapped in sticky situations.

As for Carina, I didn't want to tell her and make it so we were *both* keeping this secret from Scarlett. It was better for me to shoulder this alone.

"I've said this a dozen times, but thank you for letting him stay with you," Scarlett said. "He likes to pretend he's okay and that the obsessed fan stuff doesn't bother him, but it does."

"I know," I said softly. I could tell whenever Vincent was putting on a brave face for the world because I did the exact same thing. The clues were there if you knew what to look for—the too-bright smile, the overly casual tone, the air of forced nonchalance because wearing a mask was more palatable than making the people you love worry.

I tamped down my guilt and adopted a breezy tone. "Anyway, no need to thank me. He's paying rent, so it's not like I'm doing this out of the goodness of my heart. I just wish the police weren't so useless. They haven't made a bit of progress since we found the photo on his car."

"So what, they're waiting until Vincent gets attacked before they do something? Not that he's going to get attacked," Carina said quickly when Scarlett's face paled. "It's a hypothetical."

"I don't know. Probably." Great. Now I was the buzzkill for talking about potential murder. I pivoted to a lighter topic. "Also, I forgot to tell you guys, but I'm going with him to the Zenith dinner on Wednesday. He, um, needed a plus-one."

Carina's eyebrows winged up. "Like...a date?"

"*No*. It's strictly business. He needed someone for appearances' sake, and I wanted to eat at a nice restaurant. That's all." I snuck a peek at Scarlett. The dinner news was my way of gauging how she might react if I told her about the bet, but her expression was unreadable.

"Nice," she said. "I've been to a few business dinners with Asher. The food's usually good, but the conversations are so boring. They use the word 'synergy' way too much."

"I told him he owes me twenty pounds if that word ever comes up during our meal."

Scarlett grinned. "Genius." If she was weirded out by me joining her brother for dinner, she didn't show it.

Our conversation eventually shifted to our weekend plans, but I couldn't stop thinking about Wednesday night.

It's not a date, I repeated to myself. I'd said yes specifically because it *wasn't* one.

But that didn't stop the butterflies in my stomach from multiplying.

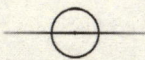

"Thanks again for doing this," Vincent said. "I owe you one."

"You're welcome, and don't worry," I said as we followed our hostess to a private dining room. "I'm already thinking of all the ways you can pay me back."

His mouth twitched up into a smile as his gaze ran over my outfit. "I forgot to tell you earlier, but you look great." Perhaps I was imagining it, but his voice sounded a touch huskier than usual.

The praise sent an unwanted spark down my spine. "So do you."

It was the night of the big Zenith dinner, and he looked *better* than great. His blazer and jeans the other night were nice, but nothing beat seeing Vincent DuBois in a custom-tailored suit. The soft Italian wool fit his six-foot-two frame like a dream while the rich navy color contrasted perfectly against his light brown skin. He'd gotten a fresh haircut, and his Zenith sneakers were a smart but subtle nod to his potential sponsor.

No wonder every head turned to watch us pass.

I'd opted for a simple blue dress that accidentally matched his suit. It was more muted than my usual style, but tonight wasn't about me. I was here for moral support only.

My heels sank into the carpet as the hostess led us into the private dining room of some fancy steakhouse. We were greeted with a flurry of warm welcomes the instant we stepped inside.

"Vincent! So great to finally meet you!"

"Such a pleasure."

"Brooklyn, lovely to meet you as well."

"Thank you for having me." I smiled and shook everyone's hands, trying to remember their names. There were three Zenith execs at the dinner, including their CEO, Rex; their Chief Marketing Officer, Dale, and their Executive Vice President of Global Partnerships, Sandra. Lloyd rounded out our group for an even six.

Everyone was friendlier than I'd expected, but Scarlett was right: the conversation was snooze-worthy. Lots of numbers and business terms I didn't fully understand.

Vincent's contributions were the only thing keeping me awake. He had a way of speaking that made even the most boring topics sound interesting. His velvety pronunciation of the word "holistic"? Diabolical—though I was disappointed no one had used "synergy" yet.

"I can tell you'd fit right in with our team," Rex said after laughing at one of Vincent's jokes. "Although I'm getting ahead of myself, considering we haven't gotten to the real reason we're here yet."

The table quieted. The Zenith execs had avoided talking specifically about their ambassadorship all night, but it seemed the time had finally come.

As Lloyd perked up like a shark smelling blood, I set my fork down, my heart racing. I had no horse in this race, but I was strangely nervous for Vincent.

His expression didn't waver, but beneath the table, his knuckles whitened around his knee.

I didn't think about it. I simply reached over and curled my hand over his before I could talk myself out of it.

His skin was warm to the touch, and my pulse beat a little faster. *Moral support.* That's all this was.

Vincent didn't openly acknowledge my gesture, but I caught the deep bob of his Adam's apple before his grip relaxed.

"We won't beat around the bush any longer." Rex spoke again. "This probably doesn't come as a surprise, but you're on our shortlist for potential ambassadors. This dinner is for both parties to get to know each other better. Nothing's guaranteed yet, but I think you would make a fine face for our brand. What do you think?"

The tension leaked out of Vincent's body. His shoulders relaxed, and his smile positively dazzled. "I think it would be an honor, sir."

Lloyd beamed. I could practically see the cartoon dollar signs popping up in his eyes.

Our servers brought out dessert, and the mood was light and celebratory until Dale said, "Forgive me if I'm speaking out of turn, but it's refreshing to see an athlete of your caliber in a committed relationship. Not that relationship status is a dealbreaker." He added that part hastily when Rex glared at him. "But a brand always runs the risk of scandal when they sign someone single. The affairs, the parties…"

"And you two make such a gorgeous couple." Sandra gestured toward Vincent and me. "So photogenic. I love it."

My stomach flipped. I opened my mouth, but Vincent beat me to the punch.

"Brooklyn and I aren't dating," he said, his tone apologetic but firm. I thought I heard a ripple of something else beneath the surface, but it was gone before I could pinpoint what it was. "We're just friends."

"Exactly," I said quickly. "Friends. That's all."

I released his hand and took a gulp of water, trying to cope with the sudden awkwardness. Vincent was right, of course. We *weren't* dating. The closest we'd come to a romantic relationship was our stupid bet. Maybe he wanted me and, as loath as I was to admit it, maybe I wanted him too. But hearing him deny we were dating so swiftly and resolutely was the reminder I needed.

The bet was just a bet. Nothing more, nothing less.

The Zenith execs' smiles melted, replaced with expressions of confusion. A vein pulsed in Lloyd's temple. The cartoon dollar signs had been replaced by a panicked glare.

"Oh!" Sandra looked mortified. "I apologize. I assumed…"

"It's okay." Vincent maintained a light, easy tone. "Listen, I get it. Single athletes can be a menace, and I say that as one myself." Another round of laughter chased away some of the awkwardness. "I'll be honest. I'm not married, and I don't know when I'll be married. But when I commit to something, personally or professionally, I'm all in. Loyalty is important to me, and I don't jump into a partnership for the sake of having one. I hope you understand."

Vincent fucking DuBois.

That was the most masterful pivot I'd ever seen, and judging by the execs' nods, it'd worked.

I almost made a joke about how married celebrities were *more* prone to scandal, but I didn't want to accidentally fuck things up, so I kept my mouth shut the way I had all night.

The rest of dinner passed without incident. We left the restaurant together, and Lloyd waited until the execs were gone before he forced us to debrief at the valet station.

"That went pretty well, despite the relationship fiasco," he said. "I almost had a fucking aneurysm."

"I'm not going to fake date someone for a brand deal," Vincent said. He sounded annoyed. "This isn't a rom-com."

"No, it's just a *nine-figure deal* that'll set you up for the rest of your life."

I almost choked on my spit. *Nine figures?* That was at least a hundred million dollars. I couldn't wrap my head around such a sum. They might as well be talking about Monopoly money.

They had a quick discussion about timelines. The holidays were coming up, so Lloyd didn't expect any concrete news until after the new year.

Then the valet pulled up with Vincent's car, ending the conversation. I climbed into the passenger seat while Vincent turned the radio on.

"Don't forget to check your email!" Lloyd yelled after us. "There's a lot of end-of-year paperwork coming your way!"

"Wow," I said after we pulled away. "He needs to chill, or he'll have a heart attack by forty."

Vincent's mouth quirked. "I tell him that all the time, but he's incapable of chilling. If he's not working, he's thinking about working. It's an obsessive thing." He glanced at me. "Sorry about what happened at dinner. I didn't expect them to jump to the conclusion that we were dating."

"Well, you brought me as your plus-one, and we accidentally matched outfits." I forced a light tone. "It wasn't that big of a jump, even though the idea of us dating is absurd."

"Totally absurd."

"Doesn't even make sense."

"Nope."

I shifted in my seat. Vincent cleared his throat and raised the volume on the radio. Smooth jazz filled the pockets in our conversation.

Make a move. The business portion of the night was done. We were alone, I was dressed up, and we were so close, I got a lungful of his scent every time I inhaled. This was the perfect opportunity for me to try and win the bet—to prove that he really did want me and that he would break first.

I shifted positions again so the folds of my dress slipped aside, exposing my bare thigh. Vincent's eyes flicked over for a brief second before they returned to the road. Other than that, he didn't react at all.

I felt a sting of disappointment. My legs were one of my best features, but maybe they weren't a great strategy when he was driving. I didn't want us to crash, but I wanted him to...I don't know, do *something*. Show he was affected, if only a little.

I changed tactics and leaned over to adjust the volume. My fingers grazed his forearm on my way back, the touch light but deliberate.

Once again, no reaction. His eyes remained fixed ahead.

The sting turned into a burn of frustration and something else I didn't want to name. My attempts were subtle, but if he was interested, they would've elicited a twitch, a sigh—anything except cool, silent indifference.

"Have you made a decision about Blackcastle yet?" Vincent asked. His voice sounded a little tight.

He wanted to talk about *work*? I gave up.

"Not yet." I kept the grumble out of my reply. "I'm still weighing the pros and cons."

Typically, candidates had one or two days to decide, but when I'd asked HR for more time, they'd shockingly granted it. They didn't need a final answer from me until December, which was unusually generous.

I couldn't decide whether that was a good or bad thing. Did they want me badly enough to work with my timeline, or did they not care enough to get a quick answer?

"Want to talk about it?" Vincent asked. "You were my moral support back there. I'm happy to return the favor."

Sure. If only I could articulate what the pros and cons are. My practical needs versus my complicated feelings about Jones, my dad, and the nutrition team's culture were all tangled up in a web that I didn't have the energy to unravel right now.

"Thanks, but I'll figure it out. I just need a little more time to think." I stared out the window, my earlier angst about the bet replaced by a twinge of exhaustion. It'd been threatening rain all day, and the skies had finally opened up. Big droplets of water splattered against the window, blurring my view of the city. It was our fourth rainstorm in as many days. "God, I'm so tired of the rain. It's weeks like these that I really miss San Diego."

"I've never been. What was it like growing up there?" Vincent sounded genuinely curious.

"I loved it, for the most part. The weather is gorgeous, the beach is right there, and the people are pretty laid-back. But for a very long time, it was only Mom and me. She has more of a, shall we say, *LA personality*, so we didn't quite fit in with our neighbors. It was a constant back and forth." Growing up in San Diego was one thing; growing up with my mom was another.

"And she didn't want to move to LA?"

"She did, but it's a tough city for a single parent. I also think she liked how much smaller San Diego feels. Big fish in a little pond and all that."

Vincent made a small noise in his throat. His expression was studiously neutral, but whenever we talked about my mom, the air would shift just a little, like he was taking great pains to rein in his thoughts.

"What about you?" I asked. "What was it like growing up in Paris?"

"It had its ups and downs. It's a beautiful city. Great culture, great food, great public transport. But I didn't speak fluent French when I moved there, and it was hard to make friends at first. It got better over time, but..." He trailed off for a moment. "I don't know. I guess I never felt quite French enough."

My heart tugged. It was hard to imagine Vincent feeling like an outsider anywhere. He was magnetic, so bright and full of life that he could draw even the loneliest shadows into his fold. It was impossible to walk into a room he was in and not be sucked into his orbit.

But as the past few weeks had proved, he was also human. He hadn't been born famous, and he had the same doubts and fears as the rest of us.

"If it makes you feel better, I've lived in London for a year and a half, but I still call chips 'fries' and crisps 'chips,'" I said. "And that's just another dialect of English, not a whole new language."

A laugh escaped Vincent's lips.

I smiled, but a new text drew my eyes to my phone.

MASON

Did you figure out your schedule for Friday yet?

MASON

No pressure! Just wanted to see if I needed to change my dinner reservations :)

Crap. I completely forgot to follow up after I left him hanging last week.

Guilt cut through me.

I'm so sorry, but I couldn't get out of my work thing. I won't be able to make it on Friday after all

MASON

That's okay. Are you free another night?

I bit my lip. He was persistent.

We stopped at a red light, and Vincent's stare bore into my cheek as I debated my answer.

Should I give Mason a chance, or should I cut the thread now instead of stringing him along?

Fuck it.

I typed my reply and pocketed my phone, determined not to look at it again until I got home.

"Who was that? Scarlett?" Vincent asked casually.

"No, it was Mason. The guy I met at the arcade," I added in case he didn't remember. "He, um, asked me out."

I wasn't sure why I'd shared that information, but it was too late to take it back.

The light turned green. Vincent shifted his attention back to the road, his hands tightening near imperceptibly around the steering wheel.

"What did you say?" He sounded bored.

"I said no." As perfect as he seemed on paper, I wasn't interested in Mason like that, and I would want someone to tell me the truth if I were in his position.

Vincent didn't respond. But I swore I saw a shadow of a smile linger on his mouth for the rest of our ride home.

CHAPTER 16

VINCENT

A WEEK AFTER THE ZENITH DINNER, I LEFT FOR OUR NEXT match in Manchester. It was a four-hour drive from London, but the energy in the stadium was noticeably different. Restless, almost explosive.

The sea of red and white filling the stands was a visual reminder that we weren't on our own turf anymore. It was always hard to give up home advantage, but this match had been an especially massive shit show so far. Gallagher and Dormund were on the bench due to injuries in the first half, and we were one down with a minute left to play.

My lungs burned. My shirt was soaked with sweat, and my muscles were shot, but we were *so close* to making this a draw.

Come on, Donovan.

The crowd roared as Asher gained possession of the ball. He broke toward the goal, his—

A shrill whistle pierced the air.

Confused shouts rang out from the stands as the match stumbled to a halt. The referee jogged toward where Manchester's striker lay on the ground, clutching his knee.

My heart thundered as I ran toward the commotion. It was such an obvious dive. There was no *fucking* way the ref would give Manchester a free kick for that.

"Come on, ref!" I heard Asher yell when I got within earshot. "I barely touched him!"

The other striker groaned dramatically as if he'd been shot. Motherfucker.

"I saw the whole thing. He fell by himself," I argued, backing Asher up. "Look at him! There's no way he's really hurt."

The official was unmoved. He awarded the other team a free kick, and I watched, my pulse hammering, as the Manchester player took his shot.

The ball sailed toward the net. Noah knocked it back out to a chorus of jeers, but his save wasn't enough.

The "foul" cost us our momentum, and when the final whistle blew less than a minute later, my chest had already caved in with disappointment. The stadium's celebratory cheers dulled into a roar as I stared at the final scoreboard.

Three-two.

We'd lost.

To cheer us up, Adil insisted we attend a "consolation celebration" later that night, which was how the entire team ended up packed into his hotel room after dinner.

We weren't returning to London until the morning, and normally, we'd have a night out after an away game, but the mood had been glum all evening. Although today's match had been a regular Premier

League match that didn't count toward the UCL, it never felt good to lose.

Adil's solution to that? Dinosaur erotica. The craziest part was, it seemed to be working.

"I now call this meeting of the Blackcastle Book Club to order." Adil banged his mini gavel against the table. "I hope you all had a chance to look over the discussion questions I emailed—"

"Oy, Chakir, get on with it already," Gallagher called out. His injury was minor, but he was still grumpy about getting subbed out. "We've suffered enough today, yeah? Don't need a whole song and dance when we already know how this goes."

Adil glowered at him. "Obviously you don't because the book club rules *clearly* state that whoever holds the gavel has the floor. For that, I use the power vested in me as the president of this club to strip you of your book-choosing privileges next month."

"What? That's not fair!" Gallagher spluttered. "It was my turn to choose!"

"You should've thought of that before you broke the rules. Now, as I was saying..."

I tuned out the rest of Adil's introduction. I wasn't surprised that he'd consider a book club meeting a consolation prize or that he'd hunted down copies of our monthly pick at a local bookshop. Our meeting was originally scheduled for Friday, so we'd left our books at home.

I was more surprised by how comforting this felt. We'd started the Blackcastle Book Club in the spring at Adil's insistence, but it'd turned into a general team bonding experience. Every month, we gathered at one of our houses to discuss our latest pick. We usually only spent ten or fifteen minutes on the actual book discussion. The rest of the hour was spent chatting or, if a guy was on the outs with his girl, providing unlicensed therapy.

This month, our pick was *Fucking My Theropod Therapist* by Wilma Pebbles. If you guessed the book was about a human woman who falls in lust with her dinosaur therapist, you'd be right.

I didn't want to know how Adil was able to get that many copies on such short notice.

"Let's start with question number one." He read from his phone. "Do you think it's ethical for a therapist to sleep with their patient, even if they're fictional?"

"It's interspecies fucking, which is technically bestiality. We've passed the boundaries of ethics," Samson said.

"That doesn't count," Stevens argued. "Interspecies fucking is the *entire premise* of the genre. We have to overlook it the way we have to overlook how everyone has, like, ten orgasms at a time in these books even though that's physically impossible."

"Impossible for you, maybe," Samson said. "Don't project your inadequacies on the rest of us."

"Personally, I'm more interested in the demographics of this world." Gallagher frowned. "Were there no human therapists? Why did she go to a dinosaur? I feel like a human therapist would've been much better equipped to help her deal with her problems."

"Yeah, but would a human be able to rail her like Big T? No. That's what makes this book absolutely bonkers!" Stevens slapped his paperback against his thigh. "This is dino erotica, people! You can't have dino erotica without the dino!"

The book discussion devolved into a mess of shouting, arguments, and futile attempts by Adil to restore order.

I stayed out of it. I had enough on my mind without trying to wrangle a bunch of footballers who were arguing about dinosaur sex.

Zenith had gone radio silent since the dinner. Lloyd warned me that might happen, but I couldn't help wondering if he was right, and I'd fucked up by telling them Brooklyn wasn't my girlfriend.

My gut twisted. I didn't regret what I'd done. I didn't want to start off our relationship with a lie, but their assumption had caused—just for a millisecond—a slight stutter in my heart. A moment where I allowed myself to imagine a world where Brooklyn was my girlfriend, not just my plus-one.

In that world, I could kiss her whenever I wanted. We'd wake up in the same bed and fall asleep in each other's arms. I'd take her to my favorite restaurants, and we'd walk along the river after, hand in hand. She'd wear my shirt number to matches, but that wouldn't be all.

In that world, I would've pulled the car off to the side of the road the other night and shown her exactly who she belonged to. Not fucking Mason, who had the balls to ask her out like he deserved her. Not any of the guys on the team who secretly had a crush on her. *Me*. Because I was the one who wanted her so much that I couldn't breathe when she was near. One glimpse of her skin, one graze of her fingers, and I'd almost crashed the damn car. It'd taken all my willpower not to react when I'd been silently dying inside.

Except I didn't live in that hypothetical world. I lived in this one, where I was surrounded by a bunch of footballers arguing about dinosaur sex and Brooklyn was two hundred miles away in London.

I wish she were here. The thought struck me with a sudden swiftness. Jones traveled with the team for all our away matches, but his interns alternated turns. Henry had tagged along for today's match while Brooklyn remained at home.

What I wouldn't give to see her right now.

I swallowed, an ache sliding behind my ribcage.

"Consolation celebration, my ass," Asher said, yanking me back to the present with jarring clarity. "This is like watching a group of ten-year-olds fight."

I blinked away an image of Brooklyn's smile and forced myself to refocus. "Nah." I tried to sound like I'd been paying attention and not pining after the coach's daughter this entire time. "Wilson's daughter is ten, and she's better behaved than this. Right?" I nudged Noah, who sat on my other side.

"Definitely." He grimaced when Stevens grabbed a pillow from the bed and whacked Samson on the stomach with it. "I can't believe this is what I left Michigan for."

Noah was the only American in the Premier League at the moment, which made him a novelty for fans. He was almost as famous as Asher and me, but he kept an incredibly low profile and was never in the tabloids. It was hard to dig up dirt on someone who didn't date, didn't party, and rarely left his house except for work.

"Hey, we need you here. Your last save was nothing short of poetry," I said.

"It wasn't good enough."

"Don't start with that bullshit." Asher wasn't having it. "You did your job. The ref was the one who fucked us over."

Noah shrugged, but I could tell he was beating himself up over the goals he didn't save. He might not hang out with the team much off the pitch, but he took the game as seriously as anyone else.

Asher checked his phone. "It's Scarlett. I'll be right back."

"Do you think he's really coming back?" Noah asked when Asher disappeared into the hall.

"Nah. We won't see him again until the morning."

I lived with Asher and Scarlett for one traumatizing week. Those two could talk for hours about the most mundane topics.

Then again, Brooklyn and I had spent an afternoon at an arcade talking about our grade-school years and underwear-buying habits, so who was I to judge?

"Everything okay?" I asked when Noah frowned at his phone.

"Yeah. Evie's with her new nanny, and I'm checking in."

"How's that working out?" I asked. "This is what, her third nanny in the past year?"

Noah sighed. "Fourth. I fired the third one last week."

"What happened?"

"I came home and found her on my bed. In lingerie."

"Oh, shit. I'm sorry, man." Most men would love to find a half-naked woman waiting for them, but Noah was the opposite of most men. His only focus was football and his daughter Evie. He didn't care about dating, but given his work and travel schedule, he couldn't take care of her on his own.

Unfortunately, he'd had the worst luck trying to find the right nanny. They either fell in love with him, didn't get along with Evie, or both.

"Thanks. The new nanny is in her seventies and happily married, so the lingerie situation shouldn't be an issue," Noah said dryly. "I just hope Evie isn't giving her a hard time."

I kept my mouth shut. Personally, I'd rather set myself on fire than watch anyone between the ages of ten and twelve. Preteens were terrifying.

While Noah texted his nanny, I checked my own phone. My heartbeat tripped when I saw a text from Brooklyn. It was as though she'd heard my thoughts earlier.

BROOKLYN

> Sorry about today's match :(That last ref call was bullshit

BROOKLYN

> But at least you didn't misjudge your interception the way you did during the Holchester match. Baby steps. You're learning.

My lips curved. Trust Brooklyn to remember a small mistake

from last month.

> Thanks a lot. That makes me feel better

I wasn't being sarcastic. Talking to her was like a weird form of therapy. She could insult me the entire time, and I'd still feel better after one of our conversations than I did after a session with the team's psychologist.

BROOKLYN

You're welcome :)

BROOKLYN

Seriously though. That ref was the worst. You should've at least gotten a draw.

> It is what it is. We'll crush it next time.

I wasn't as nonchalant about the loss as I pretended to be, but I was the captain. I had to put up a strong front for everyone else.

> What are you up to?

BROOKLYN

Enjoying alone time in the flat without you. Finally.

> Define "alone time"

BROOKLYN

...

BROOKLYN

Get your mind out of the gutter, you perv

> You started it. Anyway, don't lie. You miss me and you know it

BROOKLYN

I miss you the way I miss root canals—the ones without anesthesia

> Wow, buttercup

That's not a nice joke and my feelings are hurt. You should apologize by making me pancakes when I get home

BROOKLYN

Make them yourself. I'm not your personal chef

I mean, technically...

BROOKLYN

Finish that sentence and I will sic HR on you

Not HR. C'mon, you know Lizzie's had it out for me since I accidentally ate her yogurt

BROOKLYN

You should've thought of that before stealing other people's snacks

Three dots popped up, disappeared, and reappeared.

I held my breath.

BROOKLYN

But I was thinking of you because Bake Off comes on soon

A grin stretched across my face.

Were you? Interesting

BROOKLYN

Don't read too much into it

BROOKLYN

You've brainwashed me into turning on Channel 4 every Tuesday night and I WILL make you pay for it

You're lying again. You love watching Bake Off with me

Actually, she reminded me that I needed to leave soon. The show started in ten minutes, and our book club had devolved into a half-pillow fight, half-philosophical debate about the dinosaurs' extinction.

Want to watch it together? I can regale you with hilarious commentary over the phone

I waited. Nothing. Not even the three dots.

"Who are you texting?"

The voice was so close to my ear, I instinctively jumped and nearly banged my head into Adil's nose. "Jesus! Don't sneak up on me like that. I almost punched you."

"Sorry." He plopped down in Asher's vacated spot. He'd given up on mediating a book club discussion and was eyeing me with open curiosity. "So, who were you texting? New girlfriend? You have a goofy smile on your face."

My mouth flattened into a straight line. "My smile isn't goofy."

"Hmm. I beg to differ."

"Don't make me rethink punching you."

"Okay, okay. I can take a hint." Adil held up his hands in surrender. "Actually, I wanted to talk to you because, um, I wanted to apologize again."

"For what?"

"For telling Coach about your intruder." He shifted, his brows pulled so low they formed a sharp V. "I wasn't trying to get you in trouble. He's *Coach*, you know? He always has the answers, so I thought...I don't know. I thought he might be able to help."

"You already apologized. Don't worry about it."

I'd been annoyed at the time, but I'd gotten over it. I hadn't expected Adil to still be beating himself up over it.

"Okay. As long as you're not mad at me," he said anxiously.

"I'm not." I clapped a hand on his shoulder before rising to my feet. "But I'm going to turn in early. I'll see you in the morning."

Noah was already gone. I said goodbye to the rest of the guys and slipped out before they could guilt-trip me into staying longer. I was going to miss the start of *Bake Off*, and Brooklyn still hadn't texted me back.

I tried not to think about it as I walked to my room. She was probably busy with something else. She said she'd turned down a date with Mason, so she—

A door to my left opened. "DuBois."

My steps faltered as Coach stepped into the corridor. "Hey, Boss."

He raised his eyebrows and glanced over my shoulder. Muffled shouts and laughter leaked out from Adil's hotel room. "Do I want to know what's going on in there?"

I discreetly pushed my copy of *Fucking My Theropod Therapist* deeper into my pocket. "Not really, no." I swallowed, then added, "I'm sorry we let you down today."

I hated disappointing myself, but I hated disappointing him more.

"You didn't," he said gruffly. "The entire team fought like hell out there. Sometimes that's enough. Sometimes it isn't. That's the nature of the game. What matters is getting back up after you've been knocked down. You got that?"

"Yes, sir." He'd given us a similar pep talk in the changing room after the match, but I'd needed to hear it again. This job could really fuck with your head if you let it.

"I'm glad I caught you because there's something else I wanted to discuss. It's about Brooklyn."

My whole body tensed with foreboding. Sweat slicked down my spine, and I had to fight to keep my voice even.

"Oh?" I managed. "What about her?"

He couldn't know about our living situation. If he did, he wouldn't be this calm—unless he was trying to lull me into a false sense of security.

A golf ball lodged itself in my throat.

Coach ran a hand over his face. "Normally, I wouldn't do this. I hate mixing work and family, but Jones said she still hasn't accepted his job offer. The deadline is in a month, and you're friends with her. Has she...said anything to you about it?"

"No." Technically true. She'd never told me why she hadn't accepted the offer yet. "I'm sure she's just doing her due diligence. A permanent position is different from an internship."

Coach sighed. "You're probably right. She has a good head on her shoulders. She knows what she's doing. But don't, ah, tell her that I asked, okay? I don't want her to think I'm sneaking around behind her back."

"I won't." I hesitated, then added, "Your relationship with Brooklyn is none of my business, sir, but—and this is just a suggestion— perhaps you might want to talk to her yourself instead of asking her friends. I have a feeling she'd appreciate it."

He stared at me.

Shit. Had I crossed way over the line?

I held still, worried the slightest muscle twitch would set him off.

"Get some rest," he finally said. "We have an early morning."

I didn't release my breath until he disappeared around the corner, toward the vending machines.

By the time I got to my room, *Bake Off* had already started

I checked my phone again. Still no reply from Brooklyn.

I set it aside and focused on the TV, but no matter how hard I tried, I couldn't enjoy the episode as much as I wanted to.

CHAPTER 17

BROOKLYN

I WAS A COWARD. I COULD ADMIT IT.

Instead of answering Vincent's text last night or watching *Bake Off*, which would've inevitably made me think of him the entire time, I'd holed myself up in my room to work on my ISNA essay. That way, if he asked, I could say I'd been busy and hadn't seen his text until the morning.

It wasn't the most noble response to an innocent invitation. However, his suggestion had seemed far too intimate—us on the phone together for an hour, watching a show that'd become an inside joke between us while he made quippy observations in that velvety voice of his.

No, thank you. Didn't happen, was never *going* to happen.

Thankfully, his absence gave me time to reset. I hadn't been taking our bet seriously enough recently, and the best way to restore the status quo in our relationship was to win the wager, once and for all. Once we kissed, this weird tension would evaporate, and we could move on.

I finished my coffee and placed the empty mug in the sink. I'd stayed up past midnight working on my personal statement, but I was nowhere near finished. It was like the pressure of the looming deadline had clogged my brain, and I couldn't get it to work properly.

Jones was traveling with the team, which meant I could work from home today. I was about to grab my laptop from my room when the front door slammed. My heart skipped in response.

It was sick. Practically Pavlovian. But that didn't stop a sharp thrill from bolting through me when Vincent walked into the kitchen with a duffel slung over his shoulder.

"Morning, buttercup." He dropped his bag on the floor and went straight for the fridge.

"Morning." I waited a beat. He didn't say anything else. "You're back early. I wasn't expecting you for another hour or two."

"They made us wake up at the butt crack of dawn to beat traffic." Vincent shut the fridge door without taking anything out and opened a nearby cabinet.

He wore his typical travel uniform: a Blackcastle zip-up jacket, matching track pants, and Zenith trainers. He looked a little tired, and his voice sounded a touch cooler than usual, but he was still infuriatingly gorgeous.

"What are you looking for?"

"Something to eat." He rifled his way down the row of cabinets until he was inches away from me. "Breakfast at the hotel was shit, and I'm starving."

"I haven't done a grocery run yet," I said. "But we have some baking ingredients. You can make pancakes."

Vincent paused to stare at me. "Have you forgotten the story about my first and last pancake-making attempt? Here's a refresher: Fire. Disaster. Humiliation."

"Stop being dramatic." I stepped around him and reached into one of the cabinets he'd bypassed. "You didn't have me there to supervise you the first time. Pancakes are *super* easy. We can whip up a batch in ten minutes." I brandished a bag of gluten-free flour blend like it was a trophy.

Cooking together would be the perfect activity to kick off my renewed Win the Bet campaign. The way to a guy's heart was his stomach, and his clearly needed filling.

His stomach, I meant.

He leaned against the counter and crossed his arms. "You can also burn down a kitchen in five minutes."

"Stop letting fear hold you back. Do you want to eat, or do you want to starve because you haven't healed your trauma from the pancake-induced fire?"

Vincent cocked an eyebrow. "Have you been reading self-help books again?"

"Please, no. They are so boring. I saw the fear quote spray painted on a wall somewhere." I retrieved a large mixing bowl from beneath the sink, making sure to slow down my movements for maximum visual impact.

I couldn't be too obvious about it or he'd catch on, but I did silently thank the gods I'd changed out of my ratty pajamas and into stretchy pants before Vincent got home.

This is for the bet. I straightened and faced him again. He was still leaning against the counter, his expression inscrutable.

There was something off about our interaction today. He was terser, less playful. He was probably just exhausted and upset about yesterday's loss, but maybe he was mad I'd never texted him back.

The prospect made my skin prickle.

"I'm sorry I didn't text you back last night," I said. "I was working on my ISNA application and fell asleep."

"It's okay."

"How was the episode?"

"Good."

Okay then. I ignored the sudden chasm in my stomach and put on a bright smile. "Perfect. In the spirit of *Bake Off*, let's make pancakes. The healthy version," I amended. "You can't go through life scared of a breakfast item."

Vincent slanted a glance in my direction. "I'm not scared of pancakes. I'll eat them. I just don't want to make them." But he didn't argue when I sent him to fetch the rest of the ingredients. I was using the recipe for my favorite protein pancakes, which were healthier than the regular stuff.

"Perfect. Let's mix it all together," I said when we had everything lined up on the counter.

"You know we could've gone down to the breakfast place around the corner and saved ourselves the trouble?"

"That would've taken at least an hour. This'll take minutes."

Vincent shook his head. Despite his grumbling, he'd removed his jacket and was mixing the ingredients with surprising dexterity. His arm muscles flexed with each movement, and I had to avert my eyes before he caught me staring.

I busied myself with the skillet, cleaning it and heating it over medium heat. A cloud of warmth gusted over my face.

"Done," he said.

"Good." I cleared my throat. "Now add the coconut oil to the pan. Once it's hot, swirl it around to coat the bottom…"

He worked in silence, his movements deft and graceful despite his insistence that he wasn't good in the kitchen. Pancakes were easy, but there was something mesmerizing about the way he worked.

"Then you spoon the batter into the skillet like this." I stepped in to demonstrate. "Don't use more than a quarter cup per pancake."

"Got it." Vincent's voice rumbled close to my ear.

Tingles cascaded down my spine, and I focused intently on the stove instead of the warm, solid presence at my back. Despite his reassurance, I ladled out the next two pancakes myself while he watched.

The only sounds in the kitchen were the soft exhales of our breaths and the sizzle of batter in the pan. He was so close that, if I turned my head an inch, his skin would graze mine.

"Brooklyn." He reached around me and grasped my wrist, his hold gentle but firm. "I've got it."

The tingles spread up my arms.

I quickly relinquished the wooden spatula to him and stepped aside. "Great. Cook them for, um, two to three minutes on each side or until small bubbles appear."

Vincent made a noise of acknowledgment. While heat scorched my face, he appeared coolly unperturbed by our proximity.

This was supposed to be my attempt at winning the bet, but I couldn't remember why, exactly, I'd chosen this stupid strategy. I should've stuck with the basics and worn my football shirt again.

He finished the first batch and moved them onto a plate.

I tested out a bite. "Delicious. See? You *can* do this without a visit from the firefighters."

A smirk flickered over his mouth, but he didn't respond as he started the next batch of pancakes.

My smile faded. Something was definitely off. He hadn't tried to flirt with me, he was barely holding up his end of the conversation, and although he'd stayed to make the pancakes, there was an aloofness to him that made the pit in my stomach widen.

I was so used to his warmth that I hadn't realized how much I'd miss it when it was gone.

"I really was working on my application last night," I said, trying to gauge his reaction. "I put my phone away so I could focus."

"You said that already."

"Sure." I tucked a strand of hair behind my ear. "But you seem like you're mad at me, so I want to make sure it isn't because I didn't text you back."

Vincent stilled. He looked up from the stove, his face filled with genuine surprise. "What makes you think I'm mad at you?"

"Just...your vibes." It sounded stupid when I said it out loud, but my vibe checker had never steered me wrong.

He set the spatula down. "I'm not mad at you, but I am a little insulted you think I'd get upset over one unanswered text."

I desperately regretted bringing up the text again, but it was too late to turn back. I forged ahead. "Okay. You're not mad, but you have to admit this is a little weird." I gestured between us. "We usually have a much easier time talking to each other."

His jaw twitched. "That's because I don't want to be around you right now."

I'd goaded him into it, but his words still sent me reeling. The air evacuated from my chest, and I had to breathe through the sudden pressure stinging my throat.

One. Two. Three.

I pressed my lips together and forced a tight smile. "But you say you're not mad at me."

It didn't make sense. Bet aside, I shouldn't care this much about what Vincent thought of me. If he didn't want to hang out anymore, fine. We'd always existed on the periphery of each other's lives, drawn together more by circumstance than by choice.

But did that still hold true? I'd chosen to let him live here, and he'd chosen to move in. Our texts, our talks, the Zenith dinner and the arcade—all choices we'd made to spend time together beyond what was necessary. Some of it was to further our chances at winning the bet, but not all of it was. And that scared the hell out of me.

Vincent let out a small, humorless laugh. "That's not why I don't want to be around you."

"Then what's the reason? Either tell me, or leave," I snapped.

I was tired and stressed and confused. My eyes burned for no discernible reason. I didn't have the energy to play Guess What Vincent's Talking About anymore.

"Fine. You want to know the reason?" He walked toward me, his movements precise and controlled, like a predator prowling toward its prey. "The *reason* is because I couldn't stop thinking about you while I was gone. Then I come home to see you sitting there, doing nothing except existing, and I can't fucking breathe." His voice was low and taut. "Maybe you were right. I *am* pissed at you because you can float through the kitchen, making pancakes and cracking jokes, while I'm using every goddamn ounce of willpower not to touch you. *That's* why I don't want to be around you. You're killing me, and you don't even know it."

He stepped forward with every word; I stepped back. Soon, I was pressed against the counter, trapped between cold tile and the searing heat of his body.

My mouth was so dry I could only scrounge up a whisper. "Then why'd you stay?"

"Because I can't *fucking* say no to you if I tried." The words ground through his teeth, stripped of their usual playfulness.

My heart slammed against my ribcage. The room tilted, and I

had the curious sensation of free falling despite being rooted to the ground.

Vincent and I had circled each other for weeks, taunting, flirting, and at times genuinely connecting. We'd ended up here, teetering on the precipice of something new—and I was terrified.

He sounded sincere. His eyes pinned me to the spot, and he was so close I couldn't breathe without inhaling him into my lungs.

But he didn't kiss me. Despite the intensity of his speech, he kept a minuscule distance between us, just enough for my doubts to surface.

Did he mean what he said? Or was this another ploy to win?

"Is it really because of that, or is it because of the bet?"

Vincent stilled. "The bet," he repeated, his voice flat.

I knew immediately I'd said the wrong thing. I tried to salvage the situation and somehow made it worse. "It's a fair question."

His expression iced over. "Not everything is about the bet, Brooklyn."

He straightened and took a small step back. The tension fizzled like helium leaking out of a popped balloon.

"I'm not implying you're a liar. I was—I mean I'm..." I faltered, wishing I were more eloquent. More certain. Simply *more*.

This always happened. Something good came along, and I'd find a way to ruin it. If I had a therapist, they'd probably call it self-sabotage.

I couldn't help it. People liked the shiny, bubbly version of me, but if they saw what a mess I was on the inside, they'd leave. It was easier to keep them at arm's length and to push them away first than to suffer the devastation of them abandoning me.

It was also easier to believe people had ulterior motives for softening me up. *Especially* Vincent. Especially given our circumstances. The alternative was too risky.

So why was I so crushed by our sudden distance?

"I just wanted to make sure you weren't trying to emotionally manipulate me into kissing you." I adopted a light tone, hoping it'd ease the sting of my words. "I'm *not* saying that's you, but we're both competitive. We both want to win. I just—I'd rather have a clear view of what's happening."

A muscle twitched in Vincent's jaw. "I wouldn't do that."

He didn't sound upset. He sounded…hurt.

The bubble of distrust collapsed inside me, replaced with shame. I opened my mouth, but before I could get an apology out, a sharp, acrid smell stung my nose.

Vincent and I both whipped our heads toward the stovetop, where the second batch of pancakes was burning to a crisp in the skillet.

"Oh, *putain*!" He reached for the handle.

My eyes widened. "Wait! Turn off the—"

Flames burst to life in the pan before he touched it. Billows of hazy gray smoke curled toward the ceiling, and the alarm shrieked into action.

"Shit!"

"Fuck!" This was followed by a stream of French curses I couldn't decipher.

All thoughts of our bet vanished as we rushed to put out the fire before it spread. Vincent turned off the stove while I grabbed a lid from a nearby pot and tossed it at him. "Cover it!"

He caught it easily and slapped it over the pan. The flames hissed angrily against the metal, but they gradually petered out from the lack of oxygen.

Meanwhile, the alarm wailed on, relentless. My head pounded from the noise, and I was getting a little woozy from the smoke.

Vincent darted to the windows and cracked them open while I grabbed a placemat and flapped it uselessly against the sensor.

"You need to get closer!" he shouted. "I'll get a chair."

The kitchen stools were too unstable, but he returned a minute later with the desk chair from his room. He climbed on. I handed him the placemat, but it was too floppy to work. The smoke alarm continued to shriek like it was the end of the world.

"Try this!" I grabbed my notebook from the island and shoved it at him, desperate to make the noise stop. It was so shrill I felt my bones rattle.

My neighbor pounded on the wall and shouted something I couldn't make out. The distant rumble of traffic trickled through the open windows. The smoke had cleared somewhat, but the entire flat reeked.

And amidst all this chaos, the doorbell rang. Once, twice, followed by a series of insistent knocks that were barely audible over the ruckus.

"Coming!" I yelled.

I left Vincent to take care of the alarm while I answered the door. It was either my landlord, who lived upstairs, or the fire brigade. Either way, it didn't bode well for my security deposit.

I sneezed, my eyes watering. I was so distracted by the stench of smoke that I forgot to check the peephole. The security system beeped the way it did every time someone opened the door, and I remembered belatedly that Vincent's intruder was still on the loose.

The chances of them showing up were slim, but...

I gripped the brass knob, ready to slam the door shut at the first sign of trouble. But the person on the other side wasn't a stalker determined to kidnap Vincent, *Misery*-style.

No, it was worse.

It was my dad.

I blinked, certain I was hallucinating. His image didn't waver. The gray hair, the bushy brows, the Blackcastle tracksuit—it was him to a tee.

"*Dad*?" I gaped at him. "What are you doing here?"

The last time he dropped by was over a year ago. I'd just moved in, and he'd showed up with a brand-new toolbox and toilet paper as housewarming gifts.

The smoke alarm's shrieks came to a sudden, merciful stop.

My dad opened his mouth, but something behind me caught his eye. He froze, his concerned frown hardening into a glare. He looked like he'd swallowed a lemon whole.

I turned in time to see a shirtless Vincent pop out of the kitchen. "I finally got the alarm to—oh, *shit*."

My stomach plummeted. My dismay matched the absolute horror on Vincent's face.

Oh, no. Oh no, no, no. This was bad. *Really bad.*

I whirled to face my dad again. Dozens of excuses crowded my tongue, but they withered beneath the weight of his glare.

His face reddened as his eyes darted from me to Vincent and back again. When he finally spoke, his voice boomed loud enough to make me flinch.

"What the *hell* is going on here?"

CHAPTER 18

VINCENT

LONG STORY SHORT: I DIDN'T DIE.

I did, however, *want* to die by the time Coach was done reaming us out.

"I can't believe you've been keeping this a secret from me for a month." He paced the living room, his body trembling with unsuppressed anger. "Do you know how bad this looks? The fact that my captain is shacking up with my *daughter*? Jesus!"

He scrubbed a hand over his face. A vein throbbed in his forehead, and his complexion had morphed from cherry red to a concerning purple. I wondered, somewhat inappropriately, if I'd narrowly escaped starting a house fire only to kill my coach with a heart attack minutes later.

Brooklyn and I had hastily explained the situation, reassuring him that we *weren't* romantically involved and that I was paying rent like a normal tenant, but he wasn't having it. The more we talked, the deeper his scowl got.

Brooklyn sat on the sofa while I stood by the front door, my shirt back on and my muscles rigid with tension. I'd taken my top off because it'd reeked of smoke, but the universe clearly had it out for me. Coach's timing couldn't have been worse.

"This is why we didn't tell you." Brooklyn sounded frustrated. "We knew you'd freak out."

"With good fucking reason!" Coach roared. "This is a complete violation of our no-fraternization policy, not to mention it's...it's just *wrong*!"

Technically, we hadn't violated Blackcastle's no-fraternization policy because we weren't romantically or sexually involved. The bet fell into a grayer area, but Coach didn't know about it and neither of us was stupid enough to tell him.

Is it because of the bet?

Not everything is about the bet, Brooklyn.

I pressed my lips together. If the kitchen situation had played out a little differently before the fire, Coach's concerns might've had merit.

I'd come so close to giving in. When I'd walked in and saw her sitting there, it was like taking a sucker punch to the gut— completely unexpected and almost brutal in the way she took my breath away.

I hadn't expected the bet to go this far. I'd imagined something fun and light, an entertaining way to flex my seduction skills while competing with Brooklyn. If it ended in me satiating my curiosity about how she tasted, then that was even better.

A low-stakes bet. That was it.

It wasn't supposed to make me yearn for her this much.

And it damn well wasn't supposed to hurt.

I just wanted to make sure you weren't trying to emotionally manipulate me into kissing you.

My chest pinched.

"The policy doesn't forbid us from being flatmates." Brooklyn's argument brought me back to the living room. "But of course the club is what you're worried about."

Like me, she'd started out trying to appease her dad, but his refusal to see reason had worn her down, and her tone had taken on a defiant, almost combative edge.

Coach stopped pacing long enough to glare at her. "What is that supposed to mean?"

"It means the only thing that matters to you is football. You find out your daughter is living with one of your players, and your first thought is official policy." Brooklyn's knuckles whitened around the edge of the sofa. "We're not breaking any club rules, and a normal father would be concerned about other things."

I flinched on Coach's behalf.

I didn't know much about their relationship. He'd been happy when she joined Blackcastle, and she'd never said a bad word about him. However, it hadn't escaped my notice that they didn't interact much outside of Blackcastle. This was certainly the first time I'd seen him at the flat since I moved in.

Coach's breath gusted out in shock. His shoulders sank as some of the indignation seeped out from his body, and his mouth opened and closed like he couldn't decide which response to land on.

Brooklyn's voice softened. "I'm sorry we lied to you, but this is a temporary situation. We're not going to live together forever."

Her dad's glare had lost some of its edge, but his voice remained tight. "How temporary?"

"I'll be out by the new year," I said.

Brooklyn's eyes flitted toward me, her surprise evident.

I'd pulled the time frame out of my ass, but I'd wanted to step in before their argument spiraled again.

I'd find a way to make a hotel work. I couldn't let their relationship deteriorate further because of me.

Coach examined me. It was the first time he'd focused on me since he'd arrived, and I felt like an insect under a microscope.

"Have the police caught your intruder?" His voice flattened with eerie calm.

"No."

"Do they have any leads?"

I winced. "No."

"Then how do you know you'll be out of here by the new year if your alleged reason for moving in is still a threat?"

I'd walked right into that one.

"I guess I don't. But given the current circumstances, sir, I'm happy to relocate to a hotel until the threat has been neutralized." Apparently, when I was nervous, I talked like a bad side character from a Nate Reynolds movie.

The thought of moving home still sent my nervous system into overload. I'd considered renting another place in the city, but there were too many unpredictable variables. I didn't want to rent a random house in a random neighborhood from a random person.

At least hotels had security, and I could blend into the crowd a little more.

"You're not moving into a hotel," Brooklyn interjected. "It didn't work out the first time for a reason. It's so much more public, and people can find out where you're staying as easily as they can search up your address online. You're already settled in here, *and* you pay rent, which is very helpful, by the way. There's no reason for you to uproot yourself."

She laid out her reasoning with impeccable precision. I couldn't tell if she actually wanted me to stay or if she was trying to spite her father. Either way, my pulse spiked more than it should.

Coach's scowl returned. "I can think of at least one good reason."

"Which is?"

"The *inappropriateness* of all this." He gestured around the flat. The smoke was gone, but its acrid stench lingered. "Bloody hell, Brooklyn, I'm trying to look out for you. It doesn't matter if this is a platonic setup. If people at work find out you're living with DuBois, they'll never take you seriously again. It's already hard enough when—" He stopped short.

"When what?" Brooklyn's cheeks flushed. "When I'm the only woman on the nutrition staff, and people already look at me funny because I'm your daughter?"

"That's not what I said."

"That's what you meant." She set her jaw. "If people want to talk, let them talk. And while I understand why you're uncomfortable with the situation, Vincent and I are adults. You can't tell us what we can or can't do outside of work."

"You're my daughter. I can *absolutely* weigh in on your life inside *and* outside of work."

Brooklyn's eyes flashed, and I instinctively braced myself for indirect impact. "Really? That's hilarious, considering you haven't been there for most of my life. I've lived here for over a year, and we never connect unless *I* take the initiative to plan something. When we do talk, it's almost always about football. You have *no idea* what's going on with me, and now you're trying to steamroll over me without even attempting to see things from my perspective. Respectfully, Dad, I get that you have an image and a reputation to maintain. But don't pretend you're a concerned father who cares about his daughter's personal well-being when your past behavior has indicated otherwise."

Her words landed with the force of an atomic bomb. Silence mushroomed, the heft and weight of it making my skin prickle.

Brooklyn angled her chin up, her mouth tight but her eyes suspiciously glossy. The sight cleaved through me.

I desperately wanted to cross the room and pull her into my arms, but this was a family problem. I was the one who'd inadvertently triggered the explosion, and comforting Brooklyn right now would only make things worse.

So I stood there, fingers digging into my palms and chest aching, while Brooklyn and her father stared each other down.

Coach's nostrils flared. "We'll discuss this later when we don't have company." His voice was tightly controlled. He didn't look at me, but I felt his searing condemnation from ten feet away. "Whatever your opinion about my parenting skills, you have to admit I'm right. This will get out eventually. If you want a serious future at Blackcastle, Vincent has to move out. Immediately."

"You don't have to worry about that because I'm not accepting the job offer."

My gaze flew to her face. *What the fuck?* She'd been hesitant, but she'd never indicated she would actually leave Blackcastle.

A second vein pulsed in Coach's forehead as his carefully calibrated calm cracked in half. "You're accepting the offer."

"No, I'm not."

"Why the *hell* not?" His voice slowly rose to the decibel of a shout.

"Because I don't want to work in an office where I'm constantly living in your shadow. It doesn't matter if Vincent stays or leaves. People will *always* find a reason to doubt me. If I want to be taken seriously, I have to leave the club." Brooklyn sat straight and proud, her expression resolute.

My stomach knotted. I'd grown so used to seeing her at work that I couldn't fathom the idea of her absence.

Blackcastle without Brooklyn.

I felt a little sick.

Coach gritted his teeth. "Where exactly are you going to work if not at the club?" he demanded.

"I'll figure it out."

"In other words, you don't have another offer lined up, but you're turning down a sure thing."

"Yes."

"Goddammit, Brooke. If you're doing this to spite me—"

"I'm not." The fight bled out of her, and she suddenly looked exhausted. "Not everything is about you, and you've been 'hands-off' my entire internship. You can't just swoop in at the last minute to tell me I'm making the wrong decision. I'm declining the offer, whether you like it or not. I'll make it official tomorrow."

"You—I—" Coach spluttered. He was breathing so hard I almost called 999 in anticipation of a heart attack.

I cleared my throat. "With all due respect, sir, I think we should all take a—"

"Shut it," he growled. "I'll deal with *you* later."

Fuck me. That didn't sound good.

But what the hell, I was in deep shit anyway. I might as well say my piece. "You're upset, Brooklyn's upset. Emotions are running high for understandable reasons, but I think we should all take a step back before we say anything else we regret." They glared at me with matching stony expressions. I wisely refrained from mentioning how alike they looked at that moment. "I'll move to a hotel and make it work. We'll keep this a secret, and no one will ever find out." *Besides all the people who already know.* "After that, we can move on. This isn't something to have a falling out over."

Minutes ticked by in excruciating silence. Neither of them acknowledged my suggestions, but eventually, their boiling hostility was reduced to a mere simmer.

"Why did you come by in the first place?" Brooklyn asked her dad. She appeared to be making a concerted effort to keep her voice even.

"I wanted to talk about why you haven't accepted the Blackcastle offer yet." Coach glanced at me, his mouth twisting. I suppressed another wince. My advice to him had come back to bite me in the ass in the worst way. "I guess I have my answer."

She didn't respond.

"I have to head to the clubhouse soon. We'll continue this discussion another time," Coach said abruptly. "DuBois, pack your essentials and meet me outside in ten. You can get the rest of your stuff later."

Brooklyn shot up straight again. A panicked expression spread across her face.

I stared at him, my gut twisting with foreboding. "Uh, where are we going, sir?"

"My house." His smile lacked any semblance of humor. "You're moving in with me."

CHAPTER 19

VINCENT

HAVE YOU EVER MOVED IN WITH YOUR COACH AFTER 1) he caught you shacking up with his daughter, 2) he and said daughter got into a massive fight, and 3) he vowed to make your life a living hell because of reason number one?

I don't recommend it. It's not fun.

To be fair, Coach didn't explicitly say he was going to torture me in every legal manner possible. However, his actions expressed what he wouldn't confirm verbally.

Mandatory carpools to work every day. Five a.m. runs with him every morning, including on the weekends. Killer drills at training and awkward dinners where he grilled me on obscure football trivia over what I was sure was intentionally bland chicken.

I couldn't prove it, but I was convinced he'd wired some sort of futuristic spyware into the Wi-Fi because he magically popped up every time I texted Brooklyn.

It was like bootcamp without friends. After a week, I was ready to go home and just let the intruder stab me.

To make matters worse, the team found out about my new living situation via a "leak" (aka Coach) and had proceeded to give me never-ending shit about it. Besides Asher, Adil, and Noah, everyone thought I'd moved out of a hotel and into Coach's house because I "needed a more comforting home environment."

If they used common sense, they'd know that was bullshit because Coach was about as comforting as a radioactive hedgehog.

STEVENS

Hey Cap, say hi to Coach for us, will ya? Now that you'll be braiding each other's hair every night and all

SAMSON

Don't be insensitive. Cap doesn't have enough hair for braiding. They'll be snuggling up for Bake Off night instead

Don't you dare bring Bake Off into this

GALLAGHER

It's too bad Brooklyn doesn't live with him. Imagine waking up and seeing her every day? I'd never leave the house. It'd be flatmates with benefits, y'know what I mean?

Say another fucking word about Brooklyn, and I'll knock your teeth out

STEVENS

Oooh

SAMSON

Oooooh

ADIL

Ooooooooooh

STEVENS

Cap's mad. You're in big trouble, G

GALLAGHER

Wtf? Like you don't all think she's hot!

GALLAGHER

Since when did Cap get so possessive of her anyway?

GALLAGHER

Do you have a crush on her? 👀

> She's the coach's daughter. It's about respect. Pull your head out of your ass long enough to find some

GALLAGHER

I feel like I'm being unfairly maligned for stating what everyone else is too scared to say

> Let's see if you feel unfairly maligned when my fist meets your face

ASHER

Whoa, whoa. Let's all calm down.

ASHER

Gallagher, stop being such a prick. Vincent's our teammate, and we should be supportive. He has enough problems right now

> Thank you

ASHER

Like deciding whether he should get matching PJs with Coach and picking what board game they want to play over dinner. Bonding's important

GALLAGHER

SAMSON

LMFAO. He got you good

> Fuck you all. You're dead to me. Every single one of you

> I'm uninviting everyone from my birthday trip

GALLAGHER

I can't go anyway, so idc

STEVENS

HA. You were a pity invite

GALLAGHER

You're talking a lot of shit for someone who ALSO can't go

STEVENS

That's not my fault! I told you Truffle has the Best Miniature Pig in Show competition that day! We've been training for months!

ADIL

Why are you uninviting me from the trip?? I didn't make fun of you

But if you'd stayed at my house, this wouldn't have happened. I'M JUST SAYING.

GALLAGHER

Now that you bring it up, I'm a little offended you didn't ask to live with me, Cap

I would've if you ever washed your balls properly. You stink.

SAMSON

SHOTS FIRED

GALLAGHER

That's a low blow. My balls are clean as fuck. I can prove it.

GALLAGHER

[CENSORED PHOTO]

STEVENS

Gallagher!

What the fuck!

ASHER

I'm in public. What the hell's wrong with you??

SAMSON

Hell no, I ain't opening that

NOAH

...

NOAH

Please, for the love of God, let me leave this group

NOAH

Do not add me back

NOAH WILSON LEFT THE CONVERSATION.

ADIL CHAKIR ADDED NOAH WILSON TO THE CONVERSATION.

NOAH

I hate you so much

I shook my head. The group chat was always chaos, but that didn't explain why I wanted to march over to Gallagher's house and punch him right now. He was notorious for talking shit, and it wasn't the first time he'd made suggestive comments about Brooklyn.

My jaw tightened.

I could handle his digs at me, but Brooklyn was off-limits. I had no tolerance for his sleazy jokes anymore.

I tried to breathe through the irritation. It wasn't Gallagher's fault that I was suddenly messed up in the head about Brooklyn. He had no idea what'd been going on the past month.

Still, I wouldn't mind one punch. A quick one.

"DuBois." Coach's voice pulled my attention away from the chat and to the doorway. He stood just outside my room, his expression measured.

Maybe he'd upgraded his spyware if he was showing up when I just *thought* about her.

I straightened. "Hey, Boss. What's up?"

My survival philosophy was if I acted like everything was normal, everything would eventually *be* normal.

Nevertheless, my inner alarm bell rang as he walked in and swept his eyes over my new room. A double bed covered by a navy duvet, wooden floors, a single desk and chair—it was Spartan with a capital S. The small window would've provided a welcome ray of natural light if it weren't so gray and dreary outside. It reminded me of a prison cell, which was fitting because I was basically trapped in this house outside of training and matches.

I never thought I'd say this, but I missed the stuffed animals and sparkly pink sheets in Brooklyn's flat.

I also missed Brooklyn. A lot.

We saw each other at Blackcastle, but we had an unspoken agreement not to interact unless necessary at work. Neither of us wanted to trigger Coach's anger again.

Our texts were my only lifeline, but even they lacked our old spark. Our kitchen conversation and near-kiss had smothered it. They were the elephants in the room, the topics we'd avoided talking about since I left her flat, and it was impossible to have a real conversation about anything else without addressing them first.

"I have some news." Coach stopped two feet in front of me. "We're expanding the bachelor auction at this year's gala. Every player is expected to take part, including you."

"What?" I shot to my feet, my pulse thundering. "You can't be serious."

The annual Blackcastle Holiday Gala was the club's biggest social event of the year. Everyone came—players, staff, sponsors, fans who were willing to shell out hundreds of pounds for a ticket. It was an excuse for Blackcastle fans and staff to gather in one place, eat free food, and drink copious amounts of champagne, all while raising a load of money.

The highlight of the gala was the bachelor auction. Attendees bid to win a "date night" with each player, and all proceeds went to a local children's hospital.

"I'm dead serious." Coach's mouth twitched. He was enjoying my discomfort a little too much. "This comes from the top. All players must participate so it doesn't look like we're playing favorites."

"What if I decline and donate enough money to cover the lost proceeds?"

"That's not the point."

"You're telling me *everyone* is doing this? Including Noah?"

"Yes."

Shit. If they'd roped Noah into participating, there was no chance in hell for me.

As captain, I'd pulled rank and successfully excused myself from participating years ago. Everyone thought I'd love being the center of attention, but while I thrived in the limelight, I didn't want to spend a whole evening with someone who was only using me for clout. My "date" from my first and last auction kept posting pictures of us from dinner with kissy face emojis, despite my repeated requests for her to stop. She later went to the tabloids and lied about us having sex.

Besides me, Noah was the only player who'd been exempt. I didn't know what he'd told management, but it had worked—until now.

I made a last-ditch attempt to save myself. "My intruder is still out there. What if they show up and win the bid for me?"

"If they cough up enough money to win, then I wish you two a very happy date night."

That was fucking cold.

I grumbled in resignation. At least I could comfort myself with the knowledge that Noah would be right up there with me, hating life.

Coach hesitated. He glanced at my phone, and I was gripped by the sudden fear that he'd comb through my texts. Brooklyn and I had mostly been making small talk for the past week, but if he scrolled up further, he'd definitely find some old flirty messages.

"Have you heard—" He stopped and shook his head. His brow creased into a frown. "Never mind. Don't forget, we have our run tomorrow. Five a.m. sharp."

I waited until he left before I let out a loud groan.

I stared at my cell. Like Coach, I also wanted to reach out to Brooklyn.

Unlike him, I knew our inevitable talk wouldn't mend things— it'd change them completely.

CHAPTER 20

BROOKLYN

"IS IT TRUE YOU TURNED DOWN THE BLACKCASTLE offer?" Henry rolled his chair over to my desk. "If it is, that's *bold*, especially since you, like, don't have another job lined up."

I stared fixedly at my computer, hoping he'd get the hint and go away. He didn't. His cologne also reeked of musk—a far cry from Vincent's subtle, delicious scent.

"Don't you have work to do?" I asked pointedly.

"Yeah, but I'll get it done in time. I have to take a break every now and then for maximum productivity." He leaned closer to me. I sneezed. God, *what* was he wearing? "So? Is it true?"

"It's really none of your business, but yes, it's true." There was no point in lying. I'd officially declined Blackcastle's offer last week, much to Jones and HR's shock. Jones had expressed disappointment, but he hadn't asked any further questions. That alone confirmed I'd done the right thing. If he really wanted me here, he would've made some sort of effort to convince me to stay.

Henry whistled. "Wow. What are you going to do then?"

"I'm exploring different options." By that, I meant I was searching online job sites for anything that looked remotely interesting. So far, no luck.

"Sure, sure. Hey, how's—"

"I have to speak to Lizzie about something." I pushed my chair back and walked out. "I'll be back."

I didn't actually need to speak with the head of Human Resources, but if I didn't get away from Henry soon, I was going to be arrested for murder.

I breathed in a welcome lungful of cologne-free air as I took a lap around the building. Training was over, and the players' laughter leaked out from the changing room.

Vincent was in there somewhere.

My steps slowed. We'd texted a few times since he moved out, but we hadn't talked about anything meaningful. I was still trying to wrap my head around the fact he was gone.

One minute, he was there, strutting around shirtless and almost kissing me in the kitchen. The next, he...wasn't. He moved out and left a miles-wide void in the flat.

I hated it.

I rounded the corner and bumped right into the last person I wanted to see. I knew who it was by the scuffed trainers alone.

My shoulders stiffened as I looked up at him. "Dad."

"Brooklyn."

We eyed each other warily. If this were a movie, there'd be Western showdown music playing in the background.

My dad and I hadn't exchanged a single word since our fight. We'd never been great at communicating with each other, but the strained tension was new. The air around us stretched thin and taut, like a rubber band on the verge of snapping.

"Jones told me you declined the offer. You're really leaving," he said. His voice was impassive.

Disappointment sliced through me. I'd told him the truth about how I felt last week. Our problems ran so much deeper than my career, but he still chose to focus on that instead of our inability to connect over anything other than work.

"I told you I would do that." A heavy weight settled into my bones. I already regretted leaving my office. Dealing with Henry would be better than this.

"I thought you were bluffing. I really bloody hope you're not doing this to spite me, Brooke." A trace of frustration slipped into his words.

"And I told you that's not the reason." We were a broken record, circling round and round the same topic. "I'm leaving because Blackcastle isn't the right fit."

"Not the right fit," he repeated. "You've been interning here for over a year, and you've never complained once."

"It's not about complaining. It's about…" I searched for the right term, but it was hard to think through the fog in my head.

Honestly, I was exhausted. I'd been staying up late every night working on my ISNA essay, which was still crap. My job search proved even more fruitless the second time around. The holidays were coming up, which meant gift shopping and events and anxiety. Throw in the emotional toll of fighting with my dad and the uncertainty of my relationship with Vincent, and I was primed for a meltdown.

I wasn't going to tell my dad any of that though. He already thought I was a mess. I refused to give him more ammo.

"It's about finding my own path," I finally said. "I told you the other day. If I stay here, I'll always be in your shadow. People will always have lingering doubts about whether I'm getting special treatment because my last name is Armstrong."

"You don't get special treatment, and people don't think that," he argued. "I didn't even know you were applying for an internship until you got it."

"It doesn't matter. You know how the truth gets twisted into rumors. People believe what they want to believe." I took a deep breath and made another attempt to steer this conversation where it needed to go. If I didn't captain the ship, no one would. "I got internship offers from other Premier League clubs, but I chose Blackcastle because *you* were here. I thought it would be a good bonding experience. Instead, it's been the opposite. It's like you think that because we see each other every day at work, we don't need to talk outside of that. But I don't want a boss; I want a dad. So maybe the solution is seeing less of each other in the office, not more."

"We've had...bonding experiences." He said the words slowly, like he wasn't sure what they meant. "We had that dinner. We talked about your dating life."

"That was one time in eighteen months."

He had no response to that.

"I love the team, and I'll always be the biggest Blackcastle supporter, but I have to move on. Nothing you say will change that."

"What about money? This is London! You can't survive in London on savings alone." His frustration visibly mounted again.

"I have enough to tide me over for a few months until I find a new job."

Vincent's rent money was my saving grace. It was enough to keep me afloat until summer.

"I know you won't take money from me, but I can't let you... *flounder* out there." My dad's signature frown returned. "You're moving in with me until you find a new job."

I balked. "Absolutely not." That was *not* the bonding I had in mind. Living with your parent as an adult was a surefire way to mangle the relationship, not heal it. "Besides, Vincent is living with you. Wasn't the point of that to keep us from living under the same roof?"

His mouth flattened into a thin line. He couldn't dispute my argument, and he wasn't heartless enough to kick Vincent out of his house (even if Vincent wanted him to). Maybe he was punishing Vincent for lying to him, but he also did care about his players' safety.

"You've made up your mind, so I won't try to change it anymore. But I hope like hell you know what you're doing, Brooke," he said, his tone grim. "Because I sure don't."

He walked away.

My hands curled into fists. I wanted to scream.

That was our second round of the same fight, and he *still* didn't get it. Maybe he never would. I'd moved across an entire ocean chasing a dream—a real relationship with him, plus a chance at making a name for myself—and it was starting to dawn on me that the dream might've just been a delusion.

"Wow. That was crazy." Henry came up beside me, a chocolate bar in hand. I was too tired to care how long he'd been there or how much he'd heard. "I can't believe you talked to him like that. I know he's your dad, but he's scary."

"Stop eavesdropping."

"I wasn't eavesdropping. You were both so loud, it was impossible *not* to listen in." He took a bite of his candy. "Totally get what you were saying about finding your own path and all, but if I were you, I would've taken the job. Most people would kill to work here."

"You're not staying after your internship?" I couldn't resist asking. It was my chance to find out whether he'd also gotten a job offer from Blackcastle.

Henry laughed. "Um, no. I'll be at my dad's company. He's the founder of Hydralade, the sports drink? Anyway, the plan was always for me to head up their product development team, but he wanted me to get some 'outside experience' first." He snapped his fingers. "Hey, I have an idea! You should come work for us. We have a few openings. I'll make sure you get an interview."

A metallic taste filled my mouth. "No, thanks."

"Well, if you change your mind, give me a call." He finished his chocolate and shoved the empty wrapper in his pocket. "Hey, I heard you're also applying for the ISNA award. What'd you write about for your personal statement?"

I barely heard him over the sudden roar of blood in my ears.

Thud. Thud. Thud. My heart pounded hard enough to rattle my ribcage.

Every time I blinked, the walls crept closer, threatening to squeeze the air from my lungs.

"Don't worry. I'm not going to steal your topic." Henry's voice sounded far away. "I submitted my application weeks ago. I can show you, if you'd like. I—hey! Where are you going?"

He let out a squawk of indignation when I pushed past him and speed-walked toward the restroom. Pressure clawed at my throat.

I couldn't breathe. I had to—I needed—

I burst into the restroom and rushed into the corner stall, locking it with a deafening click.

Then, and only then, did I allow myself to cry.

I sank onto the closed toilet lid as my emotions burst free. Grief, anger, self-doubt, resentment, and a thousand more I couldn't name— they surged past the dam I'd spent years painstakingly building, their currents so strong I had no hope of escaping.

So I didn't even try.

My sobs bounced off the tiled walls. Tears dripped down my cheeks, mixing with my snot. I probably looked disgusting, but I didn't care. No one could see me—so few women worked here, the ladies' restroom was almost always empty.

I buried my face in my hands, trying to ground myself in something, *anything*, but I was unraveling at the seams. The stitches that held my life together came apart, one by one, until I was nothing but frayed edges and open wounds.

There was no one around to put me back together, and that just made everything hurt a little more.

My dad, who was clueless about what I really needed.

My mom, who was too busy with her new family to give a shit.

My coworkers, whose doubts fueled my own.

Vincent, who was forbidden in so many ways.

And most of all, myself, because I'd failed to live up to the person I thought I would be.

Younger me thought I'd have it all by now—a thriving career, a loving partner, some semblance of peace when it came to my family. Yet here I was, a full-grown adult, and I was as lost as ever. Besides my friends, every aspect of my life was a mess. I didn't know how to clean it up because I didn't know how I got here in the first place.

It was the first time I'd admitted it to myself. I'd been repressing my fears and emotions for so long that releasing them was cathartic. By the time my sobs slowed to hiccups, I felt a little better despite the shittiness of my situation.

I sat there, letting myself wallow for another minute before I wiped my face with the back of my hand and exited the stall.

I sent a quick thank-you to the universe for not bringing anyone in during my meltdown. This was not how I wanted to be remembered at the end of my internship.

I winced when I saw my reflection. Frazzled hair, puffy eyes, red nose. Ugh.

I didn't have my makeup bag with me, but I fixed myself up the best I could. Once I looked somewhat presentable again, I pushed open the door and headed back to the intern office.

It was already after work hours, but I needed to finish the travel packets for the team's upcoming winter break. The meal plans were easy. However, I'd convinced Jones to let me add extra info like how to eat healthy while traveling and how to balance indulgence and nourishment during the holidays. I'd rounded it out with a few of my favorite healthy holiday recipes. He thought they were a waste of time, but I guess he didn't want to argue when I was leaving soon anyway.

"Bye, Brooklyn." Seth, the team's new kit man, waved at me in passing. He gave me a shy smile, which I returned.

We didn't interact often, but I liked him. He was a sweet kid, and kit managers were the unsung heroes of football clubs. Managing all the players' equipment and apparel wasn't as easy as it sounded.

Thankfully, Seth didn't comment on my disheveled appearance. I was hopeful I could finish my work and go home with no one else being the wiser about my breakdown until I passed by the changing room.

Someone stepped out at the exact same time I walked past.

Dark hair. Lean frame. Sculpted jaw.

Vincent.

We came to a mutual standstill, and my pulse slowed to a glacial pace as we stared at each other.

"Hi," I said, painfully aware of my ruined makeup and mascara-stained shirt. I summoned what I hoped was a convincing smile, but the sight of him made my heart twist all over again.

I missed him. I saw him every day at work, but it wasn't the same. That was Vincent the footballer. I missed *him*, Vincent the man. The one who was obsessed with the *Great British Bake Off* and played pool like he was born with a cue in his hand. Most of all, I missed how easy our relationship had been before there was a giant question mark hanging over it.

His forehead creased. His gaze swept over my face and shirt and back up again. "What's wrong? Who made you cry?" he demanded. His unexpectedly fierce protectiveness made my throat ache with fresh emotion.

"No one. It's my allergies." I sniffled and wiped my nose with the back of my hand again. "The pollen is, um, killer this week."

"Brooklyn."

One word. That was all it took.

Fresh tears scalded my cheeks as Vincent gathered me into his arms. There was no judgment, only solid, comforting strength as I buried my face in his chest and let him hold the broken pieces of me together.

"I saw my dad earlier. We talked, but it didn't—he was still mad about Blackcastle, and Henry asked about ISNA, and I can't find a single good job, and I'm just so *fucking* overwhelmed sometimes that I feel like I can't breathe." I rambled on, nearly incoherent.

I was certain I wasn't making any sense. But if crying was cathartic, then saying those words out loud was a purge. It took away their power, and Vincent surprisingly had no trouble deciphering them.

"A few things," he said when I finished. "One, your dad will come around. Two, fuck Henry. Three, you'll find the perfect job when it comes along. Waiting is better than taking a shit gig for crap pay. As for feeling overwhelmed, you're not alone. We all feel it. I'd suggest starting a group for it, but I'm still traumatized by the team's book club."

A small laugh escaped between the tears. "Who's the pep talker now?"

"I learned from the best," he said, seemingly referring to the pep talk I gave him about the Zenith partnership. "Take it from someone who's been at rock bottom. *Tout finira par s'arranger.*"

My chin wobbled. "I have no idea what that means. I stopped taking French in high school because I—" I hiccupped. "I had a crush on a German exchange student so I switched to German, but it turned out he had a girlfriend back home and I've never even *used* German after graduation!" Apparently, my penchant for bad decisions dated back to my teenage years.

I was being a little hysterical at the moment, but emotions didn't have boundaries. When one went haywire, so did the rest.

A chuckle rumbled through Vincent's chest. "It means everything will work out—unless you're talking about a relationship with the German exchange student. That obviously didn't work out."

My mouth twitched. "Don't make me laugh. I'm trying to be sad."

"You can be sad." He rubbed a soothing hand over my back. "You can be anything you want."

I melted into him. I wasn't used to having someone solid to lean on, but it made all the difference. My tears slowed to a trickle far faster than in the restroom, and when I lifted my head, I was startled to realize only a few minutes had passed since I broke down in his arms.

"Sorry I got snot all over your shirt." I hiccupped again, my face heating with embarrassment. "I'll buy you a new one, I promise."

"Don't worry about it. It's just a shirt." Vincent studied me, his eyes dark with lingering concern. "Feel better?"

I nodded. Now that I wasn't crying my eyes out, I was suddenly hyperaware of the fact that I was still in his arms. His body heat enveloped me, warming me from the inside out. One hand rested low on my back while his other thumb rubbed a lazy circle beneath my shoulder blade.

Sparks raced up my spine.

It was our first time being this physically close since our almost kiss. Vincent seemed to realize this as well because his muscles subtly tensed.

The silence between us shifted. Melancholy gave way to something thick and electric. It crackled just beneath the surface, and I could feel his heart race in response. It matched the frantic rhythm of my own pulse.

Ask him about the bet. According to our terms, the bet was valid as long as we lived together. He'd moved out, but we'd never officially called it off.

We'd also never addressed what happened in the kitchen. This was the perfect time to do it, but I didn't have the emotional bandwidth for another hard conversation today.

"Are you going home for the break?" I stuck with a safer topic.

The team was off for two weeks before Christmas. Usually, the mid-season break was in January, and we hadn't gotten one at all last year, but the Premier League's leadership decided to shake things up this year.

Vincent shook his head. "My dad's in Bordeaux for most of the break, and I don't feel like being home alone." He hesitated, then said, "My birthday's next week, and I threw together a last-minute Budapest trip to celebrate. Some of the guys and I rented a villa, but there's plenty of room. You should join us. Carina too. Scarlett's already coming with Asher, so it'll be like a girls' trip for you three."

Don't read too much into it. It was a group trip, not a romantic getaway for two. Still, my stomach fluttered.

"That sounds amazing, but considering I'll be out of a job by January, I shouldn't be going on any last-minute trips," I said reluctantly.

"It'll be all-expenses-paid, minus airfare." His dimple flashed at my shocked expression. "We've already covered the villa, food, and drinks. All you have to do is show up."

"It's your birthday. Shouldn't we be the ones paying for you?"

He shrugged. "You are. Well, the guys are. I was only responsible for the deposit on the villa."

I drew my bottom lip between my teeth. The invitation was tempting. I'd never been to Hungary, and getting away from London for a bit might be good for my mental health. I hadn't left the city since Scarlett, Carina, and I took a trip to the Cotswolds over the summer.

"It'll help clear your head," Vincent said. "Besides, how often do you get to go on a trip sponsored by professional footballers?"

"True." I made a decision before my more practical angels could talk me out of it. "In that case, I'm in."

CHAPTER 21

BROOKLYN

I DIDN'T TELL MY DAD ABOUT THE BUDAPEST TRIP. HE might find out on his own, but like with the flatmate situation, I wasn't doing anything wrong. The only reason I was hiding my trip from him was because I didn't want him to take it out on Vincent.

Besides, we hadn't talked since our hallway run in. I got my stubbornness from him, and I refused to break the ice first with a Hungary PSA.

However, my dad was the last thing on my mind when Carina and I landed in Hungary the following Friday. We were the last to arrive because she had to finish work first, but Vincent had insisted on sending a car for us. Our driver was already waiting when we exited the baggage claim, and we didn't have to do anything except sit back and relax while he whisked us to the villa.

"I wonder who else will be there besides Scar and Asher," Carina mused. "We should've asked before we said yes."

"Would you have said no to any name on the guest list?"

"Absolutely not. An all-expenses-paid holiday to Budapest? They could invite Freddy freaking Krueger and I'd still show up. I'm curious about the guest list. That's all."

"It's a bunch of footballers. Adil, maybe Samson. A few others."

"Hmm."

I narrowed my eyes. "What was that?"

"What was what?" she asked innocently.

"That *hmm*."

"Nothing." Carina examined her nails. "I just think it's interesting that Vincent invited you on his boys' trip."

"It's not a boys' trip. Scarlett will be there, and he invited you too."

"Only as your plus-one. Tell me the truth." She nudged my knee with hers. "Did something happen while you were living together?"

Heat crawled over my face and chest. "No. I'd tell you if it did."

Nothing *had* happened. If Vincent and I had actually kissed, I would've spilled the beans. That was too big a secret to keep. Until then, I was keeping my mouth shut.

Not that I expected to kiss Vincent anytime in the near future. It was a hypothetical.

Vincent's villa rental was located in what our driver assured us was one of the best neighborhoods in the city. It was a gorgeous, sprawling affair that encompassed four floors and multiple balconies, but it was so late that Carina and I didn't bother exploring. We said hi to Scarlett and Asher, who told us where our room was, and promptly passed out. We didn't even get a chance to see Vincent, who was apparently out with the other guys.

We woke up the next morning to laughter and chatter from downstairs. We got dressed and went into the living room, where everyone was eating breakfast and playing…Jenga?

"B! C! You're here!" Adil said happily. "You're just missing A!" He paused. "Wait. I can be your A! We're like the alphabet trio."

Carina eyed him. "Are you drunk?"

"Nah. He just feels left out because he doesn't drink alcohol, so he *acts* drunk all the time to make up for it." Samson was sprawled on the sofa with his arm around a beautiful brunette. "The other possibility is his parents dropped him on his head when he was young."

Laughter scattered through the group. Adil threw a Jenga tile at the grinning winger, who looked unfazed when it bounced off his forehead.

I took a quick inventory of who was here. Besides me, Carina, Adil, Samson, and Samson's date, there was Scarlett, Asher, Seth, and Noah. I was surprised by the presence of the latter two, but it made sense. Vincent was the only player who could include the newest staff member on a group trip *and* somehow convince Noah to come along.

Vincent himself wasn't here, but I held off on asking about his whereabouts. I was a little worried Scarlett would see right through me if I talked about him in front of her.

"Have you guys explored the villa yet?" she asked when we took a seat next to her. "It's wild."

"Not yet. I need breakfast first." Carina yawned. "I'm starving."

"I'll get you something from the kitchen," Seth said, bright and eager as a puppy. "You'll have plenty of time to explore later. We don't have scheduled plans until dinner."

We stayed in the living room through breakfast, and I tried my best to engage in conversations with everyone. However, my mind kept wandering back to Vincent's absence.

It was his birthday, and he never slept this late. Where was he?

Finally, I couldn't take it anymore. I had to ask. "Where's the birthday boy?" I popped a strawberry in my mouth, feigning nonchalance.

"Probably in his room," Asher said over Adil's groan. They'd moved on to poker from Jenga, and Adil had just lost. "Don't know what he's doing in there. Don't want to know."

"Oh, really? Where's his room?" I asked casually. I ignored Carina's knowing smirk. "Ours is huge, so his must be, um, huger."

Nice job, Brooklyn. Not suspicious at all.

I glanced at Scarlett, who was busy writing a birthday card.

"Fourth floor, last door on the left," Seth piped up. He'd been running around all morning, fetching drinks and cleaning up spills like he was the maid instead of a guest. "I can show you, if you'd like."

"No, that's okay," I said quickly. "But Carina and I should go take a look around. Shouldn't we?"

"Sure." She rose to her feet and stretched, the shit-eating grin still on her face. "Let's take a look around."

When we were out of the group's earshot, she added, "Want to start on the fourth floor?"

"Oh, shut up." I picked up my pace, my face burning.

"What?" She ran after me, laughing. "It makes sense. Start from the top, make your way to the bottom. Unless you like being on the bottom."

"You are *so* immature." But I couldn't help laughing with her. It was impossible to be mad at her; she was too good-natured, if also too observant for my liking.

Although I'd used the tour as an excuse to break off from the group, I was genuinely awed by the villa. It was grand enough for royalty. Besides two heated pools, one indoor and one outdoor, it boasted a twenty-person screening room, a bowling alley, and a wine cellar stocked with bottles that probably cost more than my monthly rent.

The bedrooms were spread across the third and fourth floors. Carina stopped when we reached the top landing. "I need to use the toilet," she said. "You go ahead. I don't need to see another bedroom anyway. Bye! Have fun!"

"Wait! Carina, get back—"

She disappeared down the stairs, her laughter trailing up from the bowels of the house.

I glanced down the hall and held back a groan. I couldn't knock on Vincent's door for no reason. I'd look like I was obsessed with him.

An idea clicked into place. I ran to my room on the third floor, grabbed what I needed, and went back upstairs.

Last door on the left.

I hesitated for a second before knocking. Maybe he wasn't here. Maybe—

"Come in."

My stomach flipped. I had no reason to be nervous. I talked to Vincent all the time. Seeing him in Budapest was the same as seeing him in London.

I took a deep breath and entered the room. "I..." My greeting died in my throat.

Oh, God.

I'd walked in at the worst time. Or the best time, depending on how you looked at it.

Vincent was facing away from the door, half naked and in the process of pulling a white T-shirt over his head. Gray sweatpants rode low on his hips, and I glimpsed the mouthwatering flex of his chiseled back muscles before his shirt covered it.

It wasn't my first time seeing him shirtless, but there was something about *this* particular moment that hit me like a lightning strike in a quiet field.

Every nerve ending lit up. Heat surged through me, and my palms tingled with the need to run my hands over his back and feel the hard planes of muscle beneath my fingertips.

Vincent turned. His eyes locked on mine, and I knew—I *knew*—he felt it too.

The shift.

The charge in the air.

It felt like the world had shrunk to just the two of us in this room, and we were both caught in a pull so magnetic, I could feel every inch of his presence from across the room.

Then he spoke, and the tension shattered.

"You made it. How was your flight?" He sounded way too calm compared to my racing pulse. "I figured you were going to crash last night, so I didn't say hi. I was going to find you later, but you beat me to it."

"The flight was good." I matched his unaffected tone, irrationally annoyed by his composure. If I was thrown off-balance, he should be too. "How was last night?"

"Good." His cheek dimpled, and a devilish gleam entered his eyes. "Enjoy the show?"

My cheeks flamed when I realized what he meant. *Arrogant jerk.* "I've seen better."

"There's that bad taste again."

"There's that giant ego again. We all have our faults."

"So you admit it. You have bad taste."

"I guess so. If that's the case, you probably don't want your birthday gift…" I made a show of holding up the gift bag and leaving, but I only took two steps before Vincent caught up to me.

"Wait, wait." His hand closed around my wrist. He sounded like he was trying not to laugh. "I'm sorry. I didn't mean to insult your *impeccable* taste."

My skin tingled beneath his touch, but I brushed it aside and gave him an impudent smile. "That's what I thought. So easily swayed."

"Don't act so cocky yet. Let's see what you got me first." He released me to take the gift box. "What is this? A Whoopee cushion? A T-shirt that says 'Vincent DuBois Sucks'?"

I shrugged. "Open it and find out."

Despite my feigned indifference, my stomach fluttered with nerves as he tore away the gift wrap and opened the box.

His lips parted. He stared at its contents for a long, agonizing moment before he broke into peals of rich laughter.

Relief cooled my lungs. I grinned. "Like 'em?"

"Are you kidding? I fucking love them. Where did you get these?"

"I mixed and matched. Some are from department stores. Others are from slightly sketchy websites. This one was custom-made." I pointed to a pair of boxer briefs with his face on it.

I'd spent a week agonizing over his gift. What did you give someone who already had everything? I couldn't compete when it came to money spent, so I'd opted for something humorous but heartfelt.

Vincent said he owned one type of underwear during our arcade night (black Delamonte boxer briefs—I'd checked), so I bought him a dozen more of my choosing for variety's sake.

His underwear collection now included a navy pair printed with blueberry pancakes, a white pair with an alternating pattern of footballs and boots, and a green pair with little T. rex heads in an ode to Blackcastle's book club. My favorite, however, were the custom-made black briefs plastered with Photoshopped pictures of him from the waist up, wearing dark shades and a *Happy Birthday* sash.

I was afraid gifting him underwear would be weird since that was something a girlfriend would do, but I figured he'd enjoy the cheeky humor (no pun intended).

"I'm wearing these tonight." Vincent held up the Photoshopped ones. "If I miss this opportunity, I'll never forgive myself. Actually, fuck it. I'm changing into them right now."

"This means you can't say I have bad taste ever again!" I yelled after him.

He closed the en suite bathroom door, his laughter echoing through the wood.

I couldn't wipe the smile off my face. Coming to Budapest had definitely been a good idea. My worries already seemed less all-consuming. I was healthy, I had a great friend group, and I had a decent nest egg. *I'll be fine.* Even if I didn't thrive, I'd survive.

While Vincent changed, I wandered through his bedroom. Correction: his *suite*. It was too big to be called a bedroom. It even had a balcony, though it was too cold outside to enjoy it.

His phone sat on his nightstand. It kept lighting up every two seconds, and my eyes couldn't help but be drawn to it. A flurry of texts filled the lock screen. Most of them were happy birthday messages, but the one at the very top was a calendar notification.

> 📅 **BIRTHDAY** *(Do Not Contact)*

My brow wrinkled. Why would he set a Do Not Contact reminder on his birthday?

"What are you doing?"

I startled and whirled around. Vincent stood in the bathroom doorway. His voice was neutral, but his gaze slid between me and his phone with a hint of suspicion.

"Nothing." I hadn't done anything wrong, but my heart pounded like I had. "I mean, I was checking out your room and this caught my eye." I gestured to the lamp next to his phone. A crystal swan with sapphire eyes formed the base. It freaked me out a little, and I really had been interested in it before his phone distracted me.

"Yeah, I think the owner is a big crystal guy. You should see the ballroom. Crystal chandeliers everywhere." Vincent walked over and slid his phone in his pocket. "I'm going to hit the gym for a bit, but I'll see you at dinner? Thanks again for the birthday gift." His face softened. "I love it. Really."

It was a clear dismissal. "You're welcome. I'll see you later."

I left, my brain buzzing with questions. Who was that reminder about, and why did he set it for today specifically? He didn't hang out with anyone outside of Blackcastle and his sister's friend group.

Was it an old teammate? A business partner? An ex-girlfriend?

My chest pinched at the thought.

I'd always considered Vincent a pretty open book, but I'd never seen him shut down that quickly.

Uncertainty shadowed me as I rejoined my friends downstairs.

Just when I thought I had him figured out, he surprised me all over again.

CHAPTER 22

VINCENT

IF BROOKLYN SAW MY PHONE REMINDER, SHE DIDN'T LET on. I felt bad about being so curt with her earlier, but I'd panicked.

It was stupid of me to set that alert in the first place. October third was bad enough, but after last year's spiral, I'd set one for my birthday too. Seeing the command in black and white helped rein me in. The last thing I needed was to blow everything up on what should be a happy day.

Thankfully, the rest of the afternoon passed without incident. After I finished working out, I joined my friends for lunch and a movie in the screening room. It was just the guys since the girls went sightseeing.

I was a little disappointed I didn't get to see Brooklyn, but it was probably for the best. The less we interacted in front of the others, the better. Scarlett had freakishly perceptive powers, and I was convinced she'd pick up on the newfound tension between us if she saw us together for more than two minutes.

Hopefully, Asher could distract her enough during dinner and clubbing that she wouldn't notice.

I was getting ready for my official birthday night out when my phone rang. My lips curved. I'd been waiting for her to call.

"Happy birthday!" my mum sang after I picked up. "How's my baby boy doing? Are you having a nice time in Budapest?"

"Thanks, Mum. Yeah, it's great. We've been at the villa all day, but we're headed out to dinner soon."

"Good, good. You work so hard. You should have fun with your friends, and I *adore* Budapest. Did I tell you about the fling I had there when I was on holiday from uni? Oh, he was gorgeous. I could've been an exiled prince's wife, but alas, I married your father instead." Her deep sigh rattled with regret. "The follies of youth."

"Mum, please." I grimaced. "I love you, but I don't want to hear about your love life. Ever."

"Fine, but learn from my mistakes. Be very careful about who you attach yourself to, especially given who you are. There are all sorts of people just waiting to take advantage in the wings."

"I know." That was why I had such a small circle of friends. It was hard to trust people. Everyone wanted a piece of you, and sometimes, those pieces ended up as sensational headlines in the tabloids.

Fame and money corrupted, but so did proximity to fame and money.

"Speaking of love lives..." I knew what my mum was going to say before she said it. "How's yours going? Meet anyone special yet?"

No. My default answer teetered on the tip of my tongue, but it didn't feel quite right.

I glanced into the bedroom, where the rest of Brooklyn's birthday gift lay neatly folded on the bed.

"Vincent?" my mother prompted.

I shifted my attention back to the mirror. "Not yet."

The half-lie tasted metallic on my tongue.

"Oh." Her disappointment was tangible. "Well, you still have time. I thought Scarlett would never date again after Rafael, but look at her now. She and Asher are just darling together."

"Mmhmm."

We chatted for a few more minutes about my birthday plans and her work. She was a nurse, and she always had wild stories about her patients.

"I won't keep you any longer," she said after a somewhat nauseating tale involving a patient's rectum and spiky fruit. "I just wanted to call and wish you a happy birthday. I love you."

A lump formed in my throat. "Love you too."

Do Not Contact. I blinked away the image as I hung up, but guilt shredded my insides anyway.

"Not today, DuBois," I muttered. It was my fucking birthday. I was *not* going to spiral again.

I finished getting ready and went downstairs, determined to enjoy myself instead of feeding my neuroses. It was easier when there were people around. It gave me less time to be alone with my thoughts.

"There he is!" Adil spotted me first. "The birthday boy! Looking quite dapper, I might add."

I adopted an easy smile as I went around the room and greeted everyone. I'd seen them all earlier, but dinner marked the official celebration. Their presents were already piled up on the coffee table next to glasses of champagne.

My mouth quirked as I remembered Brooklyn's gift. I'd kept my promise and was wearing the boxer briefs with my face on them for our night out. They were hands down one of the best gifts I'd ever gotten—not because they were the most expensive or the most aesthetically pleasing, but because of the time and thought she'd put into them.

She didn't explicitly say it, but I knew she'd chosen the underwear because I told her I bought one style at the arcade. It was the only explanation, and the fact she'd remembered such a small detail made my chest ache a little.

"Happy birthday, my man." Samson clapped me on the back, interrupting my train of thought. "One year closer to being geriatric."

I flipped him off with a good-natured grin.

"This is for you." Seth handed me a glass of Veuve Clicquot. "Thanks for inviting me. This is, like, the coolest trip I've ever been part of."

"Anytime, man. You're part of the team. You know that."

He ducked his head, his cheeks reddening. He was twenty, making him the youngest kit manager in Blackcastle history. But he was good at his job, if a little too earnest, and he was shy enough that I'd made an effort to include him in as many group activities as possible.

Noah gave me a terse hug, which I didn't take personally. Everything he did was terse. I was honored that he'd even shown up.

Then he stepped aside, and there she was.

My breath caught. Brooklyn was laughing with Carina about something. She hadn't noticed I was nearby yet, and I took the opportunity to drink her in.

I'd seen her in every type of outfit possible—pajamas, workout gear, fancy dresses and sexy dresses and a lady pirate costume for Halloween last year. She looked great no matter what. But there was something about her tonight that stole the air right out my lungs.

Her red dress clung to her waist and flared around her thighs, revealing miles of smooth, bare skin. Her heels added at least three inches to her height, and her hair fell in soft golden waves down her back. It wasn't just the way she dressed or looked—it was the way she moved. The way she smiled. The way she could switch from playful and charming one minute to warm and empathetic the next.

It was…fuck, it was *her*. Every piece and facet of her. They shone so brightly I couldn't look away.

The truth had always been there, waiting for its moment in the sun. It'd compelled me to invite her to Budapest even though I knew it was a bad idea, and it'd made me want to kill anyone who made her cry.

But I'd never been able to put my finger on it until now.

Fuck. Me. I wasn't just infatuated with her. I—

"Happy birthday, DuBois." Her smooth greeting carried an amused lilt.

While I'd been reeling from my revelation, she'd come up beside me, her expression quizzical as I stared at her like I'd suddenly forgotten English.

"*Merci*. I mean, thank you." I chugged the champagne Seth gave me, which was a mistake. Champagne wasn't meant to be chugged. "You look…nice."

"*Merci*." Her eyes crinkled at my expense. It was adorable.

"Carina!" I turned abruptly to the brunette. "You look great too."

"Thanks, but not as great as Brooklyn," Carina chirped. "Right?"

I blinked. What the fuck did that mean? Was she on to me? Could she read minds? Did everyone in Scarlett's friend group have some freaky ability to mess with my head?

Brooklyn glared at her, but that didn't wipe the devious smile off Carina's face.

Thankfully, Scarlett came over at that moment to hug me and say it was time to open presents. By the time we finished and arrived at the restaurant, courtesy of the SUV limo I'd hired, I'd regained some semblance of control.

I did, however, make sure I sat as far from Brooklyn as possible. I couldn't afford to slip up at a group dinner with my sister and closest friends.

As a result, I was quieter than usual, but Adil made up for it with his chatter.

"Quick! Check your texts before he gets back," he said when Samson left to use the toilet. "I have another gift for you, but I don't want to make Samson feel bad because he's not included."

I raised an eyebrow. "Your gift is a text?"

"*No*. Just open the message I sent," he said impatiently. "You're gonna *love* it."

Somehow, I doubted it. Nevertheless, I did as he asked and found a new text from him that read, "Open me!"

I clicked into it, confused, until I saw the name at the top. It was a group chat called Blackcastle Baddies. Besides Adil, the only other members were Asher and Noah.

"You've been added to the club's elite chat!" Adil beamed. "We took a group vote, and we've decided to initiate you as a Blackcastle Baddie! Congratulations!"

"I tried to veto you, but I was overruled," Asher said. Scarlett elbowed him with an exasperated laugh.

"Wait." I held up a hand. "You've had a separate chat going this *whole time*? I'm the captain!" I didn't actually care that much about the chat, but it was the principle of the matter. "How the hell did Noah make it in before me? No offense, man," I added.

"None taken," Noah said, his tone dry. "Trust me. I didn't want to be there in the first place."

"Shocker," Carina murmured under her breath.

His mouth tightened, but he didn't acknowledge her comment.

"Well, I started the chat when you and Donovan hated each other," Adil explained. "He was being shunned. I felt bad, so I added him to our bromance."

"We do not have a bromance," Noah said.

"Yeah, what the fuck?" Asher crossed his arms. "Don't make it sound like a pity invite. You begged me to join."

"Uh, negative. I don't have to beg anyone to join a group chat. I can just add them, *which I did*. You're welcome."

"What's the difference between this chat and the book club one?" I asked. "Besides the number of people."

"Nothing," Noah said. "You just get double the notifications."

"It's a sign of prestige—oh shit, Samson's back." Panic spread across Adil's face. "Tina, don't tell him about the chat. I don't want to exacerbate his feelings of inadequacy, or he'll try to overcompensate on the pitch, which never ends well."

"My name's Tamara."

"Whatever."

She rolled her eyes. "Fine. I won't tell him." She returned to taking selfies on her phone.

We used to try and keep up with Samson's dates, but we eventually gave up. The guy went through girlfriends faster than Adil went through erotic novels.

Dinner ended with Samson being none the wiser about Blackcastle Baddies. I'd successfully avoided looking at Brooklyn throughout the meal, but I could hear her from all the way down the table.

Her laugh when Seth made a bad joke, her excitement when Scarlett started planning for *her* birthday trip next year, her disbelief when Noah said he had to take part in the bachelor auction.

It was infuriating.

"I'm so excited to go out with you guys," Seth said when we left the restaurant. The limo was waiting for us a little further down the street. "I've never been to a proper club."

"*Never*?" He was young, but there were plenty of eighteen-plus clubs in London.

"No." He flushed. "My friends aren't the clubbing sort."

"That's a tragedy." Samson overheard him. "Seth, mate, we gotta show you a good time tonight and get you laid. Tell me. What's your type?" He slung an arm over the kit manager's shoulder. "I'll wingman for you at the club. You can't work for Blackcastle with no game—it looks bad for the rest of us."

Seth was still stuttering and fumbling his way through a response when they disappeared into the limo.

I glanced at the restaurant entrance. Brooklyn and Carina were still in the restroom. I should—

My phone pinged. I checked it, expecting another birthday message from a friend. I was only half right.

UNKNOWN NUMBER

> Happy birthday

UNKNOWN NUMBER

> I hope you had a nice dinner in Budapest :)

I came to an abrupt halt. It was freezing outside, but that didn't compare to the ice rushing through my veins.

This was my private cell. Only a handful of people had the number, and it wasn't searchable anywhere online.

My birthday trip also wasn't public knowledge. It was possible someone recognized me at the airport or in the restaurant and posted about it, but a quick Google search didn't turn up anything about me being in Budapest.

Even if a random fan knew I was here, how the fuck did they get my number?

Who is this?

I waited, my breaths forming small white puffs in the air.
But a reply never came.

CHAPTER 23

BROOKLYN

"REMIND ME AGAIN WHY I WORE A DRESS AND HEELS." Carina shivered as we exited the restaurant and practically ran to the limo.

"Because we're going to a club, and you look hot." I wore a thick down coat that went past my knees, but every inch of exposed skin felt like ice.

"Right. Hot. Think of heat," she chanted.

Luckily, the limo wasn't parked too far from the exit. Vincent stood near the passenger side door, his gaze fixed on his phone. My steps slowed when I took in his white knuckles and the rigid set of his shoulders.

Something was wrong.

Carina disappeared into the car like the hounds of hell were at her heels. The sounds of my friends' laughter and a warm blast of air beckoned from inside, but my feet remained rooted to the ground.

Vincent hadn't noticed me yet. He was probably answering birthday texts, and I was overthinking things, but...

"Don't tell me you're googling yourself again," I teased. It was a soft gauge to see what he was doing.

He glanced up, his mouth grim.

My smile disappeared. *Something's definitely wrong.*

"Actually, I was, but not for the reason you think." He hesitated, then said, "I got a weird text, and it's freaking me out a bit."

He handed me his phone. I skimmed the text in question, my skin pebbling with goose bumps as another gust of frigid air swept over me. "Maybe it's a friend and they got a new number?" I suggested optimistically. Still, I couldn't resist a scan of our surroundings in case someone was lurking in the shadows, watching us.

"Maybe." Vincent didn't sound convinced, and rightfully so. The unknown number and their lack of response to his follow-up were glaring red flags.

"Do you think it's the same person who left the doll and photo?" I didn't want to feed into his worries on his birthday, of all days, but I had to ask. It also hadn't escaped my notice that I was the only person he'd told about the text. If the others knew, they wouldn't be laughing in the limo.

The warmth I felt at this display of trust was tempered by burning anger. I didn't hate a lot of people, but I *hated* whoever was doing this to him. It took a special kind of twisted to mess with someone's head, disappear, and pop back up weeks later to fuck with them some more. It was psychological torture at this point.

"I hope so. I can't deal with two different people trying to mess with my head." Vincent grimaced. "Not a lot of people know I'm in Budapest, and they texted right after I left the restaurant. The timing can't be a coincidence."

"It's suspicious," I admitted. "But it's also dinnertime, so it could be a lucky guess. As for your location, some fans could've seen you and posted about it online."

No matter my personal reservations, I wasn't going to let him spiral on his birthday. This was *his* day, and we were in freaking Hungary. There was nothing we could do about the text tonight.

"You should forward that to Detective Smith, just in case," I added. "The police might be able to trace the number." Hopefully, the text was "actionable" enough for the detective to finally get off his ass and do his job.

"I will." Vincent glanced at the driver. He waited outside the limo, smoke curling from his cigarette while he watched what sounded like a sports match on his phone. "Don't tell the others about this, okay? Especially not Scarlett. I don't want them to worry."

"I won't. I promise."

"Thank you." His shoulders relaxed, and his face softened as he added, "I didn't get a chance to tell you earlier, but you look beautiful."

I blushed, the compliment washing over me in a warm wave. "Thank you." Then, because I couldn't think of anything witty to say, I grabbed his hand and pulled him into the car. "Come on. We have a birthday to celebrate."

Vincent and I didn't speak of the text again for the rest of the night. It was easier to push it to the back of my mind when we were with our friends, who were too hyped up about our next stop to ask why it took us so long to get in the car.

We were ending the night at a multi-story mega club in the heart of the city. When we arrived, a dedicated staff member escorted us inside through a private entrance and up to the VIP floor.

Despite the discretion, a few clubgoers did double takes when our group passed by.

"Oh my God! Is that who I think it is?"

"Asher! Vincent! I love you!"

"They are *sooo* hot."

"Blackcastle sucks!"

"Can you sign my boobs?"

"No, Adil." Asher grasped the midfielder's arm when he moved toward the gushing fan. "No boob signing."

"Aw, man." Adil pouted. "I never get to have any fun!"

But he perked right back up when we finally made it to the VIP area. Like the rest of the club, it resembled a hedonistic Disneyland for adults, and it was opulent enough to rival even the best nightspots in London.

The air was thick with a heady cocktail of perfume, sweat, and alcohol. Neon and strobe lights swept through the vast space, glinting off mirrors, metallic surfaces, and the glass DJ booth suspended over the dance floor. A writhing mass of bodies moved in sync with the music, and the bass was so deep, so primal, I could feel it in my bones.

"First round's on me!" Samson shouted. He beckoned one of the bottle girls and whispered something to her. She returned less than a minute later with a tray of electric blue shots. There was a non-alcoholic option for Adil, who downed his with as much gusto as the rest of us.

My gaze collided with Vincent's over the top of our shot glasses. We finished our drinks and set them back on the tray, our eyes lingering on each other.

I rarely drank hard alcohol, and the buzz was immediate. My cheeks flushed as a tingle ran through my blood. The room seemed to swirl as our friends blurred into background noise.

Vincent was the only one in focus. His wide shoulders and

sculpted form cut a commanding presence in the chaos. The sleeves of his shirt were rolled up, revealing muscled forearms, and his gaze was hooded as it slid down my face to my mouth. It rested there for half a beat longer than appropriate before it came back up to meet mine.

My pulse quickened. I felt lightheaded, my whole body fizzing with anticipation like it already knew what his touch would feel like.

"Let's dance!" Carina grabbed my hand. She sounded giddy and more than a little drunk.

The spell holding the rest of the club at bay collapsed. The noise rushed back with disorienting clarity as Carina dragged me to the dance floor, and when I looked back, Vincent was already gone.

It was impossible to keep track of the group as the night wore on. They dipped in and out, there one minute and gone the next.

Samson and Tamara, making out shamelessly.

Seth, dancing and fist pumping like he was at a rave in 1999.

Asher and Scarlett, slow dancing to a song only they could hear.

The drinks flowed, the music swirled, and the lights flashed, illuminating pockets of the room like they were snapshots in time.

I'd lost count of the hours, but we'd been here long enough that my worries felt like a bad dream. ISNA, my job, my family, none of that mattered at this moment. The outside world didn't exist, and that was exactly how I wanted it.

Carina laughed when I twirled her around. She returned the favor, but my giggles were drowned by a club remix of Riley K's latest hit. I was still breathing heavily from the quick spurt of cardio when a gorgeous guy came up to us and said something to Carina. She gestured toward me and shook her head, but I could tell she was intrigued.

Do you want to dance with him? I mouthed.

"I'm staying with you!" she shouted over the music. It wasn't a no.

"I'll be fine. Go! He's hot!"

"Are you sure?"

"*Yes*." I gently pushed her toward the guy. "Have fun! Text me if you need me!"

Carina hesitated, but when I waved her off again, she winked and mouthed, *I'll find you later.*

I grinned. I didn't mind dancing alone, and I was happy to see her interested in someone. Carina was beautiful, but she was extremely picky. She'd turned down almost every date invitation and dance offer I'd seen her receive since we met.

The music switched to an upbeat hip-hop song. I was too buzzed to think too hard about where the rest of my friends were, but I did notice Noah standing alone by the bar with a frown.

Why was he frowning? This was supposed to be fun!

I shimmied over to him. He watched me approach with a bemused expression.

"Come on, Wilson, let's get you on the dance floor! You look miserable!" I tugged at his hand, but it was like trying to pull a tree out from its roots.

"I don't dance."

"*Ever?*"

"Not to this music."

"Don't be a snob. This isn't a…a waltz or whatever you like to do, but it's still fun. No one will judge you."

"I'm fine right here."

"Noah Wilson." I planted my hands on my hips. "You are at the best nightclub in *Budapest*. You've spent the entire night watching other people enjoy themselves from the sidelines. Even Carina is dancing with someone, and she usually *never* dances with guys when we go out! You can be uptight all you want tomorrow, but at least try to loosen up tonight."

His frown deepened. A muscle ticked in his jaw, and just when I thought it was a lost cause, he set his drink down and said gruffly, "One song. That's it."

I beamed. "Deal."

He followed me onto the dance floor like a prisoner following the warden to his execution. The music transitioned again, this time to something sultrier.

He was a little stiff at first, so I tried to ease him into it. "Here. Put your hands on my waist." I stepped closer to make it easier for him. "I'll put my arms around your neck, and we can just move our feet and hips like this. One, two. One, two. See? It's easy."

A noise of complaint rumbled from his throat, but at least he stayed. His face was even more perfect up close, and if I'd met him randomly at a bar in the US when I was younger, I would've been smitten.

Now? I didn't feel a single flicker of attraction. I admired him the way I'd admire a sculpture of a Greek god—appreciative of the details but devoid of any romantic or sexual attraction.

There was only one person in this club, in this *world*, who could make my heart race, and he was nowhere to be seen.

Where is he anyway? He'd vanished after that first round of shots. Was he with the other guys somewhere, or was he with a girl?

I missed a beat and accidentally stepped on Noah's toes. I apologized profusely, my face flaming.

"It's okay." He placed a reassuring hand on my hip, steadying me. "I—"

"What's going on?"

Our heads whipped around at the same time. Vincent stood next to us, his gaze roving from our faces to Noah's hand placement and back again. His jaw was tight.

It was like I'd conjured him up with my thoughts, though my imaginary version of him was less...aggravated.

"We're dancing," Noah and I said in unison.

We glanced at each other in embarrassment before looking away.

"I see." Vincent smiled, but it didn't reach his eyes. "Do you mind if I cut in?" He slipped in between us before we could respond. He'd turned his back on Noah, effectively shutting the other man out.

Noah's frown cleared, replaced with a small smirk. "Sure." An uncharacteristic hint of laughter ran beneath his voice. "It was nice dancing with you, Brooklyn."

"You too." I waited until he was out of earshot before I glared up at Vincent. "Do you know how hard it was to convince him to dance? He promised me one song, and you interrupted it."

I ignored the butterflies zooming through my stomach. I was happy to see him, but that didn't mean I liked being robbed of my victory.

"How did you convince him to dance anyway?" Vincent ignored my last statement. His hands bracketed my hips, guiding me through the beats with effortless ease despite the stiffness in his voice. "I've known him for years, and I've never seen him on a dance floor."

"The same way I do everything else. With charm and persistence."

"He looked charmed, alright. His hands were all over you."

"I lost my balance. He was helping me."

"Is that what they call it these days?"

I stopped moving to stare at him. Vincent stared back, his eyes burning with barely concealed irritation.

"Are you...jealous?" The prospect sent a breathless thrill down my spine. It shouldn't, but our relationship was built of shouldn'ts.

"Please." He scoffed, his cheekbones tinged with red. "Why

would I be jealous of Noah?"

"You tell me." I couldn't stop a smile from blossoming.

The red darkened against his skin. He didn't respond right away, but the answer was in his heartbeat, quick and heavy against mine. Somehow, we'd ended up pressed together, our bodies moving in sync. I didn't have to think about it the way I had with Noah. Our rhythms just matched. Perfectly.

"And if I did?" Vincent's voice was low in my ear. "If I told you how fucking jealous I was when I saw you with Wilson, what would you do?"

My smile evaporated. His palm seared through my dress, and it was my turn to blush. The heat crawled over my chest, up my neck, and across my face, muddying my thoughts.

What would I do? Question of the year.

Say something. Anything. A dozen responses teetered on the tip of my tongue, but I couldn't focus on one long enough to get it out.

"Kidding. Don't think too much about it." Vincent stepped back. A chill replaced the warmth of his touch. "Actually, I'm starving. There's a great pizza place next door. Want to come with me?"

I blinked, so thrown by the abrupt shift in tone and mood that my brain scrambled to catch up. "What?"

"Pizza. You in?"

"If we leave, we won't be able to get back in." That was the first reply I could come up with.

What was happening? How did we go from jealousy and what I could've *sworn* was sexual tension to talking about freaking pizza?

Vincent cocked an eyebrow at my concern.

Right. He was Vincent DuBois. Of course he could get back in.

I looked around. The rest of our group was still MIA. Even Noah was gone. And to be honest, even if they were here, I'd choose pizza with Vincent over dancing in the club.

"Sure." I smiled past my confusion. "Let's go."

Eating pizza this late at night wasn't the healthiest choice, but what the hell. I was off the clock, and we were on break. If there was ever a time to indulge, it was now.

Vincent and I grabbed our coats from the coat check and made our way to the exit. The pizza place was literally right next door to the club. It was packed with drunk tourists, but we were able to place our orders without Vincent causing a ruckus. I assumed everyone was too inebriated to recognize him.

Since there weren't any empty tables, we took our pizzas to-go. We wandered down the street, trying to eat our slices before it got cold.

Vincent didn't mention Noah again, and I didn't ask about his sudden change in attitude. The night was too beautiful to ask questions I might not want answered.

"So, how does this birthday rank against the others?" I asked. Maybe it was the lingering alcohol in my system, but the weather didn't feel as cold as it had earlier.

We finished our pizza and washed it down with water. We tossed the empty bottles into a nearby trash bin before resuming our walk.

"Honestly, I don't remember most of them," he admitted. "Vegas? Gone. Ibiza? A blur. But if I had to guess, this one would probably rank pretty high."

"It's the villa, isn't it?" I quipped. "It looks like a palace."

We turned right onto a quieter side street. The club was located on one of Budapest's main thoroughfares. It was packed to the brim with bars and restaurants, so busy that the Saturday night crowds spilled onto the pavements outside. But the street we were on was lined with small businesses, all of which had already closed for the night. The noise from the main avenue faded the further we walked.

"Nah, it's the underwear with my face on it," Vincent said. "Best present I've ever gotten."

I laughed. "I suck at Photoshop, and it took me forever to create that image. So I'm glad you like it."

"I do. But there's another reason this trip ranks high."

"What's that?"

"You."

My laughter subsided. Vincent said it easily, as though it were no big deal, but the word landed like a match in gasoline. It was impossible to breathe through the sudden haze clouding my mind.

I came to a standstill. He followed suit, his body angling to face mine. The white puffs of our exhales mingled in the air between us.

"You enjoy my company that much, huh?" Somewhere in the distance, thunder rumbled. I barely heard it over the roar of my pulse.

"Only in comparison with other people."

"As opposed to…"

"Truffle the pig. Noise-canceling headphones. My custom Zenith sneakers." His tone was flippant, but something softer, more intense, flickered beneath the surface.

"I know you're not ranking me below a pig and footwear."

"No mention of the headphones? Interesting."

"I like them more than you too, so I understand."

"I *highly* doubt that."

"Sorry," I said with a shrug. "Bose wins over DuBois every time."

A smile shadowed his mouth. "I'm glad you're here," he said softly.

The haze in my mind thickened. "Me too."

It struck me that this was the first private moment we'd had since he moved out. The Blackcastle hallway didn't count; that was at work. And while it'd been just us that morning, when I gave him his birthday gift, we were still in the villa where our friends could walk in at any minute.

Here, on a side street at midnight in Budapest, we were alone, with only the whispers of old memories to keep us company.

I hope you stay. It wouldn't be the same without you.

Who made you cry?

I'm glad you're here.

A droplet of water landed on my nose. Thunder clapped again, followed by a streak of lightning. The skies threatened rain, but my feet were rooted to the spot.

I'd spent my whole life feeling like a background character in the movie of my own life. *There*, but insignificant. I could disappear, and the lives of those around me wouldn't change in any major way.

I wasn't arrogant enough to think I should be the main character everywhere I went. I didn't need to be the center of everyone's world. But just once, I'd like to be with someone who thought I was as important to them as they were to me.

Scarlett and Carina were the closest I'd gotten to that feeling of reciprocity. But Vincent was the *only* relationship that felt truly equal.

When he showed concern, it was genuine.

When he said he wanted me there, I believed him.

And when he looked at me the way he was doing now, with dark heat and aching tenderness, I never wanted to look away.

My heart pounded loud enough to eclipse the thunder. Thunderstorms were rare at this time of the year, but I couldn't deny what I heard.

A light drizzle misted over us, turning the streetlights into hazy orange glows.

I wanted to step into his warmth and finally give in to this pull between us. But before I did, I had to know. There was still one conversation we'd never had.

"That day at my flat. If the fire hadn't happened, and my dad hadn't shown up..." My voice sounded almost too breathy to be mine. "Would you have kissed me?"

CHAPTER 24

VINCENT

WOULD YOU HAVE KISSED ME?

The question thrummed in my blood.

This was a conversation we should've had weeks ago. I'd kept pushing it aside, worried it would upset the balance in our relationship, but fuck it.

I was tired of pretending when all I wanted was her.

"Yes," I said simply. There was no doubt in my mind.

If there had, it'd been wiped away when I saw her dancing with Noah—not because I believed they were attracted to each other, but because I'd been jealous anyway. Jealous of how close they were, of how he touched her and how he'd danced with her before I could.

It was irrational, but I was never rational when it came to Brooklyn. She was the only person in the world who could drive me out of my mind, and I wouldn't have it any other way.

She stared at me, her eyes glistening in the rain. "You would've kissed me even if it meant losing the bet?"

Her uncertainty made my heart clench. Competition was baked

into our DNA, but after everything—the talks, the comfort, this fucking trip—I was stunned she'd think I'd prioritize a stupid wager over her.

"Brooklyn." I lowered my voice, my throat strained. "I'd lose every single fucking bet in the world if it meant I could be with you."

Her breath audibly hitched. "You don't really mean that."

"No?" I took a step closer.

"No." Her whisper was nearly inaudible. Her chest rose and fell in shallow spurts when I grasped her chin between my fingers and tilted it up.

I dipped my head until our faces were so close, I could count each droplet glittering at the ends of her lashes.

"I can prove it."

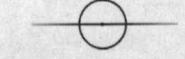

BROOKLYN

That was the only warning I got before Vincent slanted his mouth over mine and kissed me.

My whole body ignited like a bundle of dry tinder waiting for a spark to set it ablaze. Heat flooded my chest, neck, and face, and I couldn't stop a small moan from escaping as I pressed closer.

My reaction was so swift and visceral, I would've been embarrassed had I not been consumed by the sheer pleasure of the kiss. By the slide of his hand through my hair and the firm, insistent pressure of his lips. By the way his tongue coaxed me open and explored with aching sensuality. By the all-consuming *rightness* of the moment.

A hazy memory resurfaced—us in the arcade, playing pool and trading secrets.

I'm sorry your first kiss was such a terrible experience. I hope you've had better ones since then.

And I had. But every other kiss paled in comparison because this? This was the kind of kiss that upended worlds.

Vincent pulled back, his breaths heavy. "Tell me," he said roughly. "Does that taste like the kiss of someone who's lying?"

I'd lose every single fucking bet in the world if it meant I could be with you.

My throat dried.

That was all it took. One question, and I was undone again.

Instead of replying, I grabbed a fistful of his coat and yanked him toward me, my mouth finding his in a kiss that made the previous one seem positively chaste in comparison.

I'd lose every single fucking bet in the world if it meant I could be with you.

My heart threatened to pound out of my chest. I wound my arms around Vincent's neck as the rain fell steadily around us. Thunder continued to boom, shaking the dark shop windows and rattling my bones, but I barely noticed.

Our first kiss was an exploration, but this one was an expression of everything we'd been holding back for weeks, if not months—the desire, the comfort, the *craving* we had for each other. No words could adequately describe it.

Vincent fisted my hair and used it to gently tug me backward, under an awning and out of the rain. My back hit a wall, and the hard contours of his body pressed against mine in a way that drove every other thought from my mind. I wouldn't have been able to remember my name if someone asked.

His hands roamed my curves with delicious thoroughness, like he was trying to memorize every inch of me with touch alone. I arched into him, letting his warmth fill all the empty, lonely places inside me that I hadn't known existed.

Out of everything I'd tasted tonight, this kiss was the most intoxicating.

We might've stayed there forever, wrapped up in each other's arms while the world sailed on without us—had said world not intruded in the rudest way possible.

"Get a room!"

The drunken shout shattered the moment as surely as a hammer smashing through glass.

My eyes flew open, and Vincent and I broke apart in time to see a group of guys in matching fraternity sweaters stumble past. They whistled and catcalled us until one of them tripped on a loose stone and faceplanted on the pavement. His friends forgot about us after that.

A giggle climbed up my throat. Vincent looked at me, his mouth twitching, and that was all it took. We burst into laughter, our bodies shaking as I pressed my face against his chest and he buried his face in the curve between my neck and shoulder.

It was the perfect, absurd end to a perfect, absurd night.

The high from our shared amusement mingled with the high from our kiss. If I hadn't been holding onto him, I would've floated into the air.

The rain gradually stopped. The frat boys wandered off, and Vincent and I were alone again.

"We should head back to the villa and dry off," he said. "I don't want us getting sick."

"Good idea." We were both drenched. We couldn't return to the club like this, and I didn't even want to know the state of my hair and makeup. I probably looked like a drowned rat, but I didn't even care. It was worth it.

As we walked back toward the main street, Vincent's fingers interlaced with mine. Fresh warmth curled in my stomach, and I couldn't suppress a smile.

We may be in a foreign country, but I'd never felt more at home.

CHAPTER 25

BROOKLYN

"I CAN'T BELIEVE YOU AND VINCENT KISSED LAST NIGHT and you're only telling me now. It's been almost twenty-four hours!" Carina crossed her arms. "That has to be a violation of girl code."

"False. Forty-eight hours is the limit for adhering to girl code. Besides, I didn't have the chance to tell you earlier. We were with Scarlett, and she doesn't know yet."

I looked around, paranoid Scarlett could hear us even though she and Asher had left for the airport an hour ago.

It was Sunday night, aka our last night in Budapest. It was a short trip since the guys wanted time to recover before the Blackcastle gala in a few days. Everyone had booked different return flights to London, and besides Vincent and Noah, Carina and I were the last to leave.

We were currently waiting for our cab in the villa's foyer, but I was starting to regret telling her about the kiss without other distractions around. When she was bored, Carina hyperfixated on anything in her vicinity. Right now, that was me and my confession.

"I doubt anyone will be shocked, including Scar. You and Vincent have had...*vibes* for a while," she said delicately.

My cheeks heated. "We have *not*."

"Um, yes, you have. You wouldn't have run out of a nightclub to eat pizza and kiss in the rain if there hadn't been anything building up to that."

She had a point.

I glanced at the staircase. The last time I'd seen him, Vincent was packing in his room. Carina had been with me, so we hadn't exchanged more than a "goodbye" and "see you back in London."

Last night's kiss had ended there. When we returned to the villa, we'd been shocked to find half our friends had beat us there. Apparently, they'd tired of the club and, since they couldn't find Vincent or get ahold of him, they'd come back early.

They made it impossible for us to sneak off together, and when I woke up that morning, the guys had already "kidnapped" Vincent and taken him out for a boys' day in town. Scarlett, Tamara, Carina, and I spent most of the afternoon hanging out at the indoor pool and watching movies, but that meant I couldn't confide in Carina until now. The information had threatened to spill out all day.

"Does this mean you guys are dating now? Do I need to resign myself to being the fifth wheel for the foreseeable future?" she joked.

"I'm not sure," I admitted. "We didn't have 'the talk' yet."

Part of me was afraid to go there. The kiss had been so perfect. What if we ruined it by making things serious? What if he'd woken up that morning and regretted it? Unlikely, but possible.

I loathed myself for even thinking that way. I normally wasn't so insecure, but it was so much scarier to open up to someone when I actually cared about them.

"What about you?" I pivoted the conversation to Carina. "What happened with the guy you were dancing with?"

She shrugged. "Nothing. We danced. I left. That's it."

I arched an eyebrow at her unusual terseness before I caught a flash of movement from the corner of my eye. A second later, Noah walked into the foyer, dressed in black sweats with a duffel slung over his shoulder. His dark blond hair was damp from the shower.

"Hey," I said brightly. "Are you headed for the airport?"

He nodded, his expression wary. We hadn't talked since Vincent interrupted us at the club, and I wondered whether they'd discussed what happened during their boys' day.

"Do you want to come with us? Our cab's already on the way, and we have room," I offered. "It's taking forever to get a car tonight."

Noah flicked a quick glance at Carina, whose eyes were glued to her phone like it was the most fascinating thing she'd ever seen.

"Sure. If you don't mind," he said quietly.

"Not at all."

I liked Noah a lot. He was reserved, but he had a solid, self-assured presence that I found comforting. He was the type of guy I'd trust to lead us to safety if we were ever caught in a zombie apocalypse or something.

However, his arrival meant my conversation with Carina had to be put on pause. Our cab arrived a few minutes later, and the ride was silent until I attempted to make conversation.

"Are you going home for the rest of the break?" I asked.

Noah gave a curt nod. "My mother took Evie back to North Carolina already. I have to stay in London until after the gala, but I'm flying home straight after."

"I can't believe they're making you participate in the auction. People are going to go wild."

He grimaced, discomfort scrawled all over his face.

Noah wasn't as flashy or press friendly as some of the other players, but he had a solid fan base in the UK. It didn't hurt that he was also gorgeous. With his green eyes, sexy stubble, and thick, wavy hair, he could be an Armani model.

Silence fell again.

My other attempts at conversation gradually petered out, and the three of us rode to the airport like strangers forced to squeeze into a car together. Noah stared straight ahead the entire time, his expression impassive, while Carina was fixated on the scenery outside the window. She was normally a chatterbox around me, so it was very weird.

If I didn't know better, I could've sworn they were actively avoiding each other, but that didn't make sense. They barely knew each other, and they didn't have any bad blood as far as I could tell. Yet the tension in the car was so thick, I could slice it in half with a butter knife.

Thankfully, it didn't take us long to arrive at the airport. It turned out Noah was on the same flight as us, which he didn't look thrilled about. Then again, he never looked thrilled about anything, so I tried not to take offense.

After we cleared security, I left him and Carina at the food court so I could run to the restroom. I bought a pack of gum from a convenience store on my way back and was about to leave when I spotted a familiar head of dark hair near the refrigerated drinks.

Seth stared at a display of water, looking a little green.

"Partied a little too hard yesterday, huh?" I teased, coming up beside him.

He jumped, but his expression cleared when he saw it was me. "It's Samson," he croaked. "*He* parties too hard, and he took me along with him. I think I'm still hungover."

"That can happen. Did you have fun, at least?"

"Well, yes." His face flushed tomato red. He looked around furtively before he leaned in and whispered, "I kissed someone. She was really pretty."

I grinned. Say what you will about Samson, but he was an excellent wingman. "I'm glad. Everyone needs a vacation fling at least once in their life."

"I guess." Seth finally grabbed the largest water bottle from the fridge. "Speaking of which, what's going on with you and Vincent?"

My smile froze. "What do you mean?"

"I heard you came back to the villa together last night." He gave me a knowing look. Maybe he wasn't as naive as he appeared. "You both just disappeared."

I let out an awkward laugh. "Well, um, everyone did. I couldn't find anyone else at the club except for Vincent, so we got food and went back together."

I wasn't going to say a word to the team about what happened until Vincent and I talked.

"I see." Seth sounded a little skeptical, but he didn't press the issue. "He must be sad you're leaving Blackcastle though."

"Not any more or less than the other players."

"We're all going to miss you. Jones isn't nearly as fun during the presentations." I was gratified by the validation until Seth added, "I guess we should've known you would say no when Coach asked for an extension."

I froze. "What?"

Seth's eyes rounded with the horror of someone who'd just realized they'd shoved their foot in their mouth. "N-nothing. I'm going to pay for this water then head off. My flight—"

"Seth." I crossed my arms, my pulse hammering. "Tell me the truth."

The kit manager looked around frantically as though searching for someone to save him. When no one did, he swallowed hard. "I overheard Coach asking Lizzie to extend your decision period to a month instead of the usual one or two days. I guess Jones told him he wasn't sure whether you'd take the offer? I don't know— I'm just guessing," he said quickly. "I shouldn't have mentioned it. I was eavesdropping and—oh my God, Coach is going to kill me. I'm—"

"Stop. It's okay," I said. "I'm not going to tell him you told me. Don't worry."

Seth's shoulders slumped with relief. "So you're not upset?"

"Not at you."

My heart thundered with rising anger, but I kept a smile on my face until Seth and I parted ways. Once we did, I let it vanish.

"Hands-off," my ass. How could my dad ask HR for special treatment for me when he *knew* people would talk? I'd insisted on being treated like every other employee since day one, but he'd undermined me with one request.

I guess it didn't matter now since I wasn't staying at Blackcastle, but it was the fact he went back on his word *and* behind my back that bothered me. If he wanted me to stay, or he wanted me to make a quicker decision, he could've told me himself instead of trying to manipulate the situation.

I forced myself to relax my shoulders and take a deep breath before I returned to the food court, but when Carina, Noah, and I boarded our flight an hour later, I was still fuming.

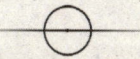

I didn't see my dad until four days later, at Blackcastle's holiday gala. We exchanged brief hellos at the start of the event, and I had to will myself not to bring up what he did. This wasn't the right time or venue for it.

The gala was the club's most anticipated celebration of the year. Two hundred attendees mingled at a fancy hotel ballroom in central London. There was a red carpet, a press line, and enough champagne to drown a small town in France. It was a big enough deal for the players to swap out their tracksuits for actual suits, though they remained firmly committed to their trainers. Trying to convince a footballer to wear dress shoes was like trying to stuff a lion into a bikini.

"You can only avoid one conversation tonight," Carina said as we entered the ballroom. "Your dad or Scarlett. Pick one. I vote for avoiding your dad."

I groaned. I'd told her and Scarlett what Seth said without mentioning he was the source, but Carina had been on me about confessing to Scarlett about the kiss too.

"I will. Tomorrow," I hedged. "I don't want to ruin her night."

"You're not going to ruin her night."

"How do you know?"

"Because I'm her best friend too, and I *know* her. This is for your own good." Carina looped her arm through mine, pulling me toward our table when I attempted to flee. "You have to tell her, or the secret will eat you alive. I love you both, and I don't want any self-cannibalism on my watch."

"Gross. Can you not talk about self-cannibalism before dinner?"

"Don't deflect, or I'll spam your inbox with the goriest videos I can find on the internet until you tell her."

I scowled, already regretting bringing her as my plus-one. She looked so innocent with her black embroidered gown and sweet smile, but she was really the devil in disguise.

"I can't tell her before I've talked to Vincent." I grasped for another excuse. "She's his sister, and he has a stake in this too. We need to wait for the right time."

Vincent and I agreed we needed to tell her, but we hadn't settled on the who, when, or how. We'd messaged a ton since Budapest, but we'd been so busy prepping for the gala that we hadn't had a chance to really sit down and *talk* about what came next.

"I get it, but knowing you two, the 'right time' means never." Carina came back swinging with the brutal truth. "Think of it this way. The longer you keep it a secret, the longer you'll have to sneak around behind Scarlett's back. It'll be exhausting, and she'll be hurt you waited so long to tell her. It's better to get it over with. I'm sure it'll work out, and Vincent will understand."

I hated to admit it, but Carina was right.

It'd been five days since the kiss, and I was already drowning in guilt from keeping it a secret from Scarlett.

"Fine," I said. "I'll tell her, but if you send me a single gory video, our friendship is over."

Carina beamed. "Deal."

I broke out into a sweat as we reached our table, where Scarlett was talking to Lizzie from HR. She'd been my first real friend in London, and the thought of hurting her made me feel a little sick.

Lizzie waved to us and bowed out gracefully to talk to Henry.

"Hey! You look beautiful." Carina bent down to hug Scarlett hello and caught my eye over her head. *You got this*, she mouthed. "I'm going to run to the loo before dinner. Be right back."

I took a seat next to Scarlett, who indeed looked stunning in a one-shoulder violet gown that contrasted perfectly with her dark hair and pale skin.

"Where's Asher?" I asked, stalling for time while I tried to think of ways to broach my confession.

Remember how Vincent and I came back to the villa together in Budapest? Well, we did more than get food beforehand.

You'll be happy to hear that Vincent and I don't bicker every day anymore. Why? It's a funny story...

Your brother and I kissed. I liked it. The end.

"He's taking a group photo with the team," Scarlett said. "I'm a little tired, so I decided to wait for him here."

I straightened, my concern temporarily overriding my anxiety. "Is it a flare-up?"

Scarlett had been diagnosed with chronic pain after her car accident years ago. It could flare up any time, though it was often exacerbated by stress or overexertion.

"I'm fine," she reassured me. "I just needed to sit for a while. Besides, I have to stay and bid on Asher or he'll never forgive me." She lowered her voice. "See that woman over there? She's been trying to 'win' him for the past three years. She freaks him out."

I followed Scarlett's gaze to where a woman with jet black hair and a tight leopard print dress had cornered a pained-looking Jones.

"He's probably right. I know a cougar when I see one, and I'm not talking about her dress," I joked.

Scarlett laughed. "This event is filled with cougars. Honestly, good for them, as long as they stay away from my boyfriend. I'd love it if they bid on Vincent though. He would die." She said this with the kind of glee that only a little sister could feel at her brother's expense.

"Yeah." I forced a matching laugh.

Tell her now. It was the perfect segue.

But when I opened my mouth, nothing came out.

Carina kept reassuring me that Scarlett wouldn't be upset. She was probably right (again), but that didn't stop the little voice of doubt in my head. The one telling me I was only a mistake away from losing the people I loved because they were only tolerating me anyway.

"Speaking of Vincent, do you think he's been acting weird lately?" Scarlett asked. "It feels like he's been avoiding me since Budapest."

I gulped. Thank God my dress was sleeveless, or it'd be marred with pit stains by now. "Um, no. He's always been weird."

What are you saying? Tell her!

"Maybe." She sounded dubious. "I feel like something happened. I'm not sure if I did anything wrong? He's usually more…" She waved a hand in the air. "You know. *There.*"

I was tempted to lie, but staring at her wide, worried eyes, I couldn't. Nor could I let her think he was keeping his distance because she did something wrong.

"Actually, I do know why he's been acting weird." I took a deep breath and willed my nerves to steady. "Before I tell you this—this next thing, I want you to know that it was *completely* unplanned and that I didn't mean to wait this long to tell you. I just didn't know how to bring it up, and I was scared you'd hate me for it. You still might."

Scarlett's brow creased. She set her drink down and focused on me, her eyes filled with equal parts curiosity and wariness.

"I kissed Vincent last weekend. In Budapest. After the club." The words tumbled out in an avalanche. "We really did just leave to get food, but then we were walking through the city and it started raining and I…it just happened."

I wasn't sure whether my run-on sentence made sense. It was hard to tell from Scarlett's reaction since her expression was unreadable.

"I'm really, really sorry I kept this from you." My pulse was racing a mile a minute. "Vincent and I haven't discussed what the kiss means for us yet, so if you're wondering whether we're dating, I have no idea. But I wanted to tell you because I couldn't keep it a secret anymore."

There was a long silence before Scarlett released a sharp breath. "You kissed Vincent," she said, the words slow and measured.

I nodded, my stomach cramping.

"On his birthday."

I nodded again.

"And it wasn't a one-night stand type of situation?"

"No. We didn't, um, sleep together."

"Oh." She slumped against her seat and closed her eyes. "Thank fucking God."

I blinked. "Uh, thank fucking God that we didn't have sex or…"

"No, thank fucking God that you kissed!" Scarlett popped up in her chair again. "It's about time. You two were killing me with all your flirting disguised as arguments. I thought I'd have to *Parent Trap* you boneheads before you realized you liked each other."

My jaw dropped. "Wait. You *wanted* us to kiss?"

"Well, 'want' is a strong word. In an ideal world, Vincent is a monk and I never, ever have to think about his love life. But you two have had…*vibes* for a while, so I'm glad you finally acted on it."

That was almost exactly what Carina said when I told her.

I couldn't believe it. I'd been twisting myself up in knots over this confession, and she'd been anticipating it the *entire time*.

"So you're really not mad?" I ventured.

"No." Her face softened. "I admit, I *am* a little nervous. He's my brother, and you're one of my best friends. I don't want you to hurt each other. Not that I think you will, but relationships are unpredictable. That's why I asked if it was a one-night stand. Those have a higher likelihood of going astray—" She broke off with a startled laugh when I threw my arms around her.

"I love you," I said, my voice muffled against her hair. "You're the bestest friend and sister ever. I'm so glad you're not pissed at me."

"I love you too." She sounded amused. "If you guys *do* end up dating, just promise not to share any explicit details with me, okay? I don't want to be traumatized."

I laughed, pressure easing from my chest. "I promise." I pulled back, my smile wide enough to split my face. I felt like someone had lifted a twenty-pound weight from my shoulders and chucked it into the river.

We didn't get a chance to talk more before Carina returned from the loo and the rest of our tablemates took their seats for dinner.

Carina raised a questioning brow and grinned when I gave her a discreet thumbs-up.

Told you it'd work out, she mouthed.

She had. I was never questioning her instincts again.

The players and coaches were all seated together near the stage since the auction was scheduled to start after the main course. I deliberately avoided looking at my dad. I was having a great night, and I didn't want to ruin it.

Right before dessert, the emcee bounded onstage to kick things off. I didn't recognize him, but he looked vaguely familiar. Maybe he was a lesser-known celebrity or sports influencer? They often emceed at these events.

"Ladies and gentleman, I apologize for interrupting your meal, but I'm happy to announce that it's time for our fourth annual Blackcastle Bachelor Auction!" he proclaimed to loud cheers and wolf whistles. He explained the rules before adding, "All proceeds will go to the St. George Children's Hospital, so get your checkbooks out because our first bachelor is already waiting to meet you. All the way from Morocco, we have the one, the only…Adil Chakir!"

More cheers as Adil jogged onto the stage and spun around in a dramatic fashion.

I cupped my hands around my mouth and yelled, "Work it, Adil!"

He grinned and did a little shimmy that had the crowd going wild. Now that the weight of telling Scarlett had been lifted off my shoulders, I could actually enjoy myself. The auction was silly and a little cheesy, but it was also fun and raised money for a great cause. It was exactly what I needed after the rollercoaster of the past few months.

The free-flowing champagne and the chance to eat dinner with a famous footballer had the bidders in a frenzy. Samson, Gallagher, and Stevens all went quickly, but Noah and Asher brought the house down—Noah because it was his first time participating, and Asher because he was Asher.

"Yes! Take that!" Scarlett said triumphantly when she "won" Asher for a whopping forty thousand pounds. He'd given her carte blanche for the auction, so he was in essence paying for himself, but he didn't look at all upset about it.

He winked at Scarlett before sauntering offstage to disappointed murmurs from the other bidders. The woman in the leopard print dress glared at her like *she* was the girlfriend, and Scarlett had robbed her of a night with her partner.

"I like this event so much more when I can participate," she said, ignoring Leopard Print's hostility. "Poor Noah though. I bet we won't see him in public again for at least six months after this."

"He might quit the team if they make him participate again next year," I said, only half joking. Noah had spent his entire time onstage looking like he'd rather swim back to the US naked than be here, but that hadn't stopped a statuesque brunette from bidding the second highest amount of the night on him.

"Finally, our last bachelor of the night needs no introduction," the emcee said. "Making his first auction appearance in years is none other than the captain himself, Vincent DuBois!"

My stomach flipped. I swallowed past a dry throat and ignored Scarlett and Carina's knowing smiles as Vincent strolled onto the stage, all easy grace and clean-cut devastation. His navy suit molded perfectly to his frame, and he greeted the ecstatic crowd with a dazzling smile. It fooled the majority of people in the room, but I recognized his fake PR smile when I saw it.

It was a little too bright, a little too forced. His eyes didn't crinkle the way they did with his genuine smiles, and a flicker of tension disrupted his jaw before he smoothed it out.

Like Noah, he was hating every second of this. He just hid it better.

Unlike with the other players, I didn't cheer as the bids quickly escalated. It was a bloodbath. People were outbidding each other before the emcee had a chance to acknowledge the last offer, and he was growing visibly flustered as he tried to keep up.

Vincent kept smiling even as his shoulders tensed.

"Twenty thousand!"

"Twenty-one thousand!"

"Twenty-two thousand!"

The bids kept going up, and the shouts kept getting louder. The front runner was Leopard Print Dress, who looked like she might murder someone if she didn't win.

"Thirty thousand!" she shouted.

The room fell silent. Vincent's smile finally wavered, and a hint of panic crept into his eyes before he covered it up.

"Thirty thousand! Wow!" The emcee beamed. "Thirty thousand going once..."

I clutched my knee with a white-knuckled hand. My heart felt like it was going to burst out of my chest.

"Thirty thousand going twice…"

Don't do it. I couldn't afford it in more ways than one.

My dad was here. My friends, my coworkers, the entire Blackcastle team—they were all here.

"Thirty thousand going three times…"

Vincent looked vaguely ill. He glanced around the room like he was desperate for someone, anyone, to save him.

The emcee raised his gavel. Before he could bang it, I jumped up from my seat and yelled, "Thirty-five thousand!"

CHAPTER 26

VINCENT

GASPS FILLED THE ROOM AS EVERY HEAD SWIVELED toward the new bidder, mine included.

Brooklyn stood on the left side of the room, chin raised in defiance. She was at the same table as Scarlett and Carina, who gaped at her with the same shock that must've been written all over my face. "Thirty-five thousand pounds," she repeated. "That's my bid."

My heart crashed against my ribcage. What the hell was she doing? She didn't have thirty-five thousand pounds to spare. Hell, even *I* wouldn't bid thirty-five grand on me.

Her eyes met mine across the room. They were a little panicked but determined, and suddenly, I knew.

She was doing this because she'd somehow sensed my discomfort, and she was bidding money she didn't have to save me from having to spend a night with the woman in leopard print.

I hadn't said a word about how much I hated being in the auction, but Brooklyn picked up on it anyway.

A tight pressure rose in my chest.

"Forty thousand!" Leopard Print yelled. She glared at Brooklyn as if daring her to one-up her offer.

Trepidation spread across Brooklyn's face before she squared her shoulders and opened her mouth. "For..." She trailed off when I gave a small shake of my head.

The thought of dinner with Leopard Print made me cringe, but I couldn't let Brooklyn spend that much money on me. If she won, I'd insist on paying her back every penny, but knowing her, she'd fight me on it. I couldn't take even the minuscule risk that she'd be hurting because of me.

She stared at me, her eyes searching my face before she finally sat down without completing her bid. She glared back at Leopard Print, whose mouth curled with triumph.

"Going once, going twice, going three times...*gone* for forty thousand pounds! Wow! What an auction!" The emcee shook his head in amazement. "That's all we have this year folks. Congratulations to the winners..."

I tuned out the rest of his closing remarks and rushed offstage before he finished talking. The auction was the last event of the night. It was late, and people were already making their way toward the exit.

My pulse clamored as I raced across the ballroom, barely acknowledging the many congratulations and back slaps I got for receiving the highest bid of the night next to Asher.

I pushed past Samson and Seth on my way to Brooklyn's table. Hopefully, she hadn't left yet because I needed to talk to her. Right now.

"Vincent!" Lloyd stepped into my path. He looked happier than I'd ever seen him, and I'd known the guy for years. "I have news."

"Can you tell me later? I have to—"

"It's about Zenith."

Any other day, I would've jumped at news about the ambassadorship, but not today. "Let's discuss—"

"They want to do a test shoot." He barreled on, oblivious to my mounting frustration. "It's not official. It's the holidays, so the execs are out of office, but I know someone who knows someone who's—"

"Lloyd." I wanted to shake him. "Get to the point."

"The point is, it's a freaking test shoot! Do you know what means?"

I stared at him blankly.

"It means you're in the home stretch." He flapped his hands in an extremely un-Lloyd-like manner. "My source says it's down to you and Filipović. Martin is out after his recent cheating scandal. Stepping out on your long-term partner for a threesome with her best friend and *your* best friend's girlfriend isn't a good look. Anyway, word is, the test shoot will be scheduled for sometime in January or February. Whoever performs better will get the deal."

"Great. Looking forward to it. Thanks." I brushed past him, trying not to calculate the number of minutes I'd lost listening to him talk about Rene Martin's personal life.

"That's it?" he yelled after me. "This is fucking Zenith, Vincent! Don't you want to know the details?"

"Email them to me!" I yelled back without slowing my pace.

I made it two steps before my phone rang. I sent it to voicemail without checking to see who was calling.

I almost made it. I was *this* close to reaching Brooklyn's table until the one person I couldn't brush off stepped into my path.

Coach.

Fuck.

"DuBois." Like the rest of the club, he was wearing a suit. He wore one to the gala every year, but that didn't make it any less weird.

It was like seeing a grizzly bear play the piano every Christmas.

"Boss." I switched to calling him "Boss" in case it endeared me more to him, though I doubted it.

We'd resumed our punishing daily schedule of early runs and awkward dinners after I returned from Budapest. I was pretty sure he didn't know Brooklyn had been on the trip, or he would've locked me up in a dungeon by now.

Then again, she'd bid on me in front of the entire ballroom. He didn't need to know about Budapest to be suspicious, as evidenced by his piercing stare.

"Tied for the highest bid of the night. Impressive," he said.

"Thank you."

"My daughter had a hand in driving that amount up."

I swallowed. "Yes, sir."

"Any idea why she bid *thirty-five thousand* pounds on her ex-flatmate?"

"Well, sir, we're friends." I searched for a plausible excuse. "And she, uh, knew I didn't want to do the auction, so she offered to bid on me if I paid her back later."

"Is that right? You looked quite surprised when she stood up."

Damn me and my slip-ups. "I...didn't know she was going to start her bid that high."

"Now that you mention it, why didn't she bid on you earlier if that was the plan?"

Sweat dotted my forehead. This was worse than getting interrogated by MI5. "It's a strategy that we found online. Wait for the small bidders to drop out, then come in at the end and take the whole thing. Like those last-minute bidders on eBay." I was pulling my answers out of my ass, and I couldn't tell whether he was buying it.

"Yet she didn't place the winning bid."

"Um…" I stalled for time. "I gave her a cap of thirty-five thousand pounds. I didn't think we'd surpass that."

Coach pressed his lips into a thin line. He obviously didn't believe me, but I'd answered his questions competently enough that he couldn't find a flaw. Yet.

"So you're not on your way to find Brooklyn," he said.

"No, sir."

"Then where are you off to in such a rush?"

"The…toilet."

"By yourself?"

"Yes. I generally don't make it a group activity. Sir," I added hastily.

"Let's go."

"To where?"

"The toilet. I have to take a piss." He jerked his chin toward the restrooms.

Fuck my life. With no other choice but to back up my lie, I followed him to the toilets, where we used the facilities in awkward silence.

"I'm headed to an after-party with some of the guys, so don't wait up for me," I said before he "offered" to drive us home. "I'll see you in the morning for our run."

Thankfully, he didn't ask any questions about my post-gala plans, but it didn't matter. By the time I returned to the ballroom, Brooklyn was gone.

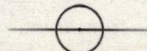

BROOKLYN

I declined Carina's invitation to go to Samson's after-party with her. Normally, I'd be down for a night of hanging out at the winger's ridiculously lavish mansion—he'd built an honest-to-God, private nightclub in the basement—but I wasn't in the mood.

I'd lingered at the gala, hoping Vincent would show up, but he'd disappeared right after the auction. He was probably at the after-party right now, living it up with the rest of Blackcastle.

It was stupid of me to assume he'd seek me out after the auction. What had I expected? That he'd be so overwhelmed by my bid, he'd run offstage and kiss me in front of everyone? He hadn't asked me to do that for him, and I hadn't even won. While part of me was relieved—the thirty-five thousand pounds would've put me in severe debt—I wished I could've punched Leopard Print in the face. She'd been way too smug about winning.

I sighed and stared at my computer. I'd already changed out of my gown and into my PJs. I was working on my ISNA application, which was due next week, but I couldn't focus.

Why was it so hard for Vincent and me to nail down our relationship? The kiss should've clarified things, but it left me more confused than ever.

Every time we moved forward, something pulled us astray before we could solidify our progress. My dad, our friends, a freaking kitchen fire. I couldn't tell if that was the universe's way of telling us we weren't meant to be or if we were just bad at communicating.

Someone knocked on the front door.

The unexpected sound echoed through the flat, and I sat up straight, my brow creasing. Who the hell would drop by this late without notice?

My mind flashed to Vincent's creepy crochet doll and the strange text he'd gotten in Budapest. Fear curdled in my stomach.

The security system he'd installed was still up and running. He'd also moved out, so the chances of the intruder showing up at my place were slim. But maybe they saw us together in Hungary, thought I was getting in their way, and came to take me out.

They knocked again.

I grabbed a cricket bat from my closet and inched into the living room, toward the front door. I peeked through the peephole, half expecting to see a masked stranger with a gun.

Instead, dark hair and a navy suit filled my vision.

My bat hit the floor with a thud, and I opened the door, my pulse skittering for an entirely different reason.

Vincent stood in the hall, his jacket slung over his shoulder and his sleeves rolled up to his elbows. His eyebrows inched up when he saw me. "You're home."

"It's midnight on a Thursday. Where else would I be?"

"The pub. The after-party. I checked both, but I thought I missed you." A trace of relief ran through his drawl.

"You checked the Angry Boar before you checked my house?"

He shrugged. "Scarlett and Asher went there after the gala."

"Ah." I suppressed a smile, my earlier uncertainties evaporating as though they'd never existed. "You could've texted to see where I was."

"True."

His gaze held mine, and little crackles of electricity danced over my skin.

"I'm sorry I didn't win the auction," I said in an effort to hide my reaction. *It's just a look.* I could not be melting over one look. "The leopard lady was freaking me out, and I tried to save you, but I didn't have enough money and it seemed like—"

"Brooklyn."

The air in my lungs turned scarce. "Yeah?"

"I'm not here to talk about the auction."

There was a beat of silence, thick with heat and unsaid words.

Then he was inside, and his mouth was on mine while my hands tugged at his shirt, trying to free it from his waistband. I wanted to feel his skin against mine. The kiss was hungry and frantic and intoxicating, but it wasn't enough. I needed *more*.

I finally freed his shirt. Vincent helped me slide it off his shoulders without breaking the kiss. He tugged my top and bottoms off, and then we were somehow in my room, our breaths heavy with want. My back hit the bed while he removed the rest of his clothing.

I wasn't wearing a bra, only panties, and a heavy pulse bloomed in my core as I watched him take off his belt and pants.

The shoulders, the abs, those *thighs*. I firmly believed that footballers had the best thighs on the planet, and Vincent proved me absolutely right. I drank him in, my eyes tracing over every sculpted ridge and shadowed curve, but a giggle erupted from my throat when I reached his groin.

He was wearing the pancake boxer briefs I'd bought him for his birthday.

"If you keep laughing at me when I'm half naked, I'm going to get a complex," he said, sounding amused.

"Sorry." I propped myself up on my elbows and cast a meaningful look at his briefs. "I was admiring your choice of underwear."

"The person who bought them has good taste." He stripped them off. "And I like to have part of her with me. Always."

My mouth dried, both at his words and at the sight of his arousal. My core pulsed again, and I let out a small whimper of anticipation when he climbed onto the bed.

His arms bracketed my body, caging me in as he lowered his head toward mine.

"Let's make another bet." His breath skimmed my skin.

"Seriously?" I whimpered again when he palmed my breast and ran a thumb over the peaked nipple. A bolt of pleasure streaked between my legs. "You want to make another bet *right now*?"

"Mmhmm." He trailed kisses over my jaw, down my neck, and across my chest. "I bet I can make you scream so loud, your neighbor will be banging down the wall. No pun intended."

My breathless laugh dissolved when he closed his mouth around my nipple and sucked.

Fuck. The bastard was trying to distract me into saying yes—and it was working.

"It's nice to know your ego is intact." I tried not to squirm when he moved to my other nipple, licking and sucking with agonizing care. My entire body flushed, but I swallowed my moan and managed to add, "I'll be lucky if you can make me come even once."

He traced my nipple leisurely with his tongue before he released it with a soft pop. He blew cool air across the wet, sensitized peak, and… *God*. My hips instinctively bucked as my moan finally broke free.

A wicked smile spread across Vincent's face. "You're going to regret saying that."

The dark promise in his voice made my toes curl.

He kissed his way down my stomach until he reached my underwear. He yanked them off and paused, taking in my bare pussy and slick thighs.

"Lucky if I can make you come once, huh?" He looked up at me, his eyes glittering with hunger. "You're already a fucking *mess*, sweetheart." He reached down and pushed two fingers inside me.

I cried out, my hips arching up again in a frantic search for more friction. *Damn* him. He was so smug, and he thought he could…he could…

My mind short-circuited when he dragged his fingers out and replaced them with his mouth. He pushed my legs farther apart and propped them on his shoulders, giving him greater access to my pussy as he licked and sucked on my clit.

My knees weakened. I fisted the sheets, my breaths heavy from the effort of holding in my cries, but I couldn't help moaning when he flicked his tongue against the *exact* spot that drove me crazy. "Oh, *fuck*."

Then he gently raked his teeth against that same spot while pushing his fingers inside me again, and my mind blanked for the second time in as many minutes. I arched up with a cry, my thighs clamping around his head while fireworks exploded behind my eyes.

The pleasure was so intense, I instinctively tried to scoot away after the first blinding wave, but strong hands held me fast. I was a ship being tossed in a storm, buffeted on all sides by sensation, and I couldn't catch my breath as the pressure built, and built, and—

Another cry, this one so loud and hoarse it hardly sounded human. My vision blurred, my toes curling as my back bowed off the mattress. Ecstasy crashed through me in waves, each more overwhelming than the last until I was utterly wrecked.

I lay there, my skin slick with sweat and my chest rising and falling in ragged bursts as the aftershocks rolled through me.

When my vision cleared, Vincent was still between my legs, his mouth glistening with the evidence of my orgasm. The sight sent a fresh, unexpected spasm of arousal through me.

"That's one," he said, his smile filled with pure male satisfaction. "*Et ça a un putain de goût, ma chérie.*"

"I have no idea what that means," I said, too spent and satiated to come up with a witty response. "But you got lucky with that one."

"You're pretty mouthy for someone who just came all over my face," he drawled, a hint of heat in his voice. He rose up on his knees, and my stomach clenched.

Holy shit. His cock was even bigger than I remembered. Harder, like eating me out had turned him on as much it had me.

"What can I say? I'm funny that way," I said breathily. I couldn't take my eyes off him.

My scrutiny didn't escape his notice.

Vincent's gaze darkened. "Open your mouth."

My clit pulsed at his soft, steely command. I obeyed, but not before I flipped us over so he was on his back and I was straddling him.

I kept my eyes on him as I wrapped my hands around his shaft and guided it in between my lips. Vincent groaned as I took more and more of him, sucking him as far down as I could go before I pulled back and swirled my tongue around the tip.

I licked every inch of his cock head before I sucked him down again, deeper this time, until saliva pooled in my mouth and the air was filled with messy slurps and gurgles.

Vincent tangled his hands in my hair, holding it back while I took him all the way. My eyes watered when he hit the back of my throat, but *God*, the guttural noise he made sounded almost as good as he tasted.

"*Fuck*, baby," he rasped. "That feels so damn good."

I moaned, loving his pants and groans, the desperate grip he had on my hair, and the way his muscles trembled, like it was taking all his willpower not to lose control.

He fisted my hair tighter into a ponytail, using it to guide me up and down as we worked up a rhythm. My entire body was flushed.

Tingles spread across my chest and clit, and when he groaned again, I felt the vibrations throb deep in my core.

"I'm going to come," he panted.

Instead of pulling away, I sucked harder until I felt his cock throb against my tongue. Thick, hot spurts filled my throat, and I made sure to swallow every drop before I released him with a satisfied smile.

Vincent let out a final groan before he slumped against the bed, his skin glistening with sweat.

"I'd say that's one for one," I purred, climbing up beside him.

His husky laugh floated between us. "Who's the cocky one now?"

"Still you."

"I did make you come so hard that you drenched my face, so I'd say that's well-deserved," he drawled, a grin playing around the corners of his mouth.

I rolled my eyes even as a blush stained my cheeks. "Yet you lost the bet." I rapped my knuckles against the headboard. "Not a peep from my neighbor."

"That was just the warm-up. We're not done yet."

My lips parted when I felt him stir against my leg. "You can't possibly be ready again. It hasn't even been two minutes!"

"What can I say? I have great stamina." Vincent's eyes gleamed at my sputters of shock. "You should know better than to tell me something is impossible. I take that as a challenge."

"There's no way." I refused to believe it. "That recovery time is not humanly possible."

"Let's test it out. Get on your hands and knees."

Moisture pooled between my thighs, but I lifted my chin in defiance just to see what he would do.

Vincent's grin disappeared. His voice turned soft but lethal. "Now, Brooklyn."

The wetness turned into a throbbing ache.

Fuck, that was hot. It shouldn't be, but it was.

If he talked to me like that outside the bedroom, we'd have a problem. But here...

A shiver of anticipation cascaded down my spine. I did as he asked while he retrieved a condom from his wallet. My breaths turned heavy again when I heard the telltale rip of foil, followed by the nudge of his cock against my entrance.

His hands gripped my hips as he pushed inside me, inch by inch. I gasped, my eyes watering again at the almost painful stretch of his cock. I'd gotten comfortable with his size while I was sucking him off, but there was a difference between taking him down my throat and taking him in my pussy. He was only halfway in, and I was already stretched so tight I might split in half if I took any more.

"Breathe," Vincent murmured. His hands grasped my hips, holding me up while a shudder rolled through my body. "That's it."

Inhale, exhale. I took a few more deep breaths until I relaxed enough for him to bury the full length of his cock inside me.

I closed my eyes, whimpers falling out of my mouth when he started moving. Then he picked up speed, his hips slamming against my ass, and those whimpers turned into moans.

The pain receded, replaced with sharp, stinging pleasure. "Yes. Yes, yes, oh, God, yes! Harder—*fuck!*" I squealed when he hit a spot inside me that made me see stars.

The world fell away, stripped of everything except the sensation of his cock pounding inside me and the sounds of his grunts mixed with my cries.

Like our kiss, this felt impossibly *right*, as though we were two lost puzzle pieces that had somehow found their way back together. Vincent filled me up so perfectly that I couldn't remember a time when he hadn't been there, and we weren't connected.

My moans were loud and desperate, and I could feel myself getting closer with every thrust.

"I'm going to come," I panted, my voice breaking. "Harder, *please*. Fuck me harder. I need to—I'm so close—"

Vincent's grip tightened around my hips. His next thrust was so brutal it sent me pitching forward on the bed, and the pressure inside me wound just a little tighter, a little closer to snapping.

"Do it," he growled. "Come for me. I want to feel that pretty little cunt drenching my cock."

That was all it took to tip me over the edge. I came with a scream, my pussy clenching around him as white-hot lightning streaked through me. It was so bright and intense, the world fractured at the edges. I was nothing more than a thousand pieces of sensation held together by one shuddering heartbeat—nerves alight, limbs trembling, mind wiped of everything except heat and pleasure and *him*.

Vincent grunted, his thrusts growing more erratic as he chased his own release. He came seconds after me, right as someone pounded furiously on the bedroom wall.

"Shut up!" My neighbor's cranky voice bled through the thin wood. "I'm trying to sleep over here!"

I was still caught up in the tail end of my orgasm, but I couldn't help my giggle. Vincent's groan of pleasure also melted into a laugh as he pulled out of me and disposed of his condom.

"Congratulations." I stretched and yawned. I always got so sleepy after sex. "You won the bet."

"Upset you lost?"

"Oh, I think I'll get over it."

He laughed again, his eyes crinkling in a way that made my chest glow. Now *that* was a real smile, not the media-trained one he'd pasted on during the auction. "Good."

He disappeared into the bathroom and returned with two small towels. He cleaned us up before sliding back into bed next to me. He wrapped an arm around my shoulders while I curled against his chest, basking in the remnants of my post-coital glow.

But now that the fun was technically over, it was time to have a long-overdue conversation.

"I told Scarlett about our kiss earlier, at the gala," I admitted.

Vincent stilled, his tone turning wary. "How'd she take it?"

"She said, and I quote, 'thank fucking God' because apparently, our repressed sexual tension was driving her nuts."

He relaxed as quickly as he'd tensed. "Classic Scarlett." He chuckled. "I should've known that would be her reaction. Not that she has any right to be angry, considering she was sneaking around with my rival behind my back for months."

"Now they're dating, and you two are besties. All's well that ends well."

His glower made me giggle again. "Asher and I are not besties."

"That's open to interpretation." I hesitated, then asked, "And us? What happens next?"

Vincent's frown softened. "What happens next is simple. We're together. Exclusively. No more games, no more uncertainty." He brushed a stray strand of hair out of my face, his voice turning tender. "In case you had any doubt, you're mine, and I'm yours. I don't care who knows. In fact, I want the whole fucking world to know because I'm done hiding."

Emotion swelled in my throat, but I swallowed it before I committed the clichéd sin of crying after sex. "It doesn't happen often, but sometimes, you know exactly what to say, DuBois."

He laughed, his arm curling more possessively around my

shoulder. "What can I say? It's one of my many talents."

"I see that." I bit my lip. "My dad's going to lose his shit."

Telling him was what I looked forward to the least. Between my relationship with Vincent and the knowledge that my dad had pulled strings for me behind my back, our next conversation was going to be a doozy.

"Probably. He stopped me after the auction and asked why you bid on me. I seriously thought he was going to throw a hood over my head and drag me to some dungeon for interrogation." Vincent grimaced. "But whatever happens, we'll deal with it. Two against one. How bad could it be?"

"Don't *say* that. Haven't you ever watched a horror movie? Asking 'how bad could it be?' is basically tempting fate." I glanced around, half-expecting my dad to pop out of the closet. Now that would be a real horror movie.

Vincent laughed again. "You're right. I'm sorry." He kissed me softly on the lips. "Lucky for us, we won't have to tell him until the morning, at the earliest. I'm thinking I should have a last meal in case I die later."

My pulse quickened at his suggestive tone. "What did you have in mind?"

Instead of telling me, he showed me. He'd been right earlier—he did have great stamina. Enough that for the next few hours, I forgot all about my dad, my neighbor, and everything else except for the man in my arms.

CHAPTER 27

VINCENT

I STAYED LONG ENOUGH AT BROOKLYN'S FLAT TO WATCH her drift off to sleep. After two more orgasms and a blowjob that nearly fried my brain, I wasn't in the best condition to walk, much less drive, but I forced myself to leave anyway.

If I had my way, I'd sleep there overnight and wake her up with breakfast...or another orgasm. Possibly both. But I wasn't living by myself anymore, and Coach would skewer me if I missed our morning run.

I parked in his drive and cut the engine. It was almost two in the morning. The windows were dark, and the house was cloaked in silence. He was most likely asleep.

I breathed a sigh of relief. We had to have a conversation about Brooklyn sooner rather than later—after tonight's auction, it was inevitable—but I needed a good night's sleep and a proper strategy first.

She was too important for me to fuck this up.

I unlocked the front door and slipped into the house. I kept my movements as quiet as possible. Coach had the supersonic hearing of a bat, but all I had to do was cross the living room, walk up the stairs, and pass by his bedroom without him hearing me.

Easy.

One step. Two steps. Three—

"Where'd you go after the gala?" The voice emanated from the darkness like a visitor from the depths of hell.

"Jesus!" I startled, my adrenaline spiking.

I searched the living room until my eyes adjusted enough to make out the familiar shapes of the furniture. Coach sat on the sofa, his burly frame unmistakable. I couldn't see his exact expression, but the crossed arms and suspicious question gave me a small hint as to how he felt.

It reminded me of when my father would wait up to yell at me every time I stayed out past curfew.

"Coach." I ironed the wrinkles of trepidation out of my voice. "You're up late."

"I was worried about you, given your intruder situation."

My shoulders relaxed an inch. "I'm—"

"I was also worried because Brooklyn hasn't answered any of my calls since the event, which is unusual." A heavy pause. "You don't happen to know why, do you?"

My muscles tensed right back up. It took every ounce of willpower not to picture what Brooklyn and I had been doing an hour ago. People couldn't read minds, but I was convinced Coach could somehow reach into my brain and squeeze out every filthy thought I'd ever had.

"She's probably sleeping." Technically not a lie. "The event ended pretty late."

Coach stood up and walked toward me. A sliver of moonlight

peeked through the window on the front door, illuminating his expression.

I expected him to look angry, which he did. But he also looked tired and a little defeated, like he'd been fighting a battle that'd lasted far longer than he thought it would.

I didn't back down, not even when he stopped a foot away from me. He wore the same suit he had on at the gala, but he'd swapped out his trainers for slippers. The sight would've been hilarious were I not drenched in cold sweat. "Now that it's just us, do you want to tell me the truth about why she bid on you at the auction?" he asked, his voice neutral.

Indecision warred inside me. I didn't want to say anything before Brooklyn got a chance to tell him herself, but they weren't on the best of terms. She might never tell him, and if she did, I could imagine their conversation devolving into cold war. They seemed to know just how to push the other's buttons.

"I didn't know she was going to bid on me." I settled on a mild version of the truth. "As for her reasons, she can tell you better than I can."

Coach's mouth tightened. I could practically see an inner war waging as he decided whether he wanted to grill me further or if he wanted to live in blissful ignorance.

"You're both adults," he finally said. "But she's my only child. She doesn't think I've been...present enough in her life, and she may be right. However, if there's anything going on that could affect either of your careers"—his glare drilled into me—"I need to know immediately. Understand?"

"Yes, sir."

"Good. Now get some rest. We have our morning run at five sharp."

I'd hoped he would forget about the run since he was up late as well, but I guess that was too much to ask.

I headed for the stairs, but the night's events kept churning in my head.

The auction. Brooklyn's bid. Coach's interrogation. Her flat and how fucking *good* it felt to give into our feelings fully and be with each other.

But as long as we kept it a secret from her dad, we could never be together in the open. What were we really afraid of anyway? She was only an employee at Blackcastle for two more weeks, which negated the club's anti-fraternization policy. It wasn't like they could fire her.

Coach would definitely lose his shit over me dating his daughter. Maybe he was overcompensating for the fact that he hadn't been a big part of her life growing up, but he seemed particularly protective of her when it came to her love life.

If he found out about us, he could punish me with tougher drills, which I could deal with, or he could ice me out.

I didn't want that. I respected him, and I'd come to see him as a second dad. But I also knew he wasn't going to come after me in a way that would affect our performance. He loved Blackcastle too much, and he wouldn't trade or bench me out of spite.

Even if he did, I'd tell him the truth anyway because if I had to choose between being with Brooklyn and staying on Coach's good side, I'd pick her. Every time, over anything.

I stopped at the bottom of the stairs, the revelation unraveling in my gut.

I could wait until the morning to tell Coach, or I could suck it up and do it now. It wouldn't make a difference. A few hours of sleep wouldn't change how I felt about her or our relationship.

I turned. "Actually, I do have something to tell you. Brooklyn didn't answer her phone because she was with me. I went to her flat after the gala."

Coach remained in the entryway. Not a single word left his mouth, and not a single movement disrupted his frame, but the air around him thickened like clouds gathering before a storm.

"When you found out we were living together, we really were just flatmates. We hadn't crossed any line that would trigger Blackcastle's anti-fraternization policy. That's no longer true." I swallowed. "Brooklyn came on my birthday trip to Budapest last weekend. We kissed. That was it. But tonight, we had a talk after the gala and, well, we're officially dating. You're the first person we've—*I've*—told. I didn't want you to hear it from someone else."

Still no reaction.

The grandfather clock ticked in the corner like the countdown timer on a bomb. The silence was painful, but I forged on.

"I understand your concerns about our relationship. Like you said, she's your only daughter, and I disagree with her conclusion that you don't care about her outside of football. I think you do care. You just don't show it in a way that she can recognize." I was toeing the line here, but Coach responded best to directness. Judging by the way his jaw worked, I'd hit a nerve. "I know I haven't had a serious relationship since I transferred to Blackcastle, and I've probably broken a few hearts along the way. I'm not proud of that. But that's because I never met anyone who made me *want* to focus on something other than football—until Brooklyn. This is real, and I'm not going to fuck it up. I promise."

Coach snorted. "You're trying to tell me you're *that* serious about my daughter."

"Yes."

"Why should I believe you?"

"You don't have a reason to. I can't say anything that'll magically wipe away your doubts. But..." The next part might actually get me punched, but it had to be said. "I'm not telling you all of this because I'm asking for your permission to date her. With all due respect, sir, that's her choice to make. Like you said, she's an adult, and she's capable of making her own decisions about her love life. However, I am telling you because I would *like* to have your blessing. You're an important part of Brooklyn's life and an important part of mine as well, so I hope you'll put aside your misgivings long enough to give us a chance. But if you don't, we're going to be together anyway. You can yell at me. You can make me run drills until I vomit. You can make me wear the fucking mascot costume and dance the 'Macarena' during halftime. It doesn't matter. I'll take it all because Brooklyn's worth it. There's nothing you can do or say that would change that."

When I said my piece, I'd imagined my words would set off an explosion—screaming, shouting, glass shattering, objects being thrown. Instead, they disappeared into the void, swallowed whole by a blanket of suffocating silence.

Coach's face appeared carved out of stone. His eyes pierced mine, and I had the eerie sense that he was mentally flaying my flesh from my bones.

But beneath the tightly leashed fury, I spotted a glimmer of something else.

Respect.

I waited, my muscles taut and my nerves frayed.

"I didn't want her mother to take her, you know." When Coach finally spoke again, his voice was quiet. I startled. That wasn't the response I'd expected. "She was so young when we divorced, and Sienna has never been the most...nurturing person. But I was coming up in my career then, and as much as I wanted Brooklyn by my side,

I thought she needed her mother. Someone who could relate to her and guide her through life in a way I couldn't. In hindsight, I'm not sure I made the right choice. But because I did make it, I missed out on some of her biggest milestones. I missed her first date, her first breakup, and her first heartbreak. I missed her senior prom and her college graduation because it was the same day as the Euro Cup final. I thought things would change when she moved to London, but it's been over twenty years. She's not the little girl I remember anymore, and I don't know how to connect with her when I've missed almost every stage of her growing up."

He fell silent. The exhaustion I'd glimpsed earlier crept back into his face, deepening the grooves around his eyes and mouth.

"I believe you think your commitment to her is sincere," he said. "But I've coached enough footballers to know how fickle they are off the pitch. Cars, women, houses. Their non-football passions rarely last in the long run. I don't have much faith that you're the exception."

I flinched. *Ouch.* He had a point about fickle footballers in general, but his assessment stung nonetheless.

"However…" Coach ground his next words out between gritted teeth. "It's clear that Brooklyn has a soft spot for you. If she wants to be with you, I won't stand in her way. Not that I could stop her if I tried." His mouth twisted with equal parts resignation and disapproval.

The tight band across my chest loosened. "Thank—"

"I'm not finished." He held up his hand, his eyes sparking with renewed ferocity. "If you hurt her in *any* way—if you so much as make her shed a single tear—I will gut you like a fish and hang you up in the park to dry. I can always find a new captain and defender. You're not irreplaceable. Is that clear?"

"Crystal." Despite his graphic threat, I couldn't stop a grin from emerging. "I hope you'll tell Brooklyn what you just told me. She'd appreciate it."

He snorted again. "The last time I took your advice, I walked in on you shirtless after you almost burned down her bloody flat."

I wisely kept my mouth shut. Some statements did not need a response for the safety of all those involved.

Just when I thought I was in the clear, he asked, "Now, what were you doing at her flat until two in the morning? Don't say talking. I wasn't born yesterday."

Was he seriously asking me that question? Didn't dads always opt for blissful ignorance in these cases?

There was no way in hell I'd ever admit to having sex with his daughter. Brooklyn could give birth to my baby, and if Coach asked, I'd claim it was an immaculate conception.

"We were playing a game." I threw out the first thing that came to mind.

"What game?"

"Uh, a variety of them."

This had to be as uncomfortable for him as it was for me. I was convinced Coach was doing this for the sole purpose of making me sweat.

"Like?" he persisted.

Of course, I forgot the name of every game I'd ever played. I scrambled for the easiest answer. "Twister?"

I wanted to take it back the second it left my mouth. Playing Twister at midnight was basically a euphemism for sex. Only an idiot would think otherwise.

Coach's eyes bore into mine. *Merde*, he was definitely flaying me alive in his mind—and probably roasting me over a fire for good measure.

Thankfully, he didn't pursue that line of questioning, but he did give me a smile that set off every alarm bell in my head.

"Fine, but I forgot to tell you, I'm changing our daily schedule," he said. "Since you had so much fun in Budapest, we need to whip you back in shape for our Boxing Day match. Meet me here at four a.m. sharp. We're going to Blackcastle for a field run."

Four a.m. was in less than two hours. Was he human or simply a Coach-shaped monster fueled by spite?

I groaned, but I didn't argue.

Fucking field runs. I *hated* those drills, and he knew it.

Even so, when I walked upstairs and finally crashed, I felt lighter than I had in months.

Brooklyn and I were together. Coach knew and tolerated it. I was one step closer to getting the Zenith deal, and I'd raised forty thousand pounds for charity in one night.

Life didn't get much better than this.

CHAPTER 28

BROOKLYN

I WOKE UP TO A SMILE, DELICIOUSLY SORE MUSCLES, AND a note from Vincent saying he'd gone back to my dad's house during the night.

Normally, I'd be more upset about a guy leaving in the middle of the night after we had sex for the first time, but I felt a curious sense of calm as I rolled out of bed and got ready for the day.

No anxiety, no worries, no insecurities. Last night's talk put all that to rest. I trusted Vincent, and given his living situation, it made sense why he had to leave.

I was dying to update my friends, but today was the last day to submit my ISNA application. Instead of texting the group chat immediately, I buckled down, put on my productivity glasses, and banged out the rest of my personal statement in the kitchen.

I wasn't sure if it was the endorphins from last night, the copious amounts of coffee, or sheer delusion, but after weeks of tearing my hair out over it, I ended up with a decent essay. It wasn't the best thing I'd ever written, but it was pretty solid, in my opinion.

I pressed Submit, and a confirmation message instantly popped up.

SUBMITTED!

CONGRATULATIONS!

You've successfully submitted your application.
All applicants will be notified of their status in late January or February.

That was it. It was done.

I took off my glasses and rubbed my eyes. I should resume my job search now that I was on a roll, but scrolling through the postings was pretty depressing. Everyone wanted crazy qualifications in exchange for shit pay and minimal benefits. I might've been able to live with that and work my way up if any of the positions sounded remotely interesting, but they didn't.

Before my Blackcastle offer, I'd applied to anything and everything, but rejecting the offer helped me realize that I didn't want just "anything." I wanted a role I was *excited* about. I just had to figure out what that was.

Maybe I should look up what my old classmates from grad school were doing. It could—

Wait a minute. I sat up straight. I'd gotten my master's degree in sports nutrition three years ago, but alumni were welcome to use the career center's resources after they graduated. Why hadn't I thought about reaching out to them before? It seemed like such a simple solution.

Granted, my program was based in the US, so its connections in London might be limited, but it was worth a shot. It couldn't be worse than doom scrolling through LinkedIn.

I pulled up my old career counselor's email and sent her a quick message. I was about to check out my school's online alumni directory when someone knocked on the door.

My heart skipped. Scarlett and Carina were at work, and there was only one other person who'd show up unannounced.

I hurried to the front door, but my smile quickly faded when I opened it and saw who was on the other side.

My dad greeted me with a stiff nod. "Can I come in?"

I quashed the petty part of me that wanted to say no. He was still my dad, and this conversation was a long time coming.

After I let him in, we took seats opposite each other in the living room. He broke the silence first. "Vincent told me everything last night. Budapest. Him visiting you after the gala. The fact that you're… together." He stumbled over the last word.

I hid a flash of surprise. Vincent and I had agreed to tell him, but I hadn't expected it to happen so fast. It'd been less than twelve hours since we got together.

Part of me was relieved. I hadn't wanted to be the one to tell my dad, and ironically, we'd swapped confessions with our family members—me to Scarlett, him to my father.

"Are you serious about being with him?" my dad asked, his tone neutral. His telltale vein wasn't throbbing in his forehead, which was a good sign. No imminent nuclear meltdown.

"I am." I answered plainly and honestly. There was no use playing coy when all our cards were already on the table.

"You told me you'd never date a footballer."

"Trust me. I'm as surprised as anyone," I said with a rueful laugh. "I really like him, Dad. I didn't want to. It would be easier on so many levels if our relationship remained platonic. But I can't choose who I have feelings for, and to be honest…I've had feelings for him for a while."

I wasn't used to talking to my parents about this kind of stuff, and the words sounded awkward coming out of my mouth.

"That's what he said too." A stern line formed between my dad's brows. "Do you know what he told me? He said that he wasn't asking, he was *telling* me that you two are together. He'd like my blessing, but if he didn't get it, he was going to be with you anyway. Because you're worth it."

I would've laughed at the mental image of Vincent talking to my dad that way had a giant lump not lodged itself in my throat.

I knew how important my dad was to his players. They all idolized him, including Vincent. That he'd risk losing my dad's permanent goodwill because he'd rather be with me...

No one had ever put me first in such an undeniable way.

Emotion swelled behind my ribcage. I blinked and tried to clear my suddenly blurry vision while my dad continued talking.

"I didn't know whether I should punch him or shake his hand for having the balls to say that to me," he said. "But I figured I shouldn't do anything and see where things go with you two, for all of our sakes."

I let the words sink in. "Does that mean you're okay with us dating?"

"I'll tolerate it," he said gruffly. "Vincent's a good captain and he has a good heart, but I don't trust any of those guys to date you, which is why I told you to stay away from them. But as he so impertinently pointed out last night, you're an adult. If I want to stay in your life, I have to let you make your own decisions. So here we are."

"Do you?" I asked quietly. "Want to stay in my life, I mean."

"Of course I do. You're my daughter." He sighed and rubbed a hand over his face. "I know our past conversations about this haven't been...the best, but you're right. I haven't been the most involved parent, and it's hypocritical of me to try and tell you what to do now. But I can't change the past. I can only do better in the future. My reactions to you leaving Blackcastle and living with Vincent may have seemed overbearing, but that was me trying to protect you. I don't…" He waved a hand around the room. "I don't know how to give you advice on relationship troubles or, I dunno, what shoes to wear with your dress. But I can set things up so that you don't get hurt. I'm not perfect, but I'm trying."

It was the most words I'd ever heard him utter in one go.

I swallowed. Part of me wanted to punish him for not being there and for leaving me with my mom for the past twenty-odd years, but did I really want to dwell on the past? Like he said, we couldn't change it. He was finally opening up, and I'd moved to London because I wanted to build a stronger relationship with him. I couldn't do that if I kept looking back instead of forward.

"I don't expect you to be perfect, Dad, but I do want you to be present. I also want our relationship to be about more than football." I took a deep breath. "Speaking of which, I know you talked to HR about extending my decision deadline. Don't ask me how I found out, but I did."

My initial anger had died down, but embers of it still glimmered whenever I thought about it.

For the first time in recent memory, my dad looked embarrassed. "I was worried when you didn't make an immediate decision. I wanted you to have enough time to think it through properly."

"I appreciate the sentiment, but by doing that, you fed into the idea that I'm getting special treatment because I'm an Armstrong. If you were concerned, you could've *talked* to me about it. That's our problem. Communication."

I expected pushback, but my dad simply said, "You're right. I've gotten so used to doing things my way that I…didn't quite think my actions through. I'm sorry," he added gruffly, his expression as uncomfortable as I'd ever seen it.

Frank Armstrong didn't apologize often, but when he did, he meant it.

I deflated, too surprised and gratified by his apology to hold on to my lingering anger.

Our conversation was calmer than I'd expected it to be, especially compared to our recent talks. But our emotions had been running high during those clashes, and there wasn't much to do after the storm except clean up the debris.

"Thank you," I said. "I'm also sorry for all the secrets I kept from you the past few months. Hopefully, we can learn to, um, communicate better in the future."

"Sure."

We sat in awkward silence for a few minutes.

"The dinner we had a few months ago. I enjoyed it," my dad said, somewhat stiffly. "We should do it more often."

I smiled, a long-held knot loosening in my gut. "I'd like that."

We gradually switched to talking about other topics—the latest blockbuster film, my trip to Budapest, our mutual loathing of creepy holiday elves. It felt stilted at times, but it was progress.

Between Vincent and my dad, I started to feel like life was looking up again—until my phone rang. I checked the caller ID, my stomach plummeting.

"Who is it?" my dad asked.

"It's Mom." My voice betrayed my shock.

I couldn't remember the last time she called without warning. Actually, I couldn't remember the last time she called, period. She was more of a text person. Less obligation to make small talk that way.

My dad's lips curled like he'd smelled something rotten. "I'll let you two chat. I should head out anyway. I have some paperwork to take care of."

We said a quick goodbye before I picked up. As the door closed behind him, part of me was worried my mom had an emergency. That was the only reason I could think of for an unscheduled call.

"Hi, Mom."

"Hello, darling," she sang. "How are you?"

"I'm good." I instantly went on alert. Okay, she wasn't in the middle of a disaster, but her cheerfulness alarmed me more. Nothing good ever came after that singsong tone. "You're calling early."

"Oh, I got up early because our nanny is off for the rest of the month and Charlie was making a fuss. Weren't you, sweetie? Yes, you were." My mother cooed at him for a full two minutes before she remembered I was on the phone. "Anyway, I'm calling because my C-section is scheduled for January—I'm sure I already told you that—and I'd love for you to be at the birth. Your new half-sibling is almost here! Isn't that exciting?"

My jaw dropped. Was she serious? "No, you didn't tell me that. Didn't you *just* get pregnant?"

"What? Of course not." She laughed. "I'm eight months along, Brooklyn. I thought you knew."

"You didn't tell me you were expecting until two months ago!"

"That can't be true."

"I have your text date stamped in my messages."

"Oh, well..." My mother sounded out of breath. The faint roar of the ocean filled the background. "I've been so busy with Charlie and Harry that I lost all track of time. Did I tell you Harry got promoted to president of his company? Between that, the pregnancy, and the bathroom remodel, I've been running around like a chicken with its head cut off."

"It must be hard to be married to a corporate executive," I

deadpanned.

"It truly is." My sarcasm went right over her head. "Regardless, I was already twelve weeks along when I found out I was pregnant. You know my periods are irregular and I didn't—Charlie, don't wave at strangers, dear. *No.* They could be bad people. What was I saying? Oh, yes, my birth. You should come. London in January is miserable anyway, and it was *so* great having you around when Charlie was born. No one gets me like you do."

All the warmth from my conversation with my dad evaporated. "I can't just fly to California on a whim."

"Why not? You moved to London on a whim."

"It wasn't on a whim. I applied to jobs here months before…you know what? Never mind." I pinched my brow. The beginnings of a headache blossomed behind my temple. "Text me the details. I'll see what I can do."

Arguing with my mom was like arguing with a brick wall. She never backed down until she got her way.

"Wonderful. I'll send them after Charlie and I get home from our walk on the beach. Say hi to Brooklyn, Charlie!" I heard his gurgling laughter in the background.

Everything in me softened. I opened my mouth to say hi when the call abruptly cut off.

She'd hung up.

I gritted my teeth. No matter how good a mood I was in, my mom had an uncanny knack for ruining it.

I fought the urge to throw my phone across the room. Instead, I texted the only person who could cheer me up and hoped to God he was free that afternoon.

Can you meet me in Covent Garden in an hour?

Covent Garden during the holidays was jam-packed with tourists and locals rushing to fit in some last-minute gift shopping. That was precisely why I'd picked it.

I'd learned that alone time after talking to my mom was always a bad thing. Her voice would echo endlessly in my head, and I needed enough noise to drown it out.

Vincent was already waiting near the Christmas market when I arrived. He wore a black coat and dark jeans with a black baseball cap pulled low over his forehead. I couldn't see his face from afar, but I'd have recognized him even if he was wearing a full ski mask. The relaxed, confident posture and aura of self-assurance were unmistakable.

"No sweats and hoodie? I'm shocked," I said when I got within earshot. "Don't tell me you dressed up just for me."

His smile flashed white beneath his cap. "I heard this is the spot to meet women during the holidays. Figured I'd give it a try."

"I hate to break it to you, but look around. There aren't many single women here. It's family and couples central."

"I don't need a ton of options."

"No?"

"No." His dimple deepened. "I just need one."

The way my chest fluttered from four simple words should be illegal. A smile spread across my face and stayed there as we slowly made our way through the crowd. The noise made it difficult to talk, so we settled into a comfortable silence instead.

It was wild to think we could go from having mind-blowing, neighbor-disrupting sex last night to this, but it worked. I'd had relationships where I only turned to the other person for one thing. Some had been for sex, some had been for comfort, and others had been for food and partying.

But Vincent encompassed everything. No matter the situation, I always wanted him there.

"My dad came by earlier," I said when we reached a quieter corner of the market. "He told me what you said." I gave him a quick summary of our conversation.

"I'm glad you two mended fences. Almost as glad as I am that he didn't punch me."

"What would you have done if he had?"

"I'd have dealt with it," Vincent said. "At the end of the day, it was a choice. I chose you."

I chose you.

It was one thing to hear my dad recount it. It was another to hear it from Vincent himself. He said it so casually, as if it was a foregone conclusion and he wasn't the first person who'd ever chosen to put me first.

Something cracked open inside me. I breathed through the ache, but despite the icy temperatures, I was a pile of melted goo inside.

Vincent and I stopped at a hot cocoa stand for refreshments. We sipped our drinks and watched the other customers pass. It was a cozy, slow-paced day, which was what I needed, but I eventually brought up my mom's call. I had to.

"I talked to my mom after my dad left." I cupped my hands around my Styrofoam cup, letting the heat warm my palms. "She has a scheduled C-section next month, and she wants me to be there for the birth."

"In California?" Vincent's eyebrow rose. "Did you do that the first time?"

"Yes," I admitted. "I was still living in San Diego then, so it wasn't a big deal. I should go again, right? It's not like I have work, and it'll be good to see Charlie. He's my half-brother. It's been a while since I've visited."

Vincent frowned. He didn't speak until we tossed our empty cups into the bin and resumed our walk through the market.

"Has she visited you since you moved here?" he asked.

"No, but it's hard to fly with a toddler."

"It's also hard to fly halfway across the world to give moral support. Her husband should be there with her. He's the dad."

"He will, but she wants me there too. That's my mom." I stopped at a stall to examine a Santa keychain. I wasn't interested in buying it, but it gave me an excuse to avoid Vincent's shrewd gaze. "She's the center of her world."

"Sure, but she's not the center of yours. You don't have to drop everything and go running every time she calls."

"Maybe not, but she's still my mom, and I do miss Charlie. Even if the rest of the trip sucks, it'll be good to see him."

Vincent opened his mouth as if to argue more, but he was cut off by a jubilant exclamation.

"Brooklyn?"

We turned at the same time. Vincent's face hardened into a scowl while I zeroed in on the familiar head of auburn hair bobbing toward us.

"Mason!" My voice lit with surprise. "Hi."

Our texts had petered out after I turned down his dinner invitation. I thought he might resent me for rejecting him, but he looked genuinely happy to see me.

"Hey." He grinned. "Fancy seeing you here. You too, Vincent," he added.

Vincent gave him a tight smile in return.

"How have you been?" I asked, just to be polite. I liked Mason well enough, but I'd rather be alone with Vincent.

While Mason launched into a monologue about his life lately, my gaze latched onto the shopping bag in his hand. It was from a sports memorabilia vendor. A Blackcastle scarf and shirt peeked from a cloud of white tissue paper.

"You got into football after all, huh?" I said after he wrapped up his story about his company's recent ugly-sweater-themed Christmas party.

"What?" He followed my gaze and blushed. "Oh, yeah, everyone in my office is obsessed with it. I figured I should start watching if I want to fit in." He fished the shirt out of the bag and thrust it at Vincent. "Actually, I hate to ask this, but do you mind signing this for me? My boss is a big fan and he'll flip out. I could really use the goodwill."

Vincent's closed-lip smile was even terser the second time around. "Do you have a marker?"

"Yep. One second." Mason dug a Sharpie from his pocket. "I always carry one on me. Notepad too. Marketing ideas can strike at anytime."

Vincent scrawled his autograph across the shirt with a little more force than necessary.

"Thanks!" Mason seemed oblivious to my boyfriend's barely concealed hostility. "I won't keep you any longer. I have a bunch more shopping to do. It was great seeing you both. Happy holidays."

I waved goodbye. "Happy holidays."

"I don't like him," Vincent said immediately after Mason was out of earshot.

I stifled a laugh at his grumpy tone. "You've told me that already."

"Well, I'm reiterating my feelings. I *really* don't like him."

"Is this because he asked me out that one time?" I teased.

I meant it as a joke, but dull red washed over Vincent's cheekbones. "No."

"Hmm."

"I'm not that jealous."

"Okay."

"I'd only be jealous of someone I considered a threat, which he isn't. He looks like a Chucky doll come to life."

I couldn't contain my laughter any longer. "No, he doesn't."

"You're blinded by the nice guy act. Trust me, that guy is weird."

Before I could respond, I spotted movement out of the corner of my eye. A woman nearby was staring at us, slack jawed. She nudged her partner, who looked over at Vincent and did a double take.

Shit. Vincent signing Mason's shirt must've tipped them off.

"Uh-oh. I think your cover's been blown. No, don't look," I whispered fiercely when Vincent turned his head. "We need to get out of here before you get mobbed."

The partner tapped one of their friends on the shoulder. The friend also did a double take when he saw Vincent. The trio started barreling toward us with determined expressions.

"Yeah. Definitely time to go." Vincent grabbed my hand and pulled me through the crowd.

I looked over my shoulder. "Oh my God, they're following us!" We picked up our pace, nearly bowling over passersby in the process. "That's unhinged."

"People are unhinged, especially during the holidays." Vincent followed my backward glance. "Jesus, they're fast! What are they on, cocaine?"

"Probably," I gasped. I hadn't planned on cardio today, but I felt like I'd been dropped into the middle of an action movie as we broke into a flat-out run through the market.

"Vincent!" the woman screamed. "Vincent, we love you!"

It wasn't funny, but the absurdity of the chase forced a giggle up my throat. Vincent's lips twitched, but he held in his laugh better than I did.

After what felt like an eternity—but was in reality less than ten minutes—we finally made it out of the market and into a quiet alleyway. I didn't hear the trio of fans screaming anymore, and when I peeked out around the corner, I didn't see anyone except for an older lady with her dog and a teenage couple in matching beanies. "I think we lost them."

I faced Vincent again, slowly catching my breath after our unexpected sprint.

That didn't last long. It took only one look before we burst into full-bodied laughter at the situation. Getting chased and harassed by fans was a real problem for him, but fuck it, laughing was better than crying.

"Running away from overzealous fans together is a relationship milestone," I said when we recovered our composure. I wiped a tear from my eye, my cheeks aching from how hard I'd laughed. "New couple goals unlocked."

Vincent's mouth curved again. "Couple," he said. "I like the sound of that."

My heart skid to a stop before beating in double time. "Yeah?"

"Yeah." He framed my face with his hands and kissed me with slow, delicious thoroughness.

Just like that, I forgot about the chase, Mason, and even my mom.

I wound my arms around his neck and kissed him back, my body melting into his.

This might've been our second kiss in the streets after Budapest, but it was every bit as good as the first.

CHAPTER 29

VINCENT

"COME ON, BLACKCASTLE!"

"Let's go!"

"We want a goal!"

The screams and chants from the stands blurred into background noise. Sweat dripped into my eyes. My lungs burned, but I was still going strong compared to half the players on the pitch.

It was Boxing Day, the day of our first post-break match, and we were playing at home. That should've given us an advantage against Newcastle, but we were still tied zero-zero in the second half with ten minutes to go, not including extra time.

One of their forwards cut inside from the right wing and sliced between our center-backs. I tracked back and intercepted, passing the ball to Stevens. He passed it on to Asher, who sprinted toward the goal but couldn't make it past the other team's defense.

The cycle continued as it had for the past eighty minutes, with our two teams trading possession of the ball but unable to score.

I sensed the mounting frustration both on the pitch and in the stands. A draw was better than a loss, but no one wanted to walk away with zero goals during our first holiday match.

The opposing striker broke past the midfield and sprinted down the left wing with the ball.

I didn't think. I ran.

My muscles ached, but I pushed harder, my eyes locked on the ball as he lined up his shot. If he got the angle right, it was going in.

I couldn't let that happen.

I slid in, timing it so my foot clipped the ball and sent it skidding away right as he kicked.

But before I could fully regain my balance, his knee collided with my ribs, knocking me backward. Sharp pain exploded up my side as I crashed onto the ground.

My teammates swarmed around me, but for once, they didn't need to argue. The referee blew his whistle and quickly made his decision.

Foul. We were awarded a free kick.

The stadium erupted with cheers, and after a quick deliberation, my team decided I should take the free kick even though that usually fell on Asher or Gallagher.

However, I'd taken plenty of free kicks in my career, and thanks to Coach's relentless conditioning over the break, I was still the freshest player on my team this late into the game.

I took a deep breath and lined up my shot. My stomach churned as I tried to drown out the noise.

"Let's have it!"

"Make it count!"

"C'mon, DuBois!"

I'd played hundreds of matches at this point. I was used to performing on a public stage, but there were certain moments when the import of it really hit me. Seventy thousand pairs of eyes, all on me, and that wasn't counting the people watching from home.

The pressure to deliver clamped down on my chest. Every player felt that pressure, but as the captain, I carried an extra weight.

Everyone's watching. Don't fuck up.

You deserve to be here.

You don't deserve to be here.

If you don't make this goal, everyone will know you're a fraud.

Voices crowded my head before I shoved them aside. This wasn't the time to wallow in imposter syndrome.

I had a goal to make.

I forced another breath until the crowd's shouts dulled to a muted roar beneath the heavy thumps of my heartbeat. A light breeze brushed my nape. My focus sharpened, locking in the angle, the curve, and the distance to the net.

My foot connected with the ball in a clean strike. It soared through the air in seeming slow motion, clearing the other team's defensive wall and sailing toward the goalkeeper. He tried to stop it, but he only managed to graze the ball with his fingertips before it sank deep into the net.

There was a beat of silence before waves of deafening cheers shook the stadium. The static muffle from my concentration fell away, and the sound washed over me all at once as my ecstatic teammates crowded around me.

A smile spread across my face as the rush of my goal finally sank in.

I fucking did it.

"Hell yeah!" Samson yelled. "That's how you take a shot!"

"Not bad." Asher slapped me on the back with a grin. "Not as good as me, but not bad."

"Fuck off, Donovan." I laughed.

We resumed our match, but the energy was noticeably lighter, at least on our side. We had several minutes and extra time left on the clock, but it was easier to defend when we were winning than try to force a tie-breaking goal.

The other team's players were tired, and their morale was down. But us?

We were fucking *back*.

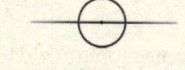

BROOKLYN

The final whistle blew minutes after Vincent's free kick, making it official.

Blackcastle had won.

"Yes!" Seth punched his fist in the air. "That's how you do it! Let's fucking go!"

I pressed my fist to my mouth, trying and failing to hide a grin. My body buzzed with so much excitement I couldn't find a proper way to express it, so I just stood there and smiled like an idiot while the rest of the team celebrated on the sidelines.

The Blackcastle players had hoisted Vincent on their shoulders and were carrying him across the pitch like a hero returning from battle. His grin dazzled even from a dozen yards away, and I was so damn proud of him I could burst.

I'd always been, and would always be, a Blackcastle supporter, but watching the matches hit different when my boyfriend was playing. The highs were higher, the lows were lower. It was like I was right there on the pitch with him, and I wouldn't have it any other way.

I finally roused myself from my daze and bypassed a giddy Seth to approach my dad. He was talking to Greely, who quickly excused himself when he saw me coming.

"Congratulations," I said. "That was a great win."

"It was okay," my dad grunted, but his eyes shone with pride.

Our relationship had improved by leaps and bounds since our talk over the break. We'd set up a weekly dinner where talking about football was off-limits, and he'd stopped scowling every time I told him I was going out with Vincent.

Things weren't perfect, but we were trying. That was what mattered.

"Are you coming to dinner tonight?" I asked.

"We'll see. I have some work to finish first. If I get it done, I'll drop by."

The team had training yesterday on Christmas Day, so Asher and Scarlett had organized a holiday dinner at their house tonight instead. Everyone at Blackcastle was invited, including the staff.

I wasn't surprised my dad was iffy on attending. He avoided big gatherings if he could help it, and since we'd had a nice father-daughter meal last night, I wasn't too upset about him potentially skipping out on what was sure to be a raucous party.

"Let me know. I'll save a plate for you if I can," I said. "No guarantees. These guys are like freaking wolves when it comes to food."

He smirked. "I will."

While he left for his post-match press conference, I checked in with Jones to see if he needed anything (he didn't) before I met Scarlett and Carina outside the stadium. We were heading to Scarlett's house early to help prep while the players spoke to the media and cleaned up.

They hugged me, their cheeks red from the cold despite the thick black-and-purple Blackcastle scarves wrapped around their necks.

"I propose we build a giant dome over the stadium for winter use," Carina said as we walked to my car. "A heated indoor pitch. How nice does that sound?"

I laughed. "Put it in the suggestion box. Maybe Vuk Markovic wouldn't mind coughing up hundreds of millions to build that dome."

"I will because we cannot keep doing this." Carina's teeth chattered. "I think I have frostbite."

"I'll buy you a portable space heater for your birthday. That way, you won't complain throughout the entire match," Scarlett said good-naturedly. "Also, just so you know, Antarctica is way colder than this."

"That's different," Carina said. "There are penguins in Antarctica. There are no penguins here to make the cold worth it."

"Maybe you'll feel differently if you date one of the players," I teased. "They can be your version of a penguin in London."

"Ha!" She snorted. "I doubt it. None of the players are anywhere near as cute."

Despite her words, I noticed a telltale blush creeping across her cheeks, but I held my tongue—for now.

We bundled into my sedan. Scarlett sat in the middle back seat, as always. Because of her accident, she had a lot of anxiety around cars. I was one of the few drivers she trusted, and I made sure to be extra careful with the speed limit when she was in the back seat.

Carina settled into the passenger seat, and we were on our way.

My nerves intensified as we got closer to Scarlett's house. Vincent and I had spent most of the break together, and it'd been a dream, filled with lingering dinners and aimless wanders through the city. But he'd told me one thing that had stuck in my mind for the past week, and I couldn't pretend it wasn't happening any longer.

"Did your dad confirm?" I glanced at Scarlett in the rearview mirror.

She nodded. "He's dying to meet you."

"Oh, great." I tried not to freak out and focused on the road instead.

I'd met Scarlett and Vincent's mom before, but I'd never met their dad. He lived in Paris, and they usually alternated holidays between their parents. But this year, he'd flown to London to celebrate with them *and* his ex-wife. It was a big deal.

"Don't worry. He'll love you," Scarlett reassured me, obviously picking up on my anxiety.

"If he doesn't, he has bad taste," Carina added.

I let out a forced laugh. "Right."

Their mom liked me. Their dad should too, right? Then again, their parents were divorced, so maybe they had different tastes in people.

My stomach cramped. I'd never felt this nervous about meeting the parents, but I'd never liked anyone as much as Vincent either. What if his dad hated me? What if he thought I wasn't good enough for his son and told Vincent to dump me?

It was unlikely, given what Scarlett and Vincent had told me about their father, but it was possible.

Scarlett's parents had skipped the match to prep the food, and their cars were already parked outside when we arrived at the house.

"Girls! It's so good to see you!" Vincent's mom was the first to greet us when we walked in. She hugged and cooed over Scarlett and Carina before stopping at me. "Oh, look at you. You're even prettier than I remembered!" She swept me up in a hug too. She was five foot one, but her big personality eclipsed her petite build. Her short blond curls smelled like fruit-scented hairspray, and her gold sequined jacket sparkled so brightly, I wished I'd brought my sunglasses.

I smiled and hugged her back. "Thank you, Ms. Hughes. You look great, too. Happy holidays."

"Happy holidays, dear." She pulled back, her eyes twinkling. "Can I just say, I'm absolutely *delighted* that Vincent came to his senses and snapped you up. I always thought you'd make the cutest couple."

"Leave the poor girl alone, Emily." A sonorous French accent interrupted before I could respond. "She just walked in, and you attack her."

Emily's smile faded as she glared at someone behind me. "I didn't attack her. I greeted her. Honestly, have you been removed from civilization for so long that you can't tell the difference?"

"I apologize for my ex-wife." A handsome man with dark hair walked over, wearing a blue Christmas sweater and holding a glass of wine. "She's very excitable, and I'm not. It's one of the reasons we divorced. That, and I hate blood pudding while she loves it."

Emily rolled her eyes and muttered something about horrid taste beneath her breath.

He ignored her and held out his hand. "I'm Jean-Paul, Scarlett and Vincent's father. You must be Brooklyn."

"Yep. I mean, yes." I blushed and shook his hand. "It's nice to meet you, sir."

"Please, call me JP. My father is the only *sir* in our family," he said good-naturedly. "So you're the girl who captured my son's heart. I'm impressed. I thought he was making you up to get us off his back about settling down."

"Oh, it's too early for that. He's still in his trial period. If he forgets to pick up his socks or put down the toilet seat, I might return him," I joked before I froze, suddenly worried I'd crossed the line with someone who wasn't familiar with my sense of humor yet.

JP blinked. But then he burst into gales of laughter, and I smiled in relief. Even though he wasn't Vincent's biological father, they shared the same infectious laugh. It was incredibly charming.

After more small talk, Scarlett, Carina, and I broke away to change and get ready for the party. We'd just come downstairs and started helping Emily with the decorations when the slam of multiple car doors echoed outside.

"The cavalry has arrived!" Adil burst into the house with dramatic flair. "Let's get this party started!"

"Perfect." Scarlett walked up to him and dumped a bouquet of flowers into his arms. "You can help set the dining table. We need more centerpieces."

His face fell. "But I was going to DJ."

"You can DJ after you set the table."

He perked up again. "Deal."

The rest of the players streamed in after him, clearly in high spirits after their win. They'd all changed out of their kits and into casual festive clothing. Not everyone could make it, but a good percentage of the team showed up, including Samson, Seth, and Noah.

Vincent was the last to walk in, but he headed straight for me before anyone else.

"There's the MVP." I stood on tiptoe to kiss him. "I'm surprised the team let you touch the ground long enough to drive. I thought they were going to parade you all the way here."

"What can I say? Your boyfriend is just that good," he drawled.

"You mean just that cocky."

"They're not mutually exclusive." He bent down to give me a longer, more searching kiss. "Hi, by the way."

Butterflies spilled into my stomach. "Hi," I breathed.

When we broke apart, I realized the entryway had fallen silent. The other guests were gathered around us in a circle, their faces plastered with shit-eating grins.

"Can I help you?" Vincent asked pointedly. He wrapped a protective arm around my shoulders.

"We're enjoying the sight of our captain in *loooove*." Samson grinned while the rest of the team catcalled us and made kissing noises.

My cheeks blazed. Our relationship was an open secret now, but this was our first time kissing in front of the team. I should've known they would tease the hell out of us for it.

"What are you all, twelve?" Vincent said dryly. "Haven't you seen people kiss before?"

"So it's official?" Stevens had brought his miniature pet pig, Truffle, who eyed us with bemusement from his arms. "You're dating?"

Vincent's arm tightened around me. "Not that it's any of your damn business, but yes."

"Vincent!" his mother scolded. "Language."

"He said damn, not cunt or fuck." JP sipped his wine. "I forgot how uptight you can be."

"Well, excuse *me* for wanting our son to behave like a proper gentleman. Not everyone can curse and smoke like a chimney, Jean-Paul."

While Vincent's parents bickered, the rest of the team carried on with their ribbing.

"Good thing Coach isn't here yet, or he'll bury you alive for touching his daughter," Gallagher cracked.

"I think it's adorable. It's about time. You've been circling each other for months." Adil held up his camera. "Smile! I'm adding this to our club's photo album."

"Sorry about them," Vincent whispered in my ear. "They're immature, but it's a rite of passage for new girlfriends."

"It's okay. It's better than getting hazed."

He laughed.

"Okay, that's enough!" Emily clapped her hands, and the catcalls fell silent. "Everyone back to work! We have a Christmas dinner to finish."

The players scattered at her direction. It was a friends and family-only event with no external vendors, so it was up to us to make it happen. However, decorations didn't take that long, and there were so many cooks in the kitchen that Emily eventually banished us to the rest of the house.

With nothing else left to do, I offered to look after Truffle while Adil roped Stevens into helping him finalize the playlist.

The dulcet tones of Mariah Carey rang through the house, followed by some sort of French rap song and "Jingle Bell Rock."

"Oh, sweetie, is it too loud for you? It's okay. Come here." I gently coaxed Truffle out from under the coffee table, where he was shivering in his mini Christmas sweater. Apparently, he was not a fan of holiday music.

He eyed me warily before inching toward my hands.

"Come here. That's it," I said as he took the final cautious step from out under the table. He grunted happily when I petted him on the head, but his ears really perked up after Vincent walked into the room.

Truffle immediately trotted over to him. The little pig bumped his nose against his shin and oinked.

"Hey, buddy." Vincent picked him up, eliciting more oinks and something that sounded suspiciously like a purr. I had no idea pigs could even purr.

"You're like the pig whisperer," I said, amazed.

"What can I say? Truffle has good taste." He petted the ecstatic pig on the head. "I missed ya, little guy. Hope Stevens has been treating you well. Pretty fucked up of him to put you in such an ugly sweater though."

An oink of agreement.

My heart freaking melted. Some women loved seeing guys hold babies, but seeing Vincent cuddle a miniature pig made my ovaries explode. He was so dominant on the pitch, but his soft side off the pitch was even more attractive.

We sat next to each other on the couch while we waited for dinner to be announced.

"My dad just texted," I said, checking my phone. "He can't make it. He's still at the office."

"Can't say I'm surprised," Vincent said. "The gala was enough socializing for him for the year."

"True." I leaned my head against his shoulder while he wrapped his free arm around me. A fire crackled five feet away, casting a glow of warmth over my face and chest.

This was what contentment felt like.

"How did your date with Leopard Dress go?" I asked.

Vincent had finally gone on his auction date earlier this week. He'd wanted to get it over with, so he'd convinced the winner to squeeze something in before Christmas, but we hadn't had a chance to debrief since he'd been so busy prepping for today's match.

"Not as bad as I thought it would. She backed down when I told her I had a girlfriend, though that didn't stop her from giving me her number at the end of the night. You know, she's not even from London? She flies here from New York every year for the auction."

"Oh!" I blinked. "That's...dedication."

"Yeah." Vincent hesitated, then asked, "Speaking of flights, did you buy your tickets for California yet?"

I hoped he didn't notice the way my shoulders stiffened. "Yeah. I leave the Friday before she's due."

I'd officially agreed to be there for my mom's C-section, but I counted down the days like a death row inmate waiting for their demise.

"Look on the bright side." Vincent rubbed my arm reassuringly. He'd definitely noticed. "At least the weather will be nicer there."

I let out a reluctant laugh. "True."

The familiar ring of his phone interrupted our conversation. Vincent picked it up, his face paling. "It's Smith."

I sat up straight and stared at him in shock. Vincent had forwarded Smith the strange text he'd received in Budapest, but other than a "message received" confirmation, the detective had been MIA.

If he was calling the day after Christmas, it had to be important, right?

I took Truffle from Vincent's arms while he answered and greeted Smith. Other than the occasional "Yes" and "I see," he didn't say much during their conversation. His expression gave even less away.

I hugged Truffle to my chest, my heart hammering.

"I understand," Vincent said. "I'll be there soon."

"What happened?" The question burst forth before he'd even hung up. I couldn't help it. I was too on edge to wait.

Vincent looked at me. His impassiveness cracked, revealing a mixture of relief and amazement. "They found the intruder."

CHAPTER 30

VINCENT

FORTY MINUTES AFTER I GOT SMITH'S CALL, BROOKLYN and I were seated in his office, listening to him explain the situation. He'd given me vague details over the phone with the promise of elaborating in person.

"It took us a while, but we were able to trace the number to the perp's burner phone," he said. "He made a mistake and connected to the internet on that phone. We found the IP address and, by extension, him. The text itself isn't incriminating enough to arrest him, but we used it to get a warrant and search his house. We found this in his bedroom."

Smith slid a photo across the table. Brooklyn and I leaned in together. Her sharp inhale mirrored the twist in my gut.

The photo showed a shrine to me. There was no other way to describe it. A giant framed photo of me sat propped against the wall. It was surrounded by news clippings, signed memorabilia, and collages of paparazzi shots. I recognized bottles of the cologne I repped as a brand ambassador and a limited-edition doll of me that came out a few years ago. It wasn't the crochet doll they'd left in my house, but it was similar enough that a shiver snaked down my spine.

"Oh my God," Brooklyn said. "That's…"

"Disturbing, yes." Smith pushed another photo across the desk. "Do you recognize him?"

I stared at the photo. A man in a Blackcastle shirt stared back. He looked like he was in his early to mid forties. Dull brown eyes, hair the color of dishwater, and a face that was unique only in its complete lack of distinction. If I passed him on the street, I wouldn't have given him a second thought.

I shook my head. "I have no idea who that is."

"Ethan Brown. He's an office manager at a paper company. Blackcastle season ticket holder, amateur sports blogger, and all-around super fan. He confessed to paying a hacker to get your private phone number and to digging through your rubbish for items to include in his DuBois shrine."

"Jesus." Bile surged up my throat.

"We've charged him with trespassing and unlawful acquisition and use of personal data. I also highly recommend you file an injunction against him."

"What do those charges mean? Will he be able to come after Vincent while he's awaiting trial?" Brooklyn asked.

She'd insisted on coming with me earlier. I hadn't argued. She was the only person I trusted to keep me levelheaded in situations like this.

"There won't be a trial," Smith said. "Trespassing is a civil offense. While his obtainment of private information is in breach of the Data Protection Act, it doesn't mandate imprisonment, especially since Vincent wasn't harmed. The most we can do is fine him."

My stomach sank. That was it? After months of anxiety and being on edge, all the perp got was a fine and a slap on the wrist?

"What about the break-in?" I said. "He left that doll in my house."

"He hasn't admitted to that crime, likely because he knows it carries a heavier sentence. We don't have concrete evidence tying him to the break-in yet, but we'll find it. We know who he is now." Smith swept the photos back into a folder. "That's why I suggested you file an injunction. If he violates it, it'll help us build our case."

"Did he say why he's fixated on Vincent in particular?" Brooklyn's brow furrowed. "What's the point of all this if he—Ethan—doesn't want anything from him?"

"Fans often form parasocial relationships with celebrities. Sometimes, they cross the line, as is the case here," Smith said. "There's no other rhyme or reason to it."

The whole thing seemed anticlimactic, but I supposed that was better than the circus a trial would bring. I filled out some paperwork, thanked Smith for his help, and left.

"I'm shocked they found the perp," Brooklyn said on our way back to my car. "I was convinced they were just sitting on the case."

"Me too." I made a mental note to call my lawyer tomorrow and file that injunction ASAP. "I guess that's it. Case closed, as long as the guy stops harassing me."

"I think he will. Now that he knows the police are onto him, he wouldn't be stupid enough to pull something new."

"Maybe." But something hitched in my mind, a missing piece that snagged like a thread on a nail. "Do you find it weird that he went to so much trouble to cover his tracks with the doll and photo, but got sloppy enough to use the internet from his burner?"

"A little," she admitted. "But everyone slips up eventually. Maybe he didn't know you could trace a burner from internet usage. I wouldn't worry too much about it. Just enjoy being free for now."

We reached my car. "Maybe."

"The best part is, you don't have to live with my dad anymore—unless you want to," Brooklyn teased. "You guys must have bonded a lot during those early morning runs."

"Sure, we bonded the way a captive bonds with their kidnapper." She laughed. My lips curved in response.

She was right. I should stop overthinking the situation and take the win. If Ethan turned out to be a vengeful monster who wouldn't back off even with a injunction…well, I'd cross that bridge when we got there.

It was the holidays. We'd won our first post-break match, and I was with the girl of my dreams. I wasn't going to put a damper on it by worrying about hypotheticals.

"My parents like you," I said as I started the engine and pulled onto the road. "They're usually in a snippy mood when they're near each other, but they stopped arguing long enough to talk to you. It's impressive."

"I like them too. I think they're hilarious." Her voice softened. "But the divorce must've been hard on you and Scarlett."

"The divorce itself was pretty civil, but the hardest part was moving to a new country." I gave her a crooked smile. "On the bright side, I learned fluent French. Girls ate it up whenever I traveled abroad."

"Of *course* that's what you cared about." Brooklyn rolled her eyes, but her face was filled with good humor. "Honestly, I love that your parents can be in the same room together. Mine can't even stand hearing the other's name."

"Was their split that bad?"

"Oh, yeah. My mom hasn't stepped foot in the UK in twenty years, and she actively hates football. But from what they've told me, they were never compatible as a couple. Their personalities were too different. But they were also young and beautiful, and...things happened. Then they had me, and they were tied together for life." Her mouth twisted into a wry smile. "I don't think my mom ever forgave me for that."

I had a lot of choice words to say about her mother, but I kept them to myself—for now. "She's lucky to have you."

"Maybe." Brooklyn stared out the window. The trace of sadness in her voice made me want to hop on a plane to California right that second. Fuck propriety. Anyone who treated Brooklyn as shittily as her mum treated her deserved a verbal lashing.

Since I couldn't do that, I settled on the next-best option. "Would you rather head back to the party or go somewhere else?"

When we left, we gave everyone a shoddy excuse about helping Coach with a "work emergency." That'd been almost two hours ago. The party was likely over. If it wasn't, we could easily explain away our absence by saying we wanted "personal time." No one would question us, given we were an official couple now.

"Where did you have in mind?" Brooklyn sounded intrigued.

I grinned. "It's your last week at Blackcastle. I think you should say a proper goodbye."

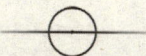

I made it a point to get to know everyone on Blackcastle's staff, from management to the maintenance staff. They were all crucial to the success of the team, and I actually enjoyed talking to them. Most of them anyway. I remembered their birthdays, bought them Christmas gifts, and asked them about their children's graduations and anniversaries. It was my way of appreciating them for the work they did.

As a result, I was beloved by the staff—and one of the perks of being beloved was my ability to ask for wild favors on short notice, like tonight.

"Where are you taking me?" Brooklyn sounded wary. "It smells like...dirt. And mildew."

"You'll find out soon."

"We're not in the back alley of the Angry Boar, are we? I know it's the team's favorite pub, but I can say goodbye to Blackcastle in other ways."

"Patience, buttercup." I laughed. "We're almost there."

I'd fashioned a blindfold out of her scarf and made her wear it before I drove us here. I'd expected her to figure out where we were going from my hints, but her brows furrowed with confusion as I guided her through the tunnel.

Nelson had pulled through for me, and the key weighed heavy in my pocket.

Two minutes later, we stopped in front of a metal door. I unlocked it, gently pushed Brooklyn through, and untied her blindfold. "Open your eyes."

The cashmere material fell away. She blinked and look around, her jaw going slack.

Rows and rows of empty seats surrounded us, stretching up to the night sky. Massive stadium lights cast a soft glow over the pitch, and the air smelled like a mixture of fresh grass and cold winter.

Blackcastle stadium.

It was electric when seventy thousand people packed the stands, their cheers so loud it shook the very earth. But when it was empty and still, with nothing but silence and the dreams of glory echoing across the pitch?

It was magic.

"How did you do this?" Brooklyn breathed.

"I had some help from the head groundskeeper. I told you I can charm anyone."

The night guard also cut off the security feed to the pitch for us so we didn't get in trouble. We had two hours before he needed to turn the cameras back on, but that was more than enough time.

"Normally, I'd humble you a bit, but I'll give you a pass this time. This is too cool." She walked onto the pitch, her eyes shining. I followed her, soaking in her awed expression. I wished I could make her look that happy every day. "I've never been here at night. It's beautiful."

"It's my favorite place in the world when it's like this. Match days are nice, but when it's empty and you can really take a good, hard look at it from this perspective...nothing else beats the feeling."

I'd played for Blackcastle for years, but nights like these still hit hard. This was my childhood dream. I'd fought and scraped and worked my ass off my entire life to stand here, to play here, to be part of history in the only way I knew how.

In moments of doubt, I wasn't sure I deserved it. I couldn't wrap my head around the fact that I'd actually made it, and I kept waiting for some higher authority to drag me out and lock me up for being an imposter.

Tonight, those doubts were nowhere to be found. It was just Brooklyn and me and the magic of an empty stadium.

I sat on the middle of the pitch and patted the ground. She sank beside me, her laugh tickling my skin when I tugged her so we were both lying on our backs instead.

"Every Blackcastle member should experience this at least once before they leave," I said. "There's no better goodbye."

She stared up at the sky, her expression wistful. "No, there isn't."

We fell silent. It was a content, comfortable quiet, the kind where we didn't have to say a word to know what the other was feeling.

I listened to Brooklyn breathe, my gut tightening when it hit me that this was really it. In a few days, she'd no longer work at Blackcastle. I wouldn't see her face every time I walked into the training facilities or hear her rhapsodize about the importance of carbs during a presentation.

Of course I could still see and talk to her any time I wanted to, but it wasn't the same. This was the end of an era, and I'd never been great with goodbyes.

Brooklyn laced her fingers through mine, as though she could hear my thoughts and wanted to reassure me. We weren't wearing gloves, and despite the winter chill, her skin was warm and soft against mine.

"This is the best Christmas present," she said. "Thank you."

"Better than the new state-of-the-art blender I bought you? That model hasn't even hit the market yet. I had to pull a lot of strings to get my hands on it early."

Her laugh washed over me. "I do love that blender, but yes, this is better."

"Good. I was testing you. If you'd said no, I would've been offended."

"You can be such a pain in the ass even when you're being sweet."

"It's one of my superpowers." My eyes traced the night sky, searching for stars. "I don't usually like the holidays, but this year has been an exception."

Brooklyn turned her head to face me. "Why don't you like the holidays?"

I fell silent. The lights hummed in the distance as I debated how much to tell her. No one knew how I felt about the season except Scarlett. I put on a good show for my parents, so they thought I loved it when my true feelings were mixed at best.

"It makes me think of my birth mum," I finally said. "It's stupid because I never knew her. We've never spent Christmas together, and I have an actual family who I can celebrate with. But there's something about the holidays that just…gets to me. Tis the season, I guess."

"Have you talked to your parents about her?" Brooklyn asked softly.

"No. They don't know anything about her. Apparently, she was adamant she wanted no contact when she gave me up, and she forbade the agency from sharing any personal details." Pressure ballooned behind my ribcage. "I feel like shit sometimes because it's been almost thirty years, and I still think about meeting her one day."

"That's normal. Most adopted children are curious about their birth parents."

"Not Scarlett. She genuinely doesn't think about hers at all, and I don't know why I can't be the same. Our parents are great. I'm so fucking glad they're my family, but it feels like a betrayal every time I think about my birth mum. It's like my desire to get to know her means I think my parents aren't…enough, but I can't help it." The pressure climbed into my throat. "Mostly I want to know why she gave me up. I was a baby. What did I do so wrong that she wanted me out of her life forever?"

"Vincent." Brooklyn propped herself up on her elbow, her voice suddenly fierce. "There is *nothing* wrong with you. Like you said, you were a baby. Completely innocent. And there are so many reasons why people choose the adoption route. Maybe she was too young to take on that responsibility, or she didn't have the resources to do so. Maybe she was forced to give you up."

It was the same thing I'd told myself on many occasions.

"I know, but that doesn't stop the situation from messing with my head." I let out a rueful laugh. "I went to therapy for a bit. It was earlier in my career, but it didn't help much. The only thing it did was make me realize that one of the reasons I'm so obsessed with winning is because I want her to see it. I want to be so fucking successful that she can't help but reach out, or at least regret giving me up. I want to be everywhere so she can't turn around without seeing my face. It's a little bit of spite, and a little bit of hope. I don't know what I'd say to her if we met, but I doubt that'll happen anyway. I'm captain, I won a World Cup, and I have billboards and sponsorships coming out of my ass. If she hasn't reached out by now, she never will."

The words spilled out of their own accord. Brooklyn didn't interrupt. She just watched me, her expression gentle, as I reached the part I'd never, ever told anyone. Not even Scarlett, who knew the half-truth.

"So..." I swallowed, the confession sticking in my throat before I forced it out. I had to get it out, or I was going to choke on it. I'd been keeping it in for far too long. "I hired a lawyer to find her for me. My adoption records were sealed, but the attorney is the best in her field. She was able to locate my birth mum somehow. I know exactly who she is and where she lives. I've known for years."

There was an audible catch in her breath.

"Charleen Davies, age forty-seven. Lives in Bristol. Works as a paralegal, married to a history professor at the local university. One kid, a son, who's currently attending uni." I rattled off the information dispassionately, like I was reciting numbers from an old phone book. "I called in sick and booked a train to Bristol the day after I found out who she was. I went to her house. It sounds creepy when I say it, but I just...I wanted to see what it looked like. What her life was like. I didn't knock on her door, but I saw her come out with her husband and son. They were dressed up for dinner, and they looked...

happy. *She* looked happy, as though she'd gotten the exact family she'd always dreamed of. And I realized in that moment that I didn't exist to her. Somehow, I just knew that when she gave me up, she'd wiped me from her memory. My lawyer couldn't find any information on my birth father, so I assume he wasn't in the picture when I was born. I was her mistake, and her current family is her do-over."

Brooklyn's hand tightened around mine. She was breathing heavier, her eyes glossy as I finished my confession.

"I came back to London that same night, but I still have her number programmed into my phone. I couldn't bring myself to delete it. I'm not tempted to contact her most of the time, but certain days are hard. Christmas. My birthday, and hers. Especially hers."

My phone burned a hole in my pocket. I wanted to take it out and chuck it into the stands, where it'd hopefully be lost forever.

"October third," I said quietly. "Every year, I want to call and wish her a happy birthday, which is so fucking stupid. The last thing she wants is to hear from me. If she does, I'm sure she'll contact my parents and tell them to keep me away. It would break their hearts. They can't know I've been sneaking around behind their backs, digging up information on my birth mum. So I set a Do Not Contact reminder for the hard days. It helps."

Clarity sharpened Brooklyn's gaze. "That's why you had the—" She broke off, her face reddening.

"The calendar reminder for my birthday?" I finished wryly. "I figured you saw, but I appreciate you not asking about it."

"I didn't mean to snoop," she said, sounding embarrassed. "Your phone kept lighting up with new texts, and the reminder was right at the top."

"It's okay. You know the whole story now anyway." I let out another, more self-conscious laugh. "I didn't mean to trauma dump on you the day after Christmas. This was not the Blackcastle goodbye I'd imagined. We were supposed to run around the pitch. Dance to shitty music from my phone. Make out. Fun stuff, not...whatever the hell I just did."

"Joke's on you, I love a good trauma dump. It makes me feel like I have my shit together when other people's lives are a mess."

My chuckle echoed in the night air. "Then we're a perfect match."

"I think so." Brooklyn squeezed my hand. "You can tell me anything at any time, you know. And whatever happens with your birth mom, I'll support it a hundred percent. If you call her for her birthday? Great. If you show up at her house to rub your success in her face? I'll go with you. If you keep her number and need a distraction a few times a year? I have plenty of ideas. If you delete her info and move on? Well..." She shrugged. "You won't need me, but I'll support the hell out of that too."

God, I didn't know what I'd done in a past life to deserve her, but if I could go back and give that version of me a big, fat thank-you, I would.

"Ride or die, huh?" I tried to keep my voice steady.

She smiled. "Like Bonnie and Clyde."

A gust of wind swept past, tousling her hair. I tucked a stray strand behind her ear, my fingers lingering against her cheek for a beat longer than necessary.

Her smile faded as the silence of the moment coiled around us, tight and breathless with anticipation.

"You ruin me," I said, my voice barely there.

Then I leaned in, my lips brushing hers in the softest of kisses, and my ruination was complete.

CHAPTER 31

VINCENT

THE KISS STARTED OUT AS NO MORE THAN A BRUSH OF warmth in the night, but that was enough to unravel me. It wasn't about the kiss itself—it was about the woman, and the fact I'd never craved someone the way I did her.

Her scent, her taste, the sound of her moans—I needed them the way I needed oxygen. In my lungs, in my blood, in every fucking molecule of my body. She was wrapped up around me, her body pressed against mine, yet I still ached from missing her.

I cupped the back of her head, drawing her closer. I slid my other palm over her thigh, savoring the hitch in her breath when I grazed the hem of her dress.

"Are you cold?" I asked huskily. "We can go inside."

Heat seeped through her tights and seared into my palms, but we were still in the middle of the pitch during winter.

She shook her head. "No," she breathed. "I'm burning up."

A slow smile spread across my face. "Good."

I crushed my mouth to hers again. Her lips parted in a soft moan, and I took full advantage, sliding my tongue against hers in a hungry, possessive sweep that made her gasp.

The kiss deepened, turning frantic, almost ravenous.

She tugged at my coat; I pushed her dress up around her waist and yanked her tights and underwear down. Despite our layers of clothing, we somehow shed them effectively enough for me to feel the press of her skin against mine.

She was smooth and warm and so fucking soft as she wound around me, urging me on with each movement. I angled her head and kissed her harder, threading my fingers through her hair and savoring her minty sweet taste.

I could stay like this forever. There could be an earthquake, a cyclone, I didn't care. The world could end, and I'd still be right here with her, where I was meant to be.

"Vincent." Brooklyn moaned, her breath catching. "I want to feel you inside me. Right now."

Fuck. She was going to be the death of me, and she didn't even know it.

I moved to roll her on her back, but she shook her head. "I want to be on top." She flipped us over so I lay on the pitch while she straddled me, looking like a goddamn goddess backlit by the stadium lights.

Her hair fell in messy, tangled waves over her shoulders. Her face was flushed and her mouth was swollen from our kiss, but the devilish gleam in her eyes sent blood rushing straight to my cock. So did the peaked points of her nipples, which poked through the delicate silk of her dress.

"You sure you want to be in charge tonight, buttercup?" A noticeable strain tempered the amusement in my voice. I was rock-fucking-hard, and the only thing I could focus on was how much I wanted to tear that silk away with my teeth and feast on her nipples.

Brooklyn smiled, the gleam in her eyes growing brighter. She freed my cock from my trousers and rolled on the condom she'd gotten out of her bag.

"Sometimes I like to be in the driver's seat. So sit back..." She wrapped her hand around my cock, and I had to bite back a stream of expletives. "Relax..." She guided me toward her pussy. "And enjoy the ride."

She sank onto me with agonizing slowness. I could feel every inch of my cock sliding inside her while she clenched around me, sending electric bolts of pleasure down my spine.

My head fell back as my breaths grew heavy. "Fuck, baby, you feel so good."

Brooklyn moaned. She placed her hands on my chest to steady herself as she rode me, and if I wasn't already on the brink of losing control, her little whimpers and the wet sounds of her pussy impaling itself on my cock would've sent me there.

Sweat broke out on my skin. I grabbed her hips, forcing her to slow down so I didn't come before I was ready.

"What's wrong?" she teased breathlessly. "Can't handle it?"

My mouth quirked even as a dangerous tone slid into my voice. "Don't make me turn you over and fuck that brattiness out of you."

Blotches of pink blossomed across her face and chest. "You wouldn't dare," she said, but the way her pussy spasmed at my words told a different story.

"Try me."

Brooklyn leaned forward, taking me at a different, deeper angle. I hissed in pleasure.

She smiled, back in control. "I'll do you one better. Remember that bet we made the first time we had sex? Let's change it up. I bet I can make you beg to come tonight."

"Sweetheart, if you can make me beg, you deserve to win."

It was a promise as much as it was a challenge, and Brooklyn never shied away from either.

She leaned back and rode me harder, squeezing her muscles so tightly it almost made me black out. When I finally returned to my senses, I grabbed the back of her head and pulled her back down for a rough kiss. I reached between us without breaking the kiss and rolled her nipple between my fingers, tugging and pinching in a way that I knew drove her wild.

Brooklyn made a noise somewhere between a moan and a cry. "Bastard," she whispered.

I smiled against her mouth. "All's fair in sex and war."

She pushed me back down. "We'll see about that."

We settled into a desperate, breathless rhythm—her riding me to the edge, then pulling back right before I came, while I did everything I could to hold back a cursed plea.

But eventually, I broke.

This was Brooklyn. I was too lost in her not to.

"*Fuck*." I cursed when she gently scraped her nails down my chest and clenched around me again. My breathing quickened. A ball of electric heat gathered at the base of my spine, building and building but never quite reaching its peak thanks to Brooklyn's fast and slow rhythm—fast enough to bring me to the edge, then slowing down once I got there. "Enough games. Let me come, sweetheart."

She scraped her nails back up under my shirt and across my nipples. Another jolt of pleasure buzzed through my nerves. "Only if you say please," she purred.

"Please." My breaths turned into pants when she moaned and picked up speed again.

I didn't care about the damn bet anymore. Brooklyn needed this as much as I did—I felt it in the way her muscles quivered and heard it in the way her voice hitched. I wanted to reach the peak with her. Right now, together.

I grabbed her ass, my fingers digging into the soft flesh as I slammed my cock up at the same time she thrust downward. Our groans and grunts blended together as she rode me faster and harder until finally, *finally*, we came at the same time with loud cries.

The sound echoed through the stadium as we caught our breath, our bodies trembling from the aftershocks of our shared orgasm.

"I won," she said with such a proud smile that I couldn't help but laugh.

"You did. Making me say 'please' is no small accomplishment." I rubbed my thumb against the soft skin of her hip. She was still straddling me, and I could feel my cock twitching again.

It should be impossible, but when it came to her, I was insatiable.

"I made you beg," Brooklyn corrected.

"Hmm. I wouldn't count one 'please' as begging."

She tsked with mock disappointment. "Don't be a sore loser."

Sore loser, huh? We'd see about that.

I gave her another minute to bask in her triumph before I grabbed her and flipped her over so she was on all fours. I pinned her beneath me, nudging her legs open with my knee and replacing my used condom with a fresh one.

Her breath stuttered. "What are you doing?" she squealed.

"You want to talk about begging?" My lips grazed her ear. "Don't act so smug when I haven't had my turn yet."

She squirmed against me, pressing her ass against my groin. My cock thickened, growing harder by the second. "Oh, I doubt you can beat my record."

"Let's see, shall we?" I reached for my phone and set the timer.

Brooklyn stilled. "Are you seriously setting a *timer* for making me come?" I could hear the shock in her voice.

"I like clear rules and guidelines," I explained. "I even gave you an extra minute out of the goodness of my heart."

"You are such an arrogant—*ungh*!" She let out a gurgled cry when I slammed into her. She was still soaked from our last session, and I managed to bury myself balls deep with ease.

"What was that?" I taunted.

Her hands curled into fists against the grass. "I said, you're such a...a...oh, *God*." She cried out again when I pulled out and pounded into her again, angling my cock so it hit her most sensitive spot.

I'd acquainted myself with her body so intimately that I knew exactly how to drive her crazy. She was so goddamn responsive, and I picked up on every detail.

The way her breath hitched when I played with her clit. The way she bucked against me when I alternated between long, smooth strokes and shorter, harder thrusts. And the way her cunt clenched and convulsed when I held her down, fucking her mercilessly in the middle of the pitch until she was begging me to let her come.

"Please. Vincent, please," she sobbed when I slowed my thrusts again. "I need to—let me—I need..."

"What do you need, sweetheart? Use your words." I leaned over her, one hand on her hip and the other braced on the ground next to her. Heat poured off her body, and I wanted to bury myself in her neck, breathing in her scent and feeling the wild flutter of her pulse against my skin.

I got off on competition, but I got off on pleasuring her more. Seeing her smile, hearing her moan—it was better than the world's strongest aphrodisiac.

"I need to come." Brooklyn whimpered. "*Please*. Let me come."

I kissed her tenderly on the shoulder. "All you had to do was ask."

I thrust into her again. At the same time, I reached around and pressed my thumb against her swollen, needy clit.

Just like that, she came apart, her scream tearing through the night right as the timer went off. It didn't take me long to join her, and when the throes of our orgasms finally receded, we collapsed next to each other in an exhausted heap.

"Let's call that a tie," she said drowsily. "One-one."

I chuckled. "I'll put it on our scoreboard." I pulled down her dress and adjusted the rest of her clothes, covering her up with her coat before I got dressed.

Now that we were cooling off, I felt the bite of the wind again. We should head inside soon, but I wanted to stay just a moment longer so I could soak her in—her happy smile and sparkling eyes, the rosy blush on her cheeks as she stretched her arms over her head.

"I take back what I said earlier. *This* was the best gift ever," she said. "Having sex on a football pitch? Inspired."

"I aim to please." I gave her a soft kiss. "Now let's get out of here before we get sick, or someone figures out we've defiled the pitch."

"I can finally check that off my bucket list. I never thought it would happen." Brooklyn's smile softened as she wrapped her arms around my neck. She brushed her lips against mine. "Happy Christmas, DuBois."

Warmth surged through my chest. My throat tightened, but I pulled her closer and murmured, "Merry Christmas, buttercup."

And as we walked back to my car, her hand in mine, I realized that the most dangerous person in my world wasn't the intruder or my birth mom or any rival footballer.

It was Brooklyn, because she was the only person alive with the power to unravel me.

CHAPTER 32

BROOKLYN

THE REST OF THE HOLIDAYS PASSED IN A BLUR. BEFORE I knew it, it was the last day of my internship.

Human Resources had organized a goodbye party for the interns in the kitchen. The "party" consisted of half a dozen balloons and a gluten-free cake, but it was the thought that counted.

We'd said goodbye to the players earlier, in case we didn't see them after training. They'd all signed individual cards for Henry and me, and the petty side of me was gratified to see I got personalized messages while his contained only their signatures.

"I guess I'll see you around. Or not." Henry popped a piece of cake into his mouth. He chewed, swallowed, and said, "I'm serious about that job though. If you want to join the Hydralade family, I can get you through the door. You might have to work your way up though, since you don't have any experience in product development. *But* there are plenty of great admin and support roles."

"Henry." I deliberately set the cake knife down. "I would rather go to the manufacturing plant, flood it with your shitty sports drink, and walk into the middle of the flood wrapped in live electric wires."

"What does that even mean?"

"It means I would rather electrocute and drown myself at the same time than work for your family's company, Henry." I emphasized his name a second time.

He blinked. "Well, that's a little dramatic, but point taken. Your loss." He shrugged and nabbed another slice of cake before sauntering out.

I blew out a breath. Interacting with him wiped away any sadness I had about leaving. Thank God I wouldn't have to work with him again.

Most of the staff had already trickled out. Jones and Lizzie were the only two left in the kitchen. They were deep in conversation, but then Lizzie excused herself, and it was just Jones and me.

He came up beside me as I threw away the empty paper plates. "Have you heard back from ISNA?"

"Not yet. Finalists don't get announced until late January or February." I wasn't sure what to expect, but I had hope that I would at least make it to the next round.

"Ah, right." Jones drummed his fingers against the table. "Well, good luck. Let me know how it goes."

"Thank you." I didn't point out that he could look up the list of finalists himself on ISNA's website. "I appreciate you writing the recommendation. And I appreciate everything you've taught me during this internship. I learned a lot."

Despite my complicated feelings about his rigid ways, his favoritism toward Henry, and the obvious boys' club at Blackcastle, I meant what I said. Working at Blackcastle had been a learning experience like no other, and as the minutes ticked down toward the end of the day, the lump in my throat grew bigger.

"You've been a great intern," Jones said. "I'm sad we won't have you with us moving forward, but I wish you the best in your future endeavors." He gave me a stiff hug.

We said our goodbyes, and that was it.

I checked the clock. It was officially after work hours. Training ended half an hour ago, and most of the players were probably already gone.

I left the kitchen and walked to the changing room. I didn't know why, but I had to see it before I left.

As expected, it was empty when I got there. I heard the faint sound of a shower running, but I was the only person in the changing room itself.

I sank onto a bench and soaked it all in. My night at the stadium with Vincent had been magical, but this was the heart of the club. It was where I'd worked with the players, where we laughed and joked around, where we celebrated our victories and mourned our losses.

I was going to miss it.

I blinked back a prickle of tears. *Get it together.* I'd made the choice to leave. I couldn't second-guess myself now.

The shower squeaked off. I startled, but before I could leave, Vincent walked out, a towel slung around his hips. He cocked an eyebrow when he saw me.

"Just taking it in while I still can," I said in response to his unasked question. "Your timing is freakishly perfect. Were you waiting to see if I'd be here before you walked out half naked?"

I wouldn't be surprised. Sometimes, it felt like he knew me better than I knew myself.

"Do I look like the type of person who would do that?"

"Absolutely."

If I hadn't been sitting, his grin would've knocked me off my feet.

He walked to his locker, a stray droplet of water sliding past the ridges of his abs and into his towel.

Despite my earlier sadness, I had the brief urge to trace the droplet's journey with my tongue. We'd already defiled the pitch. Might as well add the changing room to that list.

"Are you all packed for tomorrow?" He pulled a shirt over his head.

I sighed. Talk about ruining the view.

"Yeah, but you don't have to drive me to the airport. I can take a cab." I was flying to San Diego tomorrow morning, which was another reason it felt like my emotions were being fed through a meat grinder.

The prospect of seeing my mom always exacerbated my worst moments.

"Screw that. I can't let my girlfriend leave the country without seeing her off." Vincent finished dressing and sat next to me.

I breathed in his clean shower smell, butterflies taking wing at the word *girlfriend*. I wasn't used to it yet, but I liked the way it sounded. A lot.

"I'll be back Tuesday," I said, amused. "It's not like I'll be gone for a year."

"Four days without you is a long time, buttercup."

"Getting needy already, DuBois?"

"I always need you." His eyes gleamed with playfulness, but there was a smooth, dark edge to his voice that drove any lingering nostalgia out of my mind. Heat curled low in my stomach.

"Is there anyone in the showers?" I asked.

He shook his head. The playful gleam vanished, replaced with something more wicked. "We should—"

"*Ahem.*"

Vincent and I jumped apart like we'd been burned.

"Hi, Dad."

"Hi, Coach."

Our voices overlapped as we stared sheepishly at my dad. He stood at the entrance to the changing room, his face creased with a glower. "What are you two doing here? Alone?"

"Talking," Vincent quickly said.

"I wanted to see the changing room one last time before I left," I added.

"I stayed late so I could drive her home."

"We're innocent."

Okay, my last statement wasn't that of an innocent person, though it was, ironically, correct. Just because I'd been *thinking* about shower sex didn't mean we'd *engaged* in shower sex.

Semantics. They mattered.

My dad's eyes narrowed. "Uh-huh."

He hadn't guilt tripped me about leaving Blackcastle since our talk. He was, however, still ornery every time he saw Vincent and me alone together. He hadn't been there for my past boyfriends, and I suspected he was struggling with how to handle my love life.

"Get out of here," he finally said. "You have an early flight tomorrow. You need sleep." He paused, then added, "But if you want to skip California altogether, I'll handle the hurricane."

The "hurricane" was my mother, but not even my father could save me from the shitstorm that would ensue if I missed her C-section.

"It's okay, Dad. I'll be back before you know it."

Vincent and I left quickly before he changed his mind and decided to interrogate us some more about our changing room plans.

"Good thing I don't live with him anymore," Vincent said as I turned in my employee badge to HR. He'd filed an injunction against Ethan Brown and moved back home the weekend after Christmas. "Or else he'd be chaperoning your visits like a primary school teacher."

I laughed. "Yeah. That's a part of his parenting I never missed."

I gathered my belongings from the intern office. Vincent placed his hand on the small of my back as we headed toward the exit. I tried to think of anything I might be forgetting, but I came up with nothing.

I'd said my goodbyes. I'd done my farewell tour of the facilities, and I'd made my peace with leaving. The end of my internship wasn't the end of the world. I could still see the people I wanted to see outside the club, and while it'd be weird not to work with Vincent every day, we'd adjust. We always did.

The lump in my throat slowly dissolved.

I didn't know what the next chapter of my life would bring, but when I walked out of Blackcastle for the last time as an employee, I felt more hopeful about the future than I had in months.

CHAPTER 33

BROOKLYN

SAN DIEGO WAS EIGHT HOURS BEHIND LONDON, SO I landed bright and early in California the following day. I hadn't been back since I moved, and the salty ocean air sent a wave of nostalgia crashing through me when I exited the airport.

My mom and stepfather knew when I'd be arriving, but Harry was at work and my mom was overseeing renovations at their house, so I shelled out the absurd fees for an airport taxi to my hotel.

They had plenty of guest rooms at their place, but I would rather tear my hair out than spend an entire weekend with them.

I stared out the window as the city whizzed by. It was weird seeing the familiar spots from my childhood when I'd been gone for so long. The smoothie shop I'd frequented, the movie theater where I'd had my first (horrible) kiss, the stretch of beach where I'd learned how to surf...they all seemed so quaint, like they belonged to a different life.

The nostalgia was there, but that was it. Most of my old friends had moved away, and I wasn't close to those who'd stayed anymore. Besides my mom and Charlie, I had nothing tethering me to the city.

The realization hit hard. I'd lived in the UK for eighteen months, but a small part of me had viewed it as a temporary thing. I'd assumed I would move back to California at some point, but the thought of leaving London felt like a knife in my gut.

Vincent was there. My dad and my friends were there. My *life* was there.

"Miss!" The cab driver glanced at me in the rearview mirror. Judging by his impatient tone, he'd been trying to get my attention for a while. "We're here."

"Right. Thank you," I said, flustered.

I paid and dragged my luggage to the check-in desk, still reeling from a revelation that, in hindsight, should've been obvious. However, I didn't have time to dwell on what it meant. Maybe it didn't mean anything at all. It wasn't like it changed my plans in any way.

Thankfully, my room was ready despite my early arrival. I had time for a quick shower and a change of clothes before I needed to be at my mother's house. She'd scheduled our "arrival check-in" before her weekly salon appointment, and if there was one thing she hated, it was being late to the salon.

I called an Uber. Thirty minutes later, it dropped me off in front a Mediterranean-style mansion that was three times the size of my childhood home. My stepfather Harry was a big corporate executive, and while his house wasn't as decked-out as Vincent's or Asher and Scarlett's, it still occupied several thousand square feet of prime beachfront real estate.

My mom would've never settled for anything less.

I rang the doorbell, expecting their housekeeper to greet me. Instead, Harry answered it himself. "Brooklyn! So wonderful to see you. Come in. I hope you had a good flight."

"Thanks. I slept for most of it, so I can't complain."

"Lie-down seat?"

I shook my head.

He grimaced. "I wish you would've let me pay for your flight. I told your mother to tell you I would've been happy to spring for first class."

That was news to me.

"It's fine. Like I said, I slept most of the way." My smile felt tight and plastic. "Don't you have work today?"

"I'm going in later. Your mother wanted me to speak with the contract—ah, there she is." He beamed, and I had to give it him. He was either a great actor, or he was inexplicably still in love with my mother after four years of marriage.

It was an uncharitable thought, but I'd seen my mom love and leave enough men growing up to know that most of her relationships didn't last beyond the six-month mark. Harry was one in a million.

She waltzed into the foyer. Even at nine months pregnant, she was impeccably turned out in designer maternity clothes, freshly blown-out hair, and perfectly manicured nails. She carried Charlie in her arms.

"Hello, darling." My mom gave me a kiss on each cheek. She'd picked up the habit after her honeymoon in France and hadn't stopped using it since. "Oh, it's *so* good to see you, though you look a little pale. Must be that dreadful London weather"—she clucked her tongue, her eyes scanning my bare legs and arms—"but at least you're not bloated from all that pub food. I do wish you'd get rid of those dirty sneakers though."

"Good to see you too, Mom," I said dryly.

She was still stuck on my shoes. "What happened to those adorable Jimmy Choos I bought you for your birthday?"

"I can't wear Jimmy Choos on a plane."

"Why not? I do it all the time."

"Because it's uncomfortable and I don't want to."

She huffed out a sigh, but her annoyance visibly melted when Charlie reached his arms out toward me. "Yes, that's Brooklyn," she cooed. "That's your half-sister. Say hi to your half-sister, sweetie."

The repeated emphasis on *half*-sister felt a little pointed, but I shook it off and smiled at my favorite person in the household.

"Hi, Charlie. You've grown so much since the last time I saw you," I cooed. "You're the cutest kid on the planet, aren't you? Yes, you are."

He giggled, his eyes crinkling as he grabbed for my finger. I held out my pinky. He grasped it with both hands and a happy squeal, and my heart absolutely melted.

My mom reluctantly handed him to me when Charlie kept trying to squirm out of her arms. I held him close, my chest tightening.

I didn't have baby fever, but I ached for the unconditional love that babies had for their parents. To them, their mom and dad were their whole world.

Sometimes, I secretly resented him for being the apple of our mother's eye when she hadn't cared much for me since the day I was born. But when I saw him, all those resentments went away. It wasn't fair of me to wish the same type of childhood I'd had on him, and I truly hoped he got the best version of her because I hadn't.

"You should stay with us," Harry said, breaking me out of my thoughts. "There's no reason to pay for a hotel when we have room here. Charlie'll love having you around."

"Harry, stop pressuring her," my mother admonished. "She's already settled into her hotel. Aren't you, darling?"

"Sure."

"See? She'll enjoy the peace and quiet there more than this chaos." She waved her hand around the foyer. Other than our conversation and Charlie's babbles, it was utterly silent. "We'll have people coming in and out all weekend—you know we're installing new tiles in the guest bathrooms—and Charlie still cries through the night. Brooklyn would sleep so much better at a hotel."

"Wow. That's so thoughtful of you," I deadpanned.

I caught a small smirk on Harry's face before he covered it up with a cough.

The sarcasm passed over my mother's head. "Something's different." She tilted her head, her blue eyes narrowing into slits. "You have a special glow to you. Are you dating someone?"

My mom was as self-centered as they came, but she had an unparalleled nose for detecting new relationships.

"I am," I admitted. "It's pretty new. Really new, actually, but you might've heard of—"

"No, not there!" she snapped. I followed her gaze to where the housekeeper had entered the foyer with a vase of lilies. "Lilies go in the living room. Hydrangeas go in the foyer. Swap them, please."

"Yes, ma'am." The other woman left as quickly as she'd entered.

My mom turned back to me, her smile back in place. "I'm so thrilled you're dating someone! You have to tell me all about it at brunch tomorrow. It'll be a girls' day. So much fun!" She clapped her hands, nearly blinding me with her diamond ring.

"Do you have time for brunch? Don't you have to prep for your operation?"

"It'll be fine. My C-section isn't until Monday afternoon." She checked her watch. "I do have to leave for the salon soon. Today's the only day Yvette can squeeze me in all month, and I can't give birth with grown-out roots. Imagine how awful the pictures would be."

"I can't. It's too terrible a thought," I said. "I might have nightmares."

This time, Harry full-on snickered. Lucky for him, my mom was too busy fretting about the time to notice.

"You get it. Anyway, Harry and I have dinner plans tonight, but I'll see you tomorrow, okay? I'll text you the address of the restaurant later. Come here, Charlie." She took my brother back. "How's my sweet boy doing? Mommy has to leave you for a bit, but you're going to spend some quality time with Daddy, okay? Then on Monday, you'll get a sister, and it'll be so much fun…"

I stood there awkwardly while she fussed over Charlie. Should I stay, or should I go? She seemed to have forgotten I was there.

Harry finally took pity on me. "I'll have Roy drive you back to the hotel," he said. Roy was his chauffeur. "It's a beautiful day. You probably want to hit the beach or pool while the sun's out."

"That would be great," I said, relieved. "Thanks."

I said goodbye to Charlie and my mom, who gave me the barest of glances when I left. Fifteen minutes of face time and a dismissal summed up most of our interactions. I was used to it, but it stung every time.

When I returned to the hotel—earning myself a strange look from the front desk, probably because I'd been in and out three times in two hours—I sat on my bed and debated what to do.

I *should* trawl the job sites again, but staying in my room to sift through Indeed listings was way too depressing.

I peered out the window at the pool. It was packed with kids and what looked like a bachelorette party. Too chaotic.

I called the spa to see if they had any openings, but they were fully booked through Wednesday.

There was nothing good on TV, and I wasn't hungry.

I could go shopping or hit up the beach like Harry suggested, but leaving the hotel premises required a level of energy that I didn't have after an eleven-hour flight and a conversation with my mom.

I flopped back on the bed and stared at the ceiling. A wave of loneliness crested through me. Bright sunshine painted the room in gorgeous yellows, but I wished I were back in cold, rainy London instead.

I was perfectly capable of traveling alone. I'd backpacked through Europe solo and taken spontaneous trips to the countryside by myself. I didn't need company to have a good time, but this trip wasn't a vacation. It was an emotional vortex, and I desperately wished I had someone here to hold my hand before I got sucked into the undertow.

I checked my phone. It was dinnertime in London. Maybe I should—

Someone knocked on the door.

I groaned. I should've hung the Do Not Disturb sign on the handle.

I forced myself to my feet and walked over, feeling sluggish and restless at the same time. Hotels always did that to me.

I opened the door, expecting housekeeping, but the sight that greeted me was so unexpected that I had to blink twice to make sure I wasn't hallucinating.

Dark hair. High cheekbones. Devastating smile.

My jaw dropped. "*Vincent?*"

I blinked a third time, just to be sure. The solid outline of his frame didn't waver.

It was really him, and he was really here.

The world tilted. Little bubbles fizzled in my blood, and if I weren't caught in the gravity of him—of his presence, of that damn smile—I would've floated right off the ground.

"What are you doing here?" I asked faintly.

"I'm here to explore the great city of San Diego—which I've

never visited, if you can believe it." His gaze gentled, becoming more sincere. "And I'm here to be with you."

"But..." My thoughts scattered like leaves in the wind. I reached for the nearest one, no matter how inane it was. "Today's a training day."

"Coach approved me taking today and Monday off."

"But—"

"No more buts," he said firmly. "You were dreading this trip. I couldn't let you come without backup. You went to the Zenith dinner with me as moral support. It's only fair I return the favor."

"There's a difference between going to dinner and flying to another continent."

"A small one." Vincent's mouth tilted up in another smile. "But if you want to know a secret, the Zenith dinner was an excuse. I would've come either way."

Just like that, all the loneliness and tension of the past few hours seeped away.

I fell into his arms, and for the first time since I landed, I could breathe again.

CHAPTER 34

VINCENT

PULLING OFF MY SURPRISE TRIP TO CALIFORNIA HAD BEEN shockingly easy. I knew Brooklyn would try to talk me out of it if she caught onto my plans, so I hadn't told a soul except for Coach. I'd expected pushback, but he'd approved my days off without further questions. He knew Brooklyn didn't want to go, and he obviously didn't have a high opinion of his ex-wife. Judging by the way he'd almost smiled when I told him what I was planning, he might've actually respected me more for what I'd done.

Coach was overly protective and hardheaded, but he genuinely cared about Brooklyn.

Her mother, on the other hand, was a different story.

"Nice to meet you, Mrs. Wilker." According to Brooklyn, that was her new married name.

Brooklyn, her mother, and I were seated at a rooftop restaurant near the beach for brunch. Brooklyn had texted her mum to let her know I would be joining them and hadn't gotten a response, but she'd brought me anyway.

"Please, call me Sienna. Mrs. Wilker makes me sound so old." Sienna appeared unfazed by my presence, but her brows pulled together as she examined me. "You look familiar. Why do you look familiar?"

"I guess I just have that kind of face," I said.

Brooklyn snorted out a laugh.

"Brooklyn, please. What have I said about making those types of noises?" Sienna admonished. "It's unladylike."

"I like it." I set my menu aside and took a sip of water. "Being ladylike is overrated."

Brooklyn snuck a quick glance at me. A small smile played around her mouth while her mother's expression tightened.

"Everyone's certainly entitled to their own opinion," she said, her tone a touch cooler than before. "Let's order, shall we?"

Five minutes with her, and she lived up to every expectation I had given what Brooklyn had told me about her.

The two of them bore striking physical similarities—the same golden hair and cornflower blue eyes, the same freckles and heart-shaped face. But that was where the resemblance ended. Whereas Brooklyn was witty and empathetic, her mother was the exact opposite.

Sienna spent the majority of the meal talking about herself—the nursery she'd built for her new baby, the personal trainer she'd hired to whip her back into shape after she gave birth, the shopping spree she'd go on once she lost her pregnancy weight.

I'd tried to meet her with an open mind, but if it weren't for Brooklyn, I would've jumped off the roof by now.

"I can have my stylist pick out some items for you, darling," Sienna said. "You're always in activewear. That's for Pilates, not the public."

"Wearing comfortable clothing is part of my job," Brooklyn said.

"Which is why I don't understand why you chose *sports* nutrition." Her mum wrinkled her nose. "You have my looks. You could've been a model or an actress."

"I didn't know you were a model and actress," I interjected smoothly. "What were you in?" During our pre-brunch briefing earlier that morning, Brooklyn told me Sienna had worked in marketing before she met her current husband and quit her job.

Sienna's mouth pursed. "I didn't say *I* was." It clearly pained her to admit it. "I said Brooklyn *could've* been one of those two."

"Because she has your looks. But you also have your looks, so why didn't you go into modeling or acting?" I paused before adding, "I'm sure Hollywood would've loved you."

She stared at me, obviously trying to figure out whether my last statement was a dig or a compliment.

"It didn't work out. I had a child to raise," she finally said, somewhat pointedly. Sienna turned to Brooklyn, shutting me out. "How *is* your job going? Have they promoted you yet?"

Brooklyn's smile flickered and died. "Um, they offered me a permanent position at Blackcastle, but I turned it down. I'm between jobs at the moment."

I expected her mother to flip out. Instead, her eyes lit up like she'd won the lottery. "Are you switching fields? *Finally*! I know a wonderful photographer who can set you up with test shots. You don't have the high fashion look, but I bet they could get you a commercial booking—"

"I'm not switching fields." Brooklyn sounded tired. "I still want to be a nutritionist. I just can't stay at Blackcastle."

"Oh." The other woman pressed her lips together. "I don't understand. Then why not stay at Blackcastle?"

"It wasn't the right long-term fit."

It was as though the conversation had sent out an alert to the universe because less than a minute after they brought up Blackcastle, a youngish-looking guy with a short blond ponytail bounded over from a nearby table.

"I'm so sorry to bother you while you're eating, but are you Vincent DuBois?" he asked.

I nodded, already knowing where this was going.

His face broke out into a wide smile. "I *knew* that was you! Do you mind if we grab a selfie? I'm a huge fan."

"Sure." Some footballers refused to entertain fans during their personal time, but what the hell. We were in San Diego. There weren't a lot of football fans here—though it was a weird coincidence to run into one at brunch—and no one else seemed too bothered by my presence. It was only a problem if the selfie turned into a photo line.

When Ponytail Guy left, Sienna put the pieces together.

"Oh, you're a *soccer* player. That's where I know you from." Based on her tone, she had a lower estimation of my career than she did a wad of gum on her shoe. She slanted a glance at Brooklyn. "I should've known. It's always about soccer."

"I'm not dating him because of his job, Mom. We met at Blackcastle, but our relationship doesn't revolve around football."

"Hmm. Far be it for me to tell you who you should date, but that's one of the reasons your father and I divorced. He was obsessed with the sport. Couldn't bother to pay attention to me the entire time we were married." Sienna flicked her gaze toward me. "How long have you been dating again?"

It was the first time she'd asked about our relationship since we sat down, which was pretty wild since I was the boyfriend who'd gatecrashed their mother-daughter brunch at the last minute. Most people would be curious right off the bat.

"We've been dating for a month, but we've known each other for a year and a half," I replied.

"A month? Why am I only finding out about this now?"

"I figured I'd tell you in person since I was already going to be here," Brooklyn said. "We don't talk much on the phone anyway."

"Well, whose fault is that, darling? You can pick up the phone any time."

My reaction was swift and visceral. Every muscle in my body coiled, and I was already halfway out of my chair before I caught myself. I sat back down, my teeth grinding as the metal handle of my fork dug into my palm.

This wasn't my fight. Not yet. I didn't want to make a scene and embarrass Brooklyn in public, but God, I wanted to wipe that condescending expression off Sienna's face.

Brooklyn placed a reassuring hand on my knee underneath the table. "I'm going to use the restroom," she said calmly. "I'll be right back."

She left, her quick steps taking her across the rooftop and into the main restaurant. I waited until she was out of sight before I pounced.

"Why did you ask her to fly back here?" I'd smoothed the sharpest edges of my anger, but the rest of it seeped out with tightly controlled venom.

"Excuse me?"

"Brooklyn. You asked her to fly eleven hours to California so she can hold your hand while you give birth, yet you act like you don't want her here. Why is that?"

Sienna's fork hit her plate with a loud *clink*. Her lips parted in shock, and I'd bet my last dollar no one had talked to her like that in years, if ever.

"Because she's my daughter and this is my family, which is why it doesn't concern you. You've been dating for a month. I don't have to explain myself to you, and frankly, I don't like your tone."

"That's where you're wrong." I leaned back, my voice deceptively calm. "It does concern me when you treat her like shit. You may be her family, and Brooklyn and I may have only started dating a month ago, but I care about her. A lot. Which is more than I can say for you."

She glared at me, her mouth a thin slash against her rapidly reddening face.

I hadn't come to California with the intention of confronting Brooklyn's mother. I was here for moral support, but seeing their dynamic in real time made my stomach turn. Sienna was a true narcissist. Brooklyn was aware of that, but I think a part of her still hoped her mother would have a sudden epiphany and treat her like a real daughter one day.

The problem was, narcissists never changed. At the end of the day, they only cared about themselves. If they displayed the same pattern of behavior for almost thirty years, they'd continue that pattern for the next thirty.

I couldn't say that to Brooklyn without stepping way over the line, but I *could* give Sienna a piece of my mind.

"I'm aware we only met an hour ago," I said. "But in that hour, you've asked about her life exactly twice. You spent the rest of the time talking about yourself, berating her, or delivering some sort of backhanded compliment. You must rely on her somewhat for emotional support if you asked her to come here, yet you refuse to show her any warmth or appreciation. Or maybe you don't rely on her at all. Maybe you just wanted to see how far she'd jump for you if you asked. Either way, it's bullshit. She deserves better than this."

"You have some nerve." Sienna looked like she wanted to slap me, but she probably didn't want to make a scene in public. However, her eyes blazed with fury as she gave me the fakest smile I'd ever seen. "You think you can say whatever you want because you're a hotshot athlete, but I'll tell you this. Brooklyn is *my* daughter. I raised her. I birthed her from my fucking womb even though I didn't want to, and I kept her fed and clothed even when she ruined my chances of having a real life and career in my twenties. No matter what you think of our relationship, we're family, and she'll *always* choose family over anything else. I'm her only mom. *You* are replaceable. If I tell her to dump you, she will."

"Because she'll do anything you tell her to?"

"Because she's that desperate for my approval." Sienna shrugged. "Mommy issues. Everyone has them. Sometimes it works to my advantage."

"Does it?"

Sienna's face froze for a split second before it relaxed into another fake smile. She turned to where Brooklyn stood behind her. Judging by her devastated expression, I didn't have to guess how much she'd overheard.

My chest cracked in half. I wanted her to see her mother for who she was, but I didn't want her to find out this way. Sienna's comments had been cruel and callous, and it fucking killed me to see Brooklyn standing there, her eyes wide and clouded with hurt.

A sharp pain twisted in my gut. My hands clenched into fists beneath the table, and I had to breathe through the desire to sweep Brooklyn up in my arms and whisk her far, far away from here.

Whatever happened next needed to happen. I couldn't interfere.

"Darling, you're back. Good." Sienna gestured toward me, her gaze cutting. "Vincent was telling me what an apparently horrible mother I am. You won't believe the things he said after knowing me for, what? An hour? He waited until you went to the restroom and just attacked me." She shook her head. "I hate to say it because you so rarely bring a boy home, but he's not the sort of man you want to be dating. Imagine how much bolder he'll get if he's comfortable being *this* rude this early in your relationship? Take it from someone who has your best interests at heart. You need to dump him immediately."

"I don't think so."

Sienna's smile slipped. "Excuse me?"

"He's not going anywhere." Brooklyn had recovered from her shock. She crossed her arms and stared down her mother, though her eyes remained glossy with emotion. "Unlike you, Vincent *actually* has my best interests at heart. He flew all the way from London to be with me because he knew how much I was dreading this trip. He's comforted me, and supported me, and made me happier than you'll ever know. So don't you dare try to make him out to be the bad guy here."

My throat thickened, and something warm and fierce swelled in my chest. This wasn't about me, but her unflinching defense of me knocked the air out of my lungs.

I didn't know what I did to deserve this girl, but I knew that I was never letting her go.

Sienna's nostrils flared. "Maybe so, but people have multiple faces. Now sit down so we can continue this conversation at the table, sweetie," she said through a tight smile. "People are starting to stare."

She was right. Several nearby diners kept glancing at us in between bites. One of them looked at Sienna and whispered to their partner, who shook his head.

"I don't care." A flush spread across Brooklyn's face. "I heard what you said about how I ruined your life and how I'll do anything for your approval. I knew you resented me, but I hadn't known how much until I heard it straight from your mouth." She shook her head, her voice cracking. "God, I'm so *stupid*. This whole time, I kept thinking you'd somehow change and become a better mother to me because you're so good to Charlie, but you'll never change. You'll always hate me because you never wanted me to begin with, and you'll always exploit my hope for your own purposes. You may be my only mom, but that's just a matter of blood. If you don't act like a mother, then you aren't one. Not really."

"Don't act like a mother?" Sienna abandoned all pretenses of keeping a civil face for the public. She raised her voice, her eyes flashing. "How *dare* you say that to me? Do you know how much I've given up for you? I could've put you on the streets, but I didn't. You're here because of *me*. You got to go to college and move to London because of *me*. So don't you dare stand there and try to make me sound like I'm sort of...sort of witch!"

"You did the bare minimum," Brooklyn snapped back. "Yes, you fed me and clothed me and kept a roof over our heads. But I paid my own way through school, and I earned the London internship on my own merit. Being a parent is about more than the necessities. You were *never* there for me growing up, and you just said yourself that I ruined your life. I didn't ask to be born, so to put all your regrets and resentment on me is...it's not..." Her voice broke again. A tear slipped down her cheek, and she angrily wiped it away with the back of her hand.

"You did ruin my life. That's a fact." Sienna's words turned cold, crisp, and unbelievably cruel. My fists tightened. "I could've been a supermodel or a movie star. I could've married a billionaire. Do you think I wanted to spend my life in suburban San Diego, working in marketing and being a single mom? I don't think so. Obviously, the situation has improved now that I have Harry and the kids..." She placed a hand on her stomach. "But this was Plan B. I'll never forget the life I lost because of you and your father."

Brooklyn's face hardened. She straightened her shoulders, her voice taking on a quiet but steely firmness. "I'm glad you have Harry and the kids. Truly. Because I'm done here."

Sienna sputtered. "Where are you going?"

"Home." Brooklyn walked over and grabbed her bag from her chair. I tossed my napkin on the table and silently stood. "Send my well wishes to Harry, Charlie, and my new sister. I expect I won't be seeing them for a while."

"You can't leave! My operation is tomorrow!"

I shook my head in disbelief. She was truly delusional if she thought Brooklyn would show up and pretend like nothing happened after today.

"And you'll have plenty of support there. You don't need me, and I'm done playing your games. Goodbye, Mom."

I followed Brooklyn out of the restaurant, ignoring Sienna's apoplectic expression and the other diners' slack jaws.

Neither of us spoke until we got into my rental car. Then, and only then, did Brooklyn's tears fall. A sob ripped from her throat and tore my heart clean in half.

I held her, letting her cry it all out in the restaurant parking lot. Despite my agony at seeing her sad, I was so fucking proud of her for standing up for herself.

"I'm sorry if I overstepped back there," I said quietly, rubbing small circles on her back. "I saw the way she was talking to you, and I just...snapped."

"No, it's okay." Brooklyn hiccupped. "I needed to hear that. If you hadn't confronted her, and she hadn't responded by saying those ugly things, I would've never believed it. Not really. I had to hear it for myself. I..." She hiccupped again. "I just feel so dumb. I *knew* what kind of person she was, but I—I—"

"You're not dumb," I said firmly. "That's your family. We're programmed to think the best of our family, no matter how shitty they might be."

"Yeah." She pulled back and wiped at her face again. "I'm going to miss Charlie the most, you know? He's just a kid. He doesn't deserve such a dysfunctional family, but she actually wants him, so she'll probably treat him better. I hope." Her voice cracked again.

"He won't be a kid forever. Whatever happens, you're his sister, and you'll have a chance to reconnect, even if it's farther in the future." I grasped her chin and tilted it up, forcing her to look at me. "Do *not* let her make you feel bad about yourself. She's the villain here, not you."

Brooklyn nodded before giving me a watery smile. "This must be the quickest trip to California ever. Less than twenty-four hours, and we already have to head back."

"I'm not complaining. It's too hot here for January anyway. It's weird."

She laughed and blew her nose while I drove us to the hotel. Once we got there, I was buying the first ticket back to London.

It was time to go home.

CHAPTER 35

BROOKLYN

IT'D BEEN A WEEK SINCE I LEFT MY MOM AT BRUNCH, AND we hadn't exchanged a single word since. I wasn't surprised. She'd never contact me first after I humiliated her in public, and I had no desire to call her and make amends.

However, I *was* surprised by my indifference to our falling out. Just a month ago, her silence would've sent me into a spiral of anxiety. But ironically, hearing her say what I'd suspected all these years healed something in me. I no longer had to guess. I *knew* how she felt about me, and even if it wasn't positive, the certainty took away her power. She could no longer dangle the possibility of her approval over me.

The only thing I was sad about was not saying goodbye to Charlie or hello to my new half-sister. According to social media, my mother gave birth to a healthy baby girl named Teresa. She was adorable, all blue eyes and pink cheeks.

Maybe one day, when Charlie and Teresa were older, we could develop a relationship independent of my mother. Until then, I had to focus on the people who wanted me here.

"This is nuts! I've never seen this place so packed." Carina returned from the bar with two pints in hand. She slid into the booth next to me, cheeks flushed from battling through the crowd.

Blackcastle had won this afternoon's match against Munich. Fans and players alike had flooded the Angry Boar to celebrate, and the crowd was currently singing one of the club's songs in drunken unison.

"It's a new year. People are excited," I said.

Everyone was feeling good about Blackcastle's chances at winning the Champions League. Ever since Vincent and Asher called a truce and started playing *with* each other instead of *against* each other, we'd practically been unstoppable. Still, victory wasn't guaranteed, and I knew Vincent was more stressed about the upcoming knockout stage than he let on.

"Maybe. I can't believe Vincent scored another free kick though." Carina shook her head. "That's not usually his forte."

"It's because he's playing for Brooklyn," Scarlett said with an impish smile. "I'm his sister, so trust me when I say his performance today was definitely that of someone who wanted to look good in front of his girlfriend."

My face warmed. "Stop," I protested over my friends' knowing laughter. "I've been to every match since we started dating. He doesn't always play like that."

"Sure, but it's different now. The man flew to *California* for you," Carina pointed out. "If that isn't love, I don't know what is."

Something tightened in my gut. "It's not love. It's ego. The match, I mean. He wanted to win, and he did."

Scarlett and Carina exchanged glances. I knew what they were thinking—I was in denial, it was love and I didn't know it, so on and so forth.

But it was *way* too soon for the L word. I cared about Vincent a lot. I missed him when he wasn't there, and I couldn't stop smiling when he was. He was the only person who could comfort me without saying a word and thrill me with just a look. But those things were natural in all healthy relationships, right? They didn't mean it was love. It couldn't be. Not yet.

"Ladies!" Adil popped up next to our table with a pitcher of darkish liquid. "May I interest you in a customized, non-alcoholic refreshment? It's part lemonade, part iced tea, and part Coke with a twist of fruit. I created it myself. It's delicious."

"So it's an Arnold Palmer with Coke and a twist," I said, amused. I could always count on Adil for a welcome distraction.

"That's what people with no imagination call it," he said. "No offense. But *I* like to call it the Adil Chakir. Here. Try it."

He poured us all a glass. I took a sip and nearly spat it out. The concept was fine, but whatever ratio he used for the ingredients did *not* work. It tasted like soda that'd been left out for three days too long.

"What do you think?" he asked eagerly.

"Great," I choked out. "So...interesting."

"Right? That's what I told Stevens. He said it's so bad even Truffle wouldn't drink it, but he just has bad taste. Oy, Stevens!" He yelled across the room. "You're wrong! The girls like it!"

"They're just being nice!" Stevens yelled back.

"And you're just jealous you don't have your own drink!"

While Adil went to argue with his teammate, Asher, Vincent, and Noah came over to sit with us. Fans had been dragging them away all night to talk to them or buy them a round, but I didn't mind. This was their moment; they deserved to shine.

Still, I couldn't help but smile when Vincent slid into the booth next to me and kissed me on the cheek. "How's your night going? Miss me yet?"

I fluttered my lashes. "I was enjoying a testosterone-free chat with the girls, but I guess I'm happy you're here. You're nice eye candy."

He placed a hand over his heart. "Me, eye candy? Thank you for recognizing my contributions off the pitch. There's more to me than football, you know."

I laughed while Scarlett attempted to engage an uncomfortable-looking Noah across the table.

"First Vincent's birthday, now the pub? You've turned into a social butterfly," Scarlett teased.

Noah nodded at Vincent. "Blame your brother. He's aced the art of the guilt trip."

"I don't guilt anyone into anything. I *persuade*," Vincent corrected him. "Evie's with her grandparents until this weekend, right? So enjoy a night out before she gets back. You need to relax before you keel over from stress, and it would suck to have to replace our star keeper in the middle of the season."

Noah's mouth quirked. "I appreciate the concern."

"Don't worry. We'll make sure you relax." Scarlett patted him on the shoulder. "Maybe we'll even find a nice girl for you to dance with."

His half-smile morphed into a grimace. "Please don't."

I glanced at Carina, who hadn't looked up from her phone since he sat down. *Interesting.*

When I'd asked what was up with her and Noah after Budapest, she said she had no idea what I was talking about and that they barely knew each other. I suspected she was hiding something from me, but I'd dig into that when we were alone.

Until then, I had some news I'd been dying to share.

"No one asked, but since we're all here, I have a job-related update," I announced, trying to keep the giddiness out of my voice.

"Do you know who Derek Moore is?"

Just saying the name made my heart race—not because I was attracted to him but because he represented the potential next level in my career.

"The surfer?" Asher's eyebrows rose. "Twelve-time world champion, often regarded as the greatest professional surfer in history. *That* Derek Moore?"

I nodded, my stomach swooping with nerves and excitement. When I emailed my former career counselor back in December, I'd kept my expectations low. However, she'd finally emailed me back yesterday with a lead, and I'd done a double take when I saw what it was. I had to triple confirm it was *the* Derek Moore before I believed it.

"He's an alumnus of my school," I said. "He reached out to the dean because he's looking for a new nutritionist for his daughter. She's a gymnast, not a surfer, but she's hoping to make it to nationals this year and her old nutritionist wasn't working out." Derek was a legend, but his daughter Haley was a rising star in the women's gymnastics world. Commentators were already speculating about her chances at the Olympics in a few years. "He wanted to prioritize candidates from his alma mater this time around, which is how I landed an interview with them next week. It's a remote position, but it pays well and comes with full benefits."

Vincent already knew, but everyone else broke out into cheers and congratulations.

"That's amazing!" Carina cried, hugging me.

"The Moores would be lucky to have you," Scarlett added, her eyes shining.

"Thanks." I didn't bother hiding my grin.

I was excited about more than the Moores' high profile. Working for them would open a lot of doors career-wise, but when I read the job description, something just *clicked*. I'd always worked with sports teams and never with an individual. Vincent had asked if I was interested in being his personal nutritionist, but there were too many conflicts of interest, and I didn't want to dilute our relationship with work again.

But the more I thought about it, the more one-on-one work made sense for me. Obviously, it would depend on the employer, but overall, an individual would offer greater flexibility than a team. I'd miss the group camaraderie, but I wanted creative freedom more.

I was about to ask if anyone wanted another round of drinks when I spotted a familiar face in the crowd. I nudged Vincent. "Um, isn't that Lloyd?"

Slicked-back hair, expensive watch. Yep, that was definitely him.

His agent barreled toward us, elbowing people out of the way and leaving a string of colorful curses in his wake. He was the only one here not dressed in Blackcastle gear, but I wasn't surprised. I bet he slept in his Delamonte suits.

"Lloyd?" Vincent's eyebrows shot up when he reached our table. "What are you doing here? I thought pubs weren't your scene."

"They're not." Lloyd sniffed. "But I was having dinner nearby with Sandra, the Zenith exec. She wanted to go over your test shots with me."

The table quieted. Vincent stiffened, and I took his hand under the table in silent support.

Vincent had his Zenith test shoot last week, only a day after returning from San Diego. I was shocked they had the final results already.

"They fast-tracked everything so they could review the images as soon as possible," Lloyd said, answering my silent question. "Sandra and the rest of the exec team were *thrilled* with how yours came out. They said you, quote, 'really embodied the spirit of Zenith.'" A wide grin split his face. "You got it."

Vincent stared at him. "What?"

"The Zenith deal." Lloyd grabbed his shoulders. "You got the bloody Zenith deal! You're their new global men's ambassador!"

There was a beat of shocked silence before the table erupted. Everyone showered Vincent with congratulations while I squealed and threw my arms around him.

"Congrats! I *knew* you would get it." I kissed him, my chest swelling with pride and pure joy. "I had no fucking doubt."

Vincent's hand slid to my waist, holding me like I was his anchor. When I pulled back, his eyes were glassy and a little stunned. "I didn't think...I..." He shook his head and laughed, the sound cobbled from a mix of shock and disbelief. "Holy shit. *I got the Zenith deal!*"

It sounded like it'd finally sunk in.

"We have to tell the rest of the team so we can celebrate." Asher stood and dragged him out of the booth. "Sorry, Brooklyn. We'll bring him back in a bit. Wilson, let's go."

For once, Noah looked vaguely happy to be part of the festivities. He followed them to another table, where Adil and Stevens were still arguing over Adil's drink. Lloyd had already disappeared somewhere.

"Just bring him back in one piece!" I yelled after them.

Vincent could deny it all he wanted, but he and Asher were definitely besties. A moment later, fresh cheers arose from the team, and I laughed again.

My phone lit up with a new notification. I checked it, my laugh dying in my throat when I saw it was an email from ISNA.

Oh my God. It was my application status. It had to be.

I knew it was coming, but seeing it in my inbox was still a shock.

It felt like a thousand years had passed since I applied.

I clicked on it, my heart racing a million miles a minute. I was so nervous the words blurred into a giant wall of text.

I blinked and tried again, my eyes skipping past the date and address in search of the key words.

Dear Brooklyn,

Thank you for your interest in the International Sports Nutritionist Association's Innovator Award. After careful consideration, we regret to inform you that you were not selected as a finalist...

A loud buzzing filled my ears. I reread the opening paragraph twice, then a third time, as though that would somehow change the text.

It didn't.

I dropped my phone on my lap and sat back. The noise from the pub faded into a dull hum as ISNA's rejection echoed in my head.

We regret to inform you that you were not selected as a finalist.

You were not selected as a finalist.

Not selected.

Not. Selected.

I swallowed past the taste of sawdust in my mouth. I'd known winning the award was a long shot, but I'd hoped I would at least make it to the finals. ISNA might as well have mailed me a letter with *You're Not Good Enough* stamped across it in bold red type.

Tears stung my eyes, but I blinked them back before they could escape.

It's okay. It's just an award. You can always apply another year. But I couldn't shake the creeping fear that the rejection was a sign from the universe—proof that maybe I *didn't* know what I was doing and that I wasn't cut out for this job.

Just half an hour ago, I'd been flying high from the Moore

interview news. But an interview wasn't an offer, and I wouldn't put it past the universe to give me hope before yanking it away again.

A soft hand touched my arm. When I looked up, Carina was staring at me, her brow furrowed with concern. Scarlett had left to use the loo, but I'd forgotten Carina was still at the table. "Are you okay?" she asked. "You look upset."

"Oh, yeah." I pasted on a smile. "I'm a little overstimulated. That's all."

"Are you sure?"

"Uh-huh." I didn't want to bring the mood down by telling her about the application.

"Okay." She didn't look convinced, but she let the issue go. "If you need to talk about anything, I'm here."

"I know. Thank you." I squeezed her hand and waited until she turned away before I let my smile drop.

I glanced across the pub, where Vincent was celebrating with his teammates. They slapped him on the shoulders and said something that made him laugh. His grin dazzled, and he looked so happy, I couldn't bear to ruin the moment for him.

My chest felt so tight I couldn't breathe. I was genuinely thrilled that Vincent got the Zenith deal. He was at the top of his game, and he deserved the world. I would celebrate his accomplishments a thousand times over.

But as I sat there, surrounded by joy and revelry, I'd never felt so small.

CHAPTER 36

BROOKLYN

I LICKED MY WOUNDS IN PRIVATE FOR A WEEK BEFORE
the Moore interview. I was too embarrassed to tell anyone about the
ISNA rejection yet, even Vincent. How stupid I must look, turning
down a guaranteed job in the Premier League only to end up with no
job and no award. My only consolation was that Henry hadn't made
the final round either. At least there was some justice in the universe.

Getting the Moore job was my best shot at redemption. If they gave
me an offer, that would soften the ISNA blow, so I tried to buckle down
and put on my game face the following Friday for our video interview.

Derek was in his fifties but fitter than most men half his age.
With his salt and pepper hair, blue eyes, and tanned skin, he was
the definition of a silver fox. Haley was the sixteen-year-old female
version of him—same smile, same eyes, same down-to-earth demeanor
that instantly put me at ease. She seemed extraordinarily mature for
someone her age.

Despite my initial nerves, the interview went more smoothly than
I could've hoped.

"The Blackcastle internship is impressive," Derek said after he asked some clarifying questions about my résumé. "I admit, we don't follow soccer—"

"Football," Haley corrected. "That's what it's called in Europe."

"Sorry, sweetie," Derek said indulgently. I smiled. They obviously had a great relationship, which was unfortunately rare in elite athlete families. Too much pressure and competition. "We don't follow football closely, but even I know Blackcastle is a legendary club. I'm curious why you didn't stay on with them full-time?"

I'd expected this question, and I came prepared. "It was a great learning experience, and like you said, it's a legendary club. But with that comes a long-established system of processes and traditions that isn't always open to experimentation. As much as I loved my time there, I wanted to work in an environment with more creative freedom."

"Can you give us an example of what that creative freedom would look like?" Haley asked.

"Sure. When I'm paired with an athlete, I don't only personalize their nutrition plans. I also personalize the way we work together. People have different learning and motivation styles. It's important that we optimize for both their physical and mental idiosyncrasies." I gave them a few examples of how I'd done that with other athletes before I segued into more specific tools and strategies.

The personal statement I wrote for ISNA was actually great prep for the interview. It'd helped me hone my nutrition philosophy and made me think long and hard about what set me apart from my peers.

The more I talked, the more confident I got. Without restrictions and guidelines hemming me in anymore, the passion I felt for my job resurfaced, bubbling out in a stream of ideas and genuine enthusiasm. My mind raced as I came up with new approaches on the spot, though

I was careful to control my excitement in case I sounded *too* all over the place.

When I finished, both Derek and Haley looked suitably impressed.

"I love your point about tailoring your working style to the individual," Haley said. "That was the issue with my old nutritionist. She was more old-school and a little too rigid when it came to the daily stuff. We didn't quite mesh."

They had a few more questions about my background and my plan for taking Haley to nationals before they wrapped up the interview. I expected them to give me the usual spiel about taking time to discuss my application and calling me later, but Derek surprised me.

"I'll be straightforward," he said. "You're the last candidate we've interviewed, and I think I can speak for both Haley and myself when I say you're the best one by far."

Haley nodded. "The others were great, but I feel like you *get* it. The flexibility, the creativity, the willingness to experiment. We move fast, and we need someone who can not only keep up but also adapt."

I'd been burned by hope before, but my heart skipped nonetheless. "Thank you. That's great to hear."

"I apologize if this seems rushed, but rest assured that after weeks of searching, we know what works and what doesn't," Derek said. "Regionals are in two months, so we'd like to onboard someone as soon as possible. We'll send you details via email later, but rest assured that even though this isn't a corporate job, it'll include full benefits, a generous salary, and a bonus for everyone on our team if Haley makes it to nationals." He named a figure that almost made me choke.

I'd known about the benefits and salary, but holy *shit*. That bonus would be a lot of money.

"Nothing's official yet until we draw up the paperwork, but we wanted to make a verbal offer now," Haley added after glancing at her dad. "Is this something you're interested in?"

"Are you kidding? Absolutely! I would love to work for you." My ISNA rejection-induced funk lifted, letting in a glimmer of light.

"Excellent." A broad smile spread across Derek's face. "You'll have the paperwork by end of day today. I understand you're living in London now, so we're happy to give you an extra two weeks to sort out your affairs. We'll cover all your relocation expenses, of course, and provide any guidance you might need for moving to Chicago."

My elation screeched to a halt, and a vague sense of dread formed in my stomach. "Relocation? I apologize if I misunderstood, but I thought this was a remote position."

"Ah, yes." Derek winced. "I should've mentioned that at the start of the interview. That's my fault. This *was* originally a remote position. However, with regionals so close and the difficulties of onboarding someone in the middle of the season, we decided it would be more effective to hire an in-person nutritionist. Will that be a problem?"

"I—" I floundered, too caught off guard to come up with an immediate answer. "I'll have to think about it. I'm definitely still interested in the position, but I have to discuss the relocation with my...my family. It's a big decision."

"Of course," Derek said. "Take the weekend to think about it, but if you could give us your final answer by Monday night our time, that would be great. Like I said, regionals are coming up soon, so we need to onboard someone as soon as possible."

"I understand." I thanked them for their time and logged off, my mind spinning. The sense of dread in my stomach solidified into a two-ton brick.

Of *course* I'd land the perfect job only to find out it meant I'd have to leave London.

I was getting whiplash from the emotional rollercoaster that was the past two weeks. The confrontation with my mom, the interview offer, the ISNA rejection, and now this—it was like the universe was determined to send me flying as high as possible before dragging me back to earth again.

I stared at my closed laptop. The room was too quiet. I could hear the blood pulsing in my ears and feel the tension crawling up the back of my neck. The weight of my decision settled on my shoulders like a lead blanket, but before I could untangle my thoughts, the doorbell rang.

It was probably Vincent. He always came over after training, and he often stayed the night.

I took a deep breath and pushed my impending decision to the back of my mind. I'd deal with that later. I needed more time to marinate on it anyway.

I walked into the living room and opened the door, ready to greet him with a kiss, but he pushed past me and quickly locked the door behind him.

"Have you received any strange messages or seen anyone suspicious lately?" Vincent asked without preamble.

My brows knitted. It wasn't like him to be so abrupt. "No. Why?"

"I left training and found this on my car." He handed me a photo, his voice tight.

I took it, an ominous sense of déjà vu falling over me. It wasn't another picture of that creepy doll, thank God, but it might be even worse. It was a photo of Vincent and me kissing at the Angry Boar last week. Our friends were blurred out, and we were the only people in focus.

"There was no note, only the picture." A muscle twitched in his jaw. "It fits the intruder's MO perfectly."

"But we know who he is," I said. A sour feeling spread through my stomach. "Ethan Brown. You have an injunction against him. Can't the police use this to arrest him?"

"It's not him." Vincent's mouth flattened into a grim line. "I already called Smith. He said Ethan Brown left the city soon after they caught him. He's living in Newcastle now, and he has alibis for the entire week. One of Smith's police contacts there confirmed it. So it's true Brown texted me in Hungary, but he didn't leave me the doll. He and the intruder...they're two different people."

CHAPTER 37

VINCENT

I MOVED US TO A HOTEL THAT SAME NIGHT.

Perhaps it was an overreaction, but I couldn't risk it. It was one thing when the intruder was only targeting me. Now that they'd brought Brooklyn into it, I wasn't taking any chances.

If anything happened to her, I would never forgive myself.

"I'm getting a bodyguard." I'd already contacted an elite private security firm on my way here. "For both of us."

We were in the hotel suite's sitting room. I'd drawn all the blinds and turned every lock. We'd packed our essentials, but I didn't know how long we'd have to stay here. We might need to return home later to grab more things. If we did, I'd rather do so with physical protection.

"I don't need a bodyguard," Brooklyn said from her spot on the sofa. She hadn't argued about relocating to a hotel, but she put her foot down about someone shadowing her every move. "I understand why you're concerned, but things haven't escalated to the point that I need twenty-four-seven surveillance." She held up the photo. Just the sight of it made my blood freeze. "This was taken in public. It could've been anyone, and it doesn't necessarily mean they have malicious intentions."

"It's cute if they tag me in it on social media. It's not cute if they trespass onto private club property and leave it on my car in the exact same way the intruder left the doll photo."

Brooklyn blew out a long, shaky breath. "You're right. I was hoping…never mind." She shook her head and drew her knees to her chest. She looked exhausted, and I hated that I was the one stressing her out. But we had to talk about this. Her safety was at stake.

My throat felt tight, like something thick and sharp was lodged there, refusing to go down.

"It has to be someone who was at the pub," she said. "Did the police check their CCTV? Mac doesn't allow photos inside, so it should be fairly easy to see who broke the rules."

"He doesn't have cameras inside. Smith is checking the CCTV footage, but that's not going to help much. There must've been over a hundred people coming in and out all night."

"At least it's a start," Brooklyn reasoned. "Sifting through a hundred people is easier than investigating the millions who live in the city."

"Maybe." I sank beside her on the sofa, my own exhaustion getting the best of me. My limbs felt like lead, and a migraine had blossomed behind my temple, its dull ache quickly sharpening into a hot, pulsing throb that spread like wildfire through my head.

Life had finally been looking up. Brooklyn and I were together, I got the Zenith deal, and Blackcastle was killing it on the pitch. Then the intruder came swinging back into my life like a fucking wrecking ball, smashing my sense of control into smithereens.

If I ever caught them, I was going to strangle them with my bare hands.

I glanced at the photo again, my anger curdling into fear. The picture itself was innocent, but the warning was implied. Whoever left it was obsessed with me, and I was dating Brooklyn now. What if they considered her a rival or, worse, a threat?

My mind festered with morbid images of her dead and lying in a pool of her own blood.

A cold spike of terror plunged through my gut. It took everything I had not to cocoon her in bubble wrap and spirit her away to a private island where no one could get to us.

"Let's talk about something else." I shoved my spiraling thoughts into a box and slammed the lid shut. "How did your interview with the Moores go?"

I'd been so caught up in the intruder's reappearance that I hadn't gotten a chance to check in on her day.

"Really well. They basically offered me the job on the spot."

"That's great!" At least there was some good news this evening. But before I could celebrate further, I noticed hesitation clouding her eyes. "That *is* a good thing...right?"

"No, it is. I'm excited, but I...there's a catch." Brooklyn took a deep breath. "It's in Chicago."

The word dripped down my spine like freshly melted ice. *Chicago*.

My brain struggled to process it. I knew what it was and where it was, but I couldn't quite connect the dots between her statement and its implications.

I stared at Brooklyn for a second before I found my voice. "I thought it was a remote position."

"It was, but they changed it to an in-person one because regionals are so close and it'll make the transition easier." She looked down and twisted the hem of her sweater around her finger so tightly, the surrounding skin turned white. "I have until Monday night to decide."

That was in three days.

My stomach caved like I'd been punched in the gut. The intruder had taken the wind out of my sails, but if I hadn't already been sitting, the possibility of Brooklyn leaving would've sent me to my knees.

Her, in Chicago. Me, in London.

Thousands of miles and an ocean between us.

For the second time that day, the world tilted beneath my feet. I couldn't move. I couldn't think. I could only imagine an endless stretch of days where I'd wake up without her beside me.

"I'm so sorry. I didn't mean to spring this news on you when it's already been a shitty day. But you asked and I couldn't...I didn't want to keep it a secret from you. Not when the deadline is so close." Brooklyn glanced up again, her eyes bright with emotion. "I'm sorry," she repeated, her voice small.

"Don't be sorry." I forced a smile. If she was this torn over it, it meant she wanted the job. If she didn't, Chicago wouldn't matter—it would be an easy no. "You got a job offer from Derek and Haley fucking Moore. This should be a celebration."

She didn't smile back.

"What are you thinking?" I asked. "Let's talk it out. Pros and cons."

My response was logical, almost to the point of clinical, but I couldn't allow my emotions to gain a foothold. The Moores were a *huge* deal. Working for them could change her career, and I didn't want to influence her decision by letting her see how completely wrecked I felt.

If she saw the panic clawing up my throat or sensed the dread wrapping around my chest like a vise, she'd stay for *me*—and as much as I wanted that, I couldn't let her dim her future just to keep mine intact.

"Pros and cons," Brooklyn repeated. She sounded doubtful.

"Yeah. You have a few days to make your decision, so it'll be helpful to have a sounding board." If I smiled any harder, my face might crack.

She gnawed on her bottom lip. "Okay. Pros: I'll have a job with an amazing salary, benefits, and creative freedom. I really like Derek and Haley, and working for them will be a huge gold star on my résumé. They're almost guaranteed to take my career to the next level. Cons: I'll have to move to Chicago. Its winters are brutal, and I hate the wind. It also means I have to leave London, my dad, my friends..." Her voice caught on a whisper. "And you."

Her words settled between us on a heavy cloud of silence. The heater hummed in the background, the only sound in the room besides our breathing. Even the rush hour traffic outside had gone eerily quiet, like the world knew we were teetering on the edge of an abyss and was holding its breath too.

Don't go. I need you. I can't live without you.

The words threatened to break free from the crack in my chest.

The selfish part of me wanted to let them out. She could easily find another job in London...but could she find another job working for someone like the Moores?

Brooklyn had spent months agonizing over the future of her career. She gave up a sure thing at Blackcastle to pursue a better fit, and she'd finally found it. If I truly cared about her, how could I stand in her way?

"I told them I'll think about it, but I'm going to say no." She squared her shoulders. "I can't leave London. I'll find another job here. Now that I know what I want, it shouldn't be that hard."

"Maybe not, but this is a big deal. Take time to think about it and don't make an impulsive decision." The words scraped past my throat like razor blades. "Whatever you end up choosing, I don't want you to regret it down the road."

Brooklyn's eyes shimmered. "I'm sorry again. The timing couldn't be worse."

"I told you, you don't need to be sorry." The corner of my mouth lifted. "I'd rather get all the bad news at once. It's easier than getting shit on a little bit every day."

She let out a small, choked laugh. "In that case, I have one more thing to tell you. I didn't make it to ISNA's final round."

My gut twisted. I knew how much she'd wanted that prize. "Shit. I'm so fucking sorry."

"It's okay." She gave me a wan smile. "I've had a week to get over it, and honestly, I didn't submit the best application. I was *so* focused on the ISNA prize because it gave me a purpose when I didn't have other goals. But now that I've figured out what I want to do in my career, it hurts a little less."

I squeezed her hand, my chest burning with all the things I couldn't fix. All I could do was hold her tight and hope that was enough. "When did you find out?"

"Last Friday at the pub. You'd just gotten the Zenith deal, and I didn't want to be a buzzkill."

"Brooklyn." I stared at her, my tone leaving no room for argument. "You can never be a buzzkill. No matter what news you get or when you get it, you can tell me. I could've just won another fucking World Cup, and I'd still want to know if something big happened with you. Do you understand?"

She nodded, her eyes bright with emotion again.

"Say it."

"I understand," she whispered.

"Good." I pulled her close and kissed her forehead. My heart felt like a blade had cleaved it in half—partly for what she'd lost, and partly for what we might lose come Monday night. But that was three days away. Until then, I could hold her and pretend everything was alright, if only temporarily. "*Je serais toujours là pour toi, mon coeur. Quoiqu'il arrive.*"

CHAPTER 38

VINCENT

> I need help cheering Brooklyn up

ADIL
> Damn, you fucked up already? That has to be a record

> I didn't fuck up

> Why are you even here?

ADIL
> …I started this chat. I invited you to this chat!

> You're supposed to be on a digital detox

ADIL
> I am, but this is my daily one-hour break from the detox

ASHER
> What happened?

ADIL
> The thirty-minute break wasn't enough

ASHER
> I was talking to Vincent

She didn't make it to the final round of the ISNA Awards

ASHER

Oh shit. I'm sorry man, that sucks

ADIL

:(

ADIL

You should buy her a gift to cheer her up!

ADIL

What do nutritionists like? Hmm

NOAH

Before he thinks of an abomination and shares it with the group, here's a tip: do not listen to a word he says

ADIL

I resent that. I'm an amazing gift-giver

ADIL

Remember the potato pal I got you for your birthday?

NOAH

You mean the potato with my face printed on it?

NOAH

Unfortunately, yes

ADIL

It's funny because you show as much emotion as a potato, so a photo of your face on it doesn't make a difference.

ADIL

Get it?

NOAH WILSON LEFT THE CONVERSATION.

The weekend passed in a blur. Brooklyn and I stayed in our suite the entire time, ordering room service and watching nineties movies on pay-per-view. We didn't mention Chicago again, but the weight of her decision hung over us like a guillotine.

We told Coach, Scarlett, Asher, and Carina about the picture incident, but everyone else was on a strict need-to-know basis. I didn't want the guys getting distracted when knockouts were coming up. As expected, Coach flipped his shit and tried to get us to move into his house, but we both refused.

One, the three of us living under the same roof was a terrible idea. Two, his house wasn't properly secured. Even Brooklyn's flat was safer thanks to the security measures I'd installed a few months ago, but if the intruder was motivated enough, they could find out where she lived. I'd rather we stick with the hotel unless my new bodyguard had other ideas.

The security company I'd contacted had sent over a shortlist of candidates. I already had interviews with them scheduled over the next few days. Once I made a decision, we'd come up with a new security plan together.

I'd hoped it wouldn't come to that, but Smith's update wasn't promising. He finally called me after Monday's training and confirmed they hadn't found anything useful from the pub's CCTV footage. I'd expected it, but I was disappointed nonetheless.

"And you're sure it's not Ethan Brown or anyone associated with him?" I got into my car and locked the doors. I was grasping at straws, but fuck, it was bad enough I had one obsessed fan. Two in the space of a year would've been laughable if it didn't make my skin crawl.

"Positive," Smith said. "I'll be honest. It's hard for us to do more than we've already done because, like in the previous cases, the photo doesn't contain an explicit threat. We can't justify using additional police resources to track down the culprit."

My grip tightened around my phone. "Maybe it's not explicit, but that photo is an *implicit* threat to my *girlfriend*."

"I understand, but—"

"No, you fucking don't." My frustration boiled over into a full-blown roar. "Whoever the culprit is, they're obsessed with me. Sending me a picture of Brooklyn is a warning. They don't need to put a giant red X over her face for me to figure that out. You're the goddamn police. Are you going to do something to protect her, or are you going to wait until my next call is from the hospital or a fucking morgue?"

I didn't lose my cool often. I prided myself on keeping a level head because being smart often trumped being angry. My family and Brooklyn were the only exceptions. I cared too much about them to see reason when they were in danger, and no matter what Smith said, Brooklyn *was* in danger. Because of me.

A vise constricted around my chest.

"I agree," Smith said, shocking the hell out of me. "The intent behind leaving the photo is likely malicious, but my hands are tied. This is a low-priority case compared to everything else we're dealing with. Homicides. Missing children. Organized crime. A potential celebrity stalker with no history of violence doesn't even crack our top ten. That being said, I'll go over the surveillance footage again and see if I missed anything the first time."

I deflated, my anger draining out of me like water from a sieve. I could yell all I wanted, but Smith was right. There was too much going on for them to devote much manpower to my case.

I was hiring private security to protect Brooklyn and me, but would that be enough? I didn't know what resources the intruder had or how well-trained they were, but they were smart enough to avoid being identified this entire time.

I stared out the window. Drops of rain splattered against the windshield and turned the world gray.

It was Monday afternoon. Brooklyn needed to give the Moores an answer tonight. I'd put off thinking about it all weekend, but I couldn't avoid it any longer.

"You must've worked similar cases before," I said. "In your experience, how concerned should I be about the intruder turning violent and targeting Brooklyn?"

There was a long beat of silence. "I think you should take reasonable precautions," Smith finally said. "We don't know what the intruder's intentions are, but anyone who possesses this level of obsession and dedication will often turn violent when they're triggered. If and when that happens, the romantic partner of their fixation is often their first target."

My gut churned. I thanked Smith and hung up, feeling slightly numb as I drove back to the hotel. I made sure to take a roundabout route to throw off potential tails, and I kept an eye on my rearview mirror for suspicious cars, but my mind was a million miles away.

Smith's confirmation that Brooklyn was in danger snapped something loose inside me. I was a rope that'd been pulled too tight for too long, and I'd finally unraveled.

Everything was spinning out of control. I couldn't predict when the intruder would strike next, but I could do everything in my power to make sure Brooklyn was out of harm's way when it happened.

I pulled into the hotel's private VIP parking garage and cut the engine. The silence pressed in on me.

I'd spent my life worrying that I would lose the people I loved. My birth mum gave me up, and I was separated from my mother and sister when I was a child. I'd lost touch with my old friends in Paris after I transferred to Blackcastle—partly because of the distance, partly because of their envious reactions to my success.

Some of those broken ties were personal choices, and not all of them were permanent. But that didn't dislodge my deep-rooted fear that once someone walked away, they'd never come back. Unless I was constantly there, reminding them why I deserved a spot in their life, they'd forget about me or, worse, realize they never needed me to begin with.

But Brooklyn was different. She'd walked into my life through coincidence and stayed by choice. Yes, we had mutual friends, but she *chose* to be with me the same way I chose to be with her—through uncertainty, through fear, and through every obstacle life had thrown at us so far. She saw every fucked-up part of me and never flinched, and that terrified the *hell* out of me because I knew what I'd feel if I lost her. Not just pain. Not just regret. But a hollowing-out so complete I wasn't sure there'd be anything left.

My thoughts finally solidified into resolve.

I exited the car and took the elevator up to the penthouse. When I entered our suite, Brooklyn was sitting on the sofa, working on her computer.

"Hey." She greeted me with a smile. "How was training?"

"Fine. The usual." I kissed her, my throat closing at her familiar scent. "How was your day?"

While she told me about her afternoon, I tried to find the right words to broach the elephant in the room. But there *were* no right words, and there was no right time.

If I didn't say it now, I'd never say it. So when Brooklyn paused for breath, I looked her in the eye and let the weight of my words drop between us.

"I think you should take the job in Chicago."

CHAPTER 39

BROOKLYN

I FROZE, MY BRAIN STRUGGLING TO MAKE SENSE OF HIS words.

I think you should take the job in Chicago.

The sentiment was so sudden, so unexpected, that I couldn't break free from that mental no man's land between confusion and disbelief.

My heart rate sped up, and when I finally found my voice, it came out smaller than I wanted. "Do you want me to leave?"

The prospect of Vincent asking me to walk away from him, from *us*, sent an arrow of hurt through my chest.

I'd spent the weekend agonizing over my decision. Should I take the Moore job, or should I stay? Like I told him on Friday, my instinct was to stay, but the more I thought about it, the harder the choice became.

I loved my life in London. I couldn't fathom leaving it behind. At the same time, I couldn't say with certainty that I wouldn't regret turning down the Moores. It was the opportunity of a lifetime, and if I said no, I'd always wonder...*what if*? And I was afraid that wonder would turn into resentment and bitterness down the road.

But throughout all my internal debates, I'd banked on the fact that Vincent wanted me to stay. He didn't say it, probably because he didn't want to influence my decision one way or another, but the way he'd held me on Friday after he heard the news made me think that my leaving would devastate him as much as it would me.

But what if I was wrong? What if he didn't care whether I stayed or left?

I think you should take the job in Chicago.

A cold, hollow sensation seeped into my limbs.

"Fuck no," Vincent said, the fierceness of his denial halting the icy creep of doubt. "If I had a choice, I'd never leave your side. But this is your dream job, Brooklyn. I want you to stay, but I want you to be happy more."

I blinked hard, my throat thick with emotion. "How can I be happy when I'm not with you?"

"You will be. London to Chicago is just distance. It doesn't mean we won't be together." Vincent framed my face with his hands, his thumb brushing over my cheek with such tenderness it made my heart ache. "I want you to give the Moore job a chance because I don't want you to look back and wonder *what if*. If you don't like it, you can quit and move back. I'll be right here waiting for you. If you do like it, then fucking smash it in Chicago, and we'll find a way to make our relationship work. I promise. If you think I'd let a few thousand miles come between us, then you don't know me at all."

I laughed through a veil of tears. The *what if* part. I should've known Vincent would pick up on what I was thinking without me having to say it.

As for the rest...my chest squeezed.

I was tempted to follow his suggestion because he was right. I wasn't guaranteed to like the job once I started it, but I owed it to myself to try. Talking to the Moores had been a moment of clarity when my life finally clicked into place. For the first time since I turned down Blackcastle's offer, I had a solid vision of what I wanted my career to look like.

But despite Vincent's sincerity, I couldn't shake the sense that there was something he wasn't telling me—another reason he wanted me to take the job so badly.

"If I had to bet on you or a few thousand miles, I'd always choose you," I said. "But I'm going to ask you something, and you have to answer honestly. Are you pushing me to move to Chicago because you're afraid the intruder will come after me?"

I didn't blame him for the intruder's actions, but it was obvious how guilty he felt about putting me in potential harm's way. His willingness to hire a bodyguard—something he'd refused to do just a few months ago—proved how seriously he was taking the threat.

Vincent released a slow breath, as if he were debating whether or not to confess. "I should've known you'd see through me," he said ruefully. "I spoke to Smith after training." He gave me a brief summary of their conversation, including Smith's tacit confirmation that the intruder might come after me. "You'll be safer in Chicago. The intruder won't follow you there if I'm not with you, and I need you to be okay." His voice turned raw and rough. "If *anything* happened to you, I wouldn't survive. Do you understand? *Tu es plus que mon cœur. Tu es mon tout.*"

I didn't know what he'd said, but I felt the emotion behind it in my bones. It twisted something inside me—a mixture of fear, anguish, and inevitability that threatened to drown me.

"I don't want to leave you," I whispered, my words barely audible.

I'd never been the type to center big life decisions around a guy. When one of my friends backed out of a semester abroad in France so she could stay with her boyfriend, I'd told her she was out of her mind. When another friend moved across the country to be with someone she'd only known for a month, I'd sworn never to do the same.

But now, I understood how they felt—like the entire world hinged on one person, and my heart would crack wide open if I walked away from him. It was the sheer, devastating agony of choosing between myself and the person who felt like home.

"You won't be leaving me." Vincent's thumb brushed my cheek again. It came away wet, and it was only then that I realized I was crying. "I'll be here, just a text or phone call away. We'll talk so often you'll want to block me after two weeks."

I laughed again through a sob.

What a mindfuck this all was. It was proof that life could change in the blink of an eye, and that we could get what we wanted but still feel like we were losing everything that mattered.

Vincent made some good points, but at the end of the day, it was my decision.

Luckily, I had a few hours left before my final deadline.

Instead of responding, I wound my arms around Vincent's neck and kissed him. I poured everything I couldn't say into the kiss—all the longing, all the heartache, all the promises I couldn't voice without shattering into a million pieces.

And later, when his body slid over mine and he whispered my name like a prayer, I held on tight and pretended, for one desperate moment, that this would last forever.

The sky was still a deep, velvety indigo when I woke up a few hours later.

Vincent's arm was draped over my waist, his body strong and warm against mine. I basked in the comfort for a second before I gently disentangled myself from his embrace and slipped out of bed as quietly as possible.

He remained fast asleep, his torso rising and falling with steady breaths. A sharp pang snaked through my chest as I gazed at him.

I'd never imagined I would find someone who made me feel the way he did, like I was finally whole and *seen*. Like every broken part of me was just a little softer and more at peace when I was around him.

I'd certainly never thought that person would be the one standing right in front of me, waiting for me to realize he'd been there all along.

Don't sound so happy to see me, buttercup. I'll get the wrong idea.

Let's see who'll cave and kiss the other first.

I'd lose every single fucking bet in the world if it meant I could be with you.

If anything *happened to you, I wouldn't survive.*

A burn radiated through my chest. I turned away, my throat tight, and slipped into the suite's sitting room, where I opened my laptop and composed an email to the Moores.

I read and reread it, making sure I worded my response exactly right.

Then, before I could change my mind, I hit send.

CHAPTER 40

BROOKLYN

"I CAN'T BELIEVE YOU'RE REALLY LEAVING US." SCARLETT gave me a fierce hug, her voice thick with emotion. "This feels like way too soon."

"If you want cold, gray weather, we have that right here. You don't need to go to Chicago," Carina added. Her voice was steadier, but her eyes were red when she hugged me after Scarlett pulled away.

I laughed through the lump in my throat. "If Chicago isn't gray or cold enough for me, I promise I'll come back." I squeezed Carina tight. "Thank you, guys, for coming to see me off. You didn't have to do this."

"Are you kidding? We wouldn't miss this for the world." Scarlett gave me a sad smile. "We'll miss you."

The lump expanded. "I'll miss you too."

Great. Now I was the one crying in the middle of the airport.

After two weeks of frantic prepping and packing, it was here—the day I left London and moved to Chicago.

Things had moved quickly after I accepted the Moores' offer.

They'd set me up at a fully furnished apartment near their house, and they'd hired someone to help me pack up my flat in London. I was only bringing my clothes and other personal items to Chicago; my furniture and other nonessential belongings were in storage.

My three suitcases and carry-on surrounded us as Scarlett, Carina, and I lingered near the check-in kiosks. My dad had a match today, so we'd said goodbye that morning. He'd wanted to leave the match in Greely's hands and accompany me to the airport, but I'd insisted he be with his players instead. The match was too important, and the fact he'd offered meant more than his actual presence.

I was okay with our goodbye, but my girls? I needed as much time with them as possible.

"We promise we'll keep you updated on all the hot goss while you're gone," Carina said. "It'll be like you never left."

"I appreciate that. I do love some good gossip."

"I know. And if you need a care package with some proper tea and biscuits, we got you. Keep an eye on your mailbox."

I smiled even as melancholy curled through me.

We were stalling. None of us wanted to be the one to say goodbye first.

My friends had been stunned when I told them about my move, but neither had guilt tripped me into staying. They understood why I made the decision I did, and they were as happy for me as they were heartbroken.

The sentiment was mutual.

I'd never had girlfriends like them. I'd only known Scarlett and Carina for a year and a half, but they'd been more supportive and caring than any of my old friends. They were genuinely excited when I had good news, genuinely sad when I didn't, and they never judged or secretly tried to compete with me. Besides Vincent, they were the only people I felt truly comfortable with.

They also knew me well enough to guess what was on my mind at the moment.

"He'll be here," Scarlett said softly. "He wouldn't miss seeing you off if Satan himself tried to stop him."

"It's okay if he's not. I don't expect him to be." I smiled through the ache in my chest. "We said goodbye this morning."

Vincent was playing in today's match. He'd also wanted to call in sick and take me to the airport, but I refused to hear it. Blackcastle had a knockout match today, which meant they needed to win in order to advance in the tournament. I wasn't going to hamper their chances by taking their captain and best defender off the pitch.

"Oh, honey." Carina squeezed my arm, her eyes soft.

But eventually, we couldn't stall anymore. My flight was boarding soon, so I checked my bags, hugged my friends one last time, and made it through security and to my gate with ten minutes to spare.

Instead of milling around and waiting, I ducked into the shop across from my gate. I couldn't stay still for too long. If I did, my doubts would creep in again, and I'd run out of the airport and back to my flat because that was the easy thing to do.

I had to make it to Chicago first. Then I could sit on the floor and let the significance of what I was doing fully hit me.

But my plans for delaying my eventual breakdown shattered when I passed by the newsstand. Vincent smiled at me from the cover of *Sports UK* magazine, his dimple just visible enough to unravel me. His image was so sharp and clear, I felt like I could reach out and feel his warmth beneath my fingertips.

I tried to stop it, but it was impossible. A tide of emotion crashed over me, blurring my vision. A hot tear slipped down my cheek. I wiped it away, but another fell, and another, and soon, they came in waves too thick and fast for me to control.

My ribcage felt too tight for my lungs. I'd talked to Vincent just that morning, and I already missed him like it'd been years.

I had a plan, but what if it failed? What if I had to stay in Chicago forever? We'd promised each other we would make it work long distance, but I'd seen the statistics. Long-distance relationships lasted an average of only four and a half months, and my plan was a Hail Mary anyway.

"I know I look good, but I think that's the first time one of my pictures has brought someone to tears in public."

Great. Now I was hearing his voice in a freaking airport shop.

I hiccupped. So much for waiting until Chicago before my breakdown.

A hand brushed my shoulder, warm and so very *real*. "Brooklyn." His voice was tender. "Turn around."

My heart leapt in my throat. I whirled around, my pulse pounding when I saw the achingly familiar outline of Vincent's form. I blinked hard, both to clear the tears and to double-check I wasn't hallucinating.

No, that was really him, standing in the shop's narrow aisle dressed in his football kit. He was sweaty and his clothes had grass stains, but I'd never seen a more beautiful sight.

Spike, his new bodyguard, hovered a respectful distance away. Vincent's presence was already attracting stares and whispers, but Spike's glare kept anyone from approaching us.

"You—how—" I struggled to find the right words.

The match ended less than an hour ago, and it took place all the way across town. There was no way he could've made it here this quickly.

"We were already up by two in the last half. Coach subbed me out toward the end, and I came straight to the airport. But even if I had to play until the last minute, I would've found a way to get here in time." Vincent brushed my tears away with his thumb. "You didn't think I'd let you leave without a proper airport goodbye, did you?"

Fuck, I was going to start crying again.

I let out a strangled laugh. "Don't tell me you bought a ticket just to get past security."

"I didn't buy it *just* to get past security. I've always wanted to go to..." He checked his phone. "Fargo, North Dakota. Maybe you can take the weekend off, join me, and show me around."

"Unfortunately, I've never been there. I'll be as lost as you."

"Then we'll be lost together."

A sob hitched in my throat.

Vincent's face softened. He opened his arms, and I stepped into them, burying myself in his warmth. His heartbeat thudded against my cheek, steady and strong.

Neither of us spoke. What could we say that we hadn't said already?

I'll miss you.

I'll wait for you.

Don't forget this. Don't forget me.

No words needed. Our sentiments were obvious in the way he held me, in the fit of our bodies and the synchronized beats of our hearts.

I didn't know how long we stood there, lost in each other's embrace, but eventually, reality intruded.

"*Flight 226 to Chicago now boarding.*" The PA system crackled overhead.

That was my flight.

My stomach dropped. Vincent's arms tightened around me, and I pressed my face to his chest, trying to etch every detail of this moment in my memory.

My sobs had died down, but my entire body ached like I was being torn apart.

"I'll walk you to your gate," Vincent murmured, his voice rough with emotion.

No. I shook my head and clung to him.

Forget Chicago. I could call the Moores right now and tell them I'd changed my mind. Vincent and I would leave the airport together and head straight to one of our favorite restaurants, where we'd order a shit ton of carbs and laugh about the time I almost moved halfway across the world.

Then we'd still be together, and I wouldn't feel like my heart was breaking.

The PA system crackled again with warning. *"This is the final boarding call for passengers booked on flight 226 to Chicago. Please proceed to the gate immediately."*

I squeezed my eyes shut.

"Brooklyn, we have to go," Vincent said gently. "Or you'll miss your flight."

I couldn't put it off anymore. My fantasy of running out of here with him dissolved, and I followed him to the gate, where the attendant's eyes widened in recognition. Thankfully, she was smart enough not to bother us as Vincent kissed me, slow and lingering, as though we had all the time in the world.

His last gift to me.

"Call me when you land," he murmured.

I nodded, my voice breaking. "I will."

Then the attendant was hurrying me along, and I had to walk straight to the plane without looking back because I knew, without a shadow of a doubt, that if I looked back, I would never leave.

VINCENT

"DuBois! What the hell are you doing?" Coach yelled. "You're all over the place. Get it together!"

It was the third time he'd yelled at me during today's training.

"Sorry, Boss." I shook my head and tried to focus, but everything felt like static in my brain.

We had a knockout match against Berlin tomorrow, so a win was crucial if we wanted to make it through to the next stage. Unfortunately, my concentration was shot, and the rest of training was a disaster. I missed two easy passes, mistimed my runs, and nearly collided with Asher during a corner drill. By the time it ended, Coach was apoplectic, and the team was silent.

I saw the other players exchange glances as we filed into the changing room, but no one was brave enough to say anything. Even Asher maintained his distance, though he kept throwing worried looks in my direction.

I headed straight for my locker, my jaw tight, but my steps faltered when I closed in on the bench.

That was where Brooklyn and I had sat during her last day at Blackcastle.

I'll be back Tuesday. It's not like I'll be gone for a year.

Four days without you is a long time, buttercup.

Getting needy already, DuBois?

I always need you.

My heart twisted. I'd give up my left arm to go back to a time when a few days of separation was all we had to get through.

Brooklyn left two weeks ago, yet I saw her everywhere—on the pitch, in the canteen, behind my closed eyelids when I went to sleep at night. I smelled her perfume on my pillows and heard her voice calling my name when I walked through a crowd. Her presence haunted me, and even though she was only a call away, I felt every inch of the four thousand miles separating us.

I finished showering and getting dressed in record time, but Coach stopped me before I could leave.

"Let's talk," he said. It wasn't a suggestion.

I followed him to his office, too numb to argue or even worry about the tongue-lashing I was sure to receive after my fuckups today.

He waited until the door was closed before he spoke. "I miss her too."

My gaze flew to his. That was the last thing I'd expected him to say. "What?"

"Brooklyn," he clarified. "I assume she's the reason you looked like shit at training today."

I grimaced. "Was it that obvious?"

"Only to everyone and their dog." Coach leaned back in his chair. "So, let's hear it. What's on your mind, besides the fact she's in Chicago and you're stuck here, living in a hotel with that gloomy new bodyguard of yours?"

"That's it," I admitted. Coach didn't tolerate players who brought their personal problems onto the pitch, but Brooklyn was his daughter. Maybe he'd understand. "There's nothing else. I'm the one who encouraged her to go, and I'm glad she's safe, but I just... miss her. It's fucking with my head. I know I need to shape up for tomorrow's match, and I will. Today was just a bad day."

The intruder hadn't reared their ugly head again, but if and when they did, at least they couldn't get to Brooklyn.

Now all I had to do was get my shit together, as Coach would say.

He sighed. I'd anticipated more yelling, but he sounded surprisingly sympathetic. "That's normal. I expected you to feel that way, or we'd have a problem. I can't tell you how to handle a long-distance relationship, but as your coach, I can tell you that you can't let that shit affect your focus. If Brooklyn knows she's the reason you're messing up on the pitch, do you think she'd stay in Chicago? She'd be on the first flight back."

I swallowed. I hadn't thought of it that way.

"Like I said, I miss her too. She's my daughter," Coach continued gruffly. "But not letting her absence impact your performance is the best way to get through your separation. You can wallow off the pitch as much as you'd like. But when we're in that stadium, or any other stadium, you have to bring your A game. Use the situation to your advantage. Take all that frustration and channel it into the game. Control your emotions. Don't let them control you. Understand?"

I nodded, my throat tight. "I won't let you down."

"Good." He dismissed me. "Get some rest. I'll see you tomorrow."

I returned to the changing room, where Seth finally worked up the courage to approach me. He'd really come into his own since he first joined the club, and I was glad to see he was becoming more comfortable with the players. During his first month as kit manager, he could barely look any of us in the eye.

"Some of the players and I are headed to the Angry Boar soon," he said tentatively. "Do you want to join us? It might take your mind off...you know."

I shook my head. "I have a call with Brooklyn later, but thanks for the invite. Have fun."

"Okay." He looked a little disappointed, but he didn't pressure me into going. "Say hi to her for me."

"I will."

I grabbed my duffel and headed for the exit. Spike was waiting for me in the corridor. We walked to my car, which he'd upgraded with new armored protection, and we drove back to the hotel in silence.

We hadn't bonded much since I hired him, but he'd been the most competent candidate for the job. I normally tried to befriend everyone I worked with, but I was okay with the current state of our relationship as long as he kept the intruder at bay.

Spike did a customary sweep of my suite before I turned in for the night. Once he gave me the all clear, I locked the door, and he retreated to his room next to mine.

I checked the clock. It was eleven in the morning in Chicago. I still had some time left before our scheduled call during her lunch break.

I checked my emails while I waited. Lloyd had sent me the final Zenith paperwork, but I left it unread. I was too exhausted to comb through legal documents at the moment.

Instead, I indulged in the unhealthy habit of scrolling through old photos of Brooklyn and me.

Us kissing beneath a sprig of mistletoe during the holidays.

Us posing on Tower Bridge like tourists, our arms wrapped around each other's waists.

Us curled up on her sofa, her head on my shoulder as we grinned at the camera.

A familiar, pervasive loneliness stole through my chest. As much as I loved my team and my sister, they weren't a substitute for Brooklyn. She was the only person who made me feel whole, and her absence left a hollow ache where her presence used to be.

We talked every day, either on the phone or via text. We video called each other whenever we could, though our work hours and the time zone difference meant that didn't happen as often as I would've liked.

I was committed to making it work long distance. Even if she moved farther away to the West Coast or even Hawaii, I'd still find a way to be with her. But fuck, I ached for her more than I thought I ever could.

I checked the time again. Half an hour left until her lunch break.

I scrolled through my phone's album again and paused on a photo of us at Asher and Scarlett's holiday party. It was one Adil had taken of us kissing. Everyone around us was cheering and laughing, and we looked so damn happy I almost forgot she wasn't a half-hour drive away anymore.

The ache behind my ribs intensified.

Before I could stop myself, I switched to the web browser and looked up Chicago's football club.

Just in case. Just to see.

CHAPTER 41

BROOKLYN

"THIS IS YOUR MEAL PLAN FOR THE WEEK. I UPPED YOUR carbohydrate intake, but otherwise it's similar to what we've been doing so far. Once we get to regionals, I'll cut out any high-fat and high-fiber foods that are harder to digest. We don't want you having any stomach discomfort during the competition." I slid a packet with the pertinent information across the counter. "This is a hard copy for backup. I've also updated everything on the nutrition app so you have it on your phone."

"Thanks." Haley gave me a grateful smile. "You always think of everything."

"I try. How are you liking your meals so far?"

"They're good, and I'm so glad they taste like *something*. I swear my old nutritionist was allergic to seasoning. Her recipes were so bland, you'd think she'd explode if she added a little pepper to her chicken."

I laughed. "I am definitely not opposed to pepper."

We were in her family's kitchen, going over some last-minute items before she left for her afternoon training.

It was early March and my second week in Chicago. With regionals coming up fast in April, I'd hit the ground running the minute I arrived. Between onboarding with the Moores, trying to get situated in my new home, and collaborating with Haley to create a system that worked for her, I'd barely had time to sleep.

Thankfully, Derek and Haley were as warm in person as they'd been during my interview. They had high standards, but that only pushed me to work harder and be better, which was easy when I enjoyed what I was doing.

My instincts had been right: working with an individual athlete fit my style way better than spreading myself thin with a team. I had the freedom to experiment with different recipes and methods, and Haley was responsive to most of my suggestions.

Overall, it was a smooth start to my new life, but that didn't stop me from checking the clock every two seconds. I was itching to talk to Vincent. We didn't get to video call each other often, and my body was already thrumming with anticipation.

"I forgot to tell you earlier, but my grandparents are in town," Haley said. "My dad and I are having dinner with them earlier, so we don't need to check in tonight. You can take the rest of the day off."

My pulse sped up. "Are you sure?"

She nodded. "I know the past two weeks have been crazy, so get some rest. Let's meet back here tomorrow, same time, same place?"

"Sounds good." I said goodbye to Haley and left, my face breaking out into a grin. Her timing couldn't have been better.

I had the afternoon off, and it was evening in London, which meant Vincent and I could talk for as long as we wanted.

I practically floated on my way back to my apartment. It was only a ten-minute walk from Haley's house, but my face was already stinging from the wind by the time I got home. Chicago winters were brutal, but even that wasn't enough to ruin my high.

I quickly showered and changed into a silk nightshirt and lingerie (just because Vincent wasn't here in person didn't mean I couldn't dress up for him). I topped it off with some mascara and lip gloss before I took my laptop to my bedroom and logged on at our scheduled call time.

Vincent's face filled my screen, and my heart cartwheeled just like it had the first time we kissed.

His dimple flashed. "Hey, buttercup."

"Hi." I smiled back, soaking him in. God bless whoever invented video technology. The firm curve of his mouth, the sculpted arch of his cheekbones, the teasing gleam in his eyes—they were so sharp and vivid, it was like he was actually standing in front of me.

"Tell me about your day," he said. "I want to hear all about it."

We always started our conversations with detailed rundowns of our day, including what we ate and which errands we ran. To other people, it might seem mundane or even boring, but I lived for these moments. Now that we lived in different cities, I didn't want our connection to hinge only on big life events; I wanted to know the same details I would've been privy to if I were still in London.

After I finished, Vincent told me about training and Spike's apparent aversion to talking.

The bodyguard seemed determined to blend into the background, which was his job, I guess. I was just glad Vincent had someone looking out for him. Even though the intruder hadn't made another move since the Angry Boar photo, not a day passed when I didn't worry about him.

I kept that to myself. Vincent would worry about me worrying about him, and that was a vicious cycle we didn't need to get stuck in.

"Great match over the weekend, by the way," I said. "Defense looked good."

"Yeah?" Vincent drawled. "How good?"

"Good enough for me to look up the club's captain." I tapped my fingers against my desk and pretended to think. "Have you heard of a player named Vincent DuBois?"

"Vaguely. He sounds like a charmer."

"He is. He's good-looking too. Tall, dark, handsome…just my type."

"Is he?" Vincent said silkily. He leaned in, an ember of heat flaring in his eyes.

"Mmhmm." My breath hitched as the mood shifted from playful to something heavier, more electric. Anticipation curled low and hot between my thighs.

The hardest part of a long-distance relationship was not being able to touch each other. Our conversations filled an emotional void, but they couldn't satisfy my need for physical intimacy.

My toys got the job done, but they weren't him. Unfortunately, they'd have to do until one of us could visit the other in person. Unless…

An idea took shape in my mind. It was something I'd never had the guts to do, but this was Vincent. It was now or never. "I forgot to mention one thing."

"What's that?"

"I went shopping for some new lingerie over the weekend." I leaned back, my stomach fluttering with a mixture of nerves and excitement. "Black lace. It's gorgeous."

Vincent's eyes darkened. "Show me."

A thrill coursed through me at his command. I pushed away from my desk and knelt on the bed so he had a better view from my computer.

The air pulsed as I pulled my silk nightshirt over my head, leaving me in a semi-sheer lace bra and matching thong.

My heart raced. We'd sexted before, but we'd never sent nude pictures or engaged in cybersex. This was a whole new level of eroticism, and I would've chickened out if Vincent's sharp intake of breath didn't ignite something deep inside me.

"Do you like it?" My voice sounded almost too breathy to be mine.

His eyes traced the swell of my breasts and the curve of my hips. They lingered between my legs before they met mine again. Little fires erupted everywhere his gaze landed.

"I'd like it better if it was on the floor," he said, the steel in his tone betraying the softness of his words. "Take it off."

My heart rate sped up from a gallop into a full-fledged frenzy.

This was it. The point of no return.

Are you really going to do this?

I stared at myself onscreen.

The video version of me stared back, her cheeks pink and her lips parted as she slowly reached behind her and unhooked her bra. She tossed the scrap of black lace aside before she hooked her thumbs into the waistband of her thong and shimmied out of that too.

It felt like an out-of-body experience, but my senses returned to me when the last stitch of clothing fell off my body.

I kneeled there, fully naked and vulnerable. My body thrummed with nerves but also…a tiny thrill. It was my first time being naked on camera, and while it was scary to put all of myself out there like this, it was arousing in a way I couldn't name.

My nipples pebbled into diamond-hard points, and wetness pooled between my thighs.

I swallowed, my attention shifting back to Vincent. He'd removed his own clothes while I'd been stripping. He watched me from his desk, his eyes dark and hooded while his hand gripped the base of his impressive erection.

"Touch yourself for me," he ordered. "Play with your nipples and cunt. I want to see how you get yourself off when you're alone at night."

His words zipped through me like an electric shock. My pussy clenched with need, and I kept my eyes on his as I spread my legs wider.

I curled my forefinger and rubbed the slick, swollen nub while my other hand played with my breasts. I alternated between them, tugging at and pinching my nipples until jolts of pleasure shot straight to my clit. I was on fire, every inch of my body blazing despite the winter chill seeping through my apartment.

Vincent groaned, his hand twisting up and down his cock. Seeing him so turned on turned *me* on even more, and I couldn't hold back a moan.

"Oh, God." I whimpered, my head falling back as the beginnings of an orgasm coiled at the base of my spine. The slick, erotic sounds of Vincent jerking off mixed with my heavy pants.

I thought having sex over video would make me feel disconnected, but this strangely felt *more* intimate. We couldn't hide here. There were no sheets or dim lighting to soften the experience or conceal any insecurities. It was only us in all our raw, naked glory, taking pleasure for and with each other in the ultimate expression of trust.

I wouldn't do this with anyone else. I'd be too afraid they would pick apart my flaws or use it against me somehow, but Vincent? I trusted him whole-heartedly, and any self-consciousness I might've felt at pleasuring myself on camera was long gone.

I rubbed faster, my breaths turning erratic as my orgasm crept closer and closer and—

"Stop." Vincent's harsh command brought the impending wave to a halt.

I whined in protest but obeyed. My fingers were sticky with my juices, and my core continued to pulse after I pulled away.

Vincent hadn't come yet either, but pre-cum leaked from the tip of his cock and smeared on his stomach.

My mouth watered. I wanted to reach through the screen and lick him clean. To taste every inch of him and make him lose control the way he could make me lose mine.

"You're thinking about sucking my cock, aren't you?" Vincent drawled. His voice was still soft, still lethal.

"Yes," I breathed, too turned on to play coy.

"Is that what you think about every time you finger fuck yourself, sweetheart? Taking my cock down your throat and choking on it?" His silky tone camouflaged the filthiness of his words.

I shook my head slowly. "I don't use just my fingers."

His jaw clenched, a predatory gleam flashing in his eyes. "Show me what else you do." The silkiness was gone, replaced with a guttural growl.

I licked my lips, my skin buzzing as I scooted toward the edge of the bed and opened my nightstand drawer. I retrieved my biggest toy—a thick, ridged dildo with a flared base and curved shaft. I didn't use it often because it was a little *too* big, but I was feeling ambitious and more than a little aroused.

When I returned my gaze to the screen, Vincent was strangling his cock so hard I was surprised it didn't burst.

He didn't have to tell me what to do. I already knew.

I knelt on all fours, angling my body so he had an unimpeded side view as I slowly pushed the dildo inside me. Despite how wet I was, my muscles involuntarily clenched at its size.

I stopped three quarters of the way in, my body taut, my skin coated with sweat. The pressure was unbearable, and I could feel every nerve come alive with equal parts pleasure and torment.

"Keep going," Vincent ordered. "I want to see you take every inch of that cock like it's mine. Like I'm the one making you scream while I stretch that tight little pussy wide open."

My mind swam from the obscene picture he painted. It was the last push I needed, and I managed to take the remaining inches of the dildo until it hit the most sensitive spot inside me.

I cried out, my back bowing at the sensation. The edges of my vision darkened, but I had enough sense to pull the toy out so just the tip remained inside me. I pushed it back in, slowly working my way up to a steady rhythm. In and out, deeper and harder, fucking myself with long, mind-melting strokes that I imagined were Vincent's.

"Tell me what else you think about when you're fucking yourself."

"I...I think about you finding me like this," I panted. "You come home early, and you walk in on me playing with myself. I don't hear you enter, so you grab me and...and..." I hit that sweet spot again, and my brain short-circuited. "*Fuck.*"

"And what?" Vincent growled. "What do I do to you when I see you taking that cock like a greedy little slut?"

I could barely breathe through my lust-soaked haze. "You grab me and fuck me. Hard. You make me take your cock anywhere you want, and you won't let me come until I'm begging for it. Begging for *you.*"

He hissed, the sound low and tortured. "Does that turn you on? The thought of me punishing you for coming around a cock that's not mine?"

"*Yes.*" The confession spilled out as a whimper.

"I bet you'd like it if I pushed you to your knees and fucked that sweet little throat until you gagged, wouldn't you? You'd probably come just from my cock filling you up."

My replies turned incoherent. I closed my eyes, letting his dirty words and my imagination run wild as I fucked myself eagerly with the toy—except it was no longer a toy. It was Vincent, here with me in Chicago, his hands in my hair and on my hips. He pounded me relentlessly, and I could feel every inch of him inside me.

Our ragged breaths synced as we urged each other on, our bodies slick with want, our flesh slapping against each other in perfect unison. It was raw and fierce and primal, and I'd never felt this close to anyone, like I could spend the rest of my life lost in this moment and never tire of it.

A deep, pulsing heat coiled in my belly. Tremors quaked along my limbs. My muscles stiffened, and I was so close, so—

"Stop."

"No!" I cried. Tears of frustration sprang to my eyes. The dildo was still inside me, but this was my second ruined orgasm of the night. I was shaking, so close to breaking that I could barely remember my own name.

"I said stop, Brooklyn."

I let my hands drop in defeat. My walls continued to clench, grasping desperately for a release that hovered just out of reach.

"We're almost there." Vincent's voice turned soothing. "Do one more thing for me, and you can come."

"What is it?" Despite my disappointment, my skin tingled in anticipation of his request.

"Get another dildo from your drawer. Leave the one you have in."

My face blazed, but I didn't argue. I crawled over to my nightstand again. I could only imagine what I must look like, sweaty and messy and so fucking wanton with my pussy stretched around the toy still buried inside me. I fumbled through the drawer for a second before I selected a slightly smaller dildo.

"Good," Vincent said when I returned to my earlier spot on the bed. He was still grasping his cock, his eyes so dark they resembled pools of obsidian. "Now suck it. Show me how you'd take my cock if I were there."

My mouth watered again at his command. I gripped the base and sealed my lips around the tip of the dildo. I slowly lowered my head, imagining it was Vincent sliding past my tongue. I gagged halfway, drool leaking down my chin, but I eventually did it. The tip of my nose touched the mattress as I took the entirety of the toy down my throat.

Triumph sparked in my chest.

"Look at you." Vincent groaned. "You look so good stuffed with cock, sweetheart."

His praise washed over me, adding to the heat in my veins. I'd used multiple toys before, but never like this. Never in front of someone else, and never while they were urging me on, telling me how much they wanted me, how fucking beautiful I looked and how desperate they were to touch me.

I kept one hand wrapped around the base while the other reached behind me to steady the toy in my pussy. I fucked back against it, my mind blanking with each thrust while I continued to suck on the dildo in my mouth. I was stuffed so full I couldn't focus on anything except the pressure and sheer, blinding pleasure. My muscles trembled, my core throbbed, and my lungs burned, but I kept going until I finally, *finally* heard the magic words.

"Come for me."

That was all it took.

I exploded, my poor, hypersensitized body coming apart at the seams. The endless edging and dirty talk lit me up and tore me into a thousand pieces. It was a white-hot detonation that shredded every nerve, driving the air from my lungs and wrenching a cry from deep inside me. But my screams were muffled by the cock still lodged in my throat, and I lay there, my muscles locking and releasing in helpless spasms as the waves of my orgasm crashed over me.

I heard Vincent come with a loud grunt of his own, and I turned my head just in time to see thick, white ropes of cum spill over his fist and onto his stomach. His head was thrown back, his muscles strained, his body trembling as he came completely undone.

It was the hottest thing I'd ever seen.

My orgasm finally abated enough for me to take out my toys and catch my breath. When we both came down from our highs, we exchanged small smiles, our faces flushed with sated pleasure and quiet intimacy.

"You're perfect," he said, his voice rough but so sincere it melted what was left of my defenses.

My eyes prickled. "I miss you."

"I miss you too." His mouth tipped up. "Next time, we'll do that in person."

An ache ripped through me. "Next time" wasn't soon enough. I needed him right now, right here.

But that wasn't possible, so I gathered myself together and upped the wattage of my smile. "Only if you promise not to torture me like that again."

Vincent laughed, the sound huskier than usual. "If I do, I promise I'll make it up to you."

"Make it up to me how?"

He raised an eyebrow. "It wouldn't be any fun if I told you, would it?"

"Fine," I said with a genuine grin. "It's a deal."

We stayed on for a while longer, completely unselfconscious despite our nakedness. But eventually, we had to say goodbye, and I logged off with a familiar hollow in my chest.

Later that night, after I changed the sheets and showered for a second time, I went to bed alone and closed my eyes, imagining that Vincent was lying right there next to me.

The fantasy wasn't real, but for now, it was all I had.

CHAPTER 42

VINCENT

MARCH CAME AND WENT. THE FRIGID DAYS OF WINTER eventually gave way to early spring, and both the trainings and the pressure ramped up as Blackcastle advanced steadily toward the Champions League semi-finals.

Brooklyn and I settled into a comfortable routine of texts, phone calls, and video calls. The piercing ache of her absence had softened into a softer but steady hum in the background. It wasn't because I missed her any less; it was because I needed to control my emotions like Coach had said. I couldn't let them affect her time in Chicago or our race for the UCL title.

The intruder was still lying low, but Spike remained glued to my side. He did, however, convince me to move back home. The hotel became untenable after fans found out I was living there, and my earlier, all-consuming anxiety at moving home was more manageable with him around. In the autumn, I'd been worried about the effect the stress would have on my game, but if I could deal with the emotional toll of Brooklyn's absence, I could deal with the intruder.

On a brighter note, I kicked off my official tenure as Zenith's men's ambassador. Two weeks after I signed the official paperwork, Sandra suggested we meet at Blackcastle to shoot a promotional video for their social media. She wanted to do it after one of my trainings for "maximum authenticity." She'd swept in with a full camera and lighting crew, and we spent two hours filming in the changing room until she was happy. Lloyd was also there, silent but observant.

"We're so thrilled to have you on board," she said, beaming after we wrapped up the shoot. "Your test shots were fantastic, and we're so excited about the first campaign launching this fall. Of course, we scheduled the bulk of the promo for the summer. We don't want to distract you from the UCL finals!"

"Thank you." I smiled. "I'm excited to be part of the family and to launch the campaign."

I waited until Sandra and her crew left before I grabbed my duffel and headed for the exit myself.

"That was excellent." Lloyd fell into step with me. Since most of the players and staff were already gone, it was just us in the corridor. "That video is going to break the internet."

"Great." I honestly didn't care about how viral the video went. Strangely enough, I felt more neutral about the Zenith deal as well.

Don't get me wrong. I was thrilled about landing the ambassadorship, but the more time passed, the less *crucial* it seemed. When I was vying for the role, I'd wanted it so badly I could fucking taste it. Now that I had it, I liked it, but I wasn't obsessed with it the way I used to be.

It wasn't simply a case of wanting what I didn't have. It was the fact that its importance had been replaced by something more pressing.

"By the way, did you look into the Chicago club for me?" I asked.

Lloyd stopped and stared at me. "I thought you were joking."

"I wasn't."

"Vincent." He pinched his brow between his fingers. "Please tell me you're not seriously thinking about transferring to fucking *Chicago* for a girl. The US? Really? They don't even like real football over there!"

My temper ignited, but I kept my voice as even as possible. "I asked you to look into it. I didn't say to start preparing the transfer paperwork tomorrow."

"The fact you're even considering it is concerning," Lloyd snapped. "You're in the prime of your career. You have semi-finals coming up, and you could win a second World Cup next year." He jabbed a finger toward the changing room, where we'd shot the Zenith video. "You just landed *the most coveted brand deal of the decade*. How can you even think about giving it all up?"

"I'm not giving it all up." The restraint on my anger snapped. "*Even if* I transferred to Chicago—which I never said I would do—I could still have those things you mentioned. And if I couldn't? It's *my* career. You're my agent, and I respect your opinion. But if you think that gives you license to tell me how to live *my* fucking life, then you have a fundamental misunderstanding of what this relationship is supposed be."

Lloyd's nostrils flared. Animosity simmered between us, just hot enough to scald without exploding into something irreversible—yet.

"Look," he said in a noticeable effort to sound calm. "I understand it's your life and your decision. My job is to help you achieve your goals, but it *also* includes telling you the truth when no one else will. You've been dating Brooklyn for, what, a few months? But you've worked for this career *your entire life*. Sure, if you want to transfer to the MLS and be closer to her, I can make that happen. You're Vincent

DuBois. Any club in the world would jump at the chance to sign you. But the States simply cannot level up your skills or your career the way UK and Europe can. If you and Brooklyn break up, then what? You'll be stuck in Chicago for the duration of your contract." He pointed toward the changing room again. "And Zenith. Do you think they'll be happy about the bait and switch? They signed a *Premier League* footballer. That's what they want. That's *who you are*. Don't change that because you're infatuated with a girl."

I listened to him all the way through without interrupting. Once he finished, I said my piece. "You're right about everything except one thing. I'm not simply 'infatuated' with Brooklyn. I want to be with her. Full stop. For as long as she'll have me. Don't underplay that, or we're going to have a big fucking problem." Lloyd opened his mouth, but he closed it when I continued, "You said your job is to help me achieve my goals. Well, my goal right now is to get more information on Chicago. That's it. So either you get me what I want, or I'll find someone else who will."

Lloyd had been my agent since I was a fresh-faced eighteen-year-old playing in Paris. We'd been through thick and thin together, and we'd had plenty of disagreements in the past. But we'd never let our differences stand in the way of our partnership—until now.

His teeth ground hard enough to crack a molar, but he didn't argue with me again. "Understood."

We reached the exit. Lloyd walked off without a goodbye, and I let him.

I wasn't naive. From a business perspective, he was giving me the correct advice, and I wasn't impulsive enough to transfer out of the Premier League without serious thought.

But talking to him had unlocked a new clarity, and the more he spoke, the more my scattered thoughts crystallized into realization.

I'd spent my entire career chasing validation from brand deals and external accolades. I'd been desperate to prove myself to people I didn't know—my birth mum, the stranger at the pub, the random man on the street. I'd equated every little metric of success with self-worth, but honestly, who cared whether some random magazine editor placed me at number six instead of number one on their list of Greatest European Athletes of the Decade? Who gave a shit about me losing a wellness supplement sponsorship to another footballer, and who was paying attention to my fan rankings in online forums?

Some people, sure. But none more so than me. I was my own harshest critic, and I'd been so focused on everything I didn't have that I'd stopped appreciating the accomplishments I *did* have.

I'd done the work, and I'd put in the time. I'd won a World Cup. I'd led Blackcastle to the top of the league. I worked my ass off every day and pushed myself to be the best player and leader I could be. No matter what anyone else said, I fucking deserved to be here. I'd proven myself, and if Zenith didn't want me because I transferred to a less prestigious club, or people judged me because they thought I was throwing everything away for a girl, then let them.

I sucked in an audible breath as the truth hit me.

I still had ambitions for my career, but football wasn't the only important thing in my life anymore.

There was something—someone—I loved more, and my only regret was that it'd taken me this long to realize it.

CHAPTER 43

BROOKLYN

THE WOMEN'S GYMNASTICS REGIONAL CHAMPIONSHIPS took place in Seattle. After two months of frantic preparation, it was finally here, and I stood on the sides with Haley, her father, and her coach as we waited for her score.

Her team wasn't advancing to nationals, so she *needed* the best score to qualify for nationals as a top individual event specialist.

My stomach was a mess of knots, both for her and for me. The results were so important for so many reasons, and every second felt like an eternity as the judges deliberated.

If it were up to me, Haley would clear the competition. She'd executed her routine flawlessly, but—

The scoreboard finally flashed to life with her score.

15.2. It was best vault score of the competition, and Haley was the last to perform, which meant…

"Oh my God." She clapped a hand over her mouth as the audience exploded into claps and cheers. "I'm going to nationals." She looked a little stunned as her dad and coach hugged her and joined the jubilation. "*I'm going to nationals!*"

We looked at each other and squealed before grabbing each other's hands and jumping up and down, our girlish excitement drowned out by her father's whoops and the audience's elation.

"Congratulations! I *knew* you could do it!" I cried, my chest bursting with pride.

"I couldn't have done it without you," she said, her eyes shimmering.

Haley and I had developed a tight friendship over the past two months. Out of everyone on her team, I was the closest to her in age, and our personalities just meshed.

I'd done my best to prepare her for the competition, poring over her nutrition plans and recovery strategies, tweaking and refining and tweaking again until they were optimized to perfection. But I was only one spoke in the wheel of her success. She was the one who'd trained so hard for this, day in and day out, making sacrifices that most people would never have to make.

"This was all you," I said. "I just told you what to eat. You're the talent."

Haley shook her head. "Don't downplay your role in this. This was the result of a million different things, *including* food and nutrition." She gestured around us. "You of all people should know those things play as big a role in an athlete's performance as anything else."

Damn. I'd just been gently read to filth by a teenager.

But she was right. My knee-jerk instinct was to downplay my accomplishments even though I'd worked as hard as she had in my own way. It was a bad habit I'd yet to shake.

"You're way too wise for someone your age," I said. "Are you sure you're sixteen and not sixty?"

Haley laughed. "If I can even get on a vault when I'm sixty, then I deserve more than a spot in nationals. I deserve a Guinness World Record." She hesitated before asking, "Have you talked to my dad yet?"

My heart beat a little faster. That was the other reason I was so happy she'd advanced to nationals, though no one knew about my request besides myself and the Moores. I hadn't even told my friends in case it didn't work out. "Not yet, but I will."

"Good." She grinned. "Go get your man. Your *actual* man, not my dad," she added quickly. "That's gross."

I laughed. "Noted. Now, go celebrate. Everyone else is dying to talk to you."

While Haley left to talk to her teammates, I walked over to Derek. He finished his conversation with her coach and smiled wryly at my approach. "So," he said. "I imagine you're here to talk about London."

I nodded.

When I'd accepted this job, I'd done so on two conditions. The first was that they would let me take time off for any Blackcastle matches *if* Haley advanced to nationals. The timing was tricky because we needed to buckle down for her competition in June, but that had been non-negotiable for me. As for my second condition...well, I didn't even want to think about it in case I jinxed it.

"Well, a deal is a deal." Derek sighed, though the twinkle in his eyes suggested he wasn't as upset as he pretended to be. "It's unlucky for me that Blackcastle is such a good team."

"They're the best." I smiled. "Thank you. I'll make sure Haley is ready for nationals when I get back. I promise."

"I don't doubt it." He gave me an assessing stare. "This Vincent must be very special to you."

My smile softened. "He really is."

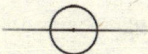

"*Ladies and gentlemen, welcome to Heathrow Airport.*" The disembodied voice over the PA system was drowned out by the clatter of luggage and the chatter of a dozen different languages as I walked toward the exit two days after Haley's regional championships.

I didn't mind the chaos or the crowds of people walking at an insufferably slow pace because I was *back*.

My feet practically floated off the ground as I stepped out onto the curb and breathed in the damp London air. The pavement was wet from recent rain, and despite the fact that it was early spring, a chill stole through my sweater and jeans.

The crisp accents, the gray skies, the ever-present drizzle…I'd never been happier.

I couldn't stop grinning even as I climbed into the back of a cab and we got stuck in traffic. Judging by my driver's side-eye, he clearly thought something was wrong with me, but I ignored his silent disapproval and soaked in the cityscape outside.

I was home for the week, and I couldn't wait to walk around and revel in the sights. Although I'd been gone for only two months, it felt like two years. I wanted to get a pint at the Angry Boar, walk along the Thames, and dress up in my Blackcastle gear and cheer them on in person.

Most of all, I wanted to see my friends and family. I hadn't told anyone I was coming except for Scarlett, Carina, and Spike. Since I didn't have my flat anymore, Carina offered her place for luggage storage until I saw Vincent. They'd wanted to pick me up at the airport, but I insisted I'd see them after work instead. I didn't want them to take a day off for me, and I was actually looking forward to some alone time first.

I needed to figure out what I was going to say to Vincent once I saw him. Should I prepare something heartfelt, or should I jump his bones and do the romantic stuff later? Maybe I'd just play it by ear and see what felt right in the moment.

Either way, we were going to be reunited in a few hours, after he finished training.

Euphoria bubbled inside me. I was so excited, I could barely sit still.

The driver glanced at me again and shook his head.

Forty-five minutes later, he pulled up in front of Carina's place. She'd given me the building's security code and left a spare key for me under her welcome mat. I used it to let myself in, drop off my luggage, and freshen up before I headed out again.

I didn't want to waste a second of my time here rattling around an empty flat, so I took the Tube to Notting Hill.

God, I even missed the *Tube*. That was how bad it was.

I had plenty of time before Vincent finished training, so I wandered through the neighborhood and popped into some of my favorite boutiques. It was a perfect, leisurely afternoon, but I couldn't concentrate on any of the shops' items, so I left Notting Hill for the Blackcastle area.

There were plenty of cafés around the stadium. I went into a quiet one, my mind consumed with thoughts of my impending reunion with Vincent.

The taste of his kiss. The feel of his touch. The sound of his voice next to my ear and the comfort of his scent in my lungs.

My chest tightened. How could I have gone so long without those things when the next *hour* felt like an eternity?

I wrapped my hands around my mug. I'd stopped for a drink and a bite, but it was so cozy here that I considered staying until it was time to head to Vincent's house.

I'd been coordinating with Spike to pull off this surprise visit. The taciturn bodyguard had been surprisingly helpful, though he'd made me send him five different videos holding that day's newspaper before he agreed to help me. He said it was to prove I was really me and that I wasn't being held hostage by some obsessed fan with nefarious intentions.

He was supposed to text me when Vincent was about to leave training, and he'd given me instructions on how to get into the house without tripping any of the alarms.

"Brooklyn!"

I looked up from my tea. My eyes widened when a familiar face stopped next to my table. "Mason?"

"Hey! Long time no see." His hair had grown out since our last run in, and his posture seemed looser, more at ease. "What are the odds? We keep running into each other. How've you been?"

"Pretty good." I smiled even as a prickle of suspicion crept down my spine. First Covent Garden, now a random café. Twice wasn't a lot, but it *was* weird that we kept bumping into each other in the oddest of places. "How about you?" Then, because he kept hovering like he was waiting for an invitation, I added, "Do you want to sit?"

"Sure." Mason slid into the seat opposite me. "I won't stay long. I'm on my lunch break, so I gotta head back to the office soon, but I saw you and had to say hi. Anyway, I've been good too. You know, I started dating someone. Her name's Lindsey…" He rambled on.

The more he talked, the more I could understand why Vincent didn't like him. He was nice enough, but he was a little too chatty even for me. It was a good thing we'd never gone on a date, or I might've stabbed myself with a fork just to get out of the conversation.

Halfway through his detailed explanation of Lindsey's allergies, I caught a flash of movement in the corner of my eye. I turned my head on instinct, but I didn't see anyone outside the window of the café. It was tucked in a side street, which was empty save for a stray cat and passing cab.

Huh. I must've imagined it.

"That's wonderful." I interrupted Mason when he segued into telling me about his new pet hamster. "I'm so sorry to cut this short, but I actually have to run. It was great seeing you though."

"Yeah, of course. I need to leave too, or I'll be late. Maybe we'll run into each other again in another neighborhood," he joked.

I hoped not. Once was cute, twice was weird, and three times was just plain creepy.

"Maybe." I said goodbye and quickly left before he could draw me into conversation again.

My phone buzzed on my way out.

SPIKE

Leaving in five

My heart skipped. *Finally*.

I hailed another cab and took it to Vincent's house, my good mood returning. Once I arrived, I followed Spike's instructions and punched in the security code.

I'd been tempted to go straight to Blackcastle and greet him when he left training, but I'd wanted our first reunion to be a private one. It was selfish, but I'd waited too long to share him with anyone else.

I stepped inside, butterflies taking wing in my stomach. Because of the intruder situation, Vincent and I hadn't spent much time at his house after we started dating, but I'd been here plenty of times before with Scarlett.

I took it all in, picking out the little pieces of him reflected in the decor—the display case with his medals and trophies, the well-worn leather sofa where he watched TV, the framed group photo he'd taken after last summer's Sport For Hope charity match.

I wandered past the living room and into the kitchen, too restless to stay in one spot. It was always my favorite room in a house, and his was as beautiful as I remembered. It was all gleaming tile and copper cookware, with big windows that overlooked the back garden.

I dropped my bag on a kitchen stool and texted Spike to let him know I'd arrived.

He didn't respond, but not long after, I heard footsteps coming from the front of the house.

I straightened, the butterflies taking flight again. *This is it.*

I double checked my reflection in the stainless steel fridge door. Hair, good. Makeup, intact. Outfit, casual but cute.

Perfect.

I turned right as the footsteps stopped.

My face broke out into an anticipatory smile, but it quickly died when I saw who was standing in the doorway. I blinked, certain I was seeing things. "What are *you* doing here?"

CHAPTER 44

BROOKLYN

"HEY, BROOKLYN," SETH SAID. "I DIDN'T REALIZE YOU were back in London."

"I flew back today. I took some time off work and was planning to surprise Vincent." I recovered from my surprise and smiled again, but the hair on my nape prickled in warning.

That was ridiculous. This was *Seth*. Sweet, earnest Seth, who was the first to comfort someone if they were feeling down and the last to leave the building every night. He wouldn't hurt a fly...so why were my inner alarm bells ringing so loudly?

"I didn't know you had a key to the house," I said as casually as possible. "Are you meeting Vincent here?"

"Oh, yeah. He gave me a key so I can drop off some items for him when he needs them." Seth smiled back. "Sometimes he leaves stuff at the club. It's hard for him to drive all the way back, you know? He has more important stuff to do, so he entrusted me to do it for him. It's an important job."

"It is." The alarm bells were deafening now. Chills skittered down my spine as I took a small step back.

Seth's story didn't add up. There was no way in hell Vincent would give his key to anyone except me and family after the intruder situation. Plus, he wouldn't leave important items behind often enough to warrant giving the *kit manager* free access to his home. That wasn't part of Seth's job.

"How's Chicago?" Seth walked toward me.

My heart slammed against my ribcage. How had I never noticed how *big* he was? He had a baby face, but he was only an inch or so shorter than Vincent and packed with muscle. It was unsettling.

"It's good." I kept my attention fixed on him. I didn't want him out of my sight, and I didn't want to let on how nervous I was. "Colder than here, but not as rainy."

"Right. So why did you come back to surprise Vincent again?" Seth stopped a few feet from me. The kitchen counter pressed against my lower back as every muscle tensed.

"Because he's my boyfriend and I haven't seen him in two months," I said somewhat pointedly.

Seth's head bobbed up and down. He wore a thoughtful expression.

I wanted out of this conversation as soon as possible, but he was blocking my path to the exit. I couldn't leave without passing him.

I didn't know why Seth was really here, but I had to keep him calm until Vincent and Spike came home. My instincts told me he was a hair trigger away from going off the rails.

"You know, Vincent was my favorite footballer growing up," he said in an apparent non-sequitur. "I had posters of him plastered all over my walls. I convinced my parents to take me to all of his matches, even the ones abroad. I even applied to work at Blackcastle because of him."

"That's...great." I glanced discreetly over Seth's shoulder. Where the hell *were* Vincent and Spike? It shouldn't take them this long if they were coming straight from the club.

"I've met a lot of celebrities, and they're often disappointing in person," Seth continued. "They're either rude, standoffish, or just not the person I built them up to be in my mind. They never appreciate their fans enough. Vincent's the only one I've met who's lived up to my expectations. I'm not just the kit man—I'm part of his inner circle. He invites me out with the team, he brought me to his birthday in Hungary, and he gives me advice when I need it. No one else would do that for me. No one else *sees* me the way he does."

A horrible foreboding crept over me. Seth didn't sound like a regular fan; he sounded obsessed. He also had access to Vincent's house and the Blackcastle facilities. Was he...?

No. It can't be. If he was the intruder, we would've spotted the red flags earlier. Right?

"He's my best friend, so I don't appreciate anyone who fucks him over." Seth's face hardened. "Like you."

My foreboding sharpened into a dagger of fear. Goose bumps pebbled my flesh, and my pulse hammered against my veins with painful intensity. "I don't know what you're talking about."

"I saw you," Seth growled. His hands clenched into fists at his side. "You were having tea with another man this afternoon, near the club. You said you came home to surprise Vincent, but that's the first thing you do after you land? Cheat on him?"

"I wasn't cheating on him. I—"

"I saw you!" His words turned shrill, almost deranged. "Don't lie to me!"

I quickly scanned the kitchen for potential weapons. The knife block was only two feet away, but I couldn't reach it without tipping him off first. My phone was in my purse, which I'd placed on a stool on the other side of the island, and everything else was either fixed in place or too light to do much damage.

Bile rose in my throat.

"Do you know devastated Vincent will be when he finds out? He's been pining after you all this time! Missing *you*! Messing up at training and getting yelled at by Coach because of *you*! He's even thinking of leaving Blackcastle and moving to Chicago *for you*!" Spittle flew out of Seth's mouth. He was completely unrecognizable from the mild-mannered man I'd known all these months. His eyes were wide, his face rapidly morphing from red to purple as he gesticulated wildly. "He thinks you're his soulmate, but he couldn't be more wrong. A soulmate wouldn't make him suffer like this."

He was bonkers. Absolutely, totally, out of his mind delusional.

I tried to keep the conversation going and stall for time. "I promise, I wasn't cheating on him. I ran into an old acquaintance and—"

"I told you to *stop lying*." There were genuine tears in Seth's eyes. "You left Blackcastle. Then you left for Chicago. You've never once considered his feelings when making those decisions. You don't deserve him."

My jaw clenched, but I forced myself to remain calm. "He was the one who told me to take the Chicago job. We *made the decision together*."

"No." Seth shook his head. "That's another lie. Why would he tell you to move away when he's so devastated over it? I can't let him follow you. I won't let him ruin his career over a lying, selfish bitch. He doesn't see the truth yet because he's under your spell, but a good friend will save him from himself. I just need to get rid of you first. As long as you're around, he'll never be free."

My fight-or-flight kicked in before he finished speaking. I lunged for the knife block, hoping the surprise from my sudden movement would slow him down. My heart beat so fast I could scarcely breathe, and my fingertips grazed one of the knives' handle before a violent tug on my hair yanked my head backward.

I cried out. Seth shoved me to the floor, and pain exploded when I hit the tile with a hard *thud*. I scrambled to my feet, my movements clumsy with terror, but Seth grabbed me from behind again before I could make it two steps. A cold blade pressed against my throat and cut my second scream short.

"I didn't want to do this." His breath was hot against my cheek. "I don't like hurting people, but you hurt him first. I just wanted to show my appreciation for him with the doll, the photo...I never wanted him to forget that there's someone out there rooting for him. But *you* convinced him I was out to get him. I should've known then that you were bad news."

Dots danced in front of my vision. I could barely think; all my attention was focused on the sharp knife nicking my skin. One quick slash, and I was as good as dead.

The taste of copper filled my mouth.

No. I won't die. I refuse.

I had too much to live for and too much I hadn't done yet. I wasn't going to let some deluded boy with a sick, parasocial obsession murder me before I saw my friends get married or hit the peak of my career or told Vincent I loved him.

The realization tore through me as surely as a bullet through the chest.

I loved him. *I loved him.* If the painful longing of the past two months hadn't made that clear, standing at death's door did. Vincent was the only thing on my mind. If I died, he would be my biggest regret; if I lived, he would be my biggest reward.

We hadn't come this far only to make it this far.

I *was* going to get out of this. Somehow.

"If you don't want him to hurt, you wouldn't do this," I said. The blade scraped against my skin with every syllable, but I forced myself to continue. "He'll never forgive you."

"He'll be upset in the short run, but he'll understand in the long run. He'll thank me for saving him when no one else would do it."

"No, he won't." My hand slowly inched up. *Keep him distracted.* "You said yourself he was willing to transfer to Chicago for me. That means giving up the Premier League. If he's willing to turn his back on *the most important thing in his life* to be with me, do you think he'll ever forgive you for taking me away forever? You won't be his friend anymore. You'll be his enemy."

"Shut up," Seth snapped. "I know what you're doing. It won't work."

But I could hear a trace of doubt in his voice, and his hold wavered for a fraction of a second.

I didn't think. I acted on pure instinct and jammed my elbow into his solar plexus as hard as I could. At the same time, I stomped on his foot, turned, and punched him in the face.

The punch was unnecessary, but it was satisfying as hell.

Seth howled. His knife clattered to the ground, and I kicked it under the counter, out of his reach, before I ran toward the exit. Adrenaline pumped in my veins, narrowing my vision to the rectangular doorway.

All I had to do was make it past the living room and through the entryway. Once I was outside, I could find help.

Almost there. Almost—

A hand grabbed my ankle. I stumbled and managed to brace

myself with my elbows before I could smash face first into the floor, but I didn't get a chance to reorient myself before Seth was on me again, more pissed than ever.

"You *bitch*," he snarled, pressing his forearm across my throat.

A lightheaded rush mixed with icy tendrils of terror. "Help!" I screamed. The sound was thin and choked, but I was beyond caring. "Someone, help—"

A heavy hand clapped over my mouth. His arm pressed tighter. Dark spots danced in front of my eyes, and the world dimmed as I fought for air.

Tears blurred my vision.

This was it. I'd tried my best, but this was how it was going to end. *I love you.*

I sent the thought out to the universe, hoping Vincent would receive it somehow. I'd been so afraid of rejection that I'd held off on admitting it even to myself, and now, I'd never get a chance to say it to him.

The tears slipped down and scalded my cheeks. If only I hadn't been in denial for so long. If only I had a little more time, and—

Something, or someone, knocked Seth's weight off me. Another cry filled the kitchen, followed by a sickening crunch of bone and a high-pitched scream of pain.

I coughed and gasped for air. My lungs burned from the sudden influx of oxygen, and I was so dizzy that I didn't notice anyone else approach until strong arms wrapped around me. A hand cradled the back of my head, and a voice cut through the fog, panicked yet heartbreakingly familiar.

"It's okay. I'm here. I got you." Vincent pressed his mouth to my forehead, his breaths ragged. "You're okay. It's okay." He sounded like he was trying to convince himself as much as he was me.

He's here. I was alive, and he was here, and I…and he…

A sob tore loose from my throat. I remained on the floor but clung to him, too drained to do anything except hold on like he was the only thing keeping me afloat.

"She's cheating on you!" Seth shouted. Spike had pinned him to the ground, and based on the earlier crunch and his grimace of pain, the guard must've broken at least one of his bones in the process. "I saw—she was—Vincent, you can't let her fool you. She'll ruin your life. I'm your best friend. You have to trust me!"

"We are *not* best friends." The abrupt shift in Vincent's voice chilled me to the bone. It was low and venomous, filled with raw, cold fury. "You're nothing but a parasite. And if you ever fucking come near Brooklyn again—if you even look at or *think* about her—I'll kill you myself."

Seth's eyes widened. He gaped at Vincent as though he couldn't believe what he was hearing. "I'm trying to *help* you."

"I don't need you to help me. I need you behind bars for the rest of your fucking life."

The boy's face turned a mottled red. His body trembled, but instead of yelling or lashing out, he retreated into a shell of glassy-eyed silence. He didn't speak or move again until the police arrived minutes later.

Detective Smith was the first on the scene. He handcuffed Seth, who let Smith yank him to the police car without protest. Vincent's harshness seemed to have broken something inside him. He passed by us, his head down and his shoulders hunched.

Even though he'd literally tried to kill me, I felt a twinge of empathy. Seth was deranged, but how lonely and neglected must he have been for him to take the small kindnesses Vincent had shown him and blow them so out of proportion?

Nevertheless, I was glad we'd caught him. The nightmare was finally over—well, almost.

The police had plenty of questions for Vincent, Spike, and me. I told them what happened so many times I got sick of hearing my own voice, but eventually, they were satisfied and left us alone. The paramedics also examined me. Thankfully, I was fine except for some cuts and bruises.

"Just so you know, this wasn't the reunion I'd imagined," I said when the EMT left to fill out some paperwork. "I'm dramatic, but not *this* dramatic."

Vincent let out a strangled laugh, his arm wrapped around my shoulders. He hadn't let me go once since he found me, not even for the paramedic's checkup. "We heard the noise as soon as we came in, but when I got to the kitchen and saw you, I thought he—I couldn't— if anything happened to you—" His voice broke.

He rarely lost his cool, and the sight of his undisguised fear made my heart squeeze.

"It didn't. I'm fine." I cupped his face with my hands, my chest swelling with so much love and relief, it almost hurt. "I also think I broke his nose during our little scuffle, so I'm very proud."

Another laugh, this one more genuine. "'Little' scuffle, huh?"

"Yep. I've been through worse. You weren't there for the Black Friday brawl of 2010. Pre-teen me was vicious."

Vincent shook his head. "You're something else."

"I'll take that as a compliment."

"It is." He kissed me softly, and when he spoke again, my breath caught in my throat. "Welcome home, sweetheart."

CHAPTER 45

VINCENT

BROOKLYN AND I SAT ON THE SOFA, MY ARM AROUND
her shoulder and her head on my chest.

The police left hours ago. The crime scene had been cleaned up,
and I'd sent Spike home for some well-deserved rest. He'd argued
vehemently, but when I told him I wanted a proper reunion with my
girlfriend, he'd relented.

We'd also called her dad and told him what happened. We
downplayed it because we didn't want Coach to have a complete
meltdown before we explained the situation in person, but that hadn't
stopped him from flying off the handle. The only reason he hadn't
marched straight to my house was because Brooklyn insisted she
needed time to rest first, but he was coming over first thing in the
morning.

Meanwhile, Seth was in police custody, and Detective Smith had
assured us he faced criminal charges that could put him behind bars
for life. Even so, I refused to let Brooklyn out of my sight, afraid that
I would blink and she'd vanish.

"That's the last time I surprise anyone," she said. "From now on, I'm letting you know exactly when and where I'll be. Preferably with a pin on Google Maps and a body cam, if necessary."

I smiled at her attempt to make light of the situation, but I couldn't shake the bone-deep cold stealing through me. That afternoon's memories sank their claws into my brain and refused to let go—Brooklyn lying on the floor while Seth tried to strangle her. Her tears and his screams. The deranged expression on his face and the overwhelming, gut-wrenching moment when I thought I'd been too late, and the earth crumbled beneath my feet.

For a split second, I'd lived in a world where she no longer existed, and that was enough to make me wish I were dust too.

My lungs tightened, and I kissed the top of Brooklyn's head again to reassure myself she was still there. Her scent was so familiar and comforting, it was like she'd never left.

There were still unanswered questions regarding Seth, like how he'd gotten the key to my house and what his motivation for harassing me had been. According to Smith, it was likely Seth didn't see his actions as harassment at all. He probably viewed them as some form of sick celebrity worship that I should be grateful for.

We wouldn't get answers until the police questioned him properly, but for all intents and purposes, the intruder situation was resolved. Brooklyn was back by my side, if only temporarily, and this should've been a happy moment, not a melancholic one.

I forced the image of Seth's arm on her neck out of my mind.

"How long are you staying in London?" I asked.

"I leave next Thursday. I need to prep Haley for nationals, but there's no way I'm missing your semi-final match."

"Next Thursday," I echoed. "That soon."

"Yes, but I have something to tell you. I wanted to wait until it was one hundred percent confirmed, but I think we both need a pick-me-up today." Brooklyn lifted her head to face me. Her eyes shone with a mixture of hope and nerves. "There's a strong possibility I'm moving back to London this summer."

My heart stopped for one glorious, shocked second before it beat again at triple speed. "What about your job? I thought you loved working with Haley."

"I do, but when I accepted their offer, I had two requests. One, if Haley advanced to nationals, which she did, I could take off for any Blackcastle matches this season. That's why I'm here—to see you guys play in the semi-finals. Two..." Brooklyn took a deep breath. "If she *places* at nationals, I can move back to London and work from home. The job was supposed to be remote anyway. They only wanted me in Chicago because of the transition and the time crunch, but I think they also wanted to see how well we worked together first. If I didn't do a good job in person, then remote would be a no-go. But they've been happy with me, and they agreed to my second request on the condition that there be a three-month probation period. That's to see how the remote work and time difference pans out."

I processed the news, my thoughts a tangle of hope, shock, and disbelief. "How likely is Haley to place at nationals?"

"She's really freaking talented, so highly likely. Plus, I'm going to do everything I can to make sure she gets a medal. I don't care if I have to carry her to the podium myself."

I laughed, but there was a catch in my throat. "Why didn't you tell me about your requests?"

"I didn't want to get anyone's hopes up in case regionals didn't pan out, but now that we've passed the first hurdle..." Brooklyn swallowed. "Honestly, I shouldn't have said anything until after nationals. But when I was in the kitchen, and I thought I was going to die, all I could think about were the things I never did. The words I never said. I don't want there to be any more secrets between us, which is why I'm telling you this now." She hesitated. "I hate to bring him up again, but while we're on the subject of secrets, Seth mentioned something interesting earlier. He said that you might transfer to Chicago."

I frowned. How did he know—

A puzzle piece suddenly clicked into place. Lloyd and I had been arguing at Blackcastle. I thought everyone had gone home, but Seth must've stayed late and overheard us.

Brooklyn had also told me about about her run-in with Mason at the cafe, which was why Seth thought she was cheating on me.

If he was that obsessed with me, I imagined something would've set him off eventually. He'd just hyperfixated on Brooklyn because she was the most obvious scapegoat.

My gut tightened with guilt, but I forced myself to shake it off. Seth was an adult. He was responsible for his own decisions, and I couldn't blame myself for his delusions.

When it came to that level of unhinged behavior, even the smallest thing would've triggered him.

"I was exploring the idea of a transfer," I admitted. "I asked Lloyd to look into it for me."

"Let me guess. He lost his shit?"

"Oh, yeah. He lost a Mount-Etna-eruption-level of shit. I thought he would keel over from a heart attack when I told him."

Brooklyn smiled, but her eyes gleamed with emotion. "I wouldn't have let you transfer anyway. You'd hate Chicago."

"Oh? You think you can 'let' me do stuff now?"

"Yes." She turned fully and wrapped her arms around my neck. "I'm very good at predicting your likes and dislikes, and there's no way in hell the captain of Blackcastle would thrive in the States. They don't like football that much over there. They don't even *call* it football."

"You sound like Lloyd," I said, amused. "I understood the risks. It was early in the process, but if push came to shove, and I had to choose between you and Blackcastle?" My voice turned tender. "I'd choose you. Every time. Because you're it for me, Brooklyn Armstrong. There's nothing and no one else I love more."

It was the first time I'd ever uttered the L word to a girlfriend. I thought it would be scary, but it felt as natural and effortless as breathing because it was *true*.

Brooklyn's eyes shone brighter. She pressed her forehead against mine. "I have one more secret to tell you," she whispered. "Earlier, when everything went down with Seth, all I could think about was you. How much I miss you. How much I need you. How much I *love* you. I was so afraid to say it before, but fuck that. It's how I feel. No secrets and no regrets, right?"

Fuck. If my realization that I loved her cracked me open, her confession that she felt the same way *destroyed* me. There was no way I'd ever be the same again, knowing that the person of my dreams thought I was hers too.

"Right." I smiled, my chest somehow tight and full all at once. "Does this mean we actually agree on something for once?"

"I think so. Hell must've frozen over."

"Probably. The heat is overrated anyway." I kissed her, deep and slow and reverent. "I love you." Now that I'd said it once, I couldn't stop saying it.

"I love you too."

We grinned at each other, our foreheads still touching, our breaths mingling in the space between us.

Maybe our repeated confessions were cheesy and a little ridiculous, but I didn't give a shit.

She was here, she was safe, and she was mine.

For the first time in my life, love didn't feel like a risk. It felt like the safest bet I'd ever made.

EPILOGUE

BROOKLYN

ONE MONTH LATER

"I CAN'T WATCH." SCARLETT GRIPPED MY HAND ON ONE side and Carina's on the other. Despite her words, her eyes were glued to the pitch. "This is torture."

I made a noise somewhere between agreement and terror.

We were packed into Wembley Stadium for the Champions League final between Blackcastle and Holchester. Blackcastle had eked out a win against Madrid in the semi-finals, but today's match was something else entirely—raw, brutal, and nerve-shredding.

We were approaching the eightieth minute, and the score was two-one with Holchester in the lead. They'd just been awarded a corner, and their fans were already on their feet, roaring loudly enough to shake the stands.

The mood in the Blackcastle box was grim, but I held on tight to hope.

Come on.

The whistle blew. The ball curled in. Holchester's captain met it cleanly with his forehead, and the ball slammed into the net.

Three-one. Holchester.

The away section erupted while silence fell over the Blackcastle side like a shroud.

"No," I breathed. It couldn't end like this. Blackcastle *had* to win.

My eyes sought out Vincent on the pitch. Like the rest of the players, he looked exhausted, his chest heaving and his skin gleaming with sweat. But even from afar, I could see the fire in his eyes.

The match wasn't over yet. Until the final whistle blew, we still had a chance.

Vincent said something to the team before Blackcastle jogged back into position.

They were too far away for anyone off the pitch to hear them, but whatever Vincent said must've worked because when the match restarted, Blackcastle played with an energy they hadn't shown since before half time.

Instead of crumbling beneath the pressure of an impending loss, they pressed like hell.

Adil to Asher.

Quick one-two on the wing.

Asher sprinted forward, weaving past the Holchester defenders with sharp, precise movements. He darted inside the box and unleashed a powerful strike. The ball flew past the goalkeeper and slipped into the bottom corner of the net.

"Goal!" I screamed a millisecond before the stadium went wild. "Goal! Goal! We made a goal!"

I sounded like an idiot, but I couldn't contain my excitement. Scarlett and Carina were right there with me, screaming and cheering as Blackcastle surged forth on a wave of renewed enthusiasm. Every pass was precise, every run more determined than the last.

Time was ticking, but we were only one down, and we were no longer fighting to stay in the game; we were fighting to win.

Vincent drew my attention again. As a defender, he wasn't the one people usually looked to for an attacking play, but tonight, everything was on the line. He pushed forward, running with the ball and joining the offense.

Stevens gained possession of the ball and passed it back to Vincent, who didn't hesitate. He slotted it to Asher, who whipped a perfect cross into the box. The ball hung in the air for a split second, just begging for someone to finish it.

And there was suddenly Gallagher—right place, right time. He connected with the ball and drove it home past the goalkeeper.

Three-three.

I couldn't think over the screams of the crowd. I could only join in the exuberance, jumping up and down as my heart fought its way out of my chest. My ears rang so fiercely I was sure I'd lost some of my hearing, but I didn't even care.

We were *so close.*

One more goal. That was all we needed.

Holchester, once calm and confident, now seemed flustered. Their players started making uncharacteristic mistakes—a missed pass here, a misjudged interception there.

Blackcastle pounced on their weakness like sharks sensing blood in the water.

They pressed harder. Asher received the ball just outside the box, danced around a defender, and fired a low shot that Holchester's keeper managed to block, but it ricocheted right into Gallagher's path.

The Blackcastle forward didn't hesitate. With one swift motion, he took a touch, lined up his shot, and smashed it toward the far post.

The goalkeeper didn't stand a chance.

Four-three. Blackcastle.

The ground shook beneath my feet as the fans stomped and cheered, and my throat was hoarse from yelling. Carina yelled something in my ear, but it was drowned out by the roar of the crowd.

We'd done it. We were in the lead. It was a comeback for the ages, and Holchester couldn't keep up. They crumbled. When the referee blew the final whistle, the chaos escalated to pure pandemonium. The crowd erupted into a frenzy, the air so thick and the sound so loud it swallowed me whole.

I hugged everyone around me, not caring whether I knew them or not. My cheeks hurt from smiling, and my eyes stung with happy tears. I was in London for only twenty-four hours—I couldn't take any more time off with nationals right around the corner—but it was worth it. Being with my family, seeing them win—I'd take an eight-hour flight every fucking day for this feeling.

"Let's go!" Scarlett grabbed my hand and pulled me toward the exit. Carina stayed behind, too caught up in the impromptu party to join us.

I followed Scarlett, my breath rushing out in an exhilarated laugh as we battled our way through the crush of people.

Family and friends weren't allowed on the pitch after a match, but this was when it paid to be Frank Armstrong's daughter. My former colleagues didn't stop us from running out onto the sidelines; they were too busy celebrating.

The team was also celebrating on the pitch—arms raised, shirts off, faces glowing with pride and pure, unfiltered joy. The sound of their laughter and triumphant shouts filled the air. The scent of freshly cut grass mixed with the unmistakable tang of sweat and victory, creating a heady, intoxicating atmosphere.

The energy was infectious. My pulse raced, and I could barely catch my breath when Vincent's eyes met mine over Asher's shoulder.

A slow smile spread across his face. He tapped his teammate on the arm. Asher turned and spotted Scarlett. He headed straight for her while Vincent jogged toward me, his movements strong and purposeful, as though nothing else mattered except getting to me.

My heart pounded in sync with the electric hum around us, but I was too impatient to wait. I ran and met him halfway, my arms winding around his neck at the same time he picked me up and wrapped my legs around his waist.

Everything else faded in the background as his mouth crashed against mine. I kissed him back with equal fervor, and when we finally pulled back, we were both breathless and flushed.

"Congrats," I breathed.

"Thanks, buttercup." His smile flashed when I shook my head.

I'd finally asked him last month why he called me by that nickname. He said it was because buttercups were beautiful but poisonous, just like me and my insults. Plus, they matched the color of my hair. His reasoning was ridiculous, but it was so him, I couldn't be mad at it.

"You're officially one of Europe's champions," I said. "How does it feel?"

He grinned. "Incredible. But not as good as I feel with you." He cupped the back of my head with one hand and kissed me again. "I don't even care that Coach can see us."

I peeked to the side. My dad was, indeed, standing right there, celebrating with Greely. For once, he was wearing a broad smile. He didn't seem bothered by Greely's victory dance, nor did he look like he was going to march over and yank Vincent off me.

After all these months, he'd finally come to terms with our relationship.

Congratulations, I mouthed.

His smile widened. He tipped his head in silent thanks and turned back to Greely, implicitly giving me more alone time with Vincent.

"I think my dad has warmed up to you as my boyfriend," I said, facing Vincent again.

"I should hope so because I plan to be your boyfriend for a very, very long time."

"That's mighty presumptuous of you."

"Maybe." Vincent's eyes gleamed with mischief. "But am I wrong?"

"No." I brushed my lips against his, my heart fluttering. "You're not."

We kissed again, and for the second time that night, the world fell away until it was just the two of us, here, together.

VINCENT
SIX MONTHS LATER

"Brooklyn! You're missing the opening credits!"

"I'm coming! I'm coming!" She ran into the room, cradling a giant bowl in her arms. "Your popcorn machine is a pain in the ass. You couldn't have bought a nicer model?"

"*You* chose that model."

"Well, couldn't you have told me to buy a nicer model?"

"No, because we'd been shopping for two hours and I would've let you buy an inflatable toaster if it meant we could leave."

"It had *not* been two hours." I scooted over so she could squeeze onto the sofa next to me. "Now shhh. This is an important episode."

Tonight was the season finale of *The Great British Bake Off*, which meant our cell phones were on silent and all interruptions were discouraged.

Brooklyn rolled her eyes, but she smiled and quieted as the episode kicked off. I draped an arm over her shoulder while she tucked her legs beneath her and curled into my side, our movements easy and effortless after months of practice.

Her hair smelled faintly of that coconut shampoo I loved. The warmth of her body pressed against mine, reminding me that she was actually here and she wasn't leaving.

It was November—five months after Haley placed second at nationals, four months after Brooklyn moved back to London, and one month after she cleared her remote work probation period.

There was no more uncertainty or waiting. She was here to stay.

My heart twinged. As invested as I was in *Bake Off*'s finale, I couldn't stop staring at Brooklyn.

Instead of having her rent another flat post-Chicago, I'd asked her to move in with me. I'd never lived with a girlfriend before, but I loved waking up next to her in the morning and listening to her breathe at night. The anxiety I'd felt over being at home was long gone now that Seth had been apprehended and tried for attempted murder, amongst other things.

Long story short: the former kit manager was going to be in prison for a long, long time. Everyone at Blackcastle had been stunned by the news, but life moved on. We'd hired a new kit man— one who had to undergo *extensive* vetting and evaluations—and we were already deep into our season. Brooklyn and I both also started therapy again, which had been extremely helpful in dealing with the Seth trauma.

Spike wasn't working for me anymore since the intruder threat had been neutralized, but I'd kept his security plans in place just in case. If Seth had taught me anything, it was that I needed to be more careful. His unfettered access to the players meant he was able to steal my house key and make a copy of it. He'd also hacked into my devices and found my security codes, so now everything was locked down per Spike's instructions.

"What are you thinking about?" Brooklyn asked during a commercial break.

"Hmm?" I traced an absentminded circle on her shoulder.

"You're too quiet, which means you're thinking hard about something."

"I'm thinking about how good those pancakes on the show look." *Bake Off* didn't feature pancakes often, but when they did, man, they looked incredible.

Brooklyn lifted her head to stare at me in horror. "Don't tell me you want to make pancakes again. Are you *trying* to die?"

After last fall's fire, Brooklyn and I were equally convinced that I was cursed when it came to pancakes. I wasn't allowed to make them ever again, not even with professional supervision. She did, however, make them for me every Sunday. In return, I made her her favorite smoothies every day. Blenders were one of the least fire-prone kitchen appliances, so I felt confident I could operate one without summoning emergency services.

I laughed. "No. But besides the pancakes, I was also thinking about you."

"Really?" She raised a playful eyebrow. "Tell me more."

"I was thinking about how good you look in this shirt…" I ran a hand over her bare thigh. She was wearing a football shirt similar to the one she'd worn during our first-ever *Bake Off* viewing together, only this one had my name on the back. "And how good you smell…" I kissed the sensitive spot below her ear. A shiver ran through her body. "And how glad I am that you're here."

"Are you trying to butter me up for something later?" she teased, but her voice hitched when I trailed another kiss down her neck.

"Maybe. Is it working?"

"Maybe." Brooklyn pulled back and tilted her head to her left. "But not in front of company."

Oh, shit.

I glanced over at where Truffle the pig stared at us from his designated armchair. He wore a black and purple shirt with *Unofficial Blackcastle Mascot* printed across the front.

Stevens was out of town for the weekend, so I'd volunteered to pet-sit while he was gone.

So far, Truffle had been an exemplary houseguest—cute, polite, and quite clean, no matter what the Angry Boar's owner said. But right now, he was definitely judging us hard.

"Sorry, buddy," I said as Brooklyn laughed. "I forgot you were there for a second."

He oinked his dissatisfaction.

I walked over, picked him up, and set him in my lap as the show resumed onscreen. My late-night plans with Brooklyn would have to wait, but I couldn't be too upset.

She snuggled up against my side again, and a wave of contentment washed over me.

I'd played in sold-out stadiums across Europe.

I'd launched a record-breaking campaign with Zenith and had more money than I could spend in a lifetime.

They were shining accomplishments in my life, but they weren't everything. I didn't need that external validation anymore. I'd even deleted my birth mum's number from my phone. After everything that had happened over the past year, I realized I couldn't care less why she gave me up.

She'd never been part of my life, and I'd rather focus on the people who wanted to be here.

I wrapped my arm tighter around Brooklyn and kissed the top of her head. She shifted slightly, settling closer to me with a happy sigh.

Nothing beat moments like this—sitting on the sofa with the woman I loved, watching my favorite show and knowing everything I needed was right here in my arms.

I'd lived in this house for years, but Brooklyn's presence changed everything.

For the first time in my life, I understood what it meant to be truly home.

Can't get enough of Vincent and Brooklyn? Download their bonus epilogue for free at anahuang.com/bonus-scenes

* * *

Thank you for reading *The Defender*! If you enjoyed this book, I would be grateful if you could leave a review on the platform(s) of your choice.

Reviews are like tips for authors, and every one helps!

xo, Ana

P.S. Want to discuss my books and other fun shenanigans with like-minded readers? Join my exclusive reader group Ana's Twisted Squad!

KEEP IN TOUCH WITH ANA HUANG

Reader Group: facebook.com/groups/anastwistedsquad
Newsletter: anahuang.com/newsletter
Website: anahuang.com
Bookbub: bookbub.com/profile/ana-huang
Instagram: instagram.com/authoranahuang
TikTok: tiktok.com/@authoranahuang
Goodreads: goodreads.com/anahuang

ACKNOWLEDGMENTS

I wrote *The Defender* after *King of Envy*, which was perhaps my darkest book yet, so it was a nice change of pace to return to the lighter, more relaxed world of Blackcastle. (Yes, there was an attempted murder in this book, but it was a relatively light attempt, you know?)

Vincent, Brooklyn, and the rest of their friend group are my feel-good place, and I wished they were real so I could cheer them on during their matches and have a pint with them at the Angry Boar afterward.

Alas, they're fictional, but the people who helped bring them to life in these pages are very real. A heartfelt thank-you to:

Becca—For always being there as a sounding board, friend, and recipient of panicked late-night texts. I can't wait to eat my way through Northern Europe with you and to celebrate all the things (after we get over our jet lag).

Brittney, Salma, and Rebecca—For being my steadfast alpha reader team and reassuring me that I do, in fact, remember how to write a book.

Ali, Kimberley, Allie, and Amélie—For sharing your expertise regarding football, Britishisms, the French language, and more. I've learned so much through you, and I'm so grateful.

Malia, Jessie, Chelé, Aishah, and Tori—For being my beta reader extraordinaires. I couldn't have done this without you.

Britt—For always polishing my books with such a keen eye. I appreciate you!

Cat—For another stunning cover I can add to my collection. Thank God blue is easier than purple, and we didn't have stress dreams about Pantone swatches this time around.

Jess—For being an all-around rockstar and the best falconry partner.

Kimberly, Aimee, and the rest of the Park, Fine & Brower team—For doing more than I can put into words and for holding my hand through all the ups and downs of this career.

Christa, Madison, and the entire team at Bloom—For your endless patience and unwavering enthusiasm. I'm so honored to be part of the Bloom family, and I wouldn't be where I am today without you.

Gina, Ellie, and the rest of the team at Piatkus and Little, Brown—For the Britishism checks and everything else that you do. I'm so happy we were able to meet up in London and Ireland, and I can't wait to see what else the future brings.

My readers—For being you. For all the love and support over the years and for making this dream career possible. Thank you for following me out of my comfort zone and into the sports romance world. I hope you love it as much as I do.

xo,
Ana

Look out for the next God of the Game . . .

THE
KEEPER

**He can resist any woman in the world . . .
except for the one he shouldn't want.**

Continue your Gods of the Game journey with
Noah and Carina's story.

Coming soon from

PIATKUS

Can't get enough of Ana Huang?

Discover the bestselling Kings of Sin series.

Fall in love with the members of the Valhalla Club today.

Available now from

PIATKUS

Don't miss Ana's bestselling Twisted series

Available now from